# A BILLION Risky Games

## WICKED HOT BILLIONAIRES

# JANE McBAY

cat whisker press
Boston

First Paperback Edition
ISBN: 978-1-957421-75-9

Published by Cat Whisker Press
Cover: Philip Ré, Rex Video Productions
Book Design: Cat Whisker Studio
Editor: Chloe Bearuski

If you enjoy homemade chocolate sauce

*This one's for you!*

# WICKED HOT BILLIONAIRES

A Billion Little Lies

A Billion Hot Kisses

A Billion Starry Nights

A Billion Last Goodbyes

A Billion Risky Games

A Billion Second Chances

# ACKNOWLEDGMENTS

I want to offer my heartfelt gratitude to the following beta readers who gave me the gift of their most precious asset, their time: Toni Young, Philip Ré, Kyrstin Poyson, Jessica Guenther, and Gail Feldman.

As always, thank you to my long-time editor, Chloe Bearuski.

Quite simply, your combined efforts made this a better book. I am exceedingly grateful. All remaining mistakes, of course, are my own.

# 1

# Lark

I spot *him*, this stranger, as soon as he enters the busy bar and grill, one of Sydney's newest hot spots. My first time here at F6 Tavern, I'm enjoying the atmosphere. Adding to the noise of endless chatter, glasses clinking, and the live band playing instrumental bluesy-rock, Charlotte, my company's VP and also my friend, is still talking business. In her singular focus, she's almost worse than I am.

"Quarterly figures . . . *blah, blah, blah.* European market . . . *blah, blah, blah.*"

I was at least three-quarters listening until I saw him. But I'm here for one simple reason, to scratch the social itch, to hook up with a guy for one night, get my jollies, and get back to work with the tension and stress released.

Charlotte isn't exactly my wing-woman, though, since she's married. Her husband, Reed, is totally confident and secure enough to let her come out with me, which I appreciate. She may or may not have known my main motive when I asked her to go for a drink after work. But I think she does. She joined in when I suggested we take a few minutes in the executive bathroom on the top floor of my company to primp.

Our hair had to have a quick brush—mine is medium blonde, hers a warm brown. Then we applied a new layer of war paint, focusing on glossy lipstick. Other than that, we're both dressed in the same Friday casual as every other female in the place. I'm wearing a lightweight denim skirt and a white T-shirt, and Charlotte has on pale pink capris and a sunny yellow blouse.

Returning to Sydney to run my family's Australian confectionery HQ, I've felt the loss of my social circle the past few months, and this night out with Charlotte is exactly what I need.

Well, the night out and *maybe something long and hard, too.*

Then *he* walks in, tall, dark-haired, and built like a bodyguard. From a distance, across a crowded bar, his skin looks like it's been sculpted from creamy milk chocolate. And as the CEO of Henley Confectionery, I do love me some chocolate.

He moves gracefully, not lumbering like some large men do. My insides clench because he's so freaking gorgeous. Every other person in the place, male or female, retreats into the blurry background. My jaw might have dropped a little, too, and I snap it shut before swallowing the sudden mouthwatering attraction I feel.

A few yards from the entrance, he stops to talk to a group at a round table. They laugh. He slaps one of the seated men on the shoulder. Then he moves on, leaning close to say something to one of the female servers who crosses his path, making her laugh, too.

With a steady purpose, he weaves his way through the place and nods at the bartender across the room. This god of a man is heading toward the back of the establishment, continuing to survey the room while he walks. Missing nothing.

Since I'm in the middle of it all, at a high top in the center, I see the moment his gaze lands on me. I'm not a supermodel, but I have my mother's good looks and my father's eyes and my own brand of style. Whatever it is about me, I get noticed. Not boasting, just saying.

In NYC, enjoying a stupidly high-profile lifestyle, I couldn't shake the suspicion that men approached me for one reason—they knew who I was, wealthy Lark Henley of *the* Henley Confectionery family. *Proven true a time or three.*

It's not as though this good-looking man trips and falls at seeing me, but he hesitates, taking me in. He assesses everything, including Charlotte. I suppose he *fancies his chances*, as my older sister once whispered to me when she had a guy on the hook, because he raises a dark eyebrow and smiles my way.

When he makes a course correction and heads over, the flutter in my stomach confirms to my brain that I'm interested in him, at least viscerally. My body knows what it wants.

Glancing at Charlotte, I don't think she's even aware of him yet. She's busy telling me about an idea for alcoholic saltwater taffy, while using her long pink nails to open pistachios from the bowl in front of her.

When I look up again, he's right in front of us, even more scrumptious up close. Luminescent blue eyes gaze wickedly out of a face the color of my morning coffee. His dark jeans fit his muscular thighs like they were crafted specially for him, and his shirt sleeves seem to be having trouble not tearing over his biceps. His dark hair is cut short, and the smile he sends me is a billion watts.

"Good evening, ladies. Everything all right?"

American accent, not Aussie. Having buried myself both *in* and *at* work pretty much since I stepped off the plane, his is one of a mere handful I've heard. It's definitely the smoothest and deepest.

*How can a voice be so sexy?*

"We're good," I say.

At my side, Charlotte is eyeing him with curiosity—on my behalf, I'm sure. But for all I know, he's interested in her, not me.

"How about yourself?" I ask.

"Doing all right," he replies. Then his eyes crinkle and he tilts his head like a smart shepherd. "American?" he asks.

Now I know he's not from here, or he would've called me a *Yank*.

"I am. My friend here is native, though."

He barely looks at Charlotte, except to give her the briefest of dazzling smiles. Then his attention is back on me. Looks like I'm the chosen one, after all. *Yay for me!*

Yay for him, too, because, unless he does or says something really stupid, he's getting lucky tonight.

"You're not native, either," I point out.

"A good ear," he says. "I'm from Massachusetts originally."

A weird coincidence. My older sister lives on Beacon Hill, and my brother recently married a woman from Boston, although they live in New York. In *my* old apartment. And Luke has *my* old job.

But that's a long story, so all I say is, "I have ties to that area."

His face breaks out in another smile. "Awesome. Small world and all that. Can I buy you ladies a drink?"

I may as well be honest. "If you'll have one, too, and drink with us." Because I very much want him to sit and chat, just so I can listen to him speak and watch his sensual mouth. The firmly curved shape of it is made for kissing.

At my words, Charlotte sends a pistachio nut flying across the table.

"Whoops," she says. "It got away from me."

Even though it bounced off the stranger's rock-hard thigh, he shrugs. "Tell me what you're drinking." I guess he's taking me up on my invitation.

"Gin and tonic," I say.

"Nothing for me, thanks." Charlotte rises to her feet. "I need to hit the loo," she announces before turning to me. "Come with," she demands.

She wants to make sure I'll be OK if she leaves me alone with Mr. Smooth and Sexy.

"I'll be fine," I tell her as we have our quick pow-wow in the ladies' room. "Go home to your handsome husband. And thanks!"

Five minutes later, after Charlotte lectured me not to do anything rash, as if my entire life hasn't been a series of rash decisions, the last one bringing me ten thousand miles from my New York City life, she leaves me to chart my own course tonight.

Returning to the dining area with its lip-smacking scent of fried shrimp, I see our table has been taken over by a couple who are already drinking pints of beer. My gorgeous new guy friend has vanished.

*Well, damn!* Disappointment courses through me until I hear, "Hey, sheila!"

That's funny, since every woman in the place turns her head, some with annoyance at the Aussie slang, some with interest. But I know his voice already, and I know it's me he's calling for.

At a small table by the kitchen door, farther from the music and the bar, my new companion for the night has two drinks at the ready. He stands when I approach.

Bonus point for behaving like a gentleman. Although I sincerely hope that doesn't carry through to the bedroom.

"This is my table," he announces by way of explanation.

Not asking what that means, assuming he's such a regular at the bar they gave him a table, I gawk when he goes so far as to pull out a chair for me before resuming his own seat with his back to the wall. The evening has taken an intriguing turn as I find myself gazing at . . .

"Your name?" I ask.

"Mitch." He waves down one of the servers.

He's nothing like the guys I was seeing at home. And I don't mean because he's ridiculously attractive, nor because he's half black and half white. But he isn't behaving in any way like the rich men in my business circle, Manhattan's elite.

Everyone was named Kyle, Ian, or Cody with hair styled more than my own and bespoke clothing, from their suits down to their underwear. Dinner was always at an elite restaurant, impossible to get into unless you had the money to bribe the staff. With food that was more artfully arranged on the plate than filling. And they would never sit by the kitchen.

"I'll have a burger, please," he tells the server. "Load on the mushrooms and some jalapenos." Mitch nods toward me. "Have you eaten?"

"Nope. I'll have the same," I tell the woman. Not because I shape myself to any guy's whim, but because it sounds delicious. "Fries too, please," I add. "And fried shrimp."

"The big basket," he says. "I want to satisfy this one." He actually winks at me, and I get a little damp in my panties.

*Satisfy this one?* My cheeks feel warm, although I know he means by buying me dinner. After she leaves, he picks up his pint glass of beer and taps it to my gin and tonic.

"And your name is?"

I do not want to be Lark Henley, CEO. Not at this moment. He will instantly lose his casual demeanor and look at me differently. Either he'll be impressed by my title, which is unnecessary since it was handed to me, first here in Australia when I was in training as co-CEO with my brother, then as CEO of Henley NYC, and now as the Sydney HQ CEO.

Or this warm and friendly guy will be wary and feel inferior. Any man who stakes out a table in a bar as his own fiefdom probably has little else going on in his life. But I'm not interested in any of that.

Not to be too crude, but a hot night of satisfying sex sounds perfect.

"Lark," I say, leaving off my last name as he did.

He raises an eyebrow, but doesn't make some weird joke about me being a cute chick or a pretty bird. Nor does he ask me if I can sing. *Thank God.*

$❤$❤$❤$

A half hour later, my dream is coming true. While we eat, it becomes obvious we're on the same track. He brushes the back of my hand with his long fingers when we both reach for a fry. Locking gazes when I don't pull away from his touch is hot, hot, hot.

His pastel-blue eyes above his sculpted cheek bones are utterly mesmerizing. I hope to see those eyes rolling back in his head during his long climax. Directly *after* mine, of course.

Right now, his sensual lips are curved in a lazy smile, so I up the flirting ante by slipping off my heeled pump. My bare foot caresses the inside of his calf and begins its trek north. When his mouth opens slightly and his eyes narrow, I go higher, managing to nestle my toes against his crotch and feel . . . a lot!

"Did your friend drive you here?" he asks, his tone a little choked, as my toes continue examining.

The stiffening package under my big toe has me feeling a little desperate. It's been too long since I . . . *Wait, what was the question?*

"Yup," I say, before sighing. "Now I'm stranded."

His smile becomes a wolfish grin. "I would never leave a lady stranded."

I shiver. It sounds sexual, even if it's not. *But I think it is.*

"Would you like me to drive you home?" he offers.

I suddenly think about my ultra expensive waterfront apartment. My brother and I bought it when we were both running Henley Sydney, before Dad retired from the NYC division. A great investment, it's the highest of the high-end residences, and I'm not sure I want Mitch to get a sense of how much money I've got.

"What about your place?" I ask.

He hesitates, and I wonder how big of a dump it is. But what he asks is, "Do you feel safe coming with me?"

I do, in fact. But what I say is, "Safer than letting a stranger know where I live."

He nods. "Fair enough. But I'm only in Sydney temporarily, so I'm staying at a place that isn't really mine."

*Interesting.* And even better than I hoped. A single night of super crazy sex, and I'll never see him again. Potentially sad but totally freeing in what I'll do with him and let him do to me.

"Why are you here?" I ask, not because I care whether he's here to paint houses or work on a fishing boat, but to get a little insight into who he is.

"Restaurant work," he says carefully. "What about you? Do you live here full time?"

"I do now," I answer, just as carefully, imagining him as a shirtless line cook, sweat glistening on his bare skin. I would pay to see it.

"Work VISA?" he asks.

"Something like that." Because of my grandparents and my father, I actually have dual-citizenship, but he doesn't need to know.

"What do you do?"

Is he asking because he gives a damn or is he merely making conversation? I swallow and look down at the partly eaten fry on my plate when I answer. "Candy," I say quietly. "I . . . I work in candy."

"I would love to taste your candy," he shoots back, snagging my full attention and my gaze again.

All sorts of sinful thoughts flitter through my brain.

"Last call," he says softly. "Another drink or are you ready?"

As if synchronized, we both stand, eager to get out of here.

"While you pay," I say, confident he can afford it since he offered, "I have to shoot off a quick text. I'll meet you out front." I decide to let Charlotte know that I'm going to be a bad girl, but that I'll leave my phone on for tracking me. JIC. I also snag the server on my way out.

"That guy I ate dinner with . . ."

"Mitch," she says.

Good to know that's his real name. Also, he must actually be a regular if she knows it. "He's a good guy?" I ask.

"He's a top bloke. In fact—"

"Thanks." I hurry toward the door, not wanting to hear any details of how he might've slept his way through the wait staff.

Outside, I'm texting under a street lamp, hearing the waves lapping at the quay, when he pulls out of the restaurant parking lot, coming to a stop at the curb in a surprisingly nice car.

A bright green Porsche!

Climbing out, he comes around to open the door, even as my hand is already on the handle. Gentlemanly bonus point number two.

"Nice car," I say, as I slide onto the gray leather seat.

"Definitely going to miss her when I leave."

I don't pry. I simply sit back and let him drive. There's something very sexy about a man who can handle a sports car. Of course, it's a standard, and I get to watch his bicep move as he shifts gears. When he's not shifting, he rests his big hand on my thigh, scorching me through the blue denim of my skirt.

I'm ready for him to slide his hand higher when we unexpectedly turn down my street. *WTF?*

I become tense as we cruise along the waterfront boulevard, windows down, the harbor breeze blowing my hair, leaving the silhouette of the Opera House behind us.

It's a drive I take often. I start to squirm as we approach . . . *and pass by!* . . . my apartment building.

Releasing the breath I'd been holding, I glance over at him, just as he finally lets his knuckles brush the warm, damp area between my legs. Directly under his fingers, my body flutters with anticipation.

About five minutes later, we park in an underground garage and ride the elevator up to a fifth-floor penthouse equally as ritzy as my own. Pretty nice for a line cook.

"Friends in high places," he mutters, his hand on my lower back when we enter his apartment.

It clicks. Neither the car nor the penthouse is his, which makes sense. I'm a little curious, but I don't ask. It's none of my business. This is going to be one and done, anyway.

And then, as if we've been pretending sanity and using the utmost restraint, we go full-on animal attraction. I drop my purse, we both kick off our shoes, and he sinks his fingers into my hair, holding me still for our first kiss.

The sheer power of this big man gently cradling my head while his mouth covers mine is all it takes for desire to flood my panties.

We're moving, he's leading, still kissing.

"What do you like?" Mitch asks when we're in his bedroom. I know what he's asking since we're tearing off one another's clothing at a fast rate.

"A little bit of everything," I confess. "Like a box of assorted chocolates."

He smiles. "Sometimes you feel like a nut."

"Something like that," I agree, as I tug off his short-sleeve shirt to reveal his oh-so-masculine shoulders, broad chest, and sculpted six-pack I'd guessed was lurking under the innocent cotton.

Unexpectedly, a big-ass, polished gemstone swings on a black leather cord between his smooth, strong pecs. I nearly groan. It is so much sexier than a tattoo. I want to watch that deep-purple stone swing when he pounds me.

Once we're stripped down, I tell him the truth because I don't want to waste this experience. "I like a little pain to push me over the edge. Not always, but sometimes." I hold my fingers up, pinching my thumb and first finger. "Just a little . . . something."

Clearly, I haven't shocked him. He kisses me again as though it's our last moment on earth. His tongue strokes mine before he gently bites my lower lip, tugging on it as he draws back. Then he looks down at me with those luminescent blue eyes, so clear and understanding. My heart is hammering at the promise of what's to come.

"Your honesty," he says, "is brave and sexy as hell."

When I'm on my back on copper-colored satin sheets, the lights dimmed, he disappears for half a minute before returning to the bedroom. I can't see what's behind his back.

"Close your eyes," he orders.

I'm being crazy. I don't know anything about this guy except how everyone liked him at the bar. How he made people laugh, myself included. And how he made me wet between my legs with little more than a glance.

So here I am, taking a chance that he can satisfy me the way that burger took care of my hunger. I close my eyes.

Mitch palms one of my breasts, like he's gently weighing a juicy peach, stroking his thumb over my nipple. I want to see his face, and my eyes open.

He grins, then pretends to be serious. "No peeking."

"No fair," I say, but I shutter my eyelids again.

His mouth closes over one of my nipples, and intense heat shoots straight to my ladybits, like a tsunami of liquid fire. My body needs this, *needs him*, so badly, I'm shaking. He sucks my nipple to a peak and then . . . *snap*.

I gasp, but keep my eyes closed.

"It's a chip clip," he informs me. "Doing OK?"

I moan my response, mainly because that's all I can do, barely able to breathe. But he seems to get it, that I'm more than OK. After a hot lick across my other nipple, he draws it between his supple lips. I'm already trembling, knowing what's to come.

A little sucking bliss and then . . . *snap*.

"*Ohh,*" I expel a breath. The clips have springs that are a little stronger than the slight pinch of a man's fingers that I'm used to whenever a guy follows my request. They're amazing, making me lightheaded with the rush of excitement as my heart beats wildly.

Mitch trails tickling kisses down my flat stomach toward my trimmed landing strip.

"So pretty," he remarks against the smooth skin below my pierced navel. I don't know if he means the small sapphire nestled there or my trimmed landing strip.

When he blows a puff of air across my pussy, and I can no longer breathe, I figure out he doesn't give a damn about the precious gem. His eyes are on the prize.

Everything's good so far, but it would be better if he . . .

Reading my mind, he parts my nether lips with his strong fingers, before blowing softly at my already taut clit, wrenching a guttural moan from deep inside me.

My skin prickles with need.

"Again," I whisper my demand.

He does it.

"*Mmm,*" I say, mindless, nothing but nerve endings.

Then his mouth begins to play with me. A flick or two of his tongue makes me arch shamelessly, seeking more, until he closes his firm lips around me and sucks. I hope he doesn't have another chip clip because that would be too much.

He chooses that instant to reach up and flick one of the clips, making my nipple sting. Then the other. I forget how to breathe, writhing on the smooth satin beneath me.

At the same time, he tends to my clit with quick licks, and . . . I go off like a firework, bucking against his mouth, even grinding against his teeth, praying he doesn't stop until I'm finished.

When the waves of ecstasy finally subside, I'm breathless and boneless, my skin flushed and sensitive. Mitch kisses his way back up my body, removing the clips with gentle care that makes me shiver all over again.

Then I hear myself apologizing. "I'm sorry I came so fast."

"You're incredible," he murmurs against my neck, and I feel the rumble of his voice through my whole body.

"You did everything," I remind him, still catching my breath.

My hands explore the hard planes of his chest, skimming the ridges of muscle that indicate some dedication to weight-lifting. Briefly, I grasp his leather cord, run my hand over the smooth stone attached. I want to ask about it, but I also don't want to know anything more about him beyond how I can give him pleasure.

And then I enclose the thick diameter of his cock with my fingers, watching him draw in a ragged breath. We've already had *the talk* while in his car.

Clean? *Yes.* Tested? *Yes.* Condoms available? *Yes.*

Without looking, he scrabbles in the top drawer of his nightstand. I don't think about how many times he might've done this. Tonight, for one night only, he's mine.

When he hands me the shiny packet, I tear at it, before opening it with my teeth as though I'm an expert. He sees through my act when I start to fumble with the condom itself, trying to quickly figure out which way is which.

After a second or two, he takes over and unrolls it onto his massive erection.

Flat on his back, he says, "Get on top and ride me."

Sounds good. I straddle him like I'm on one of the horses at my grandparents' ranch. When Mitch holds the tip to my slippery wet opening, I brace my palms on his shoulders so I can lean forward and ease down onto the largest penis I've ever seen in real life.

"Here goes," I mutter, making him chuckle while also causing his cock to bob. And then I'm easing down onto him, slowly, inch-by-glorious-inch, being stretched the way I've read about in books but never experienced.

*Hot, full, a little painful, deep, and perfect.* It's crazy awesome.

"God, Lark," he says on a low groan. "You're so tight."

Even though it's not really an accomplishment, I feel rather pleased with myself. More so when I fit about half his length into me without hitting an ovary. An overachiever, I'm determined to make it all the way down his shaft.

Mitch distracts me from the slight burning sensation where my body is opening wide for him, by brushing his thumbs over my nipples. Then he gives them each a tug. As usual, an invisible highway of pleasure travels from them right to my clit.

Leaning into his palms, I slide down the rest of the way until my butt is on the top of his firm thighs.

"You're going to have to help me here," I say, still adjusting to his size. I need to go up and glide down or he's not going to get any closer to an orgasm, but I'm almost afraid to move.

"It's taking all I have not to thrust," he says.

That's when I notice sweat pop out on his forehead. I want to giggle at his strained tone.

"I don't want to hurt you," he adds.

"Put your hands on my waist," I suggest. "Move me as you want."

In seconds, I'm thrilled by the sight of his bulging biceps using my entire body to stroke and squeeze his cock. "Good?" I ask.

"Yes," he hisses, closing his eyes and creating a steady rhythm, lifting me before drawing me down. The gloves are off, so to speak, and gentleness gives way to his own desperate need for release. *Rise up, ram down.*

His hips get in on the thrusting action, and now I'm riding a bucking bronco. *For the win!*

"Touch yourself," he orders, and I do.

The feeling of his big hands at my hips while his cock glides in and out, filling me, stretching me, causes my brain to short-circuit, like I'm tipsy or high. My own urgent fingers work on my throbbing clit at the same time, bringing on another orgasm fast and furious.

"Mitch," I say his name like a word of surrender. "I can't wait."

"Let go," he orders, his voice husky.

I fly apart, moaning as I climax again. Looking down at his tense, attractive face, I watch the moment he comes, while feeling it deep inside me. He has me pinned to his hips with both his strong hands as he grinds against me. *Sweet mercy!*

Tangled in his sheets, I'm tired but energized at the same time, my body filled with adrenaline. I'm ready to make my escape, and call an Uber, which won't take long in this neighborhood on a Friday night.

"Stay." The single word is soft but commanding. His arms tighten around me. "Unless you have somewhere you need to be?"

I should leave. This is a one-night fantasy. But when I look into those blue eyes, seeing the genuine desire there, my resolve crumbles.

"I suppose I could stay a little longer."

His smile is pure male satisfaction. "Good. Because I'm not nearly done with you yet."

My body reacts with a deep shudder, because I'm ready to squeeze out every drop of delight from this man. Over the next hour, he worships—*there's no other applicable word*—every curve and valley of my body. His focus makes me forget my own name, let alone the responsibilities that usually keep me on the edge of stress at all times.

Without even intending to, I take a little snooze, startling awake to see him doing the same. And then we start again, goosebumps, craving, friction, and climax. By the time we finally collapse, exhausted and sated, the sky outside is beginning to lighten with the first hints of dawn.

"Sleep," he murmurs against my hair, pulling me back against his chest. "We can figure out the rest in the morning."

*The rest?* Like our last names. Our real lives. The complications that daylight will surely bring. Not gonna happen.

Yet wrapped in his arms, listening to his breathing slow and deepen, I let myself have this moment. A few more perfect minutes with a man who sees me as simply a woman, not a Henley. Not an heiress. Not a CEO with the weight of a legacy on her shoulders.

*Just Lark.*

Even if it can't last. Even if as soon as he's deeply asleep, I'll be gone.

# 2

## Mitch

This woman is still trembling in my arms, her breath coming in soft pants against my chest. And I'm enchanted.

*Christ!* When did I last feel like this? Like I've been struck by lightning and blessed by an angel all at once. The scent of her—*I swear it's vanilla and cinnamon mixed with pure femininity*—fills my senses as my breathing returns to normal.

It was just sex. Great sex, but still, nothing more than a roll in the sheets. A roll that I should have taken slower. Should have savored every moment instead of rushing at her like some hormone-crazed teenager. But the moment I spotted her at my bar, next door to my newest restaurant, I was done for.

In the same way the city of Sydney inspired me to open a casual second venue when the building next to Franklin 6 came on the market, Lark inspired me to make fast moves, even for me. Whatever it took to ensure she came home with me. And when she smiled . . .

*Shit!* I'm in trouble. Because I still want her.

Her hand traces swirly patterns on my chest, and I have to bite back a groan. Every touch from her is electric, setting off sparks under my skin. It's been years since a woman affected me like this. Maybe never, if I'm being honest.

"That was . . . ," she starts, then trails off with a little laugh that does things to my insides.

"Yeah," I agree, restraining myself from pressing a kiss to the top of her head because that's cringey. "It was."

The thing is, I almost wish we hadn't. Not because it wasn't incredible. It was intensely powerful, creating a new high bar. But now I want more. More of the same and some extra sprinkled on top. God knows I could spend days exploring every curve, every delicate spot that makes her gasp and arch beneath me.

For the first time in a long while, I wouldn't mind putting in the effort to get to know my bed partner. At the bar, Lark was a little guarded, but also very real. She ate a burger bigger than her head, laughed loudly with me when we found something funny, and was basically fearless.

*Or stupid.* With a twinge of concern, I think how dumb it was for her to come back to my place, and I want to tell her never to do anything so risky again.

With anyone but me.

I roll my eyes at myself. None of that protective crap is in my DNA. I mean, I'll defend anyone who needs my help. But women are independent creatures with their own autonomy to have casual sex and make their own decisions.

In the past, I've found them perfectly willing to choose a night of sexual pleasure. Mutual fun. One and done.

Lark made a *really* good choice, and we both benefited from it. I brush my fingertips along the bare skin of her stomach without thinking about what I'm doing. She gasps. I'm not initiating sex again. Not this precise second. I just wanted to touch her.

Damn me if she doesn't seem like the kind of woman who'd be into the whole enchilada. Great sex, the dreaded cuddling, spending the night, monogamy, dates, etc. And she deserves it, too. Personally, I'm not "doing" relationships at the moment because I don't stay in any place long enough to make it worth the woman's time.

*Unless she wants sex with no strings attached.* As it happens, I do that very well and have done, ever since my live-in girlfriend moved out. Unexpectedly, abruptly, while leaving my stunned jaw on the floor as the circumstances played out. She was already in love elsewhere, or at least, in love with a rich older guy's connections and deep pockets.

Camille taught me a few hard lessons as a poor cooking student at Le Cordon Bleu in Paris. Women like to hook up with me, since I have big muscles and a big . . . heart. They also like my large hands and long, strong fingers. But the ones who press for more, especially in a hurry, are those who find out I'm now a billionaire. My worldwide restaurants earned me half my fortune, and my grandfather bequeathed me the rest.

If only my ex-girlfriend had known the windfall that was coming two years after she walked out. *Oh well!*

Not that I'm cynical, merely experienced. And my experience tells me Camille would leave the guy she's currently with for me and my restaurants, my money, and my lifestyle. Because as soon as a fun female like Camille, or Lark for that matter, finds out who I am, I become her meal ticket. A status symbol.

I'm a convenient rung on their social climbing ladder or a safety net if they're not quite making it.

My thoughts are fucked up. And because they are, I wouldn't start something deeper than a roll in the sack even if I suddenly decided to stay in one place and stop opening new restaurants. Not unless the woman fell hard for me before she knew I was Mitchell Franklin. *And how the hell would that ever happen?*

Lark's hand has stopped moving, and so has mine. We're silent, momentarily content in the still space between our orgasms. Me and this sensual lady, who doesn't know who I am.

Despite thinking I'm an hourly restaurant worker, she willingly gave herself to me. She didn't expect or want anything more than this night—as she made clear when we did the usual health check while I drove us here.

Now Lark believes I'm some barfly-regular who also happens to know his way around a woman's body. *Thank you very much.*

Seeing a woman basking in post-coital bliss, that's nothing new. I can feel her aftershocks. But when she shudders in my arms like she's reliving the sex, I grow hard again, thinking about being inside her.

Then I get a surprising idea—we should go on a beach walk or a picnic somewhere secluded. *Sunset would look really good on her bare skin.*

She shifts against me, her leg sliding between mine, and my body responds instantly. That's all I want from her. One night of incredible sex. I scoff at anything else. I'm certainly not planning what to put in a goddamn picnic basket, like some lovesick teen.

"You're thinking awfully hard over there," she murmurs, her voice husky with satisfaction. "Regrets already?"

"No." The word comes out more forcefully than I intended. I soften it by tracing a circle around her navel.

She bats me away. "That tickles."

Laying my palm across her narrow waist instead, I add, "Definitely no regrets. Just . . . thinking."

"I hear that can be dangerous," she quips, propping herself up on one elbow.

When the sheet slips down, revealing her breasts, my mouth goes dry and I forget what I was thinking so deeply about.

"I try to avoid thinking too much," she adds with a shrug.

I know she's clever and joking with me, and I laugh despite myself. "Yeah? How's that working out for you?"

"Usually pretty well." Her smile turns mischievous. "Tonight being a prime example."

*God, she's perfect.* Smart, sexy, funny. And she has no idea that I could buy her anything she wanted, take her anywhere in the world. She's here because she wants to be, not because of what I can give her.

The thought both thrills and terrifies me. How long do I want to stay in Sydney?

"So," she says, leaning over me, pressing her perfect tits against my chest, "what's next?"

What I want to say is, *Next, we get a few hours of sleep and after that, I want to take you to breakfast, learn your last name and your middle one, for that matter. Maybe exchange some personal info so I know what you like for music and discover whether you're a morning person.*

What comes out instead is, "Whatever you want."

She studies me for a long moment, her golden-brown eyes seeing too much. "That's a dangerous offer, Mitch."

*You have no idea*, I think. Out loud, I say, "I'm a dangerous kind of guy."

She laughs, a rich, throaty sound that goes straight to my groin. "Oh, I figured that out about three orgasms ago."

*Well, damn.* This woman is going to be the death of me, but what a way to go!

"Only three?" I flip her onto her back, pinning her wrists above her head. Her caramel-blonde hair is fanned out on the pillow beneath her. Like I thought, blessed by an angel. "Clearly I need to up my game."

"Clearly," she agrees breathlessly, arching beneath me.

But even as I lower my mouth to her breast, even as she gasps and writhes under my touch, that voice in my head won't shut up. The one reminding me that I don't do this, I don't bring women to my penthouse where the evidence of wealth is basically on display. And I don't spend all night learning what makes them scream, and lie here after thinking of fun things to do apart from sex.

I have good reasons. But with Lark under me, I can't remember them beyond disappointment over a couple bad actors who soured me, some fake feelings, broken trust. Once I introduced what turned out to be the wrong woman to my parents. I've never made that mistake again.

Casual and free has been my path lately. Easy. Uncomplicated. The woman's place or a hotel room, *not* my home no matter how temporary. And most often, first names only, like with Lark.

No promises, no expectations, no chance of getting burned again.

But here's Lark in my bed, in my space, and I brought her here without thinking twice. Worse, I want her to stay longer.

"Hey." Her voice is soft, concerned. "Where'd you go?"

Lost in my own conflicted thought, I froze while she lay naked and willing beneath me. *Smooth*, Franklin. *Real smooth.*

"Nowhere important." I capture her mouth, pouring all my confusion and want into the kiss. She responds instantly, her legs wrapping around my waist, and for a while I manage to stop thinking at all.

It's all about settling between her legs and stroking circles around her clit while I enter her. Slowly. Each time her body tenses, I pause, letting her adjust, and I wait until she nods or I feel her muscles relax.

Soon, I'm rocking in and out. Lark's head is tilted back, eyes closed, gorgeous mouth open as I dominate her. All she can do is hang on, her nails sinking into my back. Fierce, just the way I like it.

Later—much later—she stretches and glances over her shoulder toward the window where soft gray light is already glowing at the edges of the curtains.

"I should probably go," she says eventually, though she makes no move to leave.

"You should probably stay." The words are out before I can stop them, hanging in the air between us like a challenge.

She goes still against me. "Mitch . . ."

"For breakfast," I add quickly, trying to sound casual when I'm freaking out at my stupid invitation. But I'm a cook by nature, even more than I'm a trained chef. I want to feed this woman. "I make a mean omelet. And the coffee machine costs more than most people's cars, so it seems a shame not to use it."

She laughs softly. "Trying to impress me with an expensive coffee maker in a place that isn't even yours?"

If only she knew. The penthouse alone is worth eight figures, and that's before we get to the view of Sydney Harbor that real estate agents would kill to offer their buyers. But she doesn't need to know any of that. Not yet. Maybe not ever.

"Is it working?" I ask instead.

She's quiet for a long moment, and I can practically hear her thinking. There's something guarded about her, something that suggests she's doing this one-night stand for more reasons than sexual satisfaction. Maybe she's been burned before too.

"Sorry to tell you, but we have a really great coffee maker at work," Lark says finally.

Disappointment hits harder than it should. "Right. Of course."

"But . . ." She props herself up again, looking down at me with those incredible topaz eyes. "I suppose I could set an alarm and stay a little while longer."

The relief is almost embarrassing. "Yeah?"

"Don't look so pleased with yourself." But she's smiling as she says it. "And this doesn't mean anything. We're just two adults who had a good time and we're not ready to call it quits yet. That's all."

"That's all," I agree.

She settles back against me, and I pull the covers up over us. Within minutes, her breathing evens out and she's asleep, trusting me enough to be vulnerable in my space. The weight of that trust sits heavy on my chest.

*So suddenly, we're having a sleepover.* I haven't had one in a while, nor a morning-after breakfast. Tomorrow, in the harsh light of day, she'll Google the address and figure out exactly who I am. Then everything will change. It always does.

But for tonight, she's simply Lark who "works in candy." I believe it's her way of hiding the fact that she's a sales clerk in a candy store. I've stumbled upon a number of nice ones here, selling high-end chocolates, imported British candy, or colorful rock candy.

I guess she's a little embarrassed, but I wonder which one she works in.

My phone vibrates on the nightstand. I reach for it carefully, not wanting to wake her.

Two missed calls from Gary, my CFO, based out of Atlanta, who thinks he's my babysitter. And one text each from Ravi, my head chef here at Franklin 6, and from my sister, Riley, who could be anywhere in the world. I'm always slightly amazed at how much communication happens whenever I'm indisposed.

Glancing at Lark's beautiful face, I think *indisposed* is a lackluster way of describing my performance this evening.

Since neither text seems urgent, not even my sister's, I ignore them and listen to Gary's voicemail. He's still dealing with Catie, the last woman who tried to extort money from me after a one-nighter in New Orleans, two restaurant openings ago. He wants to know if I've seen the paperwork he emailed me.

I set the phone aside without responding. Gary's been with me since the beginning, helping to build the Franklin Restaurant Group, from one naively hopeful, struggling Boston venue to a hospitality powerhouse. More than anyone he understands why I have my rules about keeping my private life private. Yet I let a stranger in tonight.

"I must be nuts," I mutter.

Lark shifts in her sleep, murmuring something I can't catch. Little frown lines appear between her eyebrows, making her look stressed instead of peaceful. I take hold of one of her hands like it's the most natural thing in the world. Which it isn't.

The problem is, I'm already hooked on a few things, like her laugh, her wit, and her curvy body. Best of all was how uninhibited she was, asking candidly for what she wanted and needed.

The chip clips are still on my bedside table. *God, that was sexy.*

And she's a generous lover, giving as good as she got. Through it all, she smells like aromas from a bakery or a candy store.

Anyway, tomorrow, reality will intrude. Tomorrow, she'll leave and I'll go back to being Mitchell Franklin, CEO. Tomorrow, I'll decide if I want to give relationships another try because this woman seems worth the headache, despite knowing how it usually ends.

But tonight? I close my eyes and relax beside her. When I wake up, she's gone.

# 3

# Lark

The sunrise paints Sydney Harbor in shades of rose and gold as I slip out of Mitch's penthouse, my heels dangling from one hand. The marble lobby is mercifully empty except for a sleepy doorman who doesn't even glance up from his newspaper. *Good.*

The last thing I need is a witness to my walk of shame—though honestly, I feel anything but ashamed.

My body still hums with satisfaction, every muscle deliciously sore from our marathon night. I can still feel his hands on me, still taste him on my lips. The memory sends a shiver through me that has nothing to do with the cool morning air.

I should regret this. Should be kicking myself for the impulsive decision to go home with a stranger. But as I slide into the back of an Uber, I can't summon even an ounce of remorse. Last night was . . . transcendent. Mind-blowing.

Exactly what I needed after months of emptiness. No close friends, apart from Charlotte, no famed Manhattan social life, just boring boardroom battles, and the same stressful family expectations that I felt in NYC before I uprooted and replanted myself in Sydney. Because my brother asked me to switch. I'd do anything for family.

Besides, it's not a sacrifice by any means, but definitely a jarring adjustment.

"G'day, love," the driver says, sending me a knowing smile. "You're up early."

I'm still on a Mitch-high, so I smile right back.

"Indeed I am, and it's a lovely morning, isn't it?"

My apartment is *very* close. Alarmingly so. Point Piper is an exclusive waterfront community that Luke and I knew would only increase in value, so we bought here. Eleven streets on ninety-six acres. My grandfather has more land at his ranch.

Mitch's place, or *his friend's*, if I recall correctly, was still a hotel a couple years ago. Now it's one of the glitzier addresses.

Any evening, I might be out for a walk and meet the man who knows I like my nipples pinched. On the other hand, I spend most evenings working late and can't recall the last time I went for anything so mundane as a walk by the water.

Ten minutes later, I'm standing under the spray of my rainfall shower, hot water sluicing away the scent of him—obviously sandalwood but also something uniquely Mitch. My fingers trace the faint marks his mouth left on my skin, little reminders of our passion that make me flush all over again.

*Get it together, Lark.* I'm the CEO of a billion-dollar company, not some swooning teenager. I fully intend to open my laptop and get some work done despite it being the weekend. I'm also aware that most people my age are hitting the beach or strolling one of the marketplaces. And I'll do those things in a few more weeks when I've got every department of Henley Sydney tattooed on my brain.

At that point, I'll be overdue for the two-hour drive to see my grandparents in the Hunter Valley.

For now, at a reasonable hour, I order my breakfast delivered because my cooking skills run to making coffee and pouring a bowl of cereal.

After last night, I need some serious nourishment, and cannot help recalling Mitch's promise of a breakfast I didn't stay to collect. I like how he asked me to stay as though it meant something more than just another round in bed.

I would like to see him through the steam of a fresh cup of coffee, watching while he made me that "mean omelet." *Sigh.*

Chowing down on a slice of mushroom-and-onion quiche, a fresh-fruit cup, and a side of rösti, one of my favorite potato dishes, I scroll through the world news on my laptop, looking for anything that might affect either ingredients for our chocolate production or our distribution. This includes natural disasters, gas prices, and war.

Of course, my thoughts are fractured. While I'm totally invested in Henley Confectionery's success, I can't stop thinking about Mitch. Those bright-blue eyes that darkened with desire when his pupils dilated. The way he laughed at my dry humor, really laughed, not merely polite chuckles. The way he didn't do a single damn thing to try to impress me, like pretend the car or the apartment was his.

Mostly, the way he touched me like I was precious and powerful all at once. Nothing like the men back home who knew my net worth before a first kiss.

I contact Charlotte, as promised, once it's a decent hour for a Saturday phone call.

"Well, well. Someone's sounding chipper this morning."

"Enjoying a hearty breakfast," I deflect, but I can feel the heat in my cheeks.

"*Uh-huh.*" I can almost hear her smile. "Those must be some good eggs. Are they cooked over easy or tall, dark, and handsome?"

I make my second cup of coffee because it's going to be a work day at home. "I have no idea what you're talking about."

"Lark Henley, you are the worst liar in the entire southern hemisphere." I can hear a whirring sound.

"Are you on your treadmill?" I ask, trying to imagine having the dedication to work out at this or any hour.

"I hear your condemnation," she jokes. "Wait until you're a decade older, Ms. Firm and Perky. Anyway, I know you're calling to let me know you're safe, and I appreciate it. Please tell me you got his number for a second date."

"I . . ." The lie dies on my lips. Charlotte's not just my VP. She's become my closest friend here. "There was no first date, so no, I didn't get his number. We were in agreement that it was a one-off."

No need to tell her it was like a four-off, not that I was counting.

She sighs. "Kind of a shame. I was hoping he was the real deal, but then, I only saw him for about five seconds."

I nearly blurt out how very real he was. But I know what she means. Real as in *boyfriend material*. Would a boyfriend put up with a woman who plans to spend her day sourcing Aussie cocoa beans, so Henley can move toward a claim of local and sustainable? I have no other frontier to conquer, so that's become my focus.

"It might've been a one-off, but it was incredible."

"Details. Now." I hear the treadmill slow and stop in the silence. "Was he as gorgeous without his clothes?"

"Better," I admit, heat flooding my cheeks. "So much better. And he was . . . God, he was perfect. Funny, charming, attentive. He really made me laugh. And he made me feel—" I cut myself off, not ready to voice the dangerous thoughts swirling in my head.

"Like a woman instead of a CEO?" Charlotte supplies gently.

"Exactly." I stir honey into my coffee. "He doesn't know who I am. Mitch thinks I work with candy. Probably assumes I'm standing behind a glass case somewhere. We connected as nothing but a man and a woman."

"I get it. I have to keep reminding Reed that just because I'm the VP of one of the most successful chocolate companies in the world, that doesn't mean he has to worship me quite so hard."

We both laugh. She's always complaining that her husband pretends not to grasp the finer points of laundry and vacuuming. And they've been married since she was still in the Henley marketing department, working her way up.

"It's been a long time since I was certain someone wanted me for me," I say. "Not for my last name, not my family's money, not the connections I could provide. Just . . . me. I know I sound strident about this, but Mitch being a regular guy is the only reason I let my guard down with him. If he'd been a power-player, I wouldn't have gone home with him."

Charlotte's voice softens. "I can't believe you didn't get his number."

"Don't you see, if we saw each other again, eventually, he'd find out who I am." I think about how he already has someone else's car and apartment. "I don't want to become his sugar mama."

We both chuckle. Although I didn't get the mooch vibe off him. Not at all. And I can't deny I would love a repeat of last night.

"I know where he lives, but . . . ," I trail off, having opened my email program. Red flags pepper my inbox. "*Uh-oh.*"

"What?" she asks.

"Three emails from Jim at the factory. All marked urgent." My stomach drops as I click the first one from our production manager.

**Production's hit a major snag.**

The lust-filled haze evaporates as I read through increasingly dire messages.

**Retailers right across the region are kicking up a storm.**

**Chocolate tastes *off*. Faint, swampy aftertaste.**

By the third one, I'm reeling with the nasty shock, as well as mystified.

**Texture problems, like the chocolate's fighting to melt properly on the tongue, with an unusual graininess.**

The bright side is there are no reports of illness, and all the issues are within the continent. Nothing international yet. When he tried to call me late last night, my phone went right to voicemail.

As Jim put it, he knew it was "turned off" and therefore went the email route.

There was nothing you could do on a weekend anyway.

Apparently he doesn't know me as well as he thinks he does.

"Charlotte, I'm going to call Jim but first I'll forward you everything. I know it's Saturday, but can you get up to speed and also send me the quality control data from any shipments he's flagging?"

"I'm on it, boss," she says, hanging up.

Within minutes, Jim Peters is on speakerphone.

"G'day, Lark." He's known my brother and I since we were kids and supervised us when we had to learn every job at the factory, the way our dad once did. Today, his usually calm voice is tight with stress.

"Tell me what's happening."

"Kicked off late yesterday," he says straight to the point. "Complaints came through customer service from a handful of vendors who'd copped it from their customers, and these were relayed to me. Woke up to half a dozen more reports this morning."

He pauses, and I wait, knowing how thorough Jim is.

"I've been trying to pin down the problem since yesterday. Seems to be confined to two batches of dark choc we used in the premium bars and in three of the assorted varieties."

*Well, shit!* He was doing that while I was . . .

I push my ill-timed escapades aside. "What's your assessment? Have you figured out the cause?"

"I believe it's the sugar."

I freeze. "Are you sure?"

"Only new ingredient, but I'm testing everything."

*New ingredient?* Then it's my fault. "Are you saying this is from the supplier I contracted with last month?"

When I got back to Sydney, I wanted to start building up a Henley partnership with Aussie businesses, in an effort to become more *home-grown* in whatever large or small way that I could. It used to be that way, when my grandparents founded the company. Yet as we grew and went international, our suppliers did too, coming from an ever-expanding pool. Fewer and fewer were Aussie based.

Quietly, without making a fuss or consulting with my brother or father in New York, I chose a new sugar supplier for our factory here, not for the U.S. one. Not merely based in Australia, the supplier sells locally grown and produced raw and refined sugars and syrups.

"Yep," Jim breaks into my thoughts. "This choc was the first run with the new sugar. Nothing else in the line has changed."

"Have you already got our quality control team on this?"

"Of course. I've been around the traps a time or two," he scoffs.

I shouldn't have asked. He's a professional, and we have our own quality-control lab. But sometimes, it's difficult not to be a micromanager when the Henley brand is on the line.

"The sugar's at our lab. With your go-ahead, I'll send it to an independent one tomorrow."

"Yes, do it," I tell him. We both know this could escalate to the Food Standards board.

I'll have to call Charlotte back to contact our legal department and handle damage control. While I'm praying no one has become sick from chocolate that tastes "off," I ask, "How much product are we talking about?"

"I'll flick you the batch numbers. They line up with a two-week production run. And there's more bad news," Jim adds.

"Lay it on me," I say, mentally bracing myself.

A part of me wishes I'd never crept out of Mitch's bed. The other part wishes I'd never crawled into it. I'd be twelve hours ahead of this fiasco if Jim had been able to reach me.

"This chocolate went into the gift boxes for the Sydney Business Association dinner. Three hundred boxes, all wrapped and ready, sitting in the warehouse. Plus, all the assorted product for the dessert platters."

My stomach lurches, and I lower my forehead to my dining room table. The SBA dinner is one of the biggest networking events of the year. And it's this Friday evening. Henley Confectionery has been a sponsor for nearly two decades.

We can't show up with potentially contaminated chocolate, but we can't show up empty-handed either. After a moment, I sit up straight.

"How fast can we remake them?" I ask, already knowing the answer won't be good.

"If we run double shifts all week, we might be boxing by Thursday. But Lark, that'll muck up our regular orders, make no mistake. And without the new sugar, our supply is low."

I stand, pacing to the window. The city sprawls below me, oblivious to my crisis.

"I'll find a sugar supplier who can deliver by dawn."

"On Sunday?"

*Fuck me.* "Yes," I say, but less certainly. I don't care what it costs, but I won't be the CEO who destroys our reputation at the SBA.

"Jim, call in everyone. All three of our chocolate-makers."

Because we do bean-to-bar at Henley, there's no one to call for additional chocolate for our products. It's us or no one.

"Promise them overtime, double time, whatever it takes. We are not missing that dinner."

Charlotte agrees to meet me at the office so we can work more efficiently. The rest of the day blurs together in a haze of phone calls between me and the legal team, and the special gift box manufacturer, and the printer who will do a rush job to print "Henley Confectionery Presents Our Finest at the Sydney Business Association" with the date stamped in royal blue on the new boxes.

Everything has to be a do-over and a rush job, and therefore commands a premium cost that will make our CFO weep when he eventually finds out. Plus, there's the financial loss of the candy that has to be dumped. And the lab fees for testing the sugar and testing basically *everything* in our Wetherill Park factory just to be safe.

By the time I look up from my desk, it's past eight and my temples are throbbing. I told Charlotte to go home and to switch her phone off an hour ago *after* she secured extra sugar, which is arriving on a goddamn Sunday afternoon. The price would indicate each individual granule is being carried by a magic fairy.

My phone buzzes. I open a text from an unknown number.

*Hungry? There's a hot meal with your name on it if you want to claim it. -M*

My heart does a stupid little flip. *Mitch?* Either that or my mother has flown over from upstate New York.

For a few seconds I wonder how he got my number, then scroll up to see my phone sent a text to his at three this morning. I'd turned it back on and set my alarm. His sneakiness puts a smile on my face, although I should be pissed off. I should delete his text and his number and tell him he's bordering on being a creepy stalker.

Instead, I stare at his text, thumb hovering over the keyboard. Every practical bone in my body is warring with every last remnant of fun-loving Lark. But I have a crisis to manage, a reputation to protect, a company to run. I don't have time for . . . whatever this is.

Despite not having eaten since Charlotte forced some crunchy energy bar on me around two o'clock this afternoon, I have to decline. Even though I'm ready to pack it in, knowing I can't make any good decisions this late.

Yes, I want more than anything to lose myself in his incredible glacial-blue eyes for an hour, I know I should go home. After what's happened today, I'm not thinking clearly, and I'm bound to grow reckless. Again!

*Rain check? Work emergency. Maybe next week?*

Instantly I regret the exhaustion-fueled text. *Rain check?* On meeting up after a one-night stand? *No, no, no.* And a "work emergency" for a store clerk? I shake my head at my stupidity.

Three dots appear immediately.

*Candy melting in the heat?*

What can I say?

*Something like that*

More like Henley Confectionery going down in flames. Then I send another that maybe makes sense.

*Inventory issue*

That about sums up my nightmare. He texts back:

*At this hour? How late is your store open?*

I don't even know what to respond. I'm too tired to lie. When I don't answer, he sends another.

*I'll bring the food to you. Address?*

I bite my lip. That's crossing a line. Inviting him into my professional world? *Impossible.* And I'm not about to give him my home address. The jig would be up, as they say, once he found out my apartment is also on Point Piper. Equally luxurious, equally expensive, and actually *owned by me*, not like his temporary squatting arrangement.

My stomach growls, but I don't give in.

Impatiently, he texts again.

*Let me feed you. Nothing else.*

Why does that make my ladybits flutter? I text back:

*Feed me?*

He sends a laughing face.

😄 *It's what I do. I'm a cook, remember?*

I battle my smarter self, then all at once, I think *Why not?* I can't possibly do any more damage to my family's company today. But I need to find neutral territory.

*I could use some air. There's a bench near the Opera House steps? Twenty minutes?*

It's on my way home anyway. Sort of.

Three dots appear immediately.

*By the gelato stand, right? I'll find you.*

I shouldn't be doing this. But soon, I'm driving to the waterfront, about fifteen minutes away. Once I've parked, I check myself in the rearview mirror and recoil. No make-up, hair in ponytail, wearing T-shirt and shorts, I never bothered to change when I went into work. It was just me and Charlotte all day.

Opening my car door, I start toward the bench. The night air hits my face, cool and tangy with salt from the sea. Utterly refreshing. This place is an old fave for people-watching when I used to live here with my brother. I'm pretty sure I had more friends then, and I remind myself to get in touch with some of them. It might stop me meeting strangers for food drops.

Making my way toward Circular Quay, the Opera House glows like illuminated shells against the dark water in front of me. And the bench is exactly where I remembered—tucked between two jacaranda trees, facing the harbor with a perfect view of the bridge's lights reflected in the water. And bonus, it's empty. I sink onto it, letting the breeze lift my ponytail while I think how far I am from NYC. Is that good or bad?

"Rough day, Willy Wonka?" His voice makes me jump.

Mitch appears out of the darkness, holding a big white paper bag with handles and a cardboard tray with two cups. When he's under the lamplight, I see a mischievous smile playing at his lips. He's wearing tan shorts and a navy shirt that makes his bright blue eyes look even lighter in the streetlight. His body is as fantastic as I remember, all lean, sculpted muscles.

"Something like that." I scoot over to make room, trying not to notice how good he smells when he settles beside me. "You weren't kidding about feeding me."

"Lady, I never kid about food." He unpacks the bag with efficient movements—unleashing an aroma that makes my mouth water.

"Bite-sized, spicy beer-battered cod and crispy fries," he says, opening a separate container to reveal thick wedges. "I recall you love fries." He also opens the lid on what looks like a chocolate milkshake that has me groaning at the first sip.

"When was the last time you ate actual food?" he asks.

"Charlotte, she's my . . . *ah* . . . supervisor. She forced a granola bar on me around noon." I'm not lying when I add, "I had access to all the candy I wanted. But I got busy."

Our break room at work keeps boxes of assorted chocolates, and it's unlike me to go a day without choosing at least three. On the other hand, I don't usually go into the office on a Saturday for an all-out emergency, and I barely left my office.

He hands me the to-go container of fish, as well as a packet of malt vinegar, which I tear open with my teeth and sprinkle over everything I can see, including the fries I've heaped onto my plate.

Practically diving in head first, taking massive unladylike bites and moaning in between, I barely hear his sarcastic words, "Please, go ahead and eat. Don't hold back. Doctor's orders."

After I've devoured a piece of fish and am holding the next one, I quip, "You're a doctor now?"

"Of fry-ology." He grins when I snort with laughter. "Serious medical condition when someone forgets to eat. Could lead to fainting into vats of melted caramel."

"That would be a sticky situation," I manage between bites, then groan at my own terrible pun.

"Did you just—?" He shakes his head, but he's fighting a smile. "That was awful."

"I'm frazzled. My humor cortex is compromised." I steal one of his fries since I've already demolished mine. I like how easy this is, free of awkward tension, despite us both being naked last time we laid eyes on one another. "This is amazing, by the way. Where's it from?"

"I made it. Learned my best techniques by watching my dad cook in our small kitchen in Boston."

I pause mid-chew, picturing a young Mitch, learning at his father's side. Not unlike Luke and me being taught the chocolate business by our dad and our grandfather.

"Wow! You are an amazing cook."

"Thanks. I appreciate an enthusiastic eater."

I lick tartar sauce off my thumb, then freeze when I catch him staring. The air between us shifts, thickens. Suddenly I'm hyper aware of how close we're sitting, how his thigh presses against mine, even though he could move farther along the bench.

"Lark . . ." His voice drops an octave, and my name sounds like a prayer on his lips.

"I should tell you something," I blurt out, needing to break the spell before I do something stupid like climb onto his thighs in public.

"No." He presses a finger to my lips, and I forget how to breathe. "No, you absolutely shouldn't. Unless you're married or a lesbian or leaving Sydney in the next hour."

I shake my head. "None of those things."

"Whatever it is, whatever's had you stressed and starving yourself all day, it can wait. Tonight, you're just Lark who works with candy and has terrible jokes. And I'm Mitch who makes insanely good fish and chips."

I should insist, should come clean about who I really am, what I really do. But his finger traces along my lower lip, and all my good intentions evaporate.

"OK," I whisper against his touch.

He pulls his hand back, but the heat in his eyes doesn't dim. We sit in charged silence for a moment before he deliberately lightens the mood.

"So, catastrophic candy crisis aside, how's Sydney treating you? Missing the States?"

"Sydney has its moments," I admit, grateful for the subject change even as my lips still tingle from his touch. "The coffee culture here puts to shame the one in . . . anywhere in the U.S."

I nearly said New York and caught myself, because I don't want Mitch thinking of a Lark in NYC who is now in Sydney. My last name might spring to mind.

"It's outstanding," he agrees. "Have you tried the Bourke Street Bakery yet?"

"Tourist trap," I say, my tone one of mock disdain, although it was a favorite of both my brother and me.

"Tourist trap?" He clutches his chest dramatically. "You wound me. Their croissants alone are worth the queue."

"Spoken like a restaurant snob," I say, realizing a cook is a great guy to hang around with if you're a foodie. "Or at least a guy who knows his way around a kitchen."

Bumping his shoulder with mine, being chummy in a goofy way, I immediately regret the contact when heat spreads from the point of impact to all parts family-friendly and private.

Needing to cool down, I take another sip of the milkshake, which is frankly obscene in its creamy richness. "This shake is ridiculous, by the way. What's in it?"

"Trade secret." He winks. "Though I might be persuaded to share if you agree to go out with me."

"Extortion. Not a good dating tactic." Wanting to dodge the question, I aim for playful, but fatigue creeps into my voice. Mitch, more than anyone, knows why I had very little sleep.

His expression softens. "You look ready to collapse, Lark. Beautiful, but exhausted."

The casual compliment makes my stomach flip. I stare out at the harbor, watching a late ferry cut through the dark water. If I sit here much longer, I'll be either asleep on a bench for the first time in my life, or I'll be spilling my guts about contaminated sugar.

"I better get going." Standing, I stretch and can't suppress a yawn. "Thank you for the food."

"Anytime." Mitch looks like he's going to reach for my hand, but stops himself. "Maybe next time, something a little more upscale."

"Next time?" I try for teasing, but it comes out breathless.

"If you'll let me." Those piercing eyes search mine. "How about to a club? I know we jumped right into the good stuff, but I'd like to take you out before . . ."

He trails off. *Before we jump into bed?* We both know we would have sex again if given the opportunity, but I'm glad he didn't say it.

"Friday night?" he asks.

*Friday!* The SBA dinner. The chocolate platters. The gift boxes. My stomach drops as reality crashes back like a powerful May wave at Narrabeen Beach. I'll be scrambling all week to fix our sugar crisis on time.

Shaking my head like going out with him is the last thing in the world I want to do, I tell him, "I can't Friday. Work thing."

He stares hard at me in the quickening darkness. He probably thinks I'm blowing him off, since not many sales clerks have "work things."

Finally, Mitch says, "Not a problem."

Before I start explaining myself, getting in deeper, I hurry away, leaving all the trash for him to take care of. *Like an ungrateful ass!*

But I can't let him offer to walk me to my car. It's Luke's sporty black Audi R8, which is rather expensive for a candy store worker. I don't relax again until I'm heading home, enjoying the fact that Mitch took care of me tonight, fed me, and asked me out—all while *not* knowing I'm Lark Henley.

# 4

# Mitch

Folding my arms across my chest, I lean against the wall next to the hallway connecting the ballroom of the InterContinental Sydney to the kitchen where my staff is at work. It's a good vantage point.

The room pulses with the quiet power of the city's business elite, gathered for the Sydney Business Association's yearly dinner. Crystal chandeliers cast a golden glow over tables draped in white linen. Each setting is meticulously arranged with sterling silver and fine china.

There's a hum of conversation, the powerful making chit-chat or striking deals. The clink of glassware as people toast their recent or upcoming business success.

The event is a rehearsal of sorts for the larger All-Australia Business Conference that's also held in Sydney, but four months later, at the conference center. In a way, the SBA's smaller venue is more important for those doing business in the city because the yearly dinner is where deals are made, alliances formed, and reputations cemented—or destroyed.

Also, it's unlikely I'll still be around by the time of the AABC. Franklin 6 is running smoothly and has been for nearly two months. I'm starting to get excited about my next restaurant venture back in the U.S., conquering new territory in Montana.

As the new kid in town, it's a great honor to be catering this prestigious dinner for 250. Ironically, my restaurant had to close tonight to handle the workload, although F6 Tavern remains open. Otherwise, it would be a slap in the face to the hard-won regulars.

Scanning the crowd of black-tie, well-dressed business people, I'm confident my head chef, Ravi, has everything under control. The rest of our staff are executing their jobs flawlessly, with the precision I demand.

They've been circulating with hors d'oeuvres that have been universally met with appreciative murmurs, the wine is flowing, and I've already shaken hands with most of the Fortune 500 CEOs in Australia, as well as those from the Forbes 2000 list.

Everything is perfect. So why do I feel on edge?

*Because Lark ate my food and turned me down.*

And because seeing her again confirmed the fact that I don't want to let her get away. Something with her feels different. So much so that I spent too many of my free hours this week looking for her. After our harborside picnic, when Lark rushed off clutching that milkshake like it contained the elixir of life, I realized I still knew almost nothing concrete about her.

*A woman who works with candy and has a supervisor named Charlotte.*

*She is spectacular in bed, giving as good as she gets.*

*Sassy and sweet, sexy and submissive.*

I visited every high-end chocolate shop in greater Sydney and even a couple bakeries. No Lark. If the store she works for got its shit together, then they might have a business owner here tonight. And maybe that owner would be smart enough to bring along the prettiest employee, one who could charm the women and captivate the men.

I'd sneak Lark into a coat closet and kiss her senseless. Or better yet, book a room upstairs for tonight.

"Mitch." Ravi appears at my elbow. "Plating first course, serving in five minutes."

I know he made one of his incredible appetizers, a salad with ingredients that make people pause for a second before jumping in and finishing every scrap. This one has smoked salmon on it, along with avocado and pears. At the restaurant, it's served as an entree.

"How has everything turned out?" I ask.

"All good, mate," Ravi says, which I know means *absolutely perfect.*

He and I debated, tested, and finally decided on a main course of spiced duck breast for the meat eaters and wild mushroom ravioli for the vegetarians. I'm not concerned, except for the dessert. We wanted to honor them with one of Australia's classic traditions. It would be a disaster to mess it up.

"And the pavlova?" I ask.

"Bloody ripper," he confirms.

If it's perfect, which it better be, the meringue base has a crisp outer shell and a soft, marshmallowy center. Our signature pavlova, served at Franklin 6, is topped with fresh cream and seasonal fruit. Despite being known for my rich chocolate sauce, Franklin Darkly, I purposefully didn't choose a chocolate dessert, knowing the legendary Henley Confectionery, with roots stretching back three generations, would be showcased here tonight.

Their corporate headquarters is in Sydney. Old money, old chocolate, but new ideas that keep the company ahead of competitors in the cutthroat confectionery world. I'm looking forward to meeting their representative.

"I'll be at my table," I tell Ravi. "Text if you need me."

I weave through the crowd toward a table near the makeshift stage and the podium. That's when I see her.

First, it's simply a shimmer of emerald green that catches my eye. On the other side of the room, she stands in profile, champagne flute balanced delicately between her fingers, head tipped back in laughter at something a silver-haired gentleman is saying. Her caramel-colored hair swaying across her bare back, glowing in the light of the chandeliers. But it's the gown that makes my pulse race. Shimmering silk that hugs the curves I've already memorized with my hands and my mouth.

*Lark.*

My heart hammers against my ribs like an eager fist. Six days since I last saw her. Not that I've been keeping track.

She looks different here—polished, sophisticated, completely at ease among Australia's elite. Not at all like a store clerk. I start toward her, mumbling apologies as I brush past shoulders of those in their seats. I have to get to her before she disappears again.

The microphone crackles to life, and I glance over, seeing Jenny Parsons, the president of the Association. She taps it twice before smiling broadly at the assembled guests.

"While our hard-working wait staff brings out our magnificent dinner, I'd like to acknowledge two special guests joining us tonight. We're fortunate to have culinary royalty gracing our tables."

I pause, halfway across the room. *Culinary royalty?* She must mean me and some other chef. Perhaps Elena Marone from the super chic Venetian Waters? I scan the crowd, trying to spot familiar faces from the Sydney food scene.

"First, the brilliantly creative mind behind the Franklin Restaurant Group, whose restaurants have redefined fine dining across three continents. Please welcome Mitchell Franklin, who has personally overseen tonight's exquisite menu."

A spotlight finds me, frozen in the middle of the ballroom. I force a smile and raise a hand in acknowledgment as polite applause ripples throughout. The light is blinding, but I can just make out Lark's silhouette. She is turned toward me now, her posture stiff as a mannequin's.

"And we're equally honored to have with us the CEO of Henley Confectionery's Sydney division, recently returned from conquering New York's competitive chocolate scene."

The spotlight swings across the room and lands squarely on . . . Lark!

*Not* shopgirl Lark.

*Not* the woman who casually mentioned working "in candy" like she was some counter clerk at a mall kiosk.

Lark Henley. *The* Lark Henley.

In the busy past few months of setting up not one but two Sydney venues, I guess I missed that she and her brother had switched jobs, because last I heard, Luke Henley was the CEO.

Time stops as our gazes lock across the sea of tables. The polite applause around us is nothing but white noise as comprehension blooms across her face—the same stunned realization that's currently slamming into me.

"Her family's company has sponsored tonight's delectable gift boxes," Mrs. Parsons continues, "including their signature chocolates you'll be taking home tonight. But you don't have to wait. An assortment will be served with dessert alongside Mr. Franklin's already renowned take on our beloved pavlova."

Lark and I keep staring, taking in the identity of the passionate lover behind our one sizzling night.

"If everyone will please take their seats, Ms. Henley is presenting our keynote address while you enjoy Mr. Franklin's first course," Mrs. Parsons says, oblivious to the silent charge zapping between the so-called royals.

Although I don't like being duped, fair is fair, and I gave as good as I got. Besides, I'm relieved I don't have to worry about her using me as a meal ticket. There's virtually nothing I can give Lark that she can't give herself.

*Except for my body and all that I can do with it to pleasure her.*

I see the exact moment when Lark's surprise transforms into anger. Her lips part, her shoulders straighten, and her eyes—those captivating burnished golden eyes I've been dreaming about—narrow into slits sharp enough to slice through steel. Two statues in a garden of movement, we remain locked in our silent standoff for a few seconds too long while any guests still standing find their seats.

Mrs. Parsons coughs politely, then says, "Lark, please come to the podium." The spotlight clicks off her as she makes her way to the mic. Conversation resumes briefly. The waitstaff continues circulating with practiced efficiency. But I watch Lark until she turns and faces the room. Her eyes find me once again, and I belatedly take my seat at the VIP table, realizing the empty chair must be for her.

"Thank you," she says, "and good evening. I promise I'll be brief, as I cannot wait to taste what Mr. Franklin has dished up. If he can cook up a duck as well as he cooks up a tall tale, then I'm sure we're all in for a treat."

Having let me know she's exceedingly unhappy finding out who I am this way, she finally sweeps her glance over the room. And then she proceeds to charm her audience. She compares Sydney to NYC, making sure the former comes out on top in all aspects. She tells a few Henley company stories of challenge and triumph, and ends on an encouraging note.

"I am thrilled to be back in Sydney where I spent so many formative and happy years. I hope to be a part of new growth and expansion in our thriving business community. But tonight, I'm simply elated to share with you some of Henley's finest confectionery, most of it dreamt up by our master chocolatier, Julian Cartier."

Everyone claps, by now having devoured most of their salad. The mouthwatering aroma of the main course yet to come is tantalizing, and the energy in the room is high. She briefly stops at various tables, talking to admirers, like a princess.

Lark Henley's reputation is exactly that, royalty in the family dynasty, commanding her father's NY division with skill while also dazzling Manhattan's social scene. At least, that's my impression from any press I read about her. Before she reaches us, my phone pings with an urgent request from Ravi to join him by the hallway to the kitchen. Reluctantly, I excuse myself.

"What's up?" I ask, keeping my gaze on Lark, still working the room.

"Sorry to hassle you, Mitch, but table ten wants to know the duck was treated right—happy life, gentle send-off, maybe even a lullaby before it landed on the plate." We smile at each other and refrain from rolling our eyes. *Comes with the territory.*

"Your word as head chef wasn't enough?"

"Nah. This bloke wants the *executive* chef. And play nice, mate. He's a bigwig, at a table of bigwigs. That's what Mrs. Parsons said when she asked me to send you over."

"Got it." I'd rather approach Lark and have a frank discussion, but I head over to the table Ravi indicated. They're all super nice, as it turns out, just curious. That's often the case when people see that I'm a large, biracial, black man. For some, that's not the image they have of Mitch Franklin, a French-trained chef and entrepreneur.

I charm the pants off them. Five minutes later, they're all happily eating duck and one woman wants Franklin 6 to cater her daughter's wedding. "Only slightly more guests than are here tonight," she says without blinking.

Then I take a few steps toward my table and see Lark finally reaching her seat. An attractive guy rises to draw out her chair. *Her date?* My stomach twists with something that feels dangerously like jealousy. I had tried to invite her to this very event when we were devouring fish and chips, thinking it would be a real treat for a candy store worker. *What an idiot!*

Lark doesn't sit. Instead, she exchanges a few words with him before reaching down and snagging what might be a piece of succulent duck. I watch her pop the food between her sweet lips and hope she loves the taste. Her gaze finds mine again. Then she puts her hand on the man's shoulder, urging him to sit once more, before making her way through the crowd.

Not toward another table of people trying to wave her down.

Not toward the ladies' room.

Toward me.

Her emerald dress whispers against the floor as she approaches, drawing appreciative glances from the men she passes. The silk clings to her curves, revealing enough skin to be seductive while maintaining understated elegance. This is no shop clerk. This is a woman born into great wealth, who has never known an uncertain day in her privileged life.

*How could I have mistaken her for anything else?*

"Mitchell Franklin," she says, her voice honey-coated venom. "Restaurant mogul. The man with the Midas fork."

"Lark Henley," I counter, struggling to recalibrate everything I thought I knew about her. "Third-generation chocolate heiress. Recently back from New York where you were, what was it again? Oh right. According to Mrs. Parsons, you were conquering the competitive chocolate scene."

"You lied to me." Her tone doesn't match the public smile frozen on her face. Around us, Sydney's business elite continue eating my food, oblivious to the war being waged under the chandeliers.

"Ditto," I retort childishly, then I add, "Anyway, I didn't lie. I told you I worked in restaurants."

"You own like five—"

"Six," I interrupt. "Franklin 6, remember? Plus F6 Tavern where we met."

Her mouth twists, then she continues, "Six restaurants on three continents?" The last word comes out on a hiss, her smile never faltering for the benefit of any onlookers. "That's like saying the Pope 'works in religion.'"

"And you casually mentioned you work in 'candy'—as if you're not the heir to a chocolate empire worth millions."

"A billion, actually."

My hands clench at my sides. "Do you know how many candy shops I've been to this week, looking for you?"

A glimmer of something—*surprise? maybe satisfaction?*—crosses her pretty face before she masks it with renewed indignation.

"I don't owe you my resume, Mitch. It was supposed to be one night, with a guy who wasn't a rich poser. The last thing I need is another millionaire—"

"That's billionaire, with a *b*, lady."

Again, she looks surprised, so I shrug. "Not all from restaurants. I have a retail product that sells worldwide, and I made the rest the old-fashioned way. I inherited it." I'd love to tell her about my grandfather's illustrious career as a research scientist, who patented things probably in her medicine cabinet right now. But this is hardly the place. Besides, she's obviously not in a receptive mood.

"A billionaire," she mutters. "Even worse." Oddly, her gaze flickers, vulnerability peeking through her armor for a mere instant. Then it's gone. "You were deliberately misleading, with your grungy little table by the kitchen door."

"Pot, meet kettle," I retort, then lower my voice as a couple passes too close. "And speaking of misleading, who's the guy you brought tonight? Moving on rather quickly, aren't you?" *Damn.* I wish I could take that back.

She shakes her head. "What are you talking about?"

"Your date." I jerk my chin toward the scrawny dude she'd spoken to before charging like a freight train toward me. "The one who looks like he stepped out of a men's fragrance commercial, if you like the androgynous type."

"Jules?" A startled laugh escapes her. "He's my master chocolatier. A valued Henley employee, but that's all."

"Right." The acid in my voice burns even my own ears. "I'm sure you always bring a *valued* employee, a chocolate-maker, to a black-tie gala."

"Actually, yes. But Jules doesn't *make* chocolate. We have superb chocolate-makers, but he isn't one of them. He's a chocolatier, creating our best confectionery. In a class by himself. And at Henley, we reward talent. Recognize it, develop it, and publicly acknowledge it." Her eyes narrow. "Unlike some people, who take credit for their staff's work."

That cuts deep. I've built my reputation on being hands-on, working alongside my chefs to develop everything we serve. "You're crossing a line," I warn, voice dropping lower. "I've always—"

"Given credit where it's due?" She steps closer, the familiar scent of her perfume, vanilla and cinnamon, makes me hard when I don't need lust clouding my brain. "Then why are you standing here in a tuxedo while your staff sweats in the kitchen? Why aren't they here, being duly acknowledged for the meal everyone's praising you for?"

I grip her elbow, steering her toward a quieter corner where potted palms create the illusion of privacy. She could pull her arm from my grasp and make a scene, but she doesn't.

"My name on the door doesn't diminish their contributions, but I *am* the executive chef of every Franklin restaurant. And for your information, while Franklin 6's head chef Ravi has been too busy feeding two hundred and fifty people to be standing around wearing a tux and chatting, I've mentioned him to every person who's complimented the food tonight."

"How magnanimous of you," she says, voice dripping with sarcasm. "Your majesty allows the peasants to take a bow."

"You're one to talk," I remind her. "Born with a silver spoon—or should I say, a chocolate truffle—in your mouth. At least I built my business from scratch."

Something flashes in her eyes, and I don't like having caused it. Just because she's a Henley by birth, it doesn't mean she hasn't worked hard at her job. I'm ready to apologize when she snaps, "You know nothing about me."

"I know enough to recognize when someone's playing games." I lean closer, our faces inches apart. "Why the charade, Lark? Why pretend to be something you're not?"

"That's rich coming from you." Finally, she yanks her arm free. "Tell me, Mitch, does it make you feel powerful when you seduce someone you pick up in your very own bar, especially someone you think is so beneath you in status that you hide your identity? It seems a little unethical."

Her words hit like a slap. "Is that how you remember it? That I was slumming it? Trolling for poor girls I could use and ditch? If you recall, you invited me to have a drink."

"After you offered to buy me one," she shoots back. If she'd been a man, she would be puffing up her chest and pressing it against mine in one of those macho pissing contests. Maybe poking my shoulder like a douchebag.

"*Christ*, Lark, I was instantly attracted to you. I didn't care what you did for a living. You could've been the CEO of a chocolate company for all I knew. Wait, you are!"

"And yet you never mentioned you owned the bar, or who you were."

"Neither did you."

We've reached an impasse, circling each other like wounded predators. We each have our own demons, making us behave overtly hostile. The air between us sizzles with something dangerous—anger, betrayal, and beneath it all, the same electric attraction that pulled us together in the first place. Logically, I know that whatever is angering her is not really about me. It's about something some prick has done to her, and I'm just paying the price.

Over her shoulder, I see her date—her master chocolatier—watching us with thinly veiled concern. He has risen to his feet again, clearly uncertain whether to intervene.

"Your boy's worried," I murmur, nodding in the guy's direction.

Lark doesn't turn. "He's not my boy. And I'm perfectly capable of handling myself."

"That much is clear." Despite my own irritation, which boils down to how much I don't like being squarely matched in the game of hiding one's wealth, I can't help but admire her composure. Even now, with fury radiating from her like heat, she maintains the perfect public face—back straight, smile fixed, voice controlled. "You've had practice at this."

"At what?" she demands.

"Playing roles. Being who people expect you to be."

Her eyes widen fractionally, a direct hit I wasn't even aiming for.

"You don't know me," she repeats, her voice softer now, almost sad. "One night doesn't make you an expert on Lark Henley."

"How about one night *and* take-out fish and chips," I quip, hoping for a smile. I get zilch. But I want to bring this argument down from boiling to a gentle simmer, and yes, my motive is that I want to have sex with her again. "We can agree that neither of us wanted to be who we truly are that night. We can discuss why another time. Agreed?"

For a moment, vulnerability clouds her features. Then it vanishes, replaced by cold determination.

"It doesn't matter anymore," she says, stepping back. "You're a liar. And I'm not into liars."

"Look in the mirror, lady," I mutter.

Her hand flies up, and for a heart-stopping moment, I think she's going to slap me in full view of Australia's beautiful people. At the last second, she freezes, fingers trembling in mid-air, recognition of our public setting stopping her.

"Go to hell, Mitch," she whispers, voice shaking with rage. "The duck was stringy. And your pavlova?" She leans in, her lips nearly brushing my ear. "The meringue was overbeaten. I could see the cracks when I passed the serving tray."

Then she turns on her sexy heel and walks away, directly back to her chocolatier. She places a hand on his shoulder, shaking her head slightly. Then Lark leans down to speak quietly, giving him or anyone else at the table a view of her glorious tits. My hands curl into fists at the spark of uncharacteristic jealousy that flashes through me, and I follow her.

Whatever she says makes him pause and glance at me. I hope he receives the full force of my scowl as I stalk closer. In any case, before I get there, she slips away, heading for the double doors leading to the ballroom's private balcony.

I'm conflicted. I should take my seat, make small talk with the banking executive to my right and the mining CEO to my left, and maybe pump Jules Cartier for information on why his boss is such an uptight bitch. Most definitely, I should let her go, forget about her. *Class-A nutjob and high-maintenance to boot.*

But when I reach the table, I bypass it, despite the chocolatier's gaze fixed on me. Heading to the hallway leading to the kitchen, I stop when I see one of my staff standing guard beside our state-of-the-art serving trolley that has plate warmers built in. There are still portions of duck and ravioli, although as far as I know, everyone has been served.

I can't help myself. I grab a morsel of the spicy duck. The tender meat all but melts on my tongue and explodes with flavor, which gives me a massive level of satisfaction. I should sit and eat and accept the accolades. But I give in to my desire for a woman currently alone outside while everyone is chowing down.

Lark Henley has walked out, and I need to know why. It cannot be because a one-night stand didn't tell her his full name. Which is why, instead of making crucial connections with Sydney's crème de la crème, I follow this crazy lady, drawn by the same magnetic pull that's had me searching candy stores all week like a lovesick teenager, looking for a shopgirl who didn't exist.

My phone vibrates in my pocket. Ravi, no doubt, wondering where I've disappeared to right when the main course is about to be cleared away in favor of the palate-cleansing citrus granita.

I silence it without looking. For the first time in my professional life, I'm letting someone else handle the kitchen during a major event. But I do check one of the pavlovas on my way out. It is most certainly not overbeaten and not a crack in sight!

I see her as soon as I exit the dining room. The balcony isn't huge, as it's in the old part of the hotel, a former Treasury Building built in 1851. Lark is standing with her arms wrapped tightly around herself. A silhouette of emerald silk and honey-colored hair against the lights from the Royal Botanic Gardens across the street.

Beyond it is the harbor, which she is staring at intently, shoulders drooping a little. I can almost see the strain from here.

And in a heartbeat, I melt like a Henley chocolate in the sun, ready to do anything to ease her tension and make it right between us.

# 5

# Lark

Above the hum of city traffic, I hear Mitch's footsteps and can stop wondering whether he'll follow. If I'd been betting with myself, I would've won. Releasing a big tense breath, I try to calm down. The night air helps, refreshingly cool after the crowded ballroom and the heated encounter with a man who was not supposed to be here, who turned out to be someone I could never have guessed.

Like discovering your sexy Clark Kent is actually Superman. *So not what I wanted.* I'm behaving like a spoiled brat, who just found out her down-and-dirty boy toy is a billionaire.

*Boo-hoo! Poor me!*

But in the blink of an eye, I hung so much baggage around the neck of a guy like him, it's a miracle he can walk. Unfortunately, I know too well that he can do a lot of damage.

He could tell the world what I like in bed. I shiver.

"If you've come to apologize, save it," I say without turning, pretending to enjoy the lamplit gardens. I guess I'm not done being a brat.

"I have nothing to apologize for," he says arrogantly, coming too close. I can smell the light fragrance of *Mitchness*. Must be his soap or shampoo since I'm aware most chefs don't mess with anything that might clash with the aroma of food or interfere with their ability to smell it, not when they're on the clock.

His breath tickles the back of my neck when he speaks. "You lied as much as I did."

"I never lied." Finally, I turn, noticing how the moonlight carves shadows beneath his cheekbones, making him look dangerous. In fact, he's full-on *panther in a tux*, whereas if I look anything like I feel after the past week from hell, then I'm channeling a weary hag in a designer dress.

"I said I worked in candy. I do. I said I had inventory issues. I did, as in a substantial amount of our chocolate was contaminated."

"You deliberately let me believe you were a shop assistant," Mitch points out, "working for someone named Charlotte."

"And you deliberately let me believe you were a regular guy at a bar, and afterward, at most, a line cook." I think about how much it meant to me that he wasn't rich, wasn't a player, wasn't in the spotlight or the news.

"It's fine," I add, waving my hand in his direction. "That night, you were what I needed—a normal guy with a regular job. Someone uncomplicated."

He flinches. "I'm still the same person I was that night."

"Are you?" I shoot back. I know I'm becoming all kinds of paranoid, but I'm hungry and annoyed at being tricked. "Are you the same person who told me about growing up watching his father cook in a tiny Boston kitchen? Or did you make all that up?"

My disbelieving and derisive tone is clear as a bell when I press the matter. "Who inherits millions from someone with a *tiny* kitchen?" *Dammit.* "More likely, you're another entitled hot-shot businessman playing at being authentic."

He takes a step closer, his anger flaring. Those pale-blue eyes, illuminated by the overhead balcony lighting, flare like the hottest center of a flame.

"Everything I told you was true. Every. Single. Word. I did grow up in that kitchen. My father did teach me to cook before I went to Le Cordon Bleu. I built my business from nothing. Just a food truck and an idea. The fact that I've been successful doesn't change who I am or where I come from. Nor does my grandfather selling his stocks before he died and making me and my sister stupidly rich."

*Maybe.* I sure as hell know how birth and upbringing and expectations all intertwine. He's looming over me now, and my body is humming with awareness, so I turn to stare out at the harbor lights. "You could have told me," I say, mulish and not ready to cave.

"When, exactly?"

His tone is low, like a caress, and I think he's about to touch my shoulder. And God help me, I want him to. Gripping the stone balustrade so tightly, my knuckles whiten. Waiting. Anticipating. Hoping. Dreading.

"When I was balls deep in you?"

His crude question, so at odds with the smooth tone of his voice, makes me gasp. Yeah, that wouldn't have gone over well. I would have freaked out. He continues before I can speak.

"Or should I have texted you my name sometime between you skipping out before dawn and when you ran away after the meal I brought you? You know, when you disappeared for a week."

He seems to be a little bratty himself, holding a grudge about not being able to find me. *Jeez!*

"Or maybe when you were talking about your cruel, long hours with nothing but a granola bar, like you were trapped behind a retail counter instead of in a luxurious office with take-out from any restaurant in Sydney at your disposal?"

I roll my eyes, although he can't see them.

"I never said—"

"You implied," he spits out. "And you knew exactly what you were doing." He moves to stand beside me against the cold stone railing, not looking at me but out at the harbor. "The question is, why are you reacting so strongly to my discovering who you are? And even more irate at finding out who I am?"

I don't answer. Not at first. *Do I really want to have this personal conversation?*

That almost makes me smile when I think about what I let this man do to my body. I have no fight left, at least, not tonight. My voice sounds soft, perhaps defeated, even to my own ears when I finally speak.

"I wanted to be just Lark. Not Lark *Henley*, chocolate heiress, as you called me. Not the Sydney division CEO, fighting for respect from the same people who worked for and with my brother for the last four years." I exhale slowly, trying not to let it sound like a pathetic sigh.

What I don't do is talk about my own inner critic that can't help comparing myself to Luke's success, both here and after he easily slipped into my Manhattan office.

"That night, I was simply a woman out for a drink with a friend, open to . . . opportunity, should it arise. Which it did. Then, I was a woman attracted to a man. Nothing more complicated than that."

Mitch hesitates before he speaks. "I understand what you're saying, better than you think."

When I glance up at him beside me, I wish all the shadows and slices of light were pure sunshine so I could see him better.

"Do you?" I hope my skepticism isn't evident.

"I spend a lot of time in the kitchen of whichever restaurant I'm at, because that's where I'm just Mitch. Not Mitchell Franklin, restaurant mogul. Not the guy whose face is plastered across cookbook jackets and magazine covers."

He runs a hand through his hair and looks so goddamn sexy I want to lean in and kiss him. Instead, I nod, and he adds, "I'm simply a guy who loves food, not merely the eating of it but the creating of it, the planning, the cooking, the tasting, and the devouring. That's why I still personally develop new dishes for every place I open. That's why I refuse to give up being the executive chef, supervising all my restaurants."

The tension between us shifts, eases almost imperceptibly. I study his face, and he does the same, both searching for deception.

I'm still not ready to spill my guts about the one dark and grungy example of a sly player from my past, who came on like a prince before totally screwing me over.

"So, each of us pretended," I acknowledge.

"We did." He moves closer so his arm is against mine, making me shiver. "But it wasn't all pretense, was it? The connection between us was real."

I look away, maybe not before he sees the flicker of acknowledgment I'm certain is in my eyes. Because that night was as real as it has ever been for me with any man. But that changes nothing.

"We'll call a truce," I say. "Leave the past behind us, and we can . . ." *What exactly?* "We can part as . . . friends."

"The hell we can." His voice is a growl that startles me. "We spent one night together, and I haven't been able to think straight ever since."

"That's all I was looking for," I say. "You agreed," I remind him.

He makes a face. "At least I've discovered where all the best candy stores are."

I feel a ghost of a smile cross my face before I can stop it. "While I was in corporate hell putting out fires."

"Your inventory issue."

"Sugar contaminated with geosmin." This time, I do release a long sigh. It was so unnecessary, and all my own fault, switching from the supplier my brother had been using. "Non-toxic but not particularly nice in one's chocolate bar. We didn't catch it before production."

He winces on my behalf. "That must've been a nightmare."

"Yup," I agree. "My company dug our way out of a massive disaster this week. At least I know that every chocolate in tonight's gift boxes is perfect, as well as what will be served on the plates alongside your wretched pavlova."

I can tell he doesn't take it personally, understands I'm just blowing off steam.

"Even worse, it was never supposed to be at our factory. An independent lab ID'd it as beet sugar, which we don't use." When the report came in, I nearly spit my teeth out along with my coffee.

"Someone switched out our cane sugar order *before* it landed in our warehouse in mismarked bags. And because of the high profile of tonight's sponsorship, the board's been breathing down my neck all week to remake a lot of confectionery. As if that helped!"

He makes a gruff laugh that sounds more like a groan. "And then you found out the man you spent the night with is—"

"Beet sugar, instead of cane," I mutter.

"Hardly that," he insists. "But I would love to get inside your chocolate factory."

I startle. "What?"

Mitch's smile is genuine. "I'm not using *factory* as a euphemism, although that, too," he adds, and the way he looks at my mouth creates goosebumps on my skin. "I'm honestly super curious, and I love chocolate."

Picturing him at the Wetherill Park factory, I know that no good could come of it. "The snakes and vultures wouldn't look kindly on you being inside my chocolate factory. And I am using that both in reality *and* as a euphemism."

Shaking my head, I imagine the fallout and try to explain them to him.

"Here's a few headlines: 'Henley heiress sleeps with successful restaurateur, getting a leg up, among other body parts, on international distribution in his restaurants.' Or how about, 'Has the young female Henley heir been playing at CEO, while tempting men with her chocolates?' Or maybe, 'Wholesome family business becomes *risky* business'? The tabloids would have a field day because of who I am. Too young, too inexperienced, and too blonde."

He's staring at me like I'm insane, but my perception is filtered through personal experience, as a powerful woman who often doesn't feel so powerful after all. More like I've been given a toy to play with and patted on the head.

*"Don't break the company, dear."*

"You're right about our brands being built on carefully cultivated images," he agrees. "Yours is one of family and homemade chocolates, right? Starting from your grandparents' kitchen. Mine is one of pulling myself up by my own apron strings into someone who creates eclectic risk-taking dishes. I'm considered a maverick who doesn't give a damn. A sex scandal would do me no harm at all," he concludes.

"But be potentially devastating for my family legacy," I say. "And for me professionally."

"So that's it?" Mitch asks, an edge to his voice. I recognize from personal experience that he doesn't like not being in control. Funny enough, that's what I most enjoy in the bedroom, giving any semblance of control away.

Suddenly, he strokes his thumb along my upper arm. With my emotions seesawing all night, I'm instantly wet between my legs.

"One great night and we go our separate ways, because of potential bad press?" he asks. "Or maybe it's because you're a coward?"

"A coward?" The word is like a slap. I can't help thinking he turned this personal again, because he wanted to goad me. And it works. Fury rises fresh and hot in my chest. "You dare call me a coward when I drove off into the night with you? How about when I met you alone for fish and chips?"

Mitch takes hold of my chin, looking down at me from his formidable height, his presence overwhelming on the balcony's intimate space.

"You've been running away since I met you, just like you're doing tonight."

"I'm protecting my family's legacy." The words taste bitter on my tongue. "Something you wouldn't understand. Must be nice, having only yourself to disappoint."

His jaw tightens. *Direct hit.*

"Is that what you think?" he asks, his tone harsh. "That because I built my business myself, I have no one depending on me? No one to answer to?"

The air grows thick with tension. Behind us, muffled laughter and classical music drift from the hotel where two hundred and forty-eight people are no doubt devouring Mitch's perfect pavlova.

Out here, though, it's just the two of us, and my very real and valid fear, one that I won't explain to him. Can but won't. I merely dance around the topic.

"At least your failures would be yours alone," I say, softer now. "When I fail, I drag three generations down with me."

"I'm starting to understand." He frowns, still not releasing me. I'd shake him off if that didn't seem undignified. "You're afraid of failing?" Mitch asks.

He has no idea. "I've already failed." The admission slips out before I can stop it. "The sugar contamination should never have happened. And now this . . ."

"This?" he demands.

"You." I gesture between us. "A simple night of pleasure had to become a complicated effing . . . whatever this is. *Was!*" I add.

His eyes narrow. "Whatever this could be."

The possibility hangs between us like smoke, tempting and dangerous. Finally, I turn away, and his gentle grip releases. "There is definitely no 'could be.'"

"Because I'm not good enough for the Henley dynasty?"

His words make no sense. I thought he knew how humble our roots are since he mentioned my grandparents. But I give him a truthful answer. "Because you want more than I can give. I have a major company to run, barely two hours from the Henley ranch, where Nan and Gramps started it all."

I can see by his expression he doesn't understand and try again. "Last year, the NY division created an entire new line based on classic German flavors, boosting Henley's market share by fifteen percent in eight months."

"Sounds like a reason to be proud."

"I'm very proud *of my brother*," I explain, thinking how inspired Luke was by his love for his new wife to create a candy line that honors her heritage. "But I had nothing to do with it. The success happened *after* I left. The Sydney division, with me at the helm, needs to prove itself with our own innovation. Hard enough to do when I'm totally focused. Monumentally difficult when I find out you've been searching candy stores for me all week, like some romantic hero, and I can't—" I cut myself off, breathing hard.

"Can't what?" Against all odds, we're still so close I can see the pulse above his collar bone. My back is to the cool stone balustrade, and somehow, he's inserted his hard thigh between my legs. Leaning against my lady bits, making me throb with how much I want him again, he's stolen my breath. "Can't admit it felt really good to be together?" he finishes for me.

I think of how messed up my brother got, chasing his lover all over the world until he caught her. If I did that, I'd be considered an irresponsible, flighty female, not cut out to be CEO. "It doesn't matter what I feel. I mean, felt." My voice catches. "What matters is what I need to do."

"And what's that?" Mitch's voice drops lower, intimate. "Run away again?" He reaches up and tucks my hair behind my ear, stroking its soft shell, making me shiver. "Hide behind your family name and corporate responsibilities?"

"You don't understand," I begin, but I'm starting to lean forward, hoping he'll wrap his arms around me.

"Then make me understand." His hand brushes my bare shoulder, sending an electric tingle along my skin. "Tell me why you're running."

The city lights blur before me as tears threaten. "Because I can't do both. I can't be the responsible CEO *and* the woman who wants—" I stop myself, but it's too late.

"Wants what?" His fingers trace down my arm.

"A man who makes me forget who I am. A man who gives me things I can't have."

His intense blue eyes lock onto mine. "What things?"

I groan. "Freedom to submit, to release control." The words come out as barely a whisper.

"Who says you can't do both?" he asks. "A good CEO and a great lover."

"Past experience says." I need distance to clear my head, but I can't step back so I put my hands to his firm, broad chest. Like touching a warm mountain. If only he knew the various and sundry ways I got into trouble with wealthy bad boys in NYC. "I have to adhere to what the board wants. What the shareholders deserve. What my family expects."

"And what does Lark want?" Mitch covers my hands with his. "Not Lark Henley, CEO. Just Lark."

The question scares me. *What do I want?*

The answer is even more terrifying, and I stay silent. This is too much, too fast, dancing around the subject of us starting something hot and hopeful. I'm out here, fending off my own hedonistic wish to slide my tongue into his lush mouth, instead of being in that ballroom full of business people where I belong.

That proves I can't split my attention. Before I say any of that, Mitch's hand cups my cheek, tilting my face up.

"Tell me you don't want to experience our one-night stand again. And again. Tell me you haven't thought about it every day since."

I should pull away. I should return to the SBA event, where Jules is doubtless wondering whether I've taken a long walk into the harbor. I should be the reliable, sensible head of Henley Sydney that everyone expects me to be.

Instead, I lean into his touch.

"I've thought about it," I whisper. "Still do."

His thumb traces my bottom lip. "Then why are we fighting it?"

The stone balcony beneath my feet tilts as his lips find mine, hard and fast and increasingly urgent. Our kiss tastes of champagne and possibility, dangerous and sweet. His hands slide into my hair, not too careful of how he messes it up and firm enough to keep me in place. I grip his lapels, torn between holding him and pushing him away.

Lost in the sensation of his mouth on mine, of his tongue sliding between my lips and exploring, I dissolve into nothing but yearning, hot and wet and mindless. Even the cool night air stroking my bare shoulders can't dampen the heat between my thighs or make my pulse slow from its quick trot.

For a few long minutes, I'm just a woman kissing a man who makes her feel alive.

Voices float through the air as others step onto the balcony. With them, reality rocks me, like when I was a reckless child at Bondi Beach, going in too deep, until waves crashed over my head, knocking me to my knees. I'd always come up spluttering and dazed.

I break away, breathing hard, my lips tingling.

"We can't," I whisper, even as my body screams for more. "This isn't—"

"Don't say it isn't real." His voice is rough, his eyes dark with desire. "It's as real as we make it. For however long we want."

"It's not about what's real." I smooth my gown with trembling hands. "It's about what's possible. And what's impossible."

"Everything's possible if—"

"If what?" I cut him off, bitterness seeping into my voice. "If I'm willing to risk everything I've worked for? If I'm willing to be the CEO who lets her libido and lust rule her head?"

"If you're willing to trust me." He reaches for me again, but I dodge his touch and move around him, seeing three people standing at the other end of the balcony. Way too close.

"Trust you?" I laugh, the sound hollow. "The man who let me believe he was a regular guy? For all I know, you knew all along I was Lark Henley and bedding me was a conquest."

His expression turns thunderous. "You know that's not true."

"Do I?" I refuse to allow a single tear to spill over. I sniff and blink and gather myself. Tears are for sad losers, and I'm more pissed off than sad. I need to get my head in the game and keep my clothes on. "I don't know anything about you, Mitch. Except that you're dangerous to everything I'm working for and all the people who depend upon me."

Wordlessly, he shakes his head while I walk away. I don't run, I move slowly and determinedly back toward the business world, recalling why I'm here tonight. I'm representing the Henley family company and our tradition as an industry giant in the Sydney economy.

What's more, I fully intend to find a plate of leftover duck and devour it before I head home. It's been a terrible, no-good, very bad, stressful week. That must be why I let myself become weepy over a guy I barely know. But I'm putting the week behind me, along with Mitch Franklin.

What I need is a good, long sleep. All the way till Monday.

# 6

# Mitch

Standing outside Lark's building at twilight, with the repetitive call of some loud bird getting on my nerves, I stare up at what I now know is her penthouse apartment. The irony isn't lost on me that we've been living so close to each other for months. All those nights I spent developing recipes in my kitchen, she was nearby, dreaming up new chocolate ideas.

After a restless night following our encounter at the business dinner, I spent the morning determinedly *not* thinking about Lark Henley. *Not* looking her up online to see images of her at similar ritzy events in NYC, dressed to kill, always with some handsome guy. I'm pretty sure they weren't all company employees, either.

I learned that both she and her brother, Luke, ran the Henley Sydney operation until their father retired from the New York division. Luke was supposed to be the NYC CEO. He was there for a month before doing an abrupt about-face. No reporter seemed to know why, but suddenly Lark was running Henley NYC, and Luke was here in Sydney.

Late last year, they flipped again.

By all reports, she killed it in the States. Not only as a businesswoman, either. The society pages were particularly enlightening. That is, if I *wanted* to see my competition, which I don't give a shit about. Because we were a one-night stand, and I'm not in goddamn competition with anyone.

I barely scanned the captions on her various high-profile dates, mostly photos snapped in Manhattan, with tech moguls, Wall Street types, even a prince from some small European country.

After clearing my head by baking plain old chocolate chip cookies and spending the rest of the day arguing with myself over my next move, I drove here. It was inevitable. Now, my finger hovers over her apartment buzzer.

The memory of her telling me I'm dangerous last night haunts me. I don't want to be her Sydney mistake. But her confession that she's still thinking about our night together combined with the way she melted against me means I can't walk away. Not when it's been years since I felt this interested in a woman, a little obsessed even. What's more, I know down to my bones that she feels it too.

I press the buzzer.

"Yes?" Her voice comes through crisp and professional.

"It's Mitch."

Silence stretches so long I wonder if she has walked away. Finally, she asks, "How did you find my address?"

It was ridiculously easy. "I have my ways." I lean against the intercom panel. "Are you going to let me up, or should I start singing outside your window? Fair warning—I'm tone deaf."

"That's harassment," she says, but I can hear the smile in her voice.

"That's determination." I press the buzzer again and again, just to rile her. "Come on, Lark. We need to talk."

"We talked last night."

"We also kissed, but then you walked away when I had more to say." I soften my voice. "Please."

More silence, then the door buzzes. I sprint inside before she can change her mind.

The short elevator ride to the top, on the fourth floor, gives me time to second-guess myself. Leave her alone since I'm only going to be here for a couple more months at the most. But what a great time we could have in that time.

When the doors open, her penthouse double doors are directly in front of me, and one has been left ajar. *For me.* Entering and closing it with a firm hand, I find her pacing, wearing yoga pants and an oversized T-shirt that make her look soft and touchable.

"Gorgeous, sexy, smart, and not forgetting what a powerhouse you are, there's no way you're single," I say, stepping into her space. "If Jules Cartier isn't your boyfriend, who is and where is he?"

Her eyes flash. "Which one?" she asks, lifting her chin with defiance, but I catch the slight quirk at the corner of her mouth.

She's trying to provoke me, and damn if it isn't working. Heat floods my system as I advance toward her, forcing her to step back. "We agreed to tell the truth," I remind her.

"Did we?" she asks.

"No games," I say.

She rolls her eyes. "I let you in. That should tell you everything."

"Then you're one hundred percent single."

"Am I?" Her bare feet pad backward across hardwood floors, and I notice she's painted her toenails a deep, dark chocolate brown. Even that turns me on. "Maybe I have a whole harem of men tucked away somewhere," she adds.

I want to laugh now, knowing she's kidding. But I pretend to be alarmed. "You're playing with fire, lady."

When Lark offers me a cheesy grin and starts moving more quickly, I chase her retreat until her back hits the living room wall.

"You wouldn't have looked at me the way you did at the bar if you had anyone else." I say it with certainty, because I have no doubt. Lark Henley may be a lot of things, but looking into her eyes tells me she's not into breaking hearts or keeping more than one guy on the hook.

"You seem very sure of yourself." Her breath catches when I cage her with my arms.

*You have no idea.* Born confident. And except for the blow to my ego from Camille in Paris, which was money-related to its core, I've never had any reason to doubt myself. My plans, my focus, my future, nor who I'm attracted to. Right now, I want this woman more than my next lungful of Aussie air.

"I am." I lower my head until our lips are inches apart. "Want to know why?"

She swallows hard. "Why?"

"Because you're trembling right now, like you did that first night." I brush my lips against her ear. "Because your pupils are dilated." My hand slides down her arm. "Because your skin is flushed."

"That could be anger," she whispers.

"Could be." I nip her earlobe. "But it's not."

Her hands come up to my chest, but she doesn't push me away. Instead, her fingers curl into my shirt. "This is a bad idea."

"Probably." I trail kisses down her neck. "Want me to stop?"

Her head falls back against the wall. "Yes."

"Liar." I smile against her skin. "You want this as much as I do."

Her fingers tighten in my shirt. "Mitch . . ." My name comes out of her beautiful lips as a breathy moan that sends fire straight through me.

"Tell me to stop," I challenge her again, sliding my hand under her loose T-shirt to find bare skin. Gotta love a braless female. "Tell me you don't want this."

Instead of answering, she yanks me closer and crashes her mouth against mine. The kiss is hungry, desperate, full of the tension that's been building since last night. I press her harder against the wall, lifting her slightly so she can wrap her legs around my waist.

"This doesn't change anything," she gasps between kisses.

"Shut up." I capture her bottom lip between my teeth. "Stop thinking."

My hands roam freely now, memorizing every curve. Lark arches into my touch, her head falling back to expose the elegant line of her throat. Taking full advantage, I nip a trail of kisses down her neck while she threads her fingers through my hair.

"Bedroom," she begs.

"Where?"

She points vaguely to the right, and I carry her through an archway down a hallway into a spacious bedroom with floor-to-ceiling windows overlooking the harbor. The city lights create a backdrop of twinkling stars, but I'm focused solely on the woman in my arms.

The world outside her windows fades into insignificance as I lay Lark down on her bed, her body a tempting landscape beneath me. Her eyes are dark copper pools, reflecting the hunger I feel in every fiber of my being. When I strip off my shirt, her gaze rakes over my chest, her breath hitching with anticipation.

Leaning down, my lips cover hers with a ferocity that borders on savage. Our teeth clash, tongues stroking in a fierce dance of passion. I can't get enough of her—the taste of her, the feel of her soft skin under my hands, the way she moans into my mouth when I nip at her bottom lip.

She pulls at my belt, her fingers fumbling with urgency. I help her, shedding the rest of my clothes before turning my attention back to her. Tugging at the hem of her shirt, I yank it over her head to reveal her full breasts beckoning me to take them in hand.

Palming one, I dip my head to capture a dusky nipple, sucking and biting while she writhes beneath me, her fingers tangled in my hair, pulling me closer. Her hips buck against mine, seeking friction, seeking release.

I slide my hand into her yoga pants, under her panties, finding her wet and wanting. She's so ready for me, her body opening up as I thrust first one finger, then another, inside her. Her inner walls clench around me, and I can't help but groan at the thought of how it will feel when it's my cock sheathed inside her.

"Mitch, please," she begs, her voice a desperate whisper that fans the flames of my desire.

I withdraw my fingers, and she whimpers at the loss. But I'm not gone for long. Stripping off her pants and underwear, I toss them aside before settling between her thighs. The span of my shoulders spreads her wide. Dragging my tongue along her slit, I taste her sweetness, reveling in the way she arches off the bed with a cry of pleasure.

I devour her like a man starved, my tongue and fingers working in tandem to drive her wild. I can feel her orgasm building, her body tensing, her breath coming faster and shallower. Knowing what she likes, I reach up and pinch her nipples, making her moan. When I suck on her clit, she shatters, her hips bucking against my mouth as she cries out my name.

Having this particular woman say my name as a passionate cry while she's climaxing is a head rush. Rewarding and the biggest damn turn-on.

A quick tear of a foil packet and the condom is on. I don't give Lark time to recover. I'm on her in an instant, positioning myself at her entrance, the head of my cock nudging against her slick folds. Looking into her glazed eyes, what I see there takes my breath away. Not just lust—it's deeper. Something more meaningful, like a bond of understanding so innate, that it scares me.

But fear isn't enough to stop me. I thrust into her, burying myself to the hilt in one swift motion. Lark moans, and I know my size can take some adjusting to. Aware I should have gone slower, but she feels like heaven. A tight, wet paradise that I never want to leave.

"You OK?" I ask.

"Wow," she answers, then, "God, yes."

We move together, our bodies in perfect sync. Each glide in and pulling out makes her moan, while I'm unable to keep a groan of restraint from escaping. I want to go faster, deeper, if possible, but I don't want to hurt her.

Her pussy grips me, a tight sheath that makes each of my movements more intense than the last. The room fills with the sounds of our screwing—the slap of skin on skin, our mingled gasps and moans, the creaking of the bed frame as I drive into her over and over again.

I can feel her climbing towards another peak, her nails scoring my back, her legs wrapped tightly around my waist. Angling my hips, I hit that sweet spot inside her, while I slide my hand between us, scarcely brushing her taut clit before she comes undone. Her orgasm triggers my own.

"Hang on," I warn, thrusting like a madman before my climax rolls through my lower back, tensing my hips, hardening my cock, and tightening my balls. I bury myself deep inside her, my cock pulsing when I come surrounded by her exquisite heat.

For a moment, we lie there, our bodies still intimately connected, our breathing ragged. Slowly, the world comes back into focus. The city lights. The sound of distant traffic. The soft, satisfied purr of Lark's voice as she whispers my name again.

Rolling off her and disposing of the condom on her bedside table, I pull her into the shelter of my arms. She fits perfectly against me, her head resting on my chest, her hand splayed across my stomach. I press a kiss to the top of her head, kind of a lame-ass, romantic lover's move, while inhaling the scent of her hair.

Last time, after great sex, she snuck out with no intention of seeing me again. Not gonna lie, it was a blow to my male ego. And after that, I've been in hunting mode ever since. I don't want to scare her away, but I also don't want to let her disappear again. Whatever is between us, even if it's never more than sex, is pretty damn great.

"Stay the night," I say.

She stiffens slightly, and then she starts to laugh like a fiend, as she gets my joke. After all, it's *her* apartment. But when she stops, I know she's thinking about all the reasons why this—whatever *this* is—can't work.

"Let's enjoy right now," Lark says. Not exactly what I want to hear, but I'll take it because she's right.

Much later, when it seems almost too decadent not to get out of bed, I dash home, all of seven minutes, for supplies. I've quickly learned that Lark isn't much for keeping a stocked pantry or filled fridge.

Anything I forgot to bring, we do without, as I cook dinner in her clean and basically untouched kitchen.

She perches on the counter wearing nothing but a silky robe tied by a slippery little bow. One tug and all that bare skin would be revealed. The domesticity of it all hits me hard—how right this feels, how natural.

*Get a grip,* I order myself. This weird feeling is why I've been doing one-nighters or very short stints with no sleepovers and no home-cooking for years. It's not worth the heartache if either one of us gets attached, right when I'm about to move to another continent.

*So why am I risking my sanity for Lark?*

"That smells amazing," she says, watching me stir the risotto. "Garlic always makes my mouth water."

I file that nugget of info away, but I play it cool. "Just simple mushroom risotto." I offer her a taste from the wooden spoon. "What do you think?"

She closes her pretty eyes while she savors the bite. "*Mmm . . .* perfect." I drop the spoon onto the granite counter and can't help stepping between her slender, smooth legs.

"You look incredibly sexy, even with chocolate chip smeared on your cheek." I lick my thumb and wipe it off.

She actually blushes, having been unable to stop from eating three cookies as soon as she saw them come out of the big insulated bag onto her counter.

"Those were for dessert," I scold her, while actually admiring her appetite.

She grins. Maybe to divert attention from herself, because our gazes are locked again, she says, "I have a box of chocolates to share after dinner."

"I'm counting on it." I imagine feeding her a piece at the same time as I thrust into her hot channel again. I'm instantly hard at the thought of her licking chocolate off my thumb while I feel her pussy squeeze around my cock.

"Is that why you're staying the night?" she teases. "For free chocolates."

This is the first I heard that I've been invited to stay past dessert. Kissing her, I let her know my dirty thoughts by the thrust of my tongue. Then I draw back and tell her honestly, "I'm staying the night because I want to wake up with you."

She freezes, and I can see the walls starting to go back up.

"Mitch," she says, her voice a mixture of wanting and wariness. "Last night, you asked me to trust you. Do you trust me?"

The question catches me off guard. Trust isn't something I give easily, especially in the high-stakes, cut-throat hospitality industry where betrayal can come with a hefty price tag. I've had a restaurant opening sabotaged and entire carefully planned menus stolen. But looking into Lark's eyes, I realize that I do trust her. Maybe not with my most precious recipes, not yet, but with something else. Something more ephemeral.

"Yes, Lark," I say, brushing a strand of honey-blonde hair away from her face. "I trust you."

She searches my eyes for a moment, as if looking for any hint of deception. Apparently finding none, her expression softens. "Then let's agree to be honest with each other from here on out. No more pretending. No more games."

"Agreed." I start to seal our pact with a kiss when she puts her hand on my chest.

"In all honesty, I'm really, REALLY enjoying what we're doing here," she says, big golden-topaz eyes fixed on mine, making sure I'm listening.

Mentally, I fist pump.

"But I stand by my objections from last night. I still believe having a . . . a . . ."

"A fling," I offer helpfully.

"I was going to say *relationship* but fling applies, too. Having one with you, if that's what you're after, is impossible."

*Shit! Stupid early mental fist pump.*

"At least, right now, when I'm still trying to get my feet under me," she continues. "It's not that the position is new. It's not that I haven't already been CEO before and done it well. It's that I'm trying to make the job mean something more. Trying to make a difference at Henley Sydney. Not just do the same old, same old."

"And sleeping with me will stop you from that monumental task?" I ask, dropping a kiss to her temple, then working my way down to her neck.

She leans back to give me access. "Last week was a scare for me, I was running on auto pilot, thinking I could do this job with my eyes closed. I need to get my head back in the candy game. OK?"

"And I take your head out of it?" I ask, talking against the skin over her jaw.

Finally, I claim her mouth. It's like setting a match to gunpowder. As soon as our mouths are fused, our bodies demand the same. Reaching over, I turn off the stove. It's literally the first time I can recall not giving a shit if the meal is entirely ruined.

When I tug on the bow at her waist, the silken ribbon opens easily, and I part her sassy little robe. And I groan. *Christ!* She's sitting there, entirely naked, her perfect tits with their perfect pink nipples begging for me to taste them.

Leaning down, I do precisely that, hearing her moan above me as her fingers find my shoulders. As my fingers slide along her thigh to her pussy, she hisses, and now I have ten nails digging into my skin. I've barely started stroking her when she gasps.

"Now," Lark says, her hands shaking while she fumbles with the zipper of my jeans. I help her out. Or rather, help myself by sending my pants and boxer briefs down to my ankles. I'm fitting my cock, ramrod hard, to her slit when she looks around and says, "Clothespins."

"What?" My brain is a haze of lust, and I've already got her juices on the tip of my penis. She can't be thinking of laundry.

"There," she says, sounding desperate, her eyes bright with desire.

I look where she's pointing. A small, glass bowl of clothespins is within my reach. I nearly come from thinking about what she wants me to do with them.

Then, reaching over, I almost knock the container off the counter.

"Mitch," she pleads on a mere breathy whisper.

Getting my shit together, I manage to grab two from the bowl. In a few seconds, with her watching, I've pinched each of her stiff nipples within the grip of a benign-looking, highly effective, wooden clothespin.

*"Ow,"* she cries, and I freeze.

"Too much?" I ask.

"Yes! No! Just fuck me."

She closes her eyes, head tipped back. I thrust inside her, draw back, and . . . watch her climax on my second thrust.

*Sweet mother!* She is the most sensual woman I have ever had the honor to screw.

Because she's so hot, I go off like a stick of dynamite about thirty seconds later, while she wraps her legs around me and holds on.

Both of us breathing hard, I grab for a napkin to clean up while she removes the clothespins.

As I hand her a napkin, I freak out. "Condom!"

"Birth control," she says quietly, easing herself off the counter without saying anything else. As she disappears into her bedroom, I can't help wondering if she's regretting ever meeting me.

By the time she returns in her T-shirt and sweatpants, both necessary for me to focus on cooking, I've nearly finished making dinner. The risotto with a side of sautéed spinach and pine nuts—with more garlic—is elevated far beyond its rudimentary ingredients. Not because of my skill, but because of the company.

Lark opens the Pinot Noir I brought over. After a few sips, she agrees it perfectly complements the earthy flavors of the mushrooms. Always nice to meet a woman with a good palate.

Over dinner, we talk about everything and nothing—our favorite dishes, the quirks of the food industry, our families. I tell her about my first perfect loaf of bread. Age nine.

She tells me how she astounded the company's chocolatier when she was seven years old, correctly identifying the percentage of cocoa content in three varieties of her family's chocolate. We high five our mutual *wunderkind* successes.

I learn more about her parents, her brother, Luke, whose bedroom is now a guest room, and her sister, Clover, a graphic designer in Boston. Something else she held back until this minute, despite me telling her I was from Massachusetts the moment we met.

I let it slide. We were both playing games that night. I fill her in on my parents, how they instilled in me a love for cooking and a strong work ethic. I don't say too much about my sister, respecting Riley's long-standing request.

Where I'm a social animal who loves the nightlife, the buzz of high-end restaurants, and the thrill of meeting beautiful women, Riley is an anomaly of reticence. In a high-profile career, she wants as few people to know about it as possible.

So I mention that I have a sister, not that she's a supermodel.

Anyway, a lot of info is going back and forth for two people who thought they would only ever enjoy a single sexual encounter. It's also the most engaging conversation I've had with a female in years, and I find myself thinking I wouldn't mind more evenings like this.

"What's the significance of your pendant?" she asks, out of the blue.

I can't help smiling. "Does it have to be significant?"

"No, but I'm guessing a man with no other jewelry, not an earring or even a watch, wouldn't wear it if it didn't have a story."

"Smart lady," I say. I want to express its meaning correctly without sounding like a sappy bozo. When I pause, she tilts her head.

"First," Lark says, "tell me what the stone is."

"Guess," I say.

She narrows her eyes as she leans closer, her unique perfume wafting toward me.

"Maybe amethyst. Or tanzanite."

I can't help touching her hair, when she's this close. I wind a strand around my finger, watching her pupils dilate as I do.

"Just purple glass," I confess. "Circa 1915."

Lark is watching my mouth, so I use her hair to draw her close and kiss her.

When she's hot and bothered, starting to hum against my lips, while my cock stiffens painfully in my jeans, I release her.

"Sorry," I mutter. "It's your friggin' perfume. I swear I've never smelled anything like it."

She shakes her head, looking dazed. "It's bespoke. You'll never smell it again."

Her words hit like a sledgehammer, and I don't like the message one bit, however unintentional.

"Back to the glass," she says. "Definitely not some rando piece."

"Right. OK, short story is I skimped on the quality of the shelving behind the bar of Franklin 1. Cheaper brackets meant the whole thing came down opening night from the weight of the liquor stock."

I shake my head, recalling the mess and my absolute panic at having to close the bar.

"Luckily, we had a great wine cellar," I add. "But I'd put some family heirlooms, including a couple of my great-grandmother's vinegar bottles that my mom had."

I lift the pendant. "This was a shard from one of them. Had it smoothed and mounted."

Lark nods, understanding me. "Never cut corners," she says.

"Exactly. The liquor was insured, but the lesson was priceless. I don't really need the glass to remind me to do everything at the highest quality, but I like having a piece of my family with me wherever I am. Plus that woman had some awesome pickling recipes."

We both laugh. After dinner, sitting on her balcony, sipping wine, Lark and I watch the lights of Sydney dance across the water. The night is cool, but her presence warms me. When she rests her head on my shoulder, I wrap my arm around her, holding her close. It's alarming how normal this whole scenario feels.

"Just so you know," she says, "the clothespins aren't there for *that* purpose."

A small laugh escapes me. So much for normal. I hadn't given them a second thought apart from being grateful they were so handy.

"Why then?" I ask since she brought them up.

"Speaking of family, my grandmother gave them to my brother and I when we bought the place. Kind of a weird tradition about setting up your own home and doing laundry, even though we don't have a line to hang clothes on. When I sit at the island, if I'm on the phone or watching something on my laptop, I fidget with them. Constantly. Bad habit."

She finishes eating another cookie while I help myself to assorted truffles.

"I don't usually like the chocolate in chocolate chip cookies," she says. "But these taste amazing."

I can't be too smug that she loves my cookies, because of the high-quality chips. I confess, "That's Henley's finest dark chocolate chopped up in every cookie."

"*Ohh*, no wonder they're so good." She brushes the crumbs off her hands and shirt, then she laughs. "I don't taste any contaminated beet sugar, so that's a win. In fact, I can't remember the last time I felt this content."

I'm guessing it's not merely my risotto or my cookies. And I feel the same.

"Me neither," I say. Despite the chaos since our initial meeting, being with Lark feels easy.

We sit in silence for a long while, lost in our own thoughts. Eventually, she places her hand on my thigh, and I turn to her, taking her face in my hands.

"Lark," I whisper, my voice thick with wanting her.

She answers me with a kiss, slow and full of wicked promise. Of course, I take her up on it, because it seems like we've crossed a bridge.

*From where, to where, who knows?* But our kiss says we're taking a risk. What's more, later, after sex, the old knee-jerk reaction comes over me that I need to have some space, that I should head home.

A second later, I can't think of a single reason I would want to be anywhere but beside her. When I drift off to sleep, still touching, I know I'm falling for Lark Henley, and there's not a damn thing I can do to stop it.

Except remind myself I won't be in Sydney forever.

# 7

# Lark

Staring at the quarterly reports on my laptop, I have the insane urge to sweep everything off my beautifully crafted Tassie oak desk. The next instant, I imagine Mitch leaning me back onto the cleared workspace and . . .

I sigh, trying to focus, wishing the numbers didn't blur together while my mind drifts to thoughts of the last time his hands and his mouth were on my body.

And how great the conversation was afterward.

And how nice it was to let him stay the night.

And how I made him leave by nine the following morning.

"I can't make a date with you," I told him, standing firm. Or, at least, lying-down-beside-him firm. "I can't make any plans right now."

He'd raised a dark eyebrow, looking kinda piratical, making my insides melt.

"Whatever the lady wants," he said. "I'm not here to put any pressure on you. When you're ready for round three, text me."

He'd given me a kiss that demanded I contact him soon.

And then he'd left, like I told him to.

Like I wanted.

*Sure I did.*

With an irritated grunt, I push my chair out and perform the equally pointless task of staring out the floor-to-ceiling windows of my office.

"Get it together," I mutter, pressing my forehead against the cool glass. The Sydney harbor sparkles in the near distance, but even its beauty can't distract me from the mental mess I'm in.

My assistant's voice comes directly out of the speaker on my desk. "Mrs. Bauer is on her way."

When my VP is making a surprise visit, I know it can't be good news. I don't bother acknowledging Daniel's announcement. Half a minute later, Charlotte's knock sounds at my half-closed door, soft but purposeful, before she pushes it open.

"Hey, Lark," she says, as we have never stood on formality here.

"Hey, Charlotte. What's up?" My intuition tells me it's not good.

"The board is requesting a meeting tomorrow morning."

My stomach clenches. "Both Sydney *and* New York?"

"No," she says. "Only *our* board members. Nine a.m. They're concerned about the sugar incident."

"Of course they are." I turn, squaring my shoulders, thinking more than ever that I made the correct decision with Mitch. I can't afford any distractions right now. I'd pushed him away, citing work commitments, but the truth is, I'm terrified of how quickly he's getting under my skin.

I would honestly rather be lying on a beach next to him, doing nothing, rather than doing my job. That's not like me.

"I don't know what else I can tell the board, but I'm thrilled to waste my time. I don't suppose they'd come into the modern era and do a video conference?"

Charlotte and I lock gazes, obviously both of us thinking of the chairman, Mr. Neville Wembley. And we start to laugh. An in-person board meeting, it will be.

Just then, Jules charges through the already open door before Daniel can even announce him, his enthusiasm filling the room.

"Close your eyes!" he demands, unable to stand still. "Both of you."

"Nope, but thanks," Charlotte says, heading for the door. "I've got a stickybeak brewing in the accounting department."

In her wake, thinking of the things I haven't yet done today, I say to Jules, "I don't have time—"

"Trust me." He's holding something behind his back.

With an exaggerated sigh, I comply. I hear . . . nothing. "Jules," I begin.

"I'm unscrewing a glass bottle. Chill a moment," he says as he comes closer. Then the unmistakable heady scent of chocolate fills my nostrils a moment before the sound of a metal spoon tapping on glass.

"Open up!" he suggests. "Mouth, *not* eyes. You'll taste it better."

He's right, but I grit my teeth, fully aware that Jules would never go up to my brother and tell him to close his eyes before spoon feeding him something. On the other hand, Jules wouldn't hold the door open for Luke, either. Nor would he walk on the outside of the sidewalk or occasionally bring him a pastry or cookie on the pretense of sampling the competition.

Sometimes it's wonderful being a woman. My thoughts dart instantly to Mitch, licking his way down from my nipples to my—

"Lark," Jules says, meaning I've drifted off into Mitch-world again.

Regardless, I open my eyes to see that Jules is holding a plain glass bottle filled with what appears to be liquid chocolate in one hand. In the other, a nearly overflowing tasting spoon.

"Try it," he urges.

Feeling like Alice in Wonderland and hoping I don't shrink or grow, I take the spoon from him, because I'm *not* a child, and put it in my mouth. The moment the syrup touches my tongue, my eyes widen. It's perfect—rich, smooth, with the subtlest round caramel taste, although instinctively and from tasting samples all my life, I know there's no actual caramel in it.

"This is amazing." I take the bottle from him, examining the viscosity and color before pouring another measure onto the spoon. "More body than most syrups. Not quite as thick as, say, a fudge sauce. Really interesting."

"It's the boiling time," Jules says. "To repeat this consistency, after trial and error, I now know exactly how long it needs to boil, allowing for the thickening that occurs as it cools." Then he raises an eyebrow and challenges me. "Tell me the ingredients, and lunch is on me."

I can't help smiling. I have always loved Jules's whimsical approach to research and development. Plus, he knows I'll never let him pay for lunch. Still, I play along as if a free meal is riding on this.

"Our best Belgian-style cocoa."

"That's a given," he says.

"A pinch of salt," I say because any chocolatier worth his . . . *well* . . . his salt knows the magic that happens when you add it.

"Yes, ma'am. Right again. Bonus points if you know what kind."

"It better be Aussie pink salt because I gave orders my first week here to switch over to local ingredients whenever possible."

"It is. What else?"

"A touch of vanilla. From Mexico, *not* Madagascar, unless I'm mistaken."

"You're not. I sometimes forget how amazing your palate is, Lark Henley."

I feel a warmth of pride. I'd rather we used vanilla grown in Australia, but Cyclone Jasper wiped out the burgeoning vanilla orchid production, already limited to a small sliver of north Queensland.

I take a third spoonful.

"Nearly there," Jules says.

I scrunch up my face because there's something else besides the pure spring water we use, which I mention in case he thinks I've forgotten. But another ingredient is adding a full, almost nutty flavor without being actually a nut. But first, the obvious.

"You've used some of our new shipment of sugar, obscenely expensive because of the rush delivery."

Jules makes a dreadful buzzer sound, as if I've lost the grand prize on an old-fashioned TV game show, the kind my grandmother enjoys watching.

"Wrong!" He's clearly delighted to have fooled me. "I made this with coconut sugar," he finishes proudly.

My mouth drops, then I take my fourth taste. "There's no coconut flavor," I say gratefully, because while coconut and chocolate pair well, it greatly reduces the potential application for this perfect syrup. "That's the unusual caramelized flavor I'm tasting, right? Very subtle."

"Yes. If you hadn't liked it, I would've tried maple sugar next."

I scrunch up my mouth with distaste. "I think, even if I hadn't liked this, which I do—love it, in fact!—I would've said that maple as a sweetener is out. No one wants chocolate and maple warring with one another over their buttery shortbread cookie or in their chocolate martini."

Jules nods. "Agreed. And with such a pure flavor profile, our new syrup, or sauce, if you'd rather, can be used for desserts, shakes, and cocktails."

We grin at one another at the notion of jumping into and conquering an entirely new market.

"Or straight up chocolate milk for the kiddos," I say, while also imagining it drizzled over our various candy lines.

Many Henley chocolates already have melted chocolate dripped or piped over them, as well as chocolate shards and shavings. But this will add another level of amaze-balls. Something clicks in my mind, and suddenly I'm seeing a successful future instead of last week's problems.

"This is delicious. Magical. Perfect. Imagine, though, if we took this perfection and created an entire line by adding flavors like raspberry or chili powder or espresso or—"

"I get it," Jules says, cutting me off, probably because I'm sounding manic. "But first, we develop this one and get it into production."

"Of course. Speaking of which, what inspired you to make this all of a sudden?" I'm so excited, I have another spoonful while I wait for the answer, my head buzzing with possibilities.

"I have a new friend," he begins. "We were goofing around, and that," he points to the bottle, "just sort of happened."

A red flag starts waving directly in front of me. "Hold up. Did this friend play a big part in it, or was it all you?" Please let him say it was all him. *Please. Please.*

"She doesn't cook," Jules says. "But she wanted me to make something special to pour over our crepes, and she loves chocolate. I mean, naturally, right? She's hanging out *with* me."

He laughs. I hope he knows he brings more to a relationship, even to a friendship, than free chocolate.

"And then," he continues, "I said I could make chocolate sauce. Next thing you know . . . ," he trails off.

I'm not entirely convinced his memory is working perfectly. "Regardless of whether she contributed to this a little or not at all, or made it entirely by herself after tying you up in the corner with a length of sticky taffy—"

His cheeks become a little red, and I wonder for the space of two heartbeats what Jules and his lady friend got up to this weekend.

"Regardless," I continue, "she has given you, meaning Henley Confectionery, the license to use it. Is that right?"

"Yup," he nods with his boyish energy. "She's totally cool."

Without warning, I throw my arms around Jules, knowing my brother has never hugged one of our male employees, although with some of the female ones . . .

"You're brilliant!" I tell Jules. "Do you realize what this means?"

"That I'm getting an obscenely large raise?"

I laugh. "No! Any raise I may've given you will be eaten away by the cost of using coconut sugar. It's nearly double the price of organic cane sugar, never mind regular sugar."

I pause to work out some pricing in my head, having been planning, producing, and pricing since I was eighteen.

"What this means, my dear Monsieur Cartier, is that the Henley Confectionery Company will have something brand spanking new for the Taste of Sydney exhibition. D-day is now 21 days away. All we need is a name for this deliciousness." I hold up the bottle.

"Julian's Juice," my master chocolatier says with a deadpan expression.

Suddenly, I'm thinking of all the hundreds of other things I'll need to do before I can bring a few cases of syrup to the Taste of Sydney. Like find a production facility and a bottler. Actually, the name of the product is way down on my list.

"How about just plain Henley's Syrup?" I ask.

Jules makes a face. "Kinda close to that other big H company, don't you think?"

"The name of which we cannot speak," I say softly, staring into the distance. He's right, though. If we're doing this, we might as well do it right and differently. I try something out of left field.

"What about *Aqua Chocolata*?"

"Too pretentious. Not Henley family enough," Jules says. He knows our brand as well as I do, and he's right. "Henley's Chocolate Elixir?" he suggests.

"*Elixir* makes me think of a charlatan with a potion or of nasty medicine," I say.

"How about HLC, for Henley's Liquid Chocolate?"

"Give yourself a little TLC with our HLC," I say, testing the name. We frown at one another, then slowly grin.

"Not bad," I say. "Simple but kinda elegant. We'll go with it, at least for now. Mark everything for this product as HLC and let's keep it between you, me, and Charlotte." I shrug. "And the few employees you need for limited production. I don't want this going company-wide yet. We sample and taste from now until the last possible bottling moment, then we'll do a small, soft, exclusive launch at Taste of Sydney."

I rub my hands together. At the event, we'll feature it on a simple dessert and sell small bottles. For that, I'll need packaging.

"I'll get my sister to whip up a label and keep this under her hat Stateside." More correctly, "under her shoe," because Clover loves nothing more than her shoes, except her husband.

"I've met your sister," Jules says bluntly. And I have a feeling he doesn't approve of my telling her, not if we want to keep our secret.

After considering for a second, I nod. As the only one of the three Henley siblings to go her own way—*out of the chocolate biz*—Clover's relationship with me and Luke and our board-member dad is different. She wouldn't understand how one CEO trying to prove she can make her own mark on the family brand might want to keep the other CEO in the dark. For now.

Besides, I don't want to hear Luke's suggestions or criticisms. I just don't. Not yet. The product would quickly become a joint effort. It might seem childish, but I need a Henley Sydney win right about now.

"Clover would probably tell Luke before I'd finished the word *liquid*." We agree to a test label made by someone in-house.

Within hours, I'm on the phone with a factory that can handle both the production of this liquid gold, as I already think of HLC, and the bottling, too, only until we put in the equipment we need at our own factory. We Henleys always like to have control of our own production and packaging. *Bean to bar and soon bean to bottle.*

I'm assuming, of course, that Jules's chocolate syrup is well received by everyone at the event. Of that, I have no concerns.

After working out the logistics of a small test run, I finally tell Charlotte. My VP raises a sculpted eyebrow but doesn't outright object at the way I've gone ahead with something that could be monumental WITHOUT running it by my father, who still has controlling shares in the company and a seat on the board. Or by my brother. For my part, it feels good to be excited about something work-related again.

Much later, when I'm home but still working, my laptop chimes with an incoming video call from Luke. My brother's familiar face fills the screen, his Manhattan office visible behind him. I work out the time difference, realizing he's calling me at 7 a.m.

"Hey, sis. Heard you managed to salvage the sugar situation." It's sweet that he's leading with a complimentary pat on the back. He could be holding up a spreadsheet with a negative ROI, thanks to me.

"It cost us, though," I admit, running a hand through my hair, leaning back, and swinging my feet up onto my sofa. Iced coffee in hand, new liquid chocolate coming down the pike, I'm stoked and unable to feel any lingering worry over the sugar, although we're still getting to the bottom of it.

"The board's rattled," Luke adds carefully. "But I know you did what needed to be done."

"Thanks, bro. Kinda sucks to have to fix something I shouldn't have broken in the first place."

"Why *did* you switch vendors?" That is a good question, one which I've been asking myself.

"What I'd like to do," I begin slowly, "is to use all Australian ingredients, and eventually ask you to use the same at our U.S. factory."

"Too expensive," he starts. "And frankly, I like our Belgian exporter. They're very responsive."

"I know they are. But the same suppliers would mean one hundred percent consistency in flavor and quality. And don't you think because of Nan and Gramps, it would be great to have everything Aussie-sourced, to pay tribute to the Henley brand's beginnings? You know this climate. It's great for cocoa beans and sugar and even the vanilla orchids."

*"Hm,"* is all I get from my big brother, who's scarcely a year older than me.

"I know my purist dream is a ways off," I continue. "Meanwhile, you're right. It's too expensive, and I can't source enough native ingredients at a cost that doesn't price our chocolates like they're made of gold. But the vendor I switched to for sugar was a start-up supply company in Queensland. I wanted to give them a chance."

Kindly, Luke says, "You went with your heart." At least he didn't voice his disapproval and make me feel like a kid.

I shrug, which he can vaguely see through the screen. "Seemed like a nice thing to do." I don't mention that I wanted to shake things up and not be under my brother's long, wide, impressive shadow. He was a great CEO Down Under, and everyone misses him still.

What's more, I want to tell him about the chocolate syrup, but something holds me back. Maybe it's superstition. I want to see if it's as good as I think before I start squawking.

"Just watch your step for a while, OK?" he says. "They'll be watching closely. And don't do anything crazy."

"Haven't you heard?" I ask. "The Aussie board is requesting an emergency meeting tomorrow morning. Yours truly will be on the hot seat."

"Shit! No one told me that." He pauses, then, "Shall I show up unannounced via video chat?"

"No," I say. "I appreciate it, but I can handle this myself. If our situations were reversed, you wouldn't want your sister there holding your hand, would you?"

"I guess not. But call me if you need me."

After we disconnect, I find myself reaching for my phone, thumb hovering over Mitch's number. I miss him with an intensity that frightens me. But I force myself to put the phone down. We've both maintained radio silence since I asked him to give me some space.

Business first. Always business first. I think about placing a delivery order for . . . No, not a mushroom burger from F6 Tavern. *Bad girl for even thinking of it!*

Bad girl for thinking of a lot of things to do with Mitch.

I cross my legs against the small throbbing reminder that he satisfied me like no guy ever has. And I want to be satisfied again. *Thank you very much!*

Punching in the number for Thai food, which I do at least twice a week, sometimes three times, I place an order, just squeaking under the wire before closing time. I'm a consistent customer, so they're responsive.

While I wait for the delivery, I play with drag-and-drop design software for the HLC label. Even though I've asked Charlotte to find someone in the company who can create one stat and keep it quiet, I let my creative side play and try to keep my mind on this awesome new opportunity.

And fail. I spend almost no time thinking about the board meeting other than the words *you can kiss my ass*, and all my time thinking about Mitch and how I'd like him to kiss any part of me, and vice versa.

When my food comes, I switch on the TV for company, aware as an intelligent person that it's not good to eat this late, nor to stay up watching crap. Gradually, however, I decompress, my mind stops racing.

But even while watching a 1990s sitcom, I can't help wondering if I'm making the biggest mistake of my life. Mitch is the only man in a long time who floats my boat *and* who also seems like a genuinely nice guy. What's more, he can cook.

Shaking my head, I shovel in another big bite of spicy noodles. I must be crazy to put him on hold, even temporarily, with the risky hope he'll still be available when I'm ready.

*If I'm ever ready.*

But so much can go wrong, and usually does, when I follow my heart instead of sticking to business.

# 8

## Mitch

The video call connects, and my parents' faces fill my phone screen. They're in their kitchen in Boston, and I can see Dad has already started prep for Sunday dinner. I can almost smell the roast pork.

"How's my boy?" Dad asks, while Mom, seated at the kitchen island, waves the hand clutching a newspaper. As a journalist, she still prefers to read print, rather than staring at a laptop screen.

"Business is good," I say automatically, then realize I want to tell them about something else entirely. *Someone* else. "I met someone."

Mom immediately gets down to business. "Tell us everything."

I find myself grinning. "Her name is Lark Henley."

Dad's eyebrows shoot up, and I know he recognizes the name. He's always up on food news, even the peripherals, like the world of confectionery. "As in *Henley* chocolates?"

he asks, then looks at Mom. "I doubt there are two Lark Henleys in Sydney."

"Yeah," I say, watching their expressions. "The same. Although I didn't realize she was *the* Lark Henley who'd left NYC until after we'd spent time together."

"Wait," Mom says, wiping her hands on her apron. "She's the founder's granddaughter?"

"She is. And CEO following her father's retirement." It feels like I'm discussing some European princess who has ascended the throne to lead her country. It's weird. I've never dated anyone this high-profile before. Leaning back in my chair, I prepare for the inevitable barrage of questions.

"Mitchell James Franklin!" Mom exclaims. "How long have you been seeing Lark?"

I grin. She assumes I've been hiding a relationship for ages. But *seeing Lark* is a loaded phrase. I haven't seen her for a week, the woman who has my blood thundering if I even think about the way she licks her lips after biting a french fry.

"It's complicated," I hedge, not wanting to get into the details of our hot-and-cold relationship. "We met at my bar, had a picnic, and then reconnected at a business gala." I'm behaving like a teenager who's giving a full report after staying out all night.

However, I stop myself from mentioning the last time we were together at Lark's apartment when I basically barged in because I needed to make things right. Or how she told me we had to cool it and gave me no clue as to whether or when we would be together again.

Her brush-off kinda sucked.

Regardless, I brought her up because I'm close with my family and because Lark has given me moments of utter happiness and contentment I haven't felt in forever. So, I add, "There's definitely something there."

"But what?" Mom asks, her voice carrying that journalist's prying get-to-the-bottom-of-things tone.

"Lark is focused on work right now. And honestly, so should I be." I run a hand through my hair. "The Taste of Sydney exhibition is coming up, and my head chef and I still haven't finalized what I'm presenting." Obviously, something different than the duck I showcased at the business dinner. "I want it to be really relatable and Aussie. I'm thinking Tasmanian scallops on pasta."

My dad nods, then asks, "How long do you need to keep the food at perfect plating temp and appearance?"

"The event is five hours. I'll refresh and make more."

He winces. "Still, an interesting herbal rice might sit better than pasta. You can keep it warm more easily."

I consider that. He's so damn smart. Pasta will get cold and become inedible quicker than rice, with the starch molecules becoming tightly packed. Rice is infinitely more forgiving, especially if I need to reheat it. "It'll fit better in the small tasting cups we have to use," I say. "Thanks, Dad."

"Are you offering a taste of dessert, too?" my mom asks.

"Profiteroles with Franklin Darkly."

Dad's eyes light up at the name of our family chocolate sauce. He's the trained cook. I'm just the Cordon Bleu drop-out and food truck cook who made it big. To honor him, I took the homemade syrup he used to make and serve over ice cream, and I elevated it. Less sweet, darker cocoa, and the secret ingredient that took our sauce from everyday delicious to a luxury item, both in price and taste.

Franklin Darkly is rich, but not cloying, and our unique coconut sugar recipe gives it a subtle caramel note without overpowering the chocolate. I can hardly wait for the Taste of Sydney. And it's not simply the event I'm looking forward to. I can't wait to see Lark. I already know exactly where the Henley booth will be in relation to mine, and I have no doubt she'll be there herself. She's a hands-on CEO if I ever met one.

After ending the call with my parents, I nearly text Lark. Not for the first time since I left her apartment. But I'm keeping my word to let her focus. After all, I should take it as a compliment that she begged me not to make contact. Apparently, I'm so magnificent, she fears she'll cave if I so much as crook my finger.

It's getting harder each day not to do some finger-crooking.

Instead, I head to the restaurant's kitchen where my pastry chef, Antonia, has been working on tonight's desserts. As for the Taste of Sydney, no profiteroles in sight, but the scent of baked choux pastry fills the air anyway.

"Practicing?" I ask.

"Not really . . . OK, yes, getting my choux muscles ready," she jokes. "This is a big deal and me and my elves are going to be making hundreds in a few days."

"What are you doing with the choux now?"

"Helping out Craig. He's using choux for gougères on the appetizer specials menu, and pommes Dauphine to accompany a beef dish."

"Sounds great." I peer around the kitchen. "But you do have some profiteroles, don't you?"

Antonia laughs. "Yes, boss." She carries a tray out of the walk-in fridge, letting me examine the golden puffs.

"Each one identical," Antonia says proudly.

I nod approvingly. "Perfect." Then I reach for a large-ass squeezable bottle of Franklin Darkly that we keep in the kitchen of every restaurant I own. When I trickle it over the profiteroles, it flows like liquid silk, even at room temperature.

"You going to join me?" I ask her, although a part of me wishes I was sharing these delicate pastries with Lark. In fact, I cannot wait to introduce her to my sauce. Trying to keep my thoughts clean as to exactly how I want to do that, I use a fork to cut the profiterole in half. The rich pastry cream oozes out. I mop up some chocolate sauce that has run off and take a big bite.

Franklin Darkly never disappoints. It's more than chocolate sauce—it's my father's and my legacy. That's something Lark will understand and appreciate when I present her with a plate at the Taste of Sydney.

$♥$♥$♥$

Beyond ready to see Lark again, the days drag until finally, I'm watching my staff hand out small cardboard bowls at our mobbed booth on the fourth-floor of the exhibition center.

The place is buzzing with happy voices and the indoor, air-conditioned air carries the scent of roasted meat mingled with buttery seafood, at least near me. Other halls will be rich with the aroma of coffee and tea. And farther on, where Lark is, it must smell like sweet confectionery heaven.

For the past hour, people have flocked toward the mouthwatering aroma of Franklin 6's perfectly seasoned, sautéed scallops. Dad was right about the rice, since it doesn't steal the show but does its starchy job.

Everyone who approaches takes a sample of both the savory course and the dessert. The profiteroles look elegant, two to a serving, drowning in dark, glossy sauce. My single booth is well worth the entire entrance fee to the Taste of Sydney. *In my humble opinion.*

The only blip as people buy restaurant vouchers at $100 per person and scoop up jars of Franklin Darkly with their credit cards ready is when I overhear a couple of women say my chocolate sauce tastes *exactly* like another "bloody good" one they tried in the confectionery hall.

I don't like the sound of that. Before I can question them, I hear, "Hey, Mr. Franklin."

It's the pretty chef in the booth next to mine. She shakes the hand of nearly everyone who approaches and launches into a spiel about the restaurant she works for. She's been stealing glances at my desserts since we started setting them out early this morning.

Greeting her with a nod and a wave of my hand, I decide it's time to find the Henley booth. I've given Lark time to settle in, and I need to see her. *Now!* Especially if someone else is dishing out chocolate syrup. I want her to taste mine and tell me how great it is. Then I want to kiss the sauce off her sweet lips.

Snagging a sample dessert plate with extra chocolate sauce, I haven't taken two steps when the brunette chef calls out my name again.

"G'day. Those look dangerous to the hips, mate," she says, enjoying a brief lull at her booth. "I'm Sarah."

I can't *not* engage. That would be unprofessional. Instead, I head to the front of her display and set down the profiteroles.

"Help yourself," I say. In return, one of her staff hands me a sample of what they're cooking. A chicken dish, it smells OK, but doesn't make me desperate to try it. Regardless, I have to be polite. I eat a forkful.

"It's good," I say, although I think it's bland and could use something surprising, like miso butter and fresh ginger. I almost blurt it out but restrain myself. If I say anything, it'll be at the end of the event, so she's not second-guessing what they're serving all day.

Sarah nods, but doesn't speak. She's too busy wolfing down the profiteroles without even sharing with either of the other people working at her booth. In a moment, I've given them each their own sample.

"Wow!" Sarah says when she finishes the last bite. "The chocolate syrup is bonza!"

"Family recipe," I reply, but my attention is elsewhere.

I can't see the Henley booth as it's in another hall, but I can feel Lark's pull as if she's in my line of sight. Having consulted the exhibitor map, I make a beeline in the right direction. Two halls over, there she is, dressed in a lightweight blue silk, knee-length dress adorned with chocolate-brown polka dots that match her toenail polish.

I groan, recalling kissing those cute toes a mere few weeks ago.

Naturally, Lark isn't behind the booth's counter, which is invisible under the mounds of merchandise. Lark is out in front, not looking the least bit like a CEO as she holds a silver platter of sample chocolates, charming people, laughing with a couple who have a baby in a stroller. She has brought classy gold-and-brown bags with handles to put purchases in. The man is carrying one, meaning a sale has been made.

Approaching closer, my steps falter. There, prominently featured in the midst of the stacks of boxed assorted chocolates, are elegant glass bottles. It's not the classy cork stoppers that make my heart thump. It's the dark-chocolate liquid inside. *When did this happen?*

Lark's face lights up when she sees me, which gives me a momentary thrill and a distraction, until she turns and sets down the platter of chocolates and picks up one of at least two hundred sample plates.

"Hey, Mitch," she says by way of greeting, holding the small plate toward me. "Try this. You're going to love it." Her tone is one of sheer excitement.

I look down at the square of yellow cake, topped with an artistic zig-zag of chocolate sauce that looks identical to my own. The consistency, the sheen, the way it coats the dessert—unmistakably the same. There are a few coconut sprinkles on top, indicating this is the Henley Confectionery's take on a classic Australian Lamington.

"The cake is from Time for Cake, over there." She gestures toward a booth down the aisle, but I don't look up.

Wordlessly, I tilt the plate to pool a little syrup on one side. Using the small wooden spork, I take a taste, purposefully avoiding getting any cake into my mouth. Only the chocolate. And there's no doubt. This is Franklin Darkly sauce.

*My sauce.* I'd know it anywhere.

The betrayal hits me like a physical blow. How did she get this recipe? And more importantly, why would she develop it as her own?

"What do you think?" Lark asks, her eyes bright as she bites her lower lip, which I'm no longer dying to kiss.

My jaw clenches. "It's great," I say, keeping my voice low. "Because it's Franklin Darkly sauce."

Her smile falters. "What?"

"This is *my* sauce, Lark. My family's recipe." I gesture to the bottles displayed prominently in her booth. "You're bottling Franklin Darkly and calling it your own."

"That's ridiculous," she says, but there's a flutter of uncertainty in her expression. "This is Jules's creation."

"Jules? Hardly," I snap at her denial. "Your 'valued employee' really outdid himself." The words taste bitter in my mouth. "What did he do? Come to my restaurant, order dessert, and take it home to analyze? Or did he buy a bottle outright and take it straight to the lab?"

Her mouth has formed into a hard line while I'm speaking, and now her eyes narrow. "You sound nuts. Why don't you go to Pennsylvania and accuse the big H of stealing your chocolate syrup, too?"

"Because theirs tastes nothing like mine, but this does. Exactly!"

She shakes her head, dismissing me and my claim. If she knew how many times I watched my dad whip this up in our kitchen, how important it is to me that our combined talent created something we could put our name on, she'd think again. She wouldn't be so flippant.

"This is corporate espionage, Lark. I want you to stop selling it. Immediately." This time, her mouth drops open at my vehemence. I can't help how harsh I sound. This is nothing to play around with.

A small crowd has gathered, drawn by our heated exchange. I hear whispers, people comparing the two sauces, agreeing they're identical.

"There are only so many ways to make chocolate sauce," Lark says defensively, but I can see the wheels turning in her head.

"Let's compare ingredients then," I challenge. "What's your sweetener?"

"Something unique," she says, "which is the reason I know—"

"Coconut sugar," I say.

Her expression tells me I've nailed it in one go. "Yes," she admits finally.

The confirmation of my suspicions makes my blood boil. "This isn't just about ingredients. This is my father's legacy, one that I've built a business on."

"You've built a business on chocolate sauce?" she asks, sounding sassy for someone who's been caught stealing.

"My desserts are a huge part of my Franklin brand," I tell her. "And the sauce—"

"Wasn't on your dessert at the business dinner," she reminds me, tilting her head and raising an eyebrow as if she's scored a point.

I want to tear my hair out. "That was for *your company's* sake, even before I knew you were CEO," I say. "When I was told Henley would be the other featured sponsor, I made traditional pavlova, so your chocolates could shine."

She pales. "As if Henley Confectionery needs to worry about your sticky syrup."

"My sticky syrup," I repeat loudly, "which you've bottled and corked to shore up your own personal reputation for being an innovative leader."

With her fists clenched at her sides, she takes a step toward me. All she does is snatch the sample cup out of my hand. "I need you to back off," she says, her voice calm. Then she tosses the cup into the nearby trash with as much force as I believe she'd like to toss me to the curb. "You're making a scene."

"I'll make more than a scene, lady. I'll take legal action if I have to."

Lark takes a deep breath. And then, in a calm voice of reason, that is also incredibly patronizing, she says, "Mitch, you're being a little crazy."

With blood pounding in my ears, I can tell by her placating tone that she has no idea what this means. She hasn't seen crazy! When someone messes with my restaurants or my food or my goddamn Franklin Darkly, I am not forgiving.

"We're having a misunderstanding of epic proportions," she continues. "These came straight from the plant last night—"

"You don't have bottling facilities at your candy factory, do you?" I demand.

"No." She looks flustered. "Not yet. This is a trial run, and I wanted to see how it was received before retooling."

By this time, I've bypassed Lark to get a closer look at the bottles in her booth. My sauce is in thick wide-mouth jars, two sizes, with a screw cap. Her mini-wine bottles have a cork stopper and a gold tag around the neck with HLC printed in chocolate brown.

"That's just a prototype," she says, as I pick up a bottle, feeling the urge to sweep them all off the table.

"Where'd you have it bottled?" I ask.

"Is there a problem here?" A woman in an event management badge asks before Lark can answer. Obviously someone summoned her when I was in my initial fit of rage. And Sandy, whom I recognize from the preliminary meetings, does not want a repeat scene.

Her authoritative manner and her question create a lull in the chatter around us.

"Yes," I say immediately. "Henley Confectionery is selling a product that's an exact copy of my proprietary recipe."

Some onlooker gasps. Sandy looks between us, first at me, then at Lark. She even glances at the remains in Lark's hands and at the mountain of chocolates behind her.

"Henley Confectionery has been a fixture at Taste of Sydney," she tells me, "since the event's inception in the eighties, Mr. Franklin. Before you were even a glimmer in someone's eye. The company is one of our most respected vendors."

The implication is clear. *I'm the newcomer here, the outsider.*

"If anyone needs to leave . . . ," Sandy lets the sentence hang.

I can't believe this. Turning back to Lark, I say, "Answer the question. Is it Tellco Bottling on Plum Street?"

She nods, and my anger boils again. For all I know the whole Jules angle is a lie and Lark paid someone at the bottling plant a hefty sum for my recipe.

"Christ!" I exclaim. "I knew you were hot shit in NYC, and I understand you need to make your mark here, but stealing my sauce is the wrong way to go about it!"

Lark folds her arms across her chest, her expression hardening. "Do you put vanilla in yours?" she demands.

I almost don't dignify her question with an answer.

"Of course," I spit out. And I can taste it in hers.

"From Madagascar?" she asks with a jaunty little tilt of her head.

Maybe there *is* a difference. "No, it's a Mexican vanilla bean infusion."

She pales, and I know hers must contain the very same. With fury and disappointment warring in my chest, I turn and start walking.

"This is not your sauce," she calls after me. And that's all it takes for me to spin around and storm back over to her.

"Do I need to call security?" Sandy asks.

"Not if she removes every damn bottle from the booth," I say, noticing that Lark's hands are shaking as she grips one of her precious HLC bottles.

"Who do you think you are?" she demands.

"Do not sell those bottles," I say, my voice nice and calm and neutral. I don't want to scare the Taste of Sydney customers or get hauled away by Sandy's so-called security. "You should close the whole damned display."

Lark gestures at the boxes of chocolates stacked artfully behind her but doesn't speak.

"Those are OK. They can stay," I say, sounding imperious to my own ears.

"You sound as though you think you're doing me some grand favor," she says. "Let me make this clear, Mr. Franklin. I don't need your permission to sell Henley's Liquid Chocolate." Her voice rises. "You don't decide what stays and what goes."

She's right. Short of knocking over everything in sight and throwing her chocolates up in the air, which would give me some small satisfaction, I can't do anything to stop her. Not at this moment, anyway. I stalk from her booth, keeping hold of the bottle. HLC! Let her come after me for the cost.

I'm a world-class idiot. I thought I knew her, as if a few perfect fucks gave me special insight. I wince at my own naiveté, while also regretting recently telling my parents about her.

I groan, recalling my mom's excitement. I was way out of my league with this chick who could *and did* put Wall Street execs in their place. I let myself believe we had a significant spark that could grow into a whole freakin' blaze.

But Lark Henley is exactly what everyone says about corporate executives willing to do anything to get ahead, especially female ones who have to work harder and do more to prove themselves. Even steal from someone she has willingly spread her legs for.

I arrive back at my booth, so angry I can't see straight. Chef Sarah starts to say something and closes her mouth with a click of her teeth. No longer feeling particularly nice, I tell her the truth.

"Your chicken needs some pep. That's code for *flavor*. Have you tried miso butter and fresh ginger before roasting it?" Her eyes widen. "How about aleppo pepper? Even orange juice and soy sauce would help?"

I could literally come up with a billion ways to fix her stupid chicken.

But I see her eyes well up with tears, and I roll my own into the back of my head.

*Seriously?* I had to be placed next to a thin-skinned, emotional chef? I didn't know those even existed any longer.

Turning away, frustrated and a little ashamed of myself, I go behind the counter of my booth and toss myself down on a too-small, folding chair. At this moment, I want to be literally anywhere but here. Lark thought she could use our sexual connection to get away with this. There's no other explanation for doing something so brazen. She must have thought I'd roll over for the chance to roll her again.

She was dead wrong. I won't let her get away with this just because I still want her. And the part of me clamoring to get her naked again can shut the hell up.

# 9

# Lark

My hands are still shaking as I watch the arrogant, infuriating man storm away from my booth. I want to throw something at his retreating back, preferably one of these bottles full of chocolate sauce he's so convinced I stole from him.

The accusation stings more than I want to admit, especially coming from him. From Mitch, who made me feel things I hadn't felt in years. Does he believe I could give myself to him so completely and then turn around and do something this underhanded and contemptible?

Because it sure seems like he was looking at me with contempt. And that makes my chest ache in a way I don't want to think about.

Event-goers mill around, pretending they haven't just witnessed the ugly confrontation, but I can hear their whispers. "Lark Henley caught in a scandal, less than six months after arriving." It happened once before, in NYC.

My chest tightens at the thought of making headlines after my father was able to keep the last debacle out of all media.

"Jenny," I call over one of my assistants from the booth. She's in her sixties and used to work in our factory. She loves doing events and being out, chatting with people. She'd stand in front of the Henley building with a tray of chocolates every day if she was needed.

"Would you lose your vendor tag, please, and go incognito over to Mr. Franklin's booth? It's on the map, two halls over. The banner should say Franklin 6." I keep my voice steady despite the turmoil inside. "Please buy a bottle of his chocolate sauce."

"Franklin Darkly," she says.

I sigh. I guess everyone knew about this superb chocolate sauce with its absurd name, except me. I think about how I absolutely should've known that the man I'd been playing footsie with had created a sensation within my field of expertise.

"I take it you're familiar with it."

"Oh, yeah," Jenny says. "Always got a jar in the pantry for ice cream and that sort of thing."

"How long has it been popular?" I ask.

Jenny scrunches up her face. "Oh, I reckon it's been about four years."

I wince.

"No worries," she says brightly. "I'll start buying Henley Liquid Chocolate from now on."

"Please don't concern yourself," I say, thinking that HLC will never make it to market now. I told Mitch our factory wasn't retooled yet. That was true, but I was so confident with the taste tests we've been running for two weeks, I went ahead and put in an order for the machinery. Worse, the concrete pad for the addition to our Wetherill Park factory has already been poured. My ass will be toast when the board hears about this.

Right on the heels of the mean and unexpected three-month probation they put me on over the sugar issue. It was shocking and quick, and I left the board meeting stunned but determined that nothing else would happen until I was a very old and wrinkly CEO.

"I'll reimburse you," I promise her, "but obviously, you can't use a credit card with my name on it or the company one."

She waves my words aside and removes her ID tag, handing it to me before she strolls away. Suddenly, I do feel like I'm involved in culinary espionage, sending Jenny in under cover. But I need to get my hands on Mitch's sauce. Fast. Despite having acted like any reasonable CEO would, excited by a new product, this screw-up feels like amateur hour on my part.

While Jenny's gone, I try to focus on the customers, but my smile is fake and my heart is not into pushing boxes of assorted chocolates. Even less into selling the few cases of HLC.

Grabbing the sign that states "HLC made with TLC," I toss it to the floor behind the booth. In between talking to people, my other helper and I start boxing up the remaining bottles. All the while, I can't stop thinking about the way Mitch looked at me—like I'd betrayed him personally.

As it turns out, maybe I have, but not intentionally.

Jenny returns ten minutes later. Mission accomplished. The Franklin Darkly packaging is completely different from ours. The HLC bottles are elegant. They're a nod to my grandfather's wine business, which he started on a small scale, having conquered chocolate in his younger years.

Mitch's wide-mouthed jars are more utilitarian, meant for regular use and big spoons.

It's a small relief in this mess. At least he can't accuse me of copying his presentation. I examine his sapphire-blue label, reminding me of his eyes. It's printed with black type, outlined almost imperceptibly in chocolate-brown. A really gorgeous design.

Later, when I get a quiet moment between Sydney's chocolate lovers wanting to ask me questions, taste, and buy, I go behind the booth with the two sauces. Upon tasting HLC and Franklin Darkly side by side, my stomach drops. My palate for all things chocolate is as good as it gets, and these sauces are identical. Even the silky texture is the same.

Closing my eyes, I let another drop of each melt on my tongue, first one, then the other. Their subtle caramel notes from the coconut sugar and the warm vanilla undertones dance across my taste buds. There's no denying it.

*How is this possible?*

The rest of the day passes in a blur. My mind keeps circling back to Jules. *Did he? Could he have?* But why would he steal a recipe? From Mitch or anyone, for that matter. It doesn't make sense. Jules has been with Henley for almost a decade, crafting original recipes that put us on the map and keep us there. He's an artist, a perfectionist. Stealing someone else's work is unquestionably beneath him.

Yet the evidence is undeniable.

By the time we start packing up, I'm exhausted and confused. The owner of the booth next to mine, a saltwater taffy maker, who had a ringside seat for Mitch's and my showdown, keeps shooting me sympathetic glances. That makes it worse.

Instead of heading straight home, as I fully intended upon leaving the convention center, I find myself driving right past my waterfront home. Parking in front of Mitch's building, I take a few deep breaths, still considering whether this is a good idea. But I need to talk this out with him, make him understand that I never meant to steal his sauce. I'm an aboveboard, ethical businesswoman.

*How else will I sleep tonight?*

After ghosting him for the better part of three weeks, it's the least I can do.

His doorman lets me in. I guess I seem harmless enough. The elevator ride feels endless. When it dings, telling me I've reached the fifth floor, where there are two penthouse suites, it occurs to me he may not be home. This could end in an anticlimactic retreat to my car. In fact, more than likely, he's gone to his bar or restaurant.

Still, I check my reflection in the shiny steel walls of the lift. My mascara is still in place, but my eyes betray my fatigue.

When I reach his door, a double-door entry like my own, I raise my hand to the doorbell. Before my thumb can press the button, it swings open.

My heart stops, and I step back in surprise.

A pretty brunette emerges. She's busty and wearing a white ribbed tank top that is stretched across her breasts, leaving little to the imagination. The jacket of her chef's whites is slung over her shoulder, and her checkered pants are more form fitting than most baggy chef's uniforms I've seen.

I'm sure the startled look she sends me is mirrored by my own face. Then she offers me a polite smile before heading toward the elevator. While I never saw the woman before, I imagine she was at the Taste of Sydney today. Or she works at Mitch's restaurant, paying a perfectly professional house call. *Sure she is.*

I stand there, frozen, while she steps into the elevator I just vacated. I should have followed her and ridden back down, because I'm not staying.

"Of course!" I mutter to myself. *Of course Mitch would have someone else.* Someone who didn't allegedly steal his precious recipe. Someone uncomplicated. Someone in his industry whom he doesn't even have to cook for. Who doesn't push him away for a month at a time while she figures out her work shit.

Finally, I'm moving, turning away from the door that the woman left ajar. I'll take the stairs for some exercise.

"Lark?"

I whirl around at the sound of his voice. Mitch has appeared in the doorway, his expression unreadable. His sleeves are rolled up, and I catch a whiff of something delicious coming from his apartment. The scent of garlic and herbs makes my mouth water. I'd be starving if I hadn't roamed the exhibits around six o'clock, filling up on a hundred small samples. Of course, I peeked at Mitch's booth from behind a potted plant, but he was gone.

"Who was that?" The words slip out before I can stop them. I hate how vulnerable I sound. How clingy, especially when I have no right.

But he doesn't gloat or look smug. He does this sexy shoulder and neck stretch before answering. "Sarah. The chef from the booth next to mine."

I'm glad for a second that she's *not* his regular chef because I cannot imagine them working side-by-side, creating recipes without getting very, very close. No way they wouldn't be sleeping together. I know I wouldn't be able to work beside Mitch in the kitchen, tasting great food off the same spoon, and not want to strip him bare and jump his bones.

Thinking how quickly Mitch picked up this woman he met today and brought her home, I start to climb onto my high horse of outrage . . . and quickly topple off when I realize the irony. Because that's exactly what he did with me, and I didn't mind one bit.

How can I fault the man for being a fast worker?

"I insulted her chicken earlier," Mitch continues. "Felt bad about it, so I invited her over to discuss some recipe ideas."

"To your apartment?" I know I sound petty, but I can't help it. "Wouldn't your restaurant have been a better place?"

Suddenly, he grins, stealing my breath with its sexiness. "Impossible," he says. "Franklin 6 is besieged right about now with hungry diners, placing orders. My head chef would kill me if I tried to invade his kitchen on a Saturday."

That makes sense. But I know what I saw. "So," I say. "Chicken recipes? In her skimpy tank top?"

He actually laughs at me. "She has great tits," he says. "Can't deny that."

Annoyed by his casual remark, I turn and start to walk. Showing up here, when I've been put on my back foot, as they say, was a mistake. I don't usually come from a place of being in the wrong or from a position of weakness. It feels terrible.

Before I can take two steps, however, his hand clamps around my upper arm.

"Hey, Lark," he says, holding me in place, but I don't look at him. "Your tits are far, far nicer."

*What an ass!* Wrenching my arm free, I'm determined to hit that elevator button before I hit him.

"I'm kidding," he says. "Come on, Lark. If something had been going on with Sarah, do you think she'd be leaving my place at seven thirty?"

He has a point, but the sight of another woman emerging from his apartment, looking totally at ease, sort of stings. It shook me more than I expected, making me know, deep down, that I don't want him to be with anyone else.

While I haven't claimed Mitch for myself, I selfishly want him to be here, alone, until I'm ready. That's the truth.

Swallowing hard, I turn slowly. "I came to talk. I need you to believe I didn't steal your sauce. I wouldn't do that." My voice cracks slightly on the last word.

He doesn't respond, simply looks at me with those intense eyes, blue and luminous, that make my knees weak. The silence stretches between us, heavy with unspoken accusations and something else. Frustrated desire, if he's feeling what I'm feeling.

Finally, he says, "Will you come in?"

I follow him back to his front door, and he stands aside so I can enter. First thing I see is an open case, half full of Franklin Darkly jars on his barstool at his kitchen island. *So benign.* A silly thing to have started a war over. I wonder if he might see it that way, too.

Facing him, I say, "It's just sauce, after all."

His expression changes, hardens. "*Just* sauce?" Quick as a horse whip on my grandfather's ranch, Mitch grabs my hand and yanks me close. I have to crane my neck to look up at him. His gaze is fixed on my brown one.

"That sauce is magic, lady. It's kept the lights on, so to speak, when my first cafe didn't take off instantly or when my third restaurant waned in popularity because I took my eye off the prize."

"Well, I only meant—"

"Let me show you why it's not *just* sauce."

He breaks away long enough to grab a bottle of Franklin Darkly from the box and open it with a quick twist. Leaving the lid behind, he dips his finger into the pool of chocolate darkness before swiping it across my lips, making me gasp. When he dips it in again, he looks at me and licks it off. More than anything, I wanted to lick it off his finger. He knows that, too. I can see it in his smug expression.

"Don't worry, it's your turn now." Before I can process what's happening, his mouth is on mine, hot and demanding. He tastes, of course, like chocolate. I melt against him as though I'm made of the stuff.

Part of me knows we should be talking about what happened today, not going along this familiar path, but my body wants what it wants. And my brain has an entire jar full of indecent ideas flitting through it.

I know Mitch has the same naughty notions, when he sucks my lip into his mouth then sinks his teeth into it. A wave of delicious heat courses through my body, leaving me twitching between my legs.

When he draws back, his eyes have darkened with intent. "Take off your dress," he says, his tone husky, making a shiver dance across my skin and my nipples harden.

I shouldn't comply. We need to discuss . . . something. *What the hell was it?* But my fingers are already reaching for the single button at the back of my neck. When I've undone it, I lift the dress over my head and toss it toward the sofa in the other room, missing by a mile. The air conditioning raises goosebumps on my skin, or maybe it's the way he's looking at me.

Standing before him in a champagne-colored bra and panties, I'm instantly wet and wishing we'd gone into his bedroom. Too late. He reaches behind me and wraps my hair around his hand, pulling my head back, exposing my neck. The first drop of room-temperature chocolate sauce hits my collarbone.

As it slides down the valley between my breasts, I draw in a ragged breath. His tongue follows the path of the chocolate, licking it away like a cat with cream. I forget why I ever thought this was a bad idea.

When he releases my hair, it's only to back me up to his glass dining room table. *Oh God!* My imagination is racing ahead, making my clit throb. Sure enough, he undoes my bra with one skilled hand and presses me back against the cool, hard surface, before stripping my panties off. Then he stands between my legs, looking down at me in silence.

"I'm going to feast on you," he says, "with my favorite topping."

*Sounds good to me.* My mouth has gone dry. All I do is nod and watch while he drizzles a slow, thin line of Franklin Darkly across both my breasts and then trails it down the flat of my stomach to my pussy. When he bends to begin his feast, my hands find his hair, holding him close as he works his way down my body. His mouth and tongue leave me trembling and desperate for more.

I arch my hips when he gets closer to my ladybits, but he doesn't go for my most sensitive area. Not yet. He blows on it and continues past, dripping sauce onto my inner thighs. In fact, the sauce is everywhere, sticky and sweet, but I don't care. All I care about is that he continues.

Which he does. After nibbling the tender areas of my now-quivering thighs, he parts my nether lips and devours, occasionally pausing to trickle more chocolate directly onto my clit. I'm scared I'll dissolve into pure pleasure.

"I'm coming," I whisper, unable to hold back. He simply slides a finger inside me, making me unravel faster, and he sucks my clit harder until my orgasm is over. That's when I draw my hands from his hair, letting my arms flop back to the table like a rag doll.

Mitch raises his head to look at me in my helpless, boneless condition.

"Not *just* sauce," he says with pride.

"You win," I say. "It's magic!"

When he enters me, right there on the edge of his dining table, I'm still so revved and my flesh so stimulated, it takes only a few deep thrusts before I'm breathing out his name.

Arching, adjusting, feeling the entire length and breadth of his cock as he rocks in and draws out, I reach down to stroke myself and I'm flying again into another shuddering orgasm.

Bracing himself with one big spread-open hand on either side of me, his climax follows shortly after mine.

"I want to collapse beside you," he says, "but I don't think this table can handle it. Shower?"

With our chocolate-smeared skin making it impossible to get dressed, there's really no other choice. Taking a shower together feels incredibly intimate, using *his* shampoo and soap, letting Mitch run a cloth over my back, like he cares for me.

Under the shower spray, our bodies are in such stark contrast. Not merely our size difference, nor the contrasting colors of our skin, but in the hardness factor. Staring while he rinses shampoo from his hair, his eyes closed, I'm mesmerized by his well-defined muscles, which I can't help but touch. For a moment, I wonder if he wants a similarly fit girlfriend. While I'm both curvy in some places and slender in others, I've never lifted weights or done any regular exercise beyond an occasional game of tennis. The idea of a gym workout bores me.

*Doesn't matter,* I remind myself. *You're not his girlfriend.*

Weirdly, we don't have sex again while under the sluicing hot water. Even weirder, I came twice on his dining table *without* needing a pinch of pain to push me over into two intense orgasms.

Maybe Mitch Franklin himself is the magic sauce!

For a few more blissful moments, I forget about everything except the feel of his hands on my skin and the lingering taste of chocolate in my mouth. It's a fantasy moment, disconnected from CEO Lark Henley.

*I want this*, the little voice in my head says while we dry off. I want him, us, this connection that feels so right even when he's on the verge of suing me. *Shut up, little voice!*

In this case, I'm not going to get what I want. Not Mitch Franklin, who's a heartbreaker and a distraction. Not in business, either. I wasted time and money for a month on an exciting new product that I have to give up.

And I haven't even told him about the board's probationary warning during the unpleasant emergency meeting three weeks ago. *Ugh!*

Just like that, reality crashes back in. Dressed and seated at his island, my sole task is to open a bottle of wine and decant it into two glasses. Practically in the time it takes me, he makes us both dinner—fettuccine noodles with a cream sauce, topped with the chicken he whipped up with that floozy female chef.

He *is* magic! Sautéed spinach with fresh garlic completes the feast, and I feel as though I'm at a four-star Italian restaurant.

"Not bad for a boy from Boston," I say.

"Boston has a superb Italian neighborhood. Smaller but as authentic as NYC's Little Italy."

It's now or never. "How about if I alter my HLC in some small way?" Which would sting, since I know it's perfect as is. "Then it wouldn't be a problem if I keep making it, would it?" I try to keep my tone light, though we both know it's anything but a casual question.

Mitch sets his fork down. He picks up the glass of deep red cab and takes a long drink. Then he stares me straight in the eyes, and I can see he is deadly serious.

"No," he says firmly. "I can't allow that. And you owe it to me to find out how you ended up with my recipe."

I'm the first to break eye contact, suddenly feeling more exposed than when I was spread atop the table we're now eating at.

"Someone is playing games," Mitch adds. "And I think you know who that is."

"Jules," I whisper. The evidence is strong, the coincidence too unbelievable.

But I don't believe it. "My master chocolatier is too good to do anything like that. He doesn't need to."

"How many syrups and sauces has he created for your company?"

"None," I say, realizing the truth.

"Yet this one came out of nowhere, perfectly crafted on his first try?"

It sounds impossible. But so does the alternative, that he purposefully stole Mitch's chocolate sauce. I cannot imagine what my brother and father will say when I bring this to them. Julian Cartier is a trusted employee and his expertise has been instrumental in maintaining our reputation for excellence.

"It might've been unintentional," I say weakly, but the words sound hollow, even to my own wishful ears. I set my own fork down, no longer hungry.

"You don't believe that." Mitch says. Then he cocks his head. "At this point, either you take care of this properly, or I begin legal action."

*Properly* meaning I fire Jules. I rise to my feet. "You would honestly sue me," I say, sputtering my words, I'm so pissed off. "After . . . after that?" I gesture at the now-closed jar of Franklin Darkly, still resting at one end of the table, like a poignant reminder of how vulnerable I let myself be with this man.

Mitch gets to his feet. "One thing has nothing to do with the other," he insists. "That was for fun. This is business."

*Fun?* It seemed like so much more than that. The slow intensity of his chocolate sauce seduction tore down any sense of self-preservation I had against giving in to this man.

If Mitch had ordered me to do anything for him . . . to him . . . with him, while we were in the throes of whatever the hell that was, I would have obeyed.

Now, in the cold light of being given an ultimatum over dinner, I am not feeling particularly obedient.

"It's pretty simple, Lark. I think this is a case of him or me."

I look at Mitch for a long moment, memorizing the planes of his face and the unusual color of his eyes. Then I slide on my shoes and walk out, as empty-handed as when I arrived. He doesn't even try to stop me.

That's the hardest part and what makes tears prick my eyes by the time I get in my car. I want him to run after me and say we can work this out amicably. In this risky little dance of strong personalities, it's his turn to concede.

*No one's going to call any lawyer.*

*No one's going to get fired.*

But he doesn't chase me down. In order to keep from making a big *mea culpa* explanation to the board about why I broke ground on an addition to the factory for a new product we can't make, I'm going to distance myself from Mitch and hope the problem goes away.

Apparently, he found it easy to make a decision, while I know I won't be sleeping well tonight. When I was the one staying away from him, I was in control, with the certainty that when I gave the word, we'd get together again. Like we just did on his dining room table.

But he has wrestled away that control. How can I choose between sacking our talented chocolatier, altering the future of my family's company, and the man I can't deny I'm falling for?

# 10

## Mitch

I can't stop staring at the dining room table where Lark lay a couple hours ago. The surface is still slightly smudged with chocolate sauce, despite my hasty wipe down before we ate dinner. I should clean it properly, but every time I look at it, I remember the way she arched beneath my touch, the sounds she made, the way she tasted mixed with chocolate sauce.

*My* sauce. The one she stole.

Except . . . I don't think she did. The confusion and regret in her eyes seemed genuine. The hurt in her voice when I gave her the ultimatum definitely was real. But I believe she's as sure as I am that it is my recipe, and the only person who could have recreated it was her chocolatier. It's up to her to do something about it before I have to.

Grabbing my kitchen sponge, I give the table another soapy wipe, but I can't clear the memory of her walking out my door without saying a word.

My phone buzzes. For a split second, I hope it's Lark, but the decade-old contact photo of my sister, Riley, lights up the screen. I keep it because I like to think of her before she became a big-shot fashion model.

"Hey, sis," I answer, wedging the phone between my ear and shoulder as I dry the table with a wad of paper towels.

"Big brother!" Riley's voice carries the same musical quality our mother's does. But for appearances, she has the same mixture of genes that I do. Mom's blue eyes. Dad's coffee-colored skin, if you take your coffee with cream. Riley's skin is even a shade lighter than mine.

"I've been meaning to call you for weeks. My schedule's been crazy. But I'm in Boston now for a few days. Mom and Dad say you've hooked up with a superstar."

I grunt noncommittally. I'm sure my parents didn't use the term "hooked up," at least not to mean what Lark and I did on my dining room table.

"Hello," Riley continues. "Is this thing on?"

"What do you want?" I ask, knowing I sound grumpy.

"All the deets, Mitch. Come on. They said you're seeing Lark Henley. The chocolate princess," Riley continues, her tone teasing.

If she doesn't like *chocolate heiress*, I know she'd hate *chocolate princess*. After tossing the paper towels into my stainless-steel bin, I hurl the sponge into the sink with more force than necessary, making a satisfying thump sound.

"Not anymore."

There's a pause on the other end. "Yikes, sorry. What happened?"

I pace the length of my apartment, running a hand through my hair. "She stole the recipe for Franklin Darkly."

"No way." Riley's voice is filled with disbelief. "Lark Henley doesn't need to steal chocolate recipes. Her family's been knee-deep in the best chocolate for three generations. There's a box on the table right now."

I can hear the noise as she opens the lid, scrabbling like a raccoon, and then takes a piece of candy from its little brown-paper nest. I wait, imagining my sister's taste buds lighting up.

"Fabulous," Riley says. "Mom said she's been buying it ever since you told her about the two of you."

"Well, Mom can stop now. Because Lark's master chocolatier got his sticky hands on my recipe. And she's backing him or covering for him. Either way, she wants to produce Henley Liquid Chocolate."

Riley takes a deep breath, and I can see her face in my mind, what she looks like when she's thinking. "And you're sure it wasn't just . . . I don't know, a coincidence?"

I bark out a laugh. "Exactly the same ingredients? Same texture? Same everything?"

"It seems unlikely," Riley maintains, which makes me want to throw more than a sponge. Besides, my sister's voice sounds like she's holding something back. Then she asks, "Did you like her? Before all this happened?"

I sink onto my couch, suddenly exhausted. I almost wish I still had the scent of Lark's perfume on my skin, but the shower removed all traces. Then I feel annoyed with myself for such a pathetic thought. But there's no point lying to Riley.

"Yeah," I admit. "I did. A lot."

"Then maybe you shouldn't let something like this ruin it. If I loved someone—"

"*Whoa!* I never said anything about love," I interrupt sharply.

"Fine," she says, sounding huffy. "If I really *liked* someone, I'd give that person the damn recipe with my blessing."

Riley can be such a dope. "You don't understand. This isn't only about business, although it certainly is because I can't be with someone who'd steal from me and expect to get away with it merely because she's great in—" I stop myself, then finish, "great in the kitchen." Which I've realized she isn't.

Lark said she can make scrambled eggs . . . maybe. "But it's also, to me, about Dad's legacy and how he let me run with it, to enhance it, add to it. Not let the damn sauce slip away to a big company that didn't earn it."

*Even on her back, Lark didn't earn the rights to Franklin Darkly.*

Riley comes back at me. "I don't understand business the way you do, at least not your business. I have a manager and an agent, so I can be nothing more than a pretty face with an empty head."

Now she's being sarcastic. We both know she's smart.

There's rustling on her end, and she's either settling into our dad's overstuffed armchair, the one we used to fight over as kids, or she's wolfing down chocolate and crinkling the little papers. Either way, I feel better simply talking to my only sibling.

That is, until she adds, "But I know a little something about Lark Henley that maybe you don't."

That gets my attention. "What? How?"

"As a freakin' supermodel, brother dear, I used to run in the same circles in New York City as she did. Same clubs, same guys in some instances."

"And?" I ask tersely because I don't want to think of Lark or Riley with a guy.

"Do you know Connor Whittel?"

The name triggers something in my memory. It's not John Smith, after all. "I don't know him, but I think I've heard the name."

"It would be more than familiar if Lark's father hadn't managed to squash the story about how badly Whittel screwed her over."

My hand tightens on the phone. "What are you talking about?"

Riley sighs. "Connor's a hotshot on Wall Street. They met at the Met Gala and started dating. Lark had recently taken over as CEO, so this is like four, maybe five years ago when she first came up from Australia, I think. I was brand-spanking new, too."

My sister gives a little self-deprecating laugh.

"Anyway, she made a rookie mistake and told Connor about her company's plan to change their cocoa bean supplier for their U.S. production. He didn't just invest in the supplier's company. He also tipped them off about Henley's plans. The supplier jacked up their prices, nearly cost Lark her job during her first three months."

My stomach churns. "Christ!"

"That's not all," Riley continues. "The whole reason she wanted to stay in New York instead of heading up their Sydney office as originally planned was because of Connor. Her brother was supposed to head up the NYC division, but he agreed to run Sydney instead."

My mouth has dropped open. I lean back, close it. "How the hell do you know all this?"

She hesitates. "I dated Connor briefly a few months after they broke up. Until I found out he's a class-A creep."

Both my sister and Lark have dated the same guy? That has all kinds of ick factor I don't want to think about.

Jumping up, I grab myself a Victoria Bitter, an Aussie favorite that has become mine, too. As the sweet malty flavor and clean hoppy tang of the beer hits my tongue, I start processing Riley's disclosure, and some pieces fall into place. Lark's initial hesitation with me, her fierce protection of her family's company, her independence, and her constant need to step back and focus on doing a good job.

"So she was burned badly," I say, more to myself than Riley.

"Burned? Try incinerated. Connor played her like a fiddle. I bet she had a hard time getting over the humiliation, although it's not like it happened yesterday. She seemed the type to leave the personal hurt in the past. I've met her a number of times, and I'd say she's tough as nails. But the professional hit she took. *Oof?*"

Riley makes a noise like my dad's sister, Auntie Wilkes, used to make if we messed up her living room.

"If something like that had happened to me when I was a rookie on the runway, I'd have curled up and gone home. I'm sure it messed with Lark Henley's confidence as CEO. Or at least made her hyper focused on never letting anything like that happen again."

My chest tightens as I think about how I treated Lark. Didn't I essentially do the same thing? Used our intimate connection against her and threatened her professionally to get what I want.

"Shit," I mutter.

"Yeah, shit is right." Riley's tone turns sharp. "Look, I get that you're protective of Franklin Darkly. It's made you rich, but I think your restaurants are more representative of the Mitchell Franklin legacy. Besides, you're established now. All your places are doing great. I bet Dad wouldn't mind if you shared the chocolate sauce."

"It's not about sharing the sauce," I argue, but my voice lacks conviction, and I retake my seat on the couch. "It's about principle."

"No, it's about pride. And maybe a little fear."

"Fear?" I scoff. "Of what?"

"You like her a lot. That's what you said. Something I haven't heard for a while."

"I've dated," I correct her, getting sick of my little sister's know-it-all attitude. Although one-night stands are not really dates.

"Dating, *schmating*," she says, sounding twelve again, instead of twenty-four. "When was the last time you fell in love, let someone own your ass, so to speak. I don't mean anything else by that. Just a good, knock-your-socks-off romance." She sighs into my uncommunicative silence. "But my big brother isn't known for letting someone into his life. Not lately."

"Are we done?"

"Are you listening?" she demands, hating being dismissed, as she always did. "I know you had a bit of bad luck with some greedy bitches. I know you've been running solo since you left Boston. Maybe it's time to consider a partner."

"Nope," I start.

"Not in business, silly. Although I don't see why not. But a life partner." She sighs. "Perhaps you're more worried about Lark Henley stealing your heart than your chocolate sauce."

I stand up, unable to sit still any longer. "You're starting to sound like Mom."

"Good. Mom's usually right." Riley laughs. "By the way, she absolutely loves that you're dating Lark Henley. Says it's like a fairy tale—the self-made entrepreneur and the chocolate princess. I'd hate for you to disappoint Mom's dreams."

"Too late. We're not dating anymore, remember? I basically accused Lark of corporate theft and threatened to sue her company."

"Then fix it, you idiot." Riley's exasperation comes through clearly. "Unless you're OK with letting another Connor Whittel-type swoop in and console her?"

The thought makes my blood boil. "That's not going to happen."

"It might. She's gorgeous, successful, and now single again. I've been to Australia. There are like a billion hot guys there. And now, thanks to you, she's available."

I walk to my window, looking out at the nightscape. To my left, I can see the illuminated outline of the Opera House. Between it and me, five minutes by car, Lark is in her waterfront home.

I wonder what her frame of mind is. Doubtless not much better than my own. We definitely have a connection, not merely sexual, but something else. Deeper. We seem to *get* one another.

Deep down, I know she would never have stolen a recipe from me. What I don't know for sure is whether, as a businesswoman, she'll let things stand or fix them. But I should've said my piece and hoped she'd handle it. I shouldn't have started throwing challenges around, like that "him or me" crap. Especially not after she took the trouble to come to my place. And not after what we did in the dining room before breaking bread together.

I've always taken seriously the time-honored tradition of welcome, openness, and trust that sharing a meal represents. Then I made her uncomfortable and provoked her, the worst thing a host can do to a guest, either in my restaurant or in my home.

"You still there?" Riley asks. "Or has your brain short-circuited?"

"I'm here." I press my forehead against the cool glass. "I really fucked up, didn't I?"

"Probably. But nothing's irreversible. Yet." She pauses. "You know what I think?"

"I'm sure you'll tell me."

"I think my big, strong brother is a little scared because you can see how deep you two might go. I scarcely know her, besides the obvious, that she's gorgeous, intelligent, and fierce. A match for you any day."

I agree with everything Riley has said so far.

"And it's easier to push her away over business than admit she could be the one."

"When did you get so wise?" I ask, deflecting because she's hitting too close to the target.

"I dated a therapist for a couple months. Picked up a few things." Riley laughs. "Look, I've got to go. Mom's waving at me to come help with dinner. But Mitch?"

"What now, you pain-in-the-ass?"

"Don't let your sauce be more important than your heart. Dad's legacy isn't simply about recipes. It's about the values he taught us. Like forgiveness. Understanding. Love."

After we hang up, I walk back to my dining room table. The surface is clean now, but the memory of Lark remains. The way she trusted me completely, gave herself to me without reservation. And how did I repay that trust? By threatening legal action.

My sister's right. I'm an idiot.

But before I can fix things with Lark, I'll need to figure out what compromise I can live with. Because despite my irrefutable feelings for her, I can't continue any type of friendship with her if she doesn't get to the bottom of what happened.

And if it was her master chocolatier, will she do the right thing as CEO?

# 11

## Lark

Staring at the phone on my desk, I will myself to pick it up and call Jules. It's all I've thought about from the moment I walked out of Mitch's penthouse. But how do I even begin that conversation with the man who's been our master chocolatier since before I was CEO in NYC? Since before Luke and I ran Sydney HQ jointly while Dad was still handling the U.S.?

Jules is about fifteen years older than I am. He started very young, as an apprentice at one of our competitors in Belgium, and then my father wooed him away from them. Dad put all his trust in the young and amazingly skilled artist.

How impertinent and disrespectful will I have to be to question him? *Hey, did you steal my lover's chocolate sauce recipe? And by the way, why would you do that to me?*

My hand hovers over the office receiver, then drops. Then I pick up my cell before once again, reconsidering.

This isn't a conversation for the phone. I need to see Jules's face when I ask him some hard questions. I want to watch his eyes, his expression.

After what happened with Connor Whittel, who could lie to me while we were spooning on his expensive sheets, I've learned to read people better. At least, I thought I had. If it turns out that Jules lied about creating HLC in his kitchen, then I guess I haven't learned anything at all.

Then there's Mitch, who totally caught me off guard. I wish we hadn't . . .

I nearly just lied to myself. I cannot regret sex on his dining room table. But I wish he hadn't made me feel like I was so utterly and completely *his*, only to turn around and threaten me.

*Mitch*. Thinking his name makes my body tingle with remembered pleasure. The way he used that damn sauce. I squeeze my thighs together, trying to keep my thoughts straight. Forget about the man who takes me on a journey of escape so amazing, I never want to return to reality.

I need to focus on my family's company, our legacy, and my responsibility to both.

The intercom buzzes. "Lark?" My assistant's voice is like a quick slap. "The quarterly reports are ready for your review." There's that responsibility I signed up for.

"Thanks, Dan." Looking at the reports before sending them off to the board will be more excruciating than usual. Not boring, though. Not with the glaring sugar expense, no doubt in bold and red, alongside the cost of the new concrete pad for the bottling production line I no longer need.

Groaning, I know I have to face the more pressing matter first. Making a quick decision, I straighten my coral-colored pencil skirt, grab my bag, and head out.

"I'm going to Wetherill Park," I tell Dan as I pass his desk in the reception area outside my office.

"Should I call ahead?" he offers, his hand moving toward the phone.

"No, thanks." The last thing I need is Jules preparing for my arrival.

Shaking my head, I can't even believe I'm thinking this way, and I don't know what I'm worried he might do. Destroy some bottles of Franklin Darkly he left lying around for testing? Hardly. But I'm dealing with such inconceivable shit right now, I have to be prepared for anything.

"Call my cell if you need me."

The morning Sydney traffic is thick, but my mind is thicker with thoughts. I'm still ruminating on how this sauce debacle could have happened, trying to come up with a reasonable explanation. The odds against it being a coincidence are astronomical. But the alternative—that Jules set me up—is equally impossible.

*Could he have thought it would never be discovered?* After all, he didn't know I was "seeing" Mitch on and off, sharing food and sex with the man. But Jules might've known that jars of Franklin Darkly would be at the Taste of Sydney, which puts me right back in the same place. It's ridiculous to think he could betray our company, leaving us open to a lawsuit.

My phone rings through the car's Bluetooth as I merge onto the M4.

"Hey, Jim," I answer, recognizing our factory manager's number.

"G'day, Lark. You busy up there in Sydney?" He sounds friendly but with a careful tone that immediately sets off warning bells.

"What's up?"

"We've got a situation. Food safety inspector's just rocked up."

My stomach drops. "Unscheduled inspection," I surmise. "Because of the sugar incident, right?"

"Word got around." Jim clears his throat. "He's asking to see everything."

"As it happens, I'm already on my way. Give him the long tour and keep him there." I press harder on the accelerator, grateful for my sports car's responsiveness. "I'll be arriving in twenty minutes."

For the rest of the drive, I'm thinking more about Mitch than about an inspector or even Jules. That alone proves I can't be trusted to have any sort of extracurricular relationship. I don't seem to be wired like other business people who can leave it all at the office door. I keep seeing Mitch's angry face at my booth when I stupidly gave him a taste of his own sauce. That was bad enough. But when he accused me of stealing his recipe, that's what haunts me.

The hurt in his eyes, the betrayal. It mirrored how I felt after Connor screwed me over. I know exactly how deep that kind of wound can cut. Even though Mitch gave me an incredible experience on his dining room table, there was something different about how he was treating me.

Maybe I'm simply being defensive, but if I had to describe it, I'd say he was having sex with someone he didn't trust. Someone he didn't even like as much as he had before. *Ugh!*

$♥$♥$♥$

The Wetherill Park factory looms ahead, its modern architecture a stark contrast to the industrial park surrounding it. I park in my reserved spot and hurry inside. Front desk security contacts Jim in the guts of the chocolate factory.

"He'll come collect you," the security officer says.

A minute later, Jim and I are walking together. "His name's Toddson. He's in the quality control lab now. He's already looked at the end-stage production lines, asking for one out of every two machines to be stopped so he could inspect it. He's taken a sample swab off a random wall, swiped right across the dairy tiles, and another from the concrete floor."

Jim sounds insulted. We both know there's nothing to worry about. His factory, from floor to ceiling, is as clean as humanly possible, and then some.

"The man's also looked at the cooling, molding, and stamping areas. Now he wants to see our sugar handling procedures."

I nod, already planning my approach. "The new protocols are in place?"

"Everything's documented and implemented." Jim hands me a tablet with the updated procedures. "Naturally, he's keener on getting samples of our sugar into his portable lab kit than worryin' about any protocols."

*Perfect.* Let him see how seriously we take quality control. My footsteps falter. We have always taken it seriously, so how did the sugar fiasco happen?

Striding into the lab, I find a middle-aged man in a crisp white coat examining our testing equipment.

"Mr. Toddson?" I extend my hand. "I'm Lark Henley, CEO. I understand you have some concerns about our sugar handling."

He looks surprised. "I wasn't expecting to meet you today, Ms. Henley," he says while shaking my hand firmly.

"We are an international company, but we are also family owned and operated. And we don't mess around with the quality of our brand," I say. "Any stains on our reputation are unwelcome anomalies. If you have any doubts, then I'm here to alleviate them."

"Just doing my due diligence, Ms. Henley. After the contamination report . . ."

"Which we addressed immediately," I interrupt smoothly. "In fact, I'd love to show you our new protocols, and while we're at it, you can inspect our entire inventory. We received a new shipment of cocoa beans today."

I've never skipped reading the morning's summary of all our incoming bills of lading, something our father told Luke and I to do every day, along with the outgoing shipments and the production rundown from the last business day. A force of habit that keeps me on top of the details.

Mr. Toddson's formidable eyebrows rise slightly. "Lead the way."

We tour the rest of the facility while I explain our enhanced quality control measures. We watch as the various types of chocolate are made and how the sugar dispenser releases into each mixture, along with milk powder. He declares our test kitchen to be spotless.

I was expecting to see Jules there, but he must've been on break.

Everything seems to be going well until we leave the production plant and head into the processing area where each shipment of beans is cleaned, roasted, winnowed, and ground. As our small group of three approaches the cocoa bean storage, I know something's wrong. The air carries a distinctly acrid aroma of something having been burned.

"What's that odor?" Mr. Toddson asks, his pen poised over his notepad.

Jim hurries ahead to the newly arrived shipment of beans. His rigid back tells me everything I need to know.

*Houston, we have a problem.* And if my nose isn't mistaken, that's the smell of scorched cocoa beans. Also the costly smell of more profits going up in smoke.

As the inspector and I follow him toward the burlap bags on our stainless-steel shelving, the odor grows stronger. Jim drags a utility knife from his back pocket and slices open a bag, right through the stamped name of the broker, Melton.

What I see spill out makes my heart literally stop for a second and then start thumping.

The premium, single-origin beans I specially ordered are toast. Not a few—all of them.

"This is unusual," Mr. Toddson comments, picking up a few and bringing them to his nose.

"Very," I agree, trying to keep my voice steady.

These aren't just any beans, either. They were from a single Australian plantation, carefully selected by me for their unique flavor profile. Not wanting them to get mixed into our regular chocolate production, I had them roasted *before* delivery. A secret move I hadn't even told the board about. Similar to when I switched sugar suppliers.

*Lark Henley trying to make her mark has again made a giant mistake.*

Holding my breath while Mr. Toddson makes notes, I'm expecting him to say he has to close our entire facility. Jim and I share a worried glance. Fortunately, the inspector is more concerned with our sugar protocols than the ruined cocoa beans.

"They aren't a safety issue the way using contaminated sugar is," he points out. "Though you might want to look into your supplier. However, back to the sugar situation . . ."

I barely pay attention to the rest of his inspection. Jim, who doesn't yet know why I bought bags of pre-roasted beans, keeps sending me inquisitive looks. My mind is racing.

*How did this happen? How could no one notice? Why did Melton even send them?*

The only thing I should be thinking about is how I'm going to explain this to the board when no Henley CEO has purchased processed beans in decades.

Satisfied that the company has taken care of any past and future sugar issues, and understanding the beet sugar was a mistake from start to finish, Mr. Toddson leaves. I'm glad to see the back of him.

Clutching a handful of the burned cocoa beans, I retreat to Jim's office on the second floor, overlooking the production line. Jim follows me in but lets me take his office chair. When he stands in the doorway and folds his arms, our manager reminds me of my father.

"Why wasn't I told about a different bean supplier?" he asks. "Especially one who delivers processed beans?"

"Surprise!" I say, wincing at his expression and dropping the beans onto his desk. I want to lower my head beside them and groan. Or maybe I want to have a hissy fit and scream. I do neither.

*Grow up, Lark,* I order myself silently instead.

"Sorry, Jim. Here's the thing. I thought it might be good for business if we started using Aussie suppliers for the majority of our ingredients. You know, creating a more genuine Henley home-grown image."

"Can't be done," he says.

"Yet. Can't be done, *yet*," I say. "I think we should source whatever we can from local cocoa bean plantations and eventually—"

He's shaking his head and interrupts me again. "Not enough local bean growers. Most of them use every last bean in their own boutique choccies. And we can't just change our beans."

Jim didn't let me finish. I was about to launch into my dream of Henley Confectionery growing our own beans. *Eventually!* The climate is ideal a scant few hours north. I want to get into the harvesting, fermentation, and drying side of production.

But I'm fully aware that's in the future. I can't believe it when he starts to lecture me about beans.

"Our supplier sends us Ivory Coast beans exclusively to maintain Henley choc's nutty flavor profile. We don't even touch Ecuador's beans. Too fruity and floral."

He's worked up and ends with a rather condescending, "You should've asked me."

I snap back, "And someone here should've refused delivery and never let those beans get unloaded into our facility."

I see his Adam's apple rise and fall as he swallows whatever remark he nearly made. Jim knows I'm right. Even the beet sugar mix-up should've been caught *before* any of it was used in production. But the last thing I want to do is start a war with the factory staff, neither with Jim nor any other employee.

"Look, I did my homework," I tell him. "There are a few growers in Queensland who have surplus cocoa beans and sell via this Sydney broker, named Melton. These beans," I point to those on his desk, "are from a grower near Cairns. I simply wanted to test a new line of artisan Aussie chocolate made with home-grown beans."

I send him what I hope is a winning, conciliatory smile. "Australia can't just be known for sheep, can it?"

Jim actually smiles back. "Lark, don't get me wrong. I like the sound of what you're saying. In theory. But small-batch choc will be pricey, not that I stick my beak into cost and marketing. Never have. At any rate, you know it'll be yonks before we can source enough local beans, and we'll have to dedicate one of the lines to it, cutting down on production of the main brand."

He rubs a hand over the back of his neck. "I'll probably be retired by then and won't have to bother with this type of right old mess."

*Right old mess?* I think he's being a bit of a Debbie Downer. "It was only a few bags, that's all," I remind him.

"How much?"

Sighing, I confess, "About a quarter of a ton."

Touching one of the scorched beans, I vow, "Melton is going to buy back every burned bean."

"The local grower might have a middle man, who processes for them, and sends them on to the broker," Jim muses aloud. "No small grower would send those charred monstrosities directly to the most well-known choccie company in Australia."

"Maybe they didn't know who Melton was selling to. In any case, I thought it was a start in the right direction, going local, rather than dealing with a Belgian importer-exporter."

"Your grandfather always reckoned Belgium was the go," Jim says. "Same with your old man and Luke. Makes the brand look a bit flash." He puffs his chest out.

"Better vibe for NYC," I mutter, belatedly noticing I'm spreading and gathering the cocoa beans in front of me, like they're a fidget toy.

"I like *flash* as much as the next CEO," I tell him, "but I think people appreciate another way of doing business. Although honestly, I cannot believe Melton shipped this garbage to us."

I smash my hand onto the small heap and send some flying. "Especially on our maiden order from him."

He shrugs, obviously thinking this is all my fault. Which, of course, it is. "This is why we roast our own beans," Jim says, giving me a look. Then he lets out a big sigh. "You want me to chase up this new broker, or what?"

"No," I say, realizing my head is aching. "Let me get a bottle of water, a cup of coffee, a handful of chocolate molasses squares, and I'll handle it."

The way I need to handle Jules and the stolen sauce situation. "Is Julian around?"

"Nope. He was here earlier, but left in a hurry. Personal matter, I think."

*Great, just great.* Perhaps I should be happy for the reprieve from that particular problem while I'm about to do my best to solve this one. Ten minutes later, I discover the broker never laid hands on the beans and is having a hard time believing what I'm telling him.

It's not that Harry Melton doubts the word of the CEO of Henley Confectionery, but he sort of does.

"The beans came unprocessed from the grower and went to a local processor," he tells me. "I trust them. Nothing like this has ever happened before."

If I was a man, I have a feeling Harry would be on the phone to the roasters in a heartbeat, making sure a new shipment of beans was in my factory by morning. Instead, he wants me to send a courier to his office with an unopened bag of the ruined goods.

"If you can't jump on this directly," I press him, "then I'll be forced to place an order elsewhere. And to be clear, if you make me wait while you inspect these beans, that will be the end of our association. Since you're not willing to make this right immediately, it's a one and done. Henley Confectionery will never source from you again."

He doesn't like that threat. Suddenly, Harry Melton is going to make the drive to Wetherill Park personally. He still wants to see the burned beans, but he tells me he'll put in a request for a stat shipment from the local processor.

"Beans will be at your factory tomorrow."

"Same local single estate?" I ask.

He hesitates. "No can do. Yours were the last available beans from that grower."

"Which is why I paid top dollar," I remind him. Then I fall silent, waiting, letting him figure out a solution.

Finally, he says, "I'll make sure they're from the same grower, even if we have to divert someone else's order to you, Ms. Henley." After another pause, he adds, "I apologize for this screw up. Will I be meeting with you later?"

"I don't normally hang around our factory all day," I tell him.

On the other hand, it doesn't hurt for me to spend time with workers on the production line, in the warehouse, and in the bean processing plant. Plus, I'll find out where Jules went, and whether he's returning today.

"But if you hurry, you'll catch me," I say. *Let Melton jump in his car and haul ass.*

Meanwhile, in case things don't work out, I make preliminary calls to a few other local growers. Each time, I come up empty. No one has any surplus. Besides, these beans were special. Unique in their flavor, like Mitch's chocolate sauce recipe.

The thought stops me cold. I would feel precisely the way he does if someone copied our signature truffles or our dark chocolate bark. I'd be furious. Just like Mitch. I certainly wouldn't have made the person a nice dinner.

Or had sex with him.

I go straight to our tasting room. It's not open to the public, except by appointment. The walls are lined with Henley's history. Photos, old advertisements, awards. My eyes fix on one particular framed photo—my grandparents in their kitchen, where it all began.

A young Evelyn is wearing an apron stained with cocoa powder, while strong-and-handsome Pat holds up a hand-rolled truffle, both of them beaming with pride.

Something inside me shifts. Hot tears prick at my eyes. Do they know about the sugar issue? What would they say if they knew I paid dearly for single-source beans from a new supplier so I could play around with some chocolate ideas?

It's time for a trip to their ranch in the Hunter Valley. Maybe this weekend. Just like my failed mission to see Jules, speaking with my grandparents is better done face-to-face.

When I leave the factory, having met with a contrite, boot-licking Harry Melton, it's dinnertime. I should go home, but I can't face my empty apartment. Instead, I find myself parking outside Mitch's impressive commercial real estate. Two venues, side by side.

Chic restaurant or loud bar and grill?

While a man holds the door open for a well-dressed woman at Franklin 6, I enter the bar and grill next to it. Of all the places in Sydney, I willingly chose *his*. Maybe because I'm a masochist. Or maybe because deep down, I hope he's here at F6, just like the night we met.

The place is busy with the after-work crowd. Most people are in groups, but there's a single seat at the end of the packed bar, and I slide onto the stool. The woman beside me has her back to me while she talks to the man beside her. That's fine. I don't have a lot of practice with solo dining and drinking, but I can deal with it.

"What'll it be, love?" asks the same cute bartender, who I noticed the night I met Mitch.

"Gin and tonic, please." I intend to order a hamburger, too, but after he sets my drink down, he's immediately called to the other end of the bar.

Scrolling through email on my phone, catching up with what I missed today, I've drained the glass without thinking and signal for another drink. By the time I've finished my second G&T, I've set my phone down and am tapping my hands on the bar in time to the music.

I have a very nice buzz going, but my stomach is rumbling. Getting the bartender's attention, I secure my third drink, but when he starts to hurry off, I grab his wrist. His startled brown eyes look at me.

"Burger, please." I close my eyes to focus. "Mushrooms, cheese. And fries."

He grins. "Righto, mate." I swear he's getting even cuter with each drink. Watching his ass as he walks away to put in my order, I drink and sigh. It's a nice one, but it's not even close to Mitch's spectacular buns.

"Maybe you should slow down."

His voice makes me jump. Glancing up, he's standing at my elbow, his blue eyes concerned. *When did he get here?*

"Maybe you should mind your own business," I reply, but there's no bite to my words. I'm too weary for anger.

He studies me for a long moment. "Bad day?"

I laugh, but it comes out more like a sob. "You could say that."

"Want to talk about it?" he offers.

"Not really." I swirl the ice cubes around my glass, hoping this last gin and tonic will do what the first two didn't—make me forget that I'm not happy.

"Nor do I want to talk about how your chocolate sauce ended up in my hot little hands." I end on a nervous laugh as I stare at his handsome face.

His jaw tightens, but his voice stays gentle. "Have you spoken to your master chocolatier yet?"

"Haven't had the chance." It's not a lie. "I tried," I add. But today's disaster pushed that conversation aside. I blink, but my eyes stay closed a few moments longer than intended. That's not right. Jules wasn't even there by the time I reached the factory. I'm tipsy, and having a hard time keeping my facts straight.

Mitch doesn't press, but I'm pretty sure he has a disapproving look on his face. I don't like his expression one bit, and I give the bar a jaunty little slap for no reason. After all, he doesn't know that Jules was MIA today. Mitch probably thinks I'm procas . . . procrasin . . . putting off dealing with the sauce issue.

"Come on," he says. "I'm driving you home."

"I have food coming."

"Jack," he calls out to the bartender. "Put a rush on the lady's order and pack it up to go. It's on the house, along with her two drinks."

I don't protest. Maybe because I'm drunk. Maybe because I miss his touch.

But I do clarify. "Three," I blurt out and down the last of the third one.

The ride is mostly silent but not uncomfortable. At some point, I say, "All my cocoa beans were scorched. Kind of like when I try to cook."

He frowns but says nothing. I guess he also disapproves of a woman who can't cook.

When we reach my building, Mitch comes around to my side of the car and helps me out. When he touches my arm, I lean into him and turn my face up for a kiss. He hesitates before he kisses me. And when he does, it's not like our previous kisses—neither hungry, nor passionate. Almost . . . comforting, it's over before I can grind up against him the way my body wants to.

"Come on." Holding my bag of food, he walks me only as far as the building's secure entrance, next to the underground parking gate. Momentarily I think about my car parked at the bar, but then the thought flits away.

He watches while I press my entry fob, easier than typing in the keycode. Pushing the door at the same time, epic fail. Try again. And again.

Finally, he snatches it and tries it, then examines it.

"This is your car fob," he says.

"The keycode is seven, seven, seven, seven, seven," I say. Even drunk, I can remember it, although I think that was a few numbers too many.

But Mitch has already found the right fob on my keychain. Once inside, he accompanies me on the elevator ride, in silence, making sure I get my own front door open. When I turn to invite him in, he steps back.

"Goodnight, Lark." Before I can respond, or thank him, he's gone.

I nearly run after him . . . or stagger, in my condition. I want him to stay so much it hurts. I don't even care about sex. I simply want to curl around him in bed and have him hold me.

*Ugh!* When did I become this needy person? This uncertain, emotional mess?

I'm Lark Henley, CEO of one of the world's largest chocolate companies. Or at least, co-CEO. What I'm not is a clingy female who needs a good cry. And apart from a dark time a few years back when I first started in New York, I've never been one to doubt myself.

And I certainly don't let men affect me like this. Not anymore.

Except lately, everything seems to be affecting me. *Mitch. My job. The weight of expectations.*

I'm suddenly so tired, I nearly lie down on the cool tile floor of my foyer. But I have a little pride. Kicking off my shoes, I walk straight through to my bedroom. Fully clothed, stretching out on my expensive silk comforter, I let the tears fall at a last. It doesn't feel particularly good or relieving. Just necessary. Then I eat, right there on my bed.

Tomorrow, I'll be strong again. Tomorrow, I'll face Jules, if I can find him. I'll study the quarterly reports, see if there's any place I can trim any bloat. I'll look for initiatives that need to be nurtured within the company.

But tonight, I allow myself to be weak, even a little pitiful.

And in the darkness, I admit something I've been trying to deny—a part of me wants to quit and go back to New York. Because right now, Sydney feels less like home and more like a battlefield where I'm losing every fight.

# 12

## Mitch

I can't stop thinking about Lark's face last night. The way her eyes couldn't quite focus. The way she leaned into me at her apartment, seeking something I wasn't ready to give. Not when she was shit-faced on my bar's gin. And not when she still hadn't confronted Jules about the sauce. I cannot imagine how or why she has let that go even another day.

But it was more than that. Something had happened—beyond our stalemate about the chocolate sauce. The way she mentioned scorched cocoa beans in passing, like it was an insignificant detail. I know better. For a chocolate manufacturer, ruined beans mean lost production, lost money, lost time. It could be a massive headache.

Which is why I put down my first cup of coffee, swipe the news away on my cell phone, and call Rich at Boston Beans Exporter.

"Mitch Franklin," I say when he answers. "Calling about a bean shipment."

"You're wicked early," Rich says, his voice cheerful as always and thick with his Southie accent. "Your next shipment to the Georgia facility ain't due for three weeks. And the Sydney factory is all set. You lookin' to bump up Franklin Darkly production?"

"No." I'm an odd duck who has my chocolate sauce produced in multiple small-batch factories rather than transporting bottles from one continent to the next. I don't want to have one massive chocolate sauce production facility. That's not how I do things.

"I need a special order. Same quality, same origin as my regular cocoa beans. I need them delivered to Henley Confectionery in Wetherill Park. Can you make that happen?"

There's a pause. "Henley? They don't buy from us, kid. And between you and me, they can afford their own beans. Plus, I heard through the grapevine, and from a buddy who was at Taste of Sydney, you've got a bit of a beef with Lark Henley."

I'm floored that he's heard about it. Pinching the bridge of my nose, I close my eyes momentarily. Sometimes I forget how small the food industry is.

"It's complicated," I tell him. "But yes, that's what I need. Can you do it?"

"Sure, but it might take me a few days to—"

"Today," I interrupt. "I need them today. Later this afternoon would be awesome."

Another pause. "Mitch, you know that's not how this works. We've gotta pull from inventory, process the paperwork—"

"I'll pay whatever rush fee you want to charge. Double it, even. Just make it happen."

Rich sighs. "For you, kid, I'll see what I can do. But no promises."

"Thanks." I hang up, knowing he'll come through. Rich and I go back years. He was one of my original suppliers when I opened my first restaurant in my home city, coincidentally nicknamed *Beantown.* Although for a different kind of bean altogether. Rich has no dealings with baked beans, only coffee and cocoa.

After breakfast, I head to my restaurant. I like the buzz in the kitchen when they're prepping for the lunch service. It's like an orchestra tuning up—metal on metal as spatula meets steel pan, the rhythmic sound of a knife blade coming down hard and clean on the wooden cutting board, even the juicy sizzle of something fatty on the stove.

Each has a familiar and comforting tune all its own.

We offer lunch only a couple days a week at Franklin 6. Sometimes Ravi is there, sometimes our sous chef is in charge. Today, I discover my head chef and Jackie, one of our chefs de partie, are chatting when I enter into an invisible but mouthwatering cloud of garlic, scallions, and parsley. Both heads swivel my way.

"You look like hell," Jackie observes.

"Thanks," I say. "Right back at you." She smiles and turns away, getting to work.

Jackie reminds me of my own raw energy in the kitchen and at Le Cordon Bleu when I thought I was going to be a head chef one day. I didn't have the stamina or the determination, as it turns out. Or maybe my vision was simply bigger than any single kitchen.

Ravi is the one who hits the target next. "Something to do with your candy girl?"

I don't answer, grabbing the sheaf of printed menu options splayed out in front of him. Some dishes are crossed out, some inked with additions. He is a culinary artist, and he'll be making changes almost up until plating.

Jackie pipes up again. "We're not talking about Lark Henley, are we? Most of Sydney heard about the epic sauce battle at Taste of Sydney. Everyone has taken a side in the great chocolate feud. Team Franklin or Team Henley."

I'm shocked it has blown up so big and that I've heard about it twice in a couple hours.

"Tell me you're kidding."

Ravi nods. "She's not. I'm on Team Henley, if you're interested."

This makes Jackie start laughing, with her back to us as she brings her knife down lightning quick on a length of cucumber. Ravi joins in with a snarky laugh of his own.

"You two are a real riot," I say, wishing I hadn't bothered coming into what's usually one of my favorite places. "There's no feud, by the way. In fact, I just sent the Henley Confectionery Company a load of cocoa beans."

Jackie's knife clatters unprofessionally, while Ravi stares at me for a moment.

"Maybe not wise. Looks a bit like she's had the win, mate," he says. "Or like you're conceding the chocolate sauce wasn't yours at all."

Jackie shakes her head, still not looking. "You've got it all wrong, mate," she tells him. "Only one reason our boss sent beans to Ms. Henley. He's got it bad for her."

"It's not like that." Even as I protest, I know it's a lie, but I find myself explaining anyway. "Her factory had an issue with their beans. I'm helping out."

"Helping your competition." Ravi looks disgusted. "Next you'll be giving them your sauce recipe. Oh wait— they already have that."

I toss the papers back down onto the stainless-steel surface.

"Enough. It's *my* business, *my* beans, and *my* decision."

Jackie finally turns and looks over her shoulder, her expression one of sympathy. Ravi holds up his hands in surrender.

"Righto. But when it all goes pear-shaped on you, don't say Team Franklin didn't warn you."

"I thought you were Team Henley," I say snidely.

I know *I* certainly am, at least when it comes to one member of that team. Anyway, they're both right. I'm totally hooked on Lark, but I might have sent the wrong message. One of capitulation. I probably should go talk to her before the beans arrive.

Meanwhile, as I sit in my office, dreaming up Franklin 7, my conversation with Riley won't leave me alone, especially her troubling disclosure of how Connor Whittel screwed Lark over—professionally and personally. Someone already betrayed her once. And now it might be happening again, with her chocolatier.

For some reason, I can't stand by and watch Lark suffer, even if, in this small sliver of the chocolate world, we're technically competitors.

An hour later, Rich calls back. "You're all set. The beans'll be there by three this afternoon. But Mitch? You owe me one."

"Name your price."

"Above the cost of the beans, I was thinking 'bout dinner at Franklin 1 with my wife this Friday. The weather's wicked nice, the city's buzzin', and I know you can hook us up with a bangin' good table."

"Deal." Rich is a great guy. And he didn't even charge me double after all.

The rest of the morning flies. There is no better spot than in an office above one of my kitchens. Whichever restaurant I'm at, I oversee all of them with daily updates, checking the receipts, even reading reviews in case something isn't working and no one in the place has realized it.

I don't forget to secure reservations for Rich and his wife at my flagship Boston restaurant. Best table, dinner on the house, and a bottle of champagne brought over when they arrive. By lunchtime, however, my mind has wandered away too many times to do anything but give in. I'm ready to deliver the news about the beans to Lark in person.

$♥$♥$♥$

The Henley headquarters downtown is housed in a sleek glass building with the company's name emblazoned across the front in brown script outlined in gold. Entering the cool, quiet lobby, I nod to a security guard at his desk and cross the polished hardwood floor toward a receptionist. The place is filled with light, and the walls are tiled in shades of chocolate—milk, white, and dark—making the space welcoming. The décor and its ambiance would work well in a restaurant.

And even though I know they don't make the candy here, I swear I can smell cocoa.

At the receptionist's desk, a woman wearing a headset is on a call. She smiles and holds up a finger for me to wait. An open box of assorted chocolates at my elbow accounts for at least some of the enticing aroma. Maybe they have a box stationed at each air conditioning vent to send the scent throughout the building.

All I know is I can't resist helping myself to a sample. My hand is large, and of course, I come away with three. I've eaten one, which turns out to have a melt-in-my-mouth caramel center, when she disconnects the call.

"Can I help you?"

"I'm here to see Lark Henley."

It's not surprising when, without checking, without even blinking, she informs me that Ms. Henley is in meetings all day. *Smart lady.*

"Understood, but would you please tell her Mitch Franklin is in the lobby and I need to speak to her about cocoa beans?"

The receptionist raises a plucked eyebrow but makes the call. While she does, I taste the second chocolate. The flavor of coffee buttercream explodes on my tongue.

A moment later, now with *both* eyebrows raised almost to her hairline, the receptionist nods at whatever she's being told before she taps off her headphone. Then she directs me to the elevators.

"Top floor. Someone will meet you."

"Thank you." In the brief trip, I eat the last sample, equally delicious. For the right person, this must be the best job ever.

When I step off the elevator, I'm greeted not by an assistant but by Lark herself. I can't help taking her in from head to toe, from the professional look of her hair swept up into a loose bun to her tailored navy dress with silver buttons. I know it isn't intentionally suggestive, but it hugs her curves all the same. She looks so damn sexy, I want to tear the buttons off with my teeth.

When I don't speak, she clears her throat, drawing my gaze back from her long legs to her face. Overall, there's no trace of last night's vulnerability in her expression. In fact, CEO Lark Henley doesn't look happy to see me.

"What are you doing here?" she demands over her shoulder, leading me into a glass-walled conference room with views of Sydney Harbor.

"Good to see you too," I reply, wondering how this room, too, can smell like chocolate. Then I see an open box in the center of the long table. "How's the hangover?"

She narrows her eyes. "I don't have time for this, Mitch. Just because I had a drink or two at your bar, that's not an invitation for you to return the visit. What's this about cocoa beans?"

I take a deep breath. "Your beans were scorched. You mentioned it last night."

"Did I?" She crosses her arms. I can't tell if she remembers saying anything about it or not. "And?" Lark prompts, still sounding as though I'm intruding in the worst way. This is *not* the warm, funny woman I've kissed and had sex with on multiple occasions.

"I've arranged for a shipment of the cocoa beans I use to make Franklin Darkly to be delivered to your factory today. They should arrive by three this afternoon."

Her expression shifts from irritation to disbelief, and she lowers her arms. "You did what?"

"I called my supplier. We go way back. He's sending the same beans that I use—premium, ethically sourced." I step closer. "You needed beans. I got you beans. We've already established they taste like yours. You know," I say, "because of the identical chocolate sauce."

Her jaw is slack. I may not be reading the room when I verbally pat myself on the back by adding, "Problem solved."

For a moment, she stares at me. I'm waiting for her to fall at my feet with gratitude. Instead, without warning, she explodes like a burst of Lark-flavored chocolate.

"Are you kidding me? You went behind my back and ordered beans for *my* company? Who do you think you are?" She paces the length of the conference table, pausing only to reach over and grab a chocolate from the box. Instead of eating it, she tosses it back and forth between her hands.

"Do you have any idea how this makes me look? Like I can't handle a simple supply issue. Like I need a man to come to my rescue."

"That's not what I—"

"I'm the CEO of a multinational corporation, Mitch. I've been dealing with supply issues, probably since before you opened your first bistro. I neither need nor want your help."

Her words sting, but I stand my ground. "This isn't about your competence. It's about getting you what I thought you needed as quickly as possible. Since my beans have the same flavor profile as yours, I thought you'd welcome the assist."

She stops pacing abruptly. "You thought wrong. I've already procured a new shipment of beans. The fault was with the processor, and the supplier had to make it right."

Lark pauses to eat the chocolate, which gives me a second to realize that I did, in fact, want to ride to her rescue. A dark knight on a chocolate horse. It was presumptuous of me, but she's turning it into an insult.

"Look," I begin, but she cuts me off.

"Besides, they weren't for our regular production. Nor did they have our usual flavor profile. They were for something special."

I nearly ask, "Whose recipe did Jules steal this time?" But I manage not to. What's more, she's gone silent as a morgue. Then she covers her mouth, while shaking her head. She takes a moment to collect herself.

"Wow!" Lark says. "I just came off like a total bitch. I'm a bit sensitive when a man tries to bail me out. Can you tell?" She wipes the edge of her mouth with the pad of her finger.

"The chocolate brought me back to the here and now. I'm sorry I snapped. It was kind of you to go out of your way for Henley Confectionery."

"*Not* for Henley," I insist, glad the fire of outrage has gone from her voice. "For you." I'm blown away by Lark's rapid recognition of her own shortcomings. Most of us aren't so self-aware. Strangely, she attributes her Jekyll-and-Hyde performance to a Henley chocolate.

She's truly unique, and I can't help but give her a smile as she sinks into one of the conference chairs.

"Why did you do this *for me*?" she asks. "I mean, after the chocolate sauce problem, you should be filing legal papers."

Taking the seat across from her, I tell her the truth. "Because I care about you. And I know what it's like to have a supply chain crisis, especially for an ingredient I depend upon. My first year in business, my pasture-fed beef supplier realized I was doing well and doubled his prices. Nearly put me under until I could find an alternate supplier."

She studies me for a long moment, then sighs. "You should call and cancel the shipment."

"It's too late. They expedited it."

She looks down at her hands, then back up at me. "You know, most men who want to impress a woman send flowers, not bags of cocoa beans."

I smile at that. "I'm not most men."

"No," she agrees softly. "You're not."

We sit in silence for a moment, the tension between us shifting into something different, something warmer.

"Thank you," she finally says, and I get to see the first small smile appear. "It was . . . thoughtful, in a completely overstepping, boundary-crossing way."

I laugh. "You're welcome. And I'm sorry for overstepping."

She stands, smoothing down her suit. "I should get back to work."

I rise as well. "Anything I can help with? Without overstepping, of course."

"Not unless you have a time machine."

"That bad, huh?"

"Welcome to corporate life." She walks me to the elevator. "About the beans . . . Maybe they'll work for a limited edition run. I promise, they won't go to waste, and I insist you let me pay for them."

"Insist away,' I say, looking into her gold-flecked tawny eyes, "but they're a gift. So, the answer is no." The elevator arrives, but there's still a massive issue between us. Sticking my arm out, I hold open the doors. "You can repay me another way."

She smirks at the same time as her cheeks redden, and I know what she's thinking. Suddenly, I'm thinking that, too, but it wasn't my intent.

Clearing my throat, I say, "You can follow through with your investigation into how your chocolatier ended up with my recipe."

Her expression turns stony. "You'll have to let me proceed with that in my own way, Mitch. But I promise you, I'm on it."

I step onto the elevator and keep my cool. "That's good enough for me." Although I wish she would address it today, head on.

When the doors start to close, I hold them again. "Lark? I meant what I said. I care about you. More than I probably should at this point."

Her lips soften. "I feel the same." She looks away, then back at me. "It's kind of baffling, and a little scary, to be honest."

Into the dragging silence that follows her words, I let the doors slide shut. Back at the restaurant, I have my own business issues to take care of, as my Miami restaurant had its liquor license pulled on a technicality.

Regardless, I can't stop thinking about Lark's parting words. *What did she mean?* That she's scared of my feelings? Or of her own?

My phone buzzes with a text message from her around six:

*The beans arrived earlier in Wetherill Park. Thank you. Really.*

I type back:

*You're welcome.*

But I don't want to let her go.

*We should talk. Not about beans or business.*

Three dots appear, disappear, then appear again. Finally, I get a response.

*I'm going to my grandparents' ranch on Friday afternoon. The guesthouse has your name on it.*

I stare at the message, beyond astonished. I wasn't expecting an invitation to meet her family.

*Won't that be awkward, given everything?*

She texts back:

*Probably. But my grandparents' wine cellar makes everything better. Say yes.*

I smile at my phone. This woman is giving me whiplash. But I'm in.

*Yes.*

She plays it cool. No smiley faces or hearts or parted lips.

*Good. I'll text you the address. It's in the Hunter Valley.*

Ravi catches me grinning at my phone. "Let me guess. Your candy girl."

"She has a name."

He shrugs. "Least you're looking happier now than you did this morning."

"She invited me to her grandparents' place for the weekend."

He whistles. "We call that 'meeting the rellies.' Not something done lightly, mate. Must be serious."

Weirdly, Lark and I *are serious*, but also we're completely uncommitted. "It's complicated."

"Not your usual style," Ravi says, without judgment.

We don't regularly hang out together, but he knows I've had a few one-night stands.

*She's different,* I think, but all I do is nod.

As the weekend approaches, I know exactly how different this is. I'm packing for a weekend away with a woman at her family home. Something I've never done before. Lark Henley has gotten under my skin in record time. And given our thorny business situation, I'm walking a fine line between professional integrity and personal feelings.

Friday afternoon, I follow Lark's directions to a sprawling estate in the Hunter Valley wine region two hours from Sydney. The vast property is as gorgeous as any land I've seen yet in Australia, and that's saying something.

A private road nestled between rolling hills leads me through Henley land. I pass a pasture with horses grazing, or whatever they do, and another with sheep. Vineyards stretch toward the horizon on one side, a barn complex is on the other, and then, at last, a single-story structure with vine-covered verandas. Its terracotta roof looks to be on fire, as it reflects the last rays of the sun. Several outbuildings all sport the same red roofs.

"Look where you are, Mitch," I say to myself.

Even though my family came into a lot of money a few years back and even though I've made a shit-ton myself, I'm still impressed easily by wealth done right. The Henley ranch couldn't be more quintessentially luxurious tempered by welcoming rustic vibes.

It's like the glamping craze, not easy to pull off. It also provides yet another restaurant design idea.

Lark meets me in front of a large ranch house that has obviously been added in a cheerfully haphazard way. She's wearing jeans and a simple white T-shirt, her hair loose around her shoulders. She looks younger, more carefree than I've ever seen her, except for when she's naked beside me.

"You made it," she says simply, as I get out of my car.

"Right to a patch of heaven, apparently. This place is beautiful."

She smiles, glancing around, seeing it through my eyes. I want to kiss her, but I glance at the house's windows. I don't know what my reception from her grandparents will be. The older generation doesn't always take kindly to their granddaughter dating a biracial man. And I don't want to blow it by making out with her in their driveway.

But Lark steps closer, letting me breathe in her honeyed-vanilla fragrance, before kissing my cheek.

"I'm glad you came," she says against my ear, giving me a brief hug that allows me to feel her breasts against my shirt. Then she slides an arm through mine and tugs me toward the door.

"This ranch has been in my family for generations. Nan and Gramps started the chocolate business right here in their kitchen when they were newlyweds. They're very nice. Come in and meet them. Patrick and Eleanor. They're going to love you."

*God, I hope so!* Because this woman means more to me every time I see her.

# 13

## Lark

I watch Mitch across the dining table of deep-red Jarrah heartwood. His laughter blends with Nan's as she tells him about the time she accidentally added salt instead of sugar in her hurry to finish a drizzle topping on a batch of truffles.

His eyes catch mine, and I feel that familiar flutter in my stomach. How is it possible that a few days ago, I was furious with him over the high-handed way he ordered beans for my company?

"That's how the Henley 'Sweet and Salty' caramel-topped truffle was born," Nan concludes, reaching for her wine glass. "Out of a right old stuff-up."

"The best innovations often are," Mitch says, his voice warm with genuine interest. He's been like this all evening—attentive, charming, completely at ease with my grandparents in a way that makes something twist inside me.

Gramps raises his glass of Henley Reserve, an oak-aged chardonnay. "Here's to cock-ups that come good."

We all clink glasses. The buttery wine slides easily down my throat, and I never fail to appreciate the notes of vanilla and toffee. Our Henley vineyard isn't massive. Gramps only makes a few cases a year and sells locally, and we, the family, drink the rest. Usually right here in my grandparents' dining room, a sanctuary—far removed from boardrooms and burned cocoa beans.

"This chicken pie is incredible, Eleanor," Mitch says, gesturing to his nearly empty plate. "The crust is flaky and flawless."

Nan beams at him. "Ta, love. It's nothing flash, but no one's ever turned their nose up at it."

"The best food isn't about fancy," Mitch says. "It's about love and tradition. I can taste both in this meal."

I swallow hard, watching my grandmother practically glow under his praise. It took Mitch approximately fifteen minutes to completely charm my grandparents with his genuine interest in the ranch's history and how they started the chocolate business.

On top of that, he offered to help Gramps move some fence posts tomorrow. Unnecessary since the hired help will be back on Monday, but I know my grandfather will hold him to it, just to test his mettle.

"What else keeps you out of mischief," Nan begins and refills Mitch's wine glass without asking, "when you're not cheffing?"

He darts a glance my way, then tells them the brief version of his training in France, his food truck, the various venues for his restaurants, and, of course, his family. "My parents live in Boston. Dad's a retired chef. Mom's not yet retired, but she has cut back. She's a journalist, now doing special assignments. And my sister, Riley, is a model."

My ears perk up. *How did I not know this?*

"Does she ever work in New York?" I ask.

He nods, not looking at me. "She works in every major fashion city, but spends a lot of time in Milan and Paris."

Still, I wonder if we ever met. True, there are over eight million people in the city, but a rather small clique of famous ones of a certain age. I would bet good money that we were at least at a night club together. Before I can ask, Nan speaks up.

"Lark reckons you've got a bit of a magic touch with chocolate."

Mitch and I both freeze, exchanging glances. I know we're both thinking of his dining room table. My cheeks feel warm.

"I might've mentioned your Franklin Darkly," I say.

Mitch looks like he wants to laugh, amused by my embarrassment. But all he says is, "That's high praise coming from a Henley."

"Don't let it go to your head," I say, but I can't help smiling.

"I'd love to cook for all of us tomorrow night," Mitch offers. "Give Eleanor a break."

"Oh, you don't have to fuss, love," Nan protests, but I can see she's pleased by the offer.

"I want to," Mitch insists. "It's the least I can do for your hospitality."

"We've got a ripper veggie garden," Gramps says, already sold. "Help yourself to whatever's there."

As the three of them discuss vegetables and herbs, I sit back, enjoying how Mitch interacts with my family. There's something about seeing him here, in this place that shaped me throughout my youth and early teen years, whenever my parents brought us over from the States, that makes my heart ache in a way I don't fully understand.

After dinner, Nan suggests a night swim. "The pool's heated, and there's nothing like bobbing about under the stars with a glass of plonk."

"Sounds perfect," Mitch agrees, glancing at me.

Ten minutes later, I have beaten him to the pool. Having changed into a hot pink bikini, I set down two glasses of Gramps' wine and slip into the illuminated water.

As I paddle around, I think about renewing my SCUBA certification, which I let lapse when I left Australia for New York. Then Mitch emerges from the guest house at the far end of the pool, and I forget what my last thought was.

In pale-blue board shorts that complement the creamy brown skin of his bare chest and muscled legs—not to mention matching his cornflower-blue eyes—he's simply gorgeous.

I try not to stare. And fail. *Why bother?* He knows I'm attracted to him.

"Your grandparents are wonderful," he says, lowering himself into the water near me. Nan and Gramps have remained in the house, giving us privacy that suddenly feels dangerous.

"They like you," I admit.

I'm bobbing near the wine glasses, my feet not touching the bottom. I love the feeling, like flying, and the weightlessness of floating, but Mitch is standing firm.

"Nan already told me you're a keeper," I confess. "She hasn't even tasted your cooking yet, but you offered, and that's enough for her."

His eyebrows lift. "A keeper, huh? And what do you think?"

I splash water in his direction, deflecting the question. "I think you're very good at charming people and their families."

"Just being myself." He wipes the droplets off his face and moves closer, water rippling between us.

It's true. He doesn't put on an act, but always seems to be genuinely Mitch, except for when he didn't tell me he was a wealthy restaurateur. But in that risky game, I didn't tell him I was an executive, so we're even.

"This place is really special," he says, near enough that I can study the dusting of cocoa-colored hair on his chest. "I understand how much it means to you, because you're definitely more chill here."

Looking around at the familiar landscape—the silhouettes of grapevines against the night sky, the warm lights from the farmhouse, and the whinnying of the horses—I'm certainly less stressed here than just about anywhere else in the world.

"This is the place I come to when everything feels too heavy. Always has been, except for when I lived in New York. Even then, I flew home twice a year because the ranch is where I can remember who I am beyond the boardroom."

"And who is that?" His voice is soft, curious, as he brushes a wet strand of hair from my face.

I meet his eyes in the dim light. "A woman who's still figuring it all out."

Both his hands slip beneath the surface and land on either side of my waist, their natural warmth contrasting with the water, making me shiver despite the pool heater.

"I like this woman very much," he says.

The moment stretches between us, fragile and charged. Slowly, he draws me against him, his palms sliding down to my butt, which he cups a second before claiming my mouth. It's so familiar and easy, as if we've been together for eons.

On the other hand, I've never known anyone like Mitch. The way he talks to me, forthrightly, letting me know what he's thinking.

His tongue touches my lips, and I open for him. Sliding my hands around his waist, I clasp my fingers together tightly. Maybe he's familiar because he's the guy I've been waiting for while going on countless disappointing dates.

The terrace slider sounds loud in the silence and we break apart. Nan steps outside, carrying a plate. Suddenly, we're both splashing backward, trying to put respectable distance between one another.

"Steady on, you two. I've brought you some Tim Tam brownies before Pat scoffs the lot. Goes down a treat with the vino." Giving me a smile, she winks at Mitch and heads back toward the house.

"Wait, Nan," I say when I find my voice. "You and Gramps can come out and chat with us."

She chuckles. "And muck up my granddaughter's social life? Not on your nelly." She disappears inside. *Who is this woman?*

"She used to be so strict," I mutter, leaning an elbow on the pool deck and snagging a brownie.

"No kissing boys in the pool?" he asks.

I burst out laughing. "As if I would dare. But how about no food in the pool?"

Taking a bite, I relish the crackle of Tim Tam pieces running through the fudgy, cakey square and close my eyes at its perfection. When I open them, I see Mitch watching me, and I feel totally exposed, like he's looking at me naked.

Since he's already done that, *more than once*, I get over myself and ask, "Do you know what a Tim Tam biscuit is?"

He doesn't answer. Mitch simply takes a big bite, consuming half the thick brownie in one go, and chews. His eyes widen.

"See," I say. "That's the brilliant addition of crunchy Tim Tams mashed up in Nan's brownie batter."

Without speaking, he shoves the rest in, chomps, and swallows. "Wow!" he whispers, as if worshipping in a cathedral "That's amazing."

I hand him a glass of wine and pick up mine. We click them together.

"This is the best night I've had since coming to Australia," he says, taking a sip. Then he grins and adds, "Second best. No, third best."

Rolling my eyes, I drink my wine and think how happy I am to be here, sharing this moment with him.

"This wine really does go well with a brownie," he says.

"It bloody well does," I say, making him laugh. "Everything my grandparents ever did turned to gold."

He cocks his head. "You say that as though all the Henley success is theirs and in the past."

I shrug, unable to imagine I'll ever do more than steer the company along the path it's already on. I don't feel inspired to make new flavors the way my brother did a year ago with his German Bridegroom line. I barely feel like going into work in the morning.

"Where did you go?" he asked.

My glance locks with his. "What do you mean?"

Mitch takes the wine from me and sets it down next to his glass. Then he wraps his arms around me.

"You're right here, in the Hunter Valley, on your beloved ranch, in your grandparents' pool. With me." He brushes his lips across my temple. "But for a few moments, you were a million miles away, and you didn't look happy."

He's good at reading me. I'll give him that.

"Kiss me again," I say. "That'll make me happy." And he does.

Eventually, when we cannot possibly go any further while my grandparents are a few yards away, we get out of the pool. I doubt Nan's newfound relaxed nature would stretch to me skinny dipping and playing tonsil hockey out in public.

A part of me—*the majority of my parts, in fact!*—wants to go straight to the guest bungalow, but then I think of a special spot. Calling through the slider, I say, "I'm taking Mitch to Dad's bench."

"Righto," Gramps calls back. "Don't go taking an accidental dip."

"What does he mean?" Mitch asks.

"You'll see." We put on Blunnies because of the nighttime critters in the grass, and I wrap a towel around my waist while he grabs a T-shirt. Five minutes later, I lead Mitch down a path through the vineyard. I'm holding a half-full bottle of wine. The night is cool but not cold. The scent of earth and vines fills the air.

"Where are we going?" he asks, following close behind me.

"Patience, Franklin." I lead him down the end of a row to our pond, looking like a big silvery mirror thanks to the full moon. At one end, a small rise overlooks the land beyond our property.

Holding hands, we climb the gentle slope to the wooden bench situated on top. From here, we can see the entire valley spread out before us, bathed in moonlight and carved by shadows.

"Best view ever," I say.

Sitting side by side, shoulders touching, we take in the earthy scent and the frogs "singing" in the pond below.

"One Mother's Day, my dad built this bench for Nan," I tell Mitch.

"And the pond?"

"Just a pond," I shrug. "It's always been here. Turtles and frogs and lily pads."

"What about the 'accidental dip'?" Mitch persists.

I can't help smiling, even as I tell him, "When I was a kid, I think I'd seen too many cartoons. I believed you could walk across the water lilies, like stepping stones."

*"Oops!"* he says.

"I think Luke egged me on, as brothers do. As the baby of the family, one year younger than him, I screamed blue murder until Clover jumped right in and got me. We found out we could stand up. But the turtles didn't appreciate the disturbance."

Recalling the nasty sensation of touching hard shells and reptilian skin, I shudder and take an unladylike swig from the wine bottle. Then I hand it to him.

"The years really speed by, though, don't they?" I say, knowing my outlook has been on the sour and gloomy side for a while. But I didn't realize I was also starting to think as though my best years were behind me.

Mitch curls his fingers around the bottle, but he's shaking his head at my words.

"You're talking like you're approaching ninety." He takes a sip. "Sure, time flies, but that makes it more important to do the most with each day. By the way, to be honest, I did my fair share of teasing my younger sister, too."

*Ah, the aforementioned Riley Franklin.* As I say her full name to myself for the first time, it hits me. I envisage a young woman with the same gorgeous blue eyes as her brother and nut-colored skin. Of course, there could be more than one Riley Franklin, but odds are not another one who models.

Besides in my memory, the resemblance between them tells me I'm right.

"I *know* her. She models in New York."

"She models in a lot of cities," he says vaguely.

"Yes, but I've been to places where she was. Like . . . I dunno . . . celebrity events." Then I recall something else.

"And night clubs," I whisper when it hits me. I saw her once at 1 Oak in Chelsea. Riley went out with the asshole *after* I did. I only knew her first name.

*Did Connor talk about me?* Maybe he and Mitch's sister had a good laugh at my expense.

Worse, she might've told the man currently drinking Henley wine everything she knows. *About me and my big fuck-up.*

When I reach for the bottle, he releases it, letting me have another sip.

Then Mitch drapes his arm around me, his damp swim trunks pressed against my thigh.

"I think there's a law that says you can't sit in a vineyard with a beautiful woman on a moonlit night without drinking wine."

"Sounds right," I agree, thinking that maybe, just maybe, Mitch doesn't know about my god-awful mistake. But I don't ask. I don't want to think about being discussed by the Franklin siblings.

"And I definitely can't sit here in this particular vineyard," he continues, "on this moonlit night without kissing you."

Turning my face toward him, I know I'd like Mitch to do more than kiss me. When his mouth covers mine, I manage to set the bottle down before sliding my hands up his chest and locking my fingers behind his neck.

The kiss steals my breath. Or maybe it's the way his hands are roaming. He removes my bikini top so swiftly, I don't realize he's done it until it falls to my lap and the night air caresses my breasts.

A second later, his hands are also caressing them. My nipples stiffen even before he takes one between his teeth and tugs. Sinking my hands into his still damp hair, I hold him to me, letting him up only long enough for him to switch breasts.

My bikini bottom grows wetter instead of drier when he cups my other breast and gives its nipple the same treatment.

"Mitch," I groan, wondering whether the bench is long enough for me to lie on it because there's no way I'm getting onto the ground. Not with a bare back.

"Me, too," he says, knowing what I want.

All at once, he strips off his T-shirt and drags it down over my head. Understanding dawns on me. Obviously, I can't return topless to the ranch house. Instead, I get to enjoy the *Mitch-scented* fabric. *Bonus!*

Jumping up, we retreat, the wine bottle forgotten until tomorrow. All I can think about is getting inside the comfiest guesthouse in the whole wide world and touching Mitch while he touches me.

I'm literally aching between my legs, my clit pulsing with anticipation.

As we round the pool, heading for the far end, I trip in my boots, nearly taking a plunge. Luckily, my savior still has hold of my hand and tugs me close while I regain my balance. We're both laughing when we crash against the guesthouse door, before I manage to reach around his hard body and turn the knob.

"Everything off," he orders, kicking the door closed behind him.

My Blunnies go first, then I whip off his T-shirt, while he steps out of his board shorts. His body is as ready as mine, his cock standing at attention.

"I said *everything*," he reminds me, but he hooks a finger into either side of my bikini bottoms before I can react.

Dropping to his knees as he tugs them down my now-shaking legs, Mitch parts my pussy and captures my clit as quickly as he kissed my mouth earlier.

He is an intense and supremely generous lover.

While he nibbles at my throbbing nubbin and licks it with the flat of his tongue, I have to hold onto his solid shoulders to keep from sinking to the floor. Holding my breath, feeling my heart beating hard in my chest, I hang on through his sensual assault when he ups the ante and slides two fingers into my channel.

He crooks them as if he's going to draw me closer, and his fingertips press my G-spot. I swear I see stars behind my closed eyelids. *When did I close my eyes?*

"Mitch, I'm going to come," I manage, futilely tapping his shoulders. Like that's going to stop him. But I don't want to be selfish. I want to be stroking him at the very least or have him deep inside me when I go off.

He doesn't stop. He slides a third finger inside me and ever so gently nips my clit with his teeth. I go off like a firecracker, and the stars become a blaze of colors, mostly orange and red.

He knows I've climaxed, and am floating back to earth, when I stop pulling his hair.

*Poor man. When did my fingers sink into his hair and try to scalp him?*

Finally, he rises to his feet. "Good?"

I roll my eyes at his stupid question but can't wipe the grin off my face. Not until his next words hit me like ice water.

"Wish I had some of my chocolate sauce with me. Don't suppose you have any HLC?"

It's an innocent, off-handed remark, but it lands like a zinger. I'm still standing with my bikini bottoms around my ankles, and I reach down quickly to pull them up.

"Lark," he begins.

"No, I know," I say. I've lost my bikini top along the way, so I quickly haul his T-shirt on again. "But we should clear the air about that, don't you think?"

His raging hard-on starts to wilt. "Now? Really?"

"Yes. I don't want to sleep with you again while you believe I stole your recipe."

"I don't think that any longer," he says, but he puts his shorts back on. "I think Julian Cartier stole my recipe."

Taking a deep breath, I counter him. "I don't believe he did."

"Then why don't you ask him? If I let myself think about it, it's infuriating." He paces across the floor. "You could put all this to bed, no pun intended, if you would simply talk to the man. He's your employee, and you are supposed to be his boss."

His bottled-up irritation is blowing its cork. Now I wish I'd addressed it sooner and let him know what was going on.

Mitch crosses his arms, his expression almost as annoyed as it was at the Taste of Sydney a week ago.

"I'm sorry I haven't managed a face-to-face with him yet—"

"As CEO, it's your job to manage," he interrupts, his tone quietly condemning.

All my goodwill and the endorphins from the orgasm evaporate.

"I know my job." And Mitch has no idea how much I hate being second-guessed. "But I invited you here to get away from all that," I remind him.

He hesitates, his obvious sexual frustration warring with his work-related frustration, both directly leveled at me. I shouldn't have to explain myself, or Jules's extenuating circumstances. A few days ago, when Mitch came to my office, he implied that he trusted me to handle it.

*Crap!* I ought to have left alone his innocent remark about having some chocolate sauce on hand. *Too late!* The mood is no longer carnal desire, merely tense. And while I'm sorry Mitch didn't get to climax, knowing he thinks I'm a piss-poor CEO sends me straight toward the door.

He honestly sees nothing wrong with telling me how to do my job.

*I need to get out of here.*

"It's been a really, really long Friday. I don't know about you, but I'm desperate for some shut-eye. Let's start fresh tomorrow. OK?"

I half expect him to protest. Instead, this conflicted man nods, his expression steadfastly neutral until my hand is on the door.

"Lark," he says.

When I turn, he sends me a small conciliatory smile. And that's enough for now. Returning it, hoping he won't leave at daybreak, I slip out the door.

# 14

## Mitch

I wake to early morning sunlight streaming through the guest house windows, the memory of last night's abrupt ending rushing into my brain. Running my hand over the space beside me where I'd imagined Lark would be sleeping, I sigh.

One step forward, two steps back seems to be our pattern.

The blame falls squarely on my shoulders this time. I had to bring up the damned sauce when we were having such a perfect moment. Checking my watch—5:45 a.m.—I throw back the covers. No point wallowing.

By 6:15, I've showered, put on a pair of jeans and a T-shirt, and I'm walking toward the main house. The morning air carries the scent of eucalyptus and something baking. Pat is on the veranda, a mug of coffee in his weathered hands.

"G'day, mate," he calls with a wave. "Sleep well?"

I nod, wondering if he suspects how close I came to spending the night with his granddaughter.

"Coffee smells amazing," I tell him. "And something's already in the oven."

"Eleanor's been up for ages. She's an early bird, that one." He gestures to the chair beside him. "Sit. Have a cuppa before we tackle those fence posts." Then he swivels his head to yell through the open window. "Hey, gorgeous. Mitch is dying for some coffee."

I can't help being startled, despite his lighthearted tone. My own mother would probably call back, "Come get it yourself then."

I hurry to say, "I don't want your wife thinking she has to wait on me."

Pat crinkles his face in a smile, as Eleanor steps onto the veranda holding a mug. "I figured you for a cream and one sugar bloke."

Accepting the steaming mug, savoring the rich aroma, I answer, "You figured right. And thank you."

"Our Lark brings the beans special from a roaster in Sydney." Eleanor's eyes crinkle at the corners. "She's always been thoughtful like that." Then she goes back inside.

I don't want to talk about Lark or beans of any kind. Luckily, Pat's and my conversation flows easily over all sorts of topics as we watch the sun rise over the vineyard. He tells me about the land and how much it has meant to him to be able to live life on his own terms, because of the lucrative chocolate company he and his wife started as newlyweds.

"It was mostly the missus. She has the magic," he adds. "She's also stubborn as a kangaroo on its hind legs. Whenever there was strife, she'd just dig her heels in and keep going."

I think of Lark, knowing she's got her grandmother's backbone. And listening, I'm enthralled by the family history, the way Henley Confectionery grew alongside the ranch until it *outgrew* it. The vineyard, Pat's pet project, came much later.

"Keeps me out of strife, mate, and I thought hanging about the crushing room would get me out from under Eleanor's feet." He laughs. "Turned out my missus doesn't mind tripping over me. More often than not, she's right there, too. Nearly as handy at wine-making as she is making choccie."

Mr. Henley's long history of entrepreneurship makes my own seem relatively new by comparison. And also, a little lonely. I have employees, but no partner in crime.

"Ready to move a few posts?" Pat asks, setting down his empty mug.

"Lead the way."

Turns out he didn't simply need "a few posts" moved. We spend the next two hours transporting fence posts from where they were delivered to the western boundary of the property, as well as measuring, digging holes, and setting them in the ground.

We even had a small water truck and quick-set cement to make sure the posts weren't going anywhere. When I ask him about the missing fence, he tells me the large section was charred by a fast-moving fire two years earlier.

"Never got around to fixing it because I had a stroke last year," Pat says matter-of-factly. "Bloody nuisance."

I think he means the stroke, not the fire. It doesn't seem to have slowed him down any. On the other hand, he doesn't rush the process. I'm learning that Lark's grandfather is meticulous. Throughout the work, he takes the time to show me how to carefully measure post holes and use a string to make sure all the posts are at the precise same height for the rails.

"I like them bang-on," he tells me after adjusting one post that was an inch too high.

I imagine his attention to detail is the reason both his chocolate company and his wine-making are so successful. Each in their own right.

"The fence's mostly for show, anyway," Pat adds. "I don't run stock up here—no horses, nor sheep—but I like my patch marked out. Bit of an ego thing, I reckon. Shows where I'm king."

We both laugh. I'm grateful for the physical labor, the way it clears my head and works out the lingering frustration from last night's *pleasure interruptus*.

Pat works away beside me, swinging the post-driver like it's nothing, age be damned.

"So," he says, casual as you like while he sinks another post, "how long've you known our Lark, then?"

"Not long enough," I tell him straight. "But I'd like to know her better."

He gives a slow nod, like that sits well with him. "She's a good one, that girl. Keeps the weight of the world on her shoulders, though."

I think about how different she is here at the ranch, more relaxed and playful, like the night we pretended we weren't ourselves. As CEO, she seems tightly wound.

"The company means a lot to her," I say diplomatically.

"Too much, sometimes," Pat says, resting on his shovel. "Her father—my son, Rick—was the same at the helm till he handed it over to his kids. Bloody genius with chocolate, my boy, but hopeless at balance." He shoots me a look. "You know how important that is, yeah?"

"Still working on it," I admit. "My restaurants chew up more of my life than they should."

Pat chuckles. "At least you've got your head around it, mate. Rick and his missus are finally having a bit of fun, but he still hangs onto the controlling stake in the company."

For a moment, he's peering into the distance at something I can't see. Maybe thinking about his chocolate business, how it grew away from him, split in two, and even crossed an ocean.

"Anyway, if you stick around Oz long enough, you'll meet Lark's folks," Pat assures me. "They swing back a couple times a year. The entire clan does. Henley blood runs through this land, and the land runs through all of us."

I nod and stay silent, taking in everything he's said, like Skywalker absorbing Yoda's wisdom. I've learned something more about Lark, too, and wonder if she knows how smart her Gramps is.

By the time we finish, my muscles are sore and my shirt is sticking to my back with sweat. Pat claps me on the shoulder when we start back.

"You're a good worker, Mitch. Not afraid to get your hands dirty."

Coming from him, it feels like high praise. Back at the house, Eleanor has prepared a massive breakfast of eggs, bacon, and a freshly baked damper loaf, slathered with her homemade jam. And I am here for it. I can't remember being this hungry in a long time.

Lark appears as we're sitting down, looking sleep-rumpled and gorgeous in a simple white-and-blue striped sundress.

"Morning," she says, her eyes meeting mine briefly before she kisses her grandparents' cheeks. "Smells delicious, Nan."

"Your young man's been working hard for hours already," Eleanor says, shooting me an approving look. "He and Pat got all the posts in, and tomorrow they'll be finishing that fence line."

Lark raises an eyebrow at me. "Is that right?"

It's the first I've heard of finishing it, but I like the idea of not leaving the job half done. We've only got the easy part left to do, sliding in and securing the rails. I shrug.

"Your grandfather did most of the work."

"Don't believe a word," Pat says around a mouthful of eggs. "Mitch knows his way round a bit of hard yakka."

Something softens in Lark's expression as she sits beside me, our elbows brushing.

"Thank you," she says quietly, so I alone can hear, while pressing her thigh against mine.

"Tuck in," Eleanor says, sliding a plate in front of Lark. "You two've got a bit of fun lined up. My granddaughter reckons you're gonna saddle up a couple of nags and give 'em a run."

"Horses?" I repeat, my stomach doing a small flip that has nothing to do with hunger.

Lark's smile turns mischievous. "Scared, Franklin?"

"Cautious," I correct, trying to sound more confident than I feel. "I've been on a horse only once in my life. It was more of a pony really."

Pat and Eleanor swap amused looks. "No worries," Pat says. "We'll chuck you on Daisy. She's as calm as they come."

An hour later, I'm uncomfortably perched atop a massive chestnut mare, while Lark sits easily on her own mount, a sleek black horse named Onyx.

"Relax," she instructs, leaning over and adjusting my hold on the reins. "Daisy can sense your anxiety."

"That's not comforting," I mutter, trying to loosen my death grip. I don't want the horse to sense anything except how sorry I am the Henleys are making her carry me. "I'm a city boy, remember? Not a lot of horses on the streets of Boston in the last century."

Lark laughs, the sound bright in the mid-morning air. "Follow my lead. We'll take it slow."

True to her word, she guides me patiently as we make our way along a trail that winds in the opposite direction to either the vineyard or the fencing project, northeast into the surrounding hills. Gradually, I find my rhythm, but not looking anywhere close to how natural Lark does in the saddle.

She's transformed out here, her posture confident, her smile easy. She points out landmarks while we ride—the creek where she and her siblings swam and fished as children, the tree house her father built one summer, which is more like a sturdy fort, the hill where they had picnics on special occasions.

"You love it here," I observe as we pause to let the horses drink from a stream.

Lark nods, her gaze traveling over the landscape. "It's home. Always will be, no matter where I live. Not just here at the ranch, either, but New South Wales." She pauses before adding, "And Queensland, too. Naturally, Victoria as well."

"So, basically all of eastern Australia," I clarify, and she smiles. "It's particularly beautiful out here," I say, meaning it.

Looking back at the rolling hills, the neat rows of grapevines, the ranch house in the distance, it's like a rustic painting, aside from the shimmering blue pool.

"What about you?" she asks, turning those thoughtful eyes on me. "I know you're from Mass, but where feels most like home to you?"

*Good question.* "I was going to say Boston, but it doesn't feel the same way as this does for you. My parents' house, sure, but it's not my childhood home, which they sold." I shrug, thinking how much fun it is to land somewhere new.

"I guess I've been an explorer most of my adult life. I have zero trouble moving to a new city to open a restaurant," I add. "Mostly because I know I'm not trapped there. I can do my job, stay for a few months, and get out."

Lark tilts her head, and I think I fall in love with her quizzical expression.

"You don't have a place that grounds you?" she persists.

Thinking about my restaurants, my current apartment in Sydney, the various places I've lived, and I come up empty.

"Not a physical place," I admit. "For me, it's more about the people. My family and friends, who are all spread out." Then it hits me. "A kitchen," I blurt out. "I can make myself at home in practically any place with a stove and oven."

She smiles at that. "I understand. You create your home wherever you go."

It's a nice way of looking at it, though I can't help but envy her deep connection to this land, this legacy. We ride in comfortable silence for a while, the horses picking their way along the trail. Despite my initial nervousness, I'm actually enjoying myself.

"I wanted to explain about Jules," Lark says suddenly, breaking the quiet.

I tense slightly, remembering our argument from last night. "You don't have to—"

"I do," she interrupts. "I drove to the factory last week to talk to him face-to-face. He left before I arrived. But I had a great time with a health inspector poking his nose all over the factory. That was when I discovered the scorched beans."

She sighs deeply. "Anyway, Jules never came back. Turned out his brother had a motorcycle accident, and he flew to France to be with him."

The defensiveness I'd been feeling dissipates. "I'm sorry to hear that."

Shame washes over me as I recall my accusations about how she ought to be able to manage her employees. "I shouldn't have jumped to conclusions last night."

"No," she agrees. "You shouldn't have." But there's no bite to her words. "And I should've explained sooner."

After guiding her horse around a fallen branch, she sends me a serious look. "I do take my responsibilities seriously, Mitch. As CEO and for the welfare of my company and my employees."

"I know that," I say, meaning it. "I've seen how dedicated you are. I lost my cool, and I regret it."

Her sudden smile is worth every uncomfortable minute in this saddle. "Race you to that big gum tree?" she challenges suddenly, nodding toward a massive eucalyptus in the distance.

"That's not fair," I protest. "You probably rode a horse when I was still on a tricycle."

She laughs, the sound carrying across the morning air. Before I can protest further, she takes off, her black horse eating up the distance with powerful strides. I barely have time to grab the pommel before Daisy decides to follow, apparently not as docile as advertised when her stablemate is running away.

"Slow down!" I yell, but I'm laughing despite my terror. The wind whips past my face as my horse gallops after Onyx, my body bouncing awkwardly in the saddle. Painfully, too, as my nuts hit the hard leather saddle over and over. Eventually, I figure out how to go up when Daisy goes up and down when she goes down.

Ahead, Lark's hair streams behind her like a golden banner, and she leans forward in the saddle.

I'm only seconds behind her, feeling exhilarated. Reaching the tree, Lark pulls up smoothly while I fumble with the reins, relief flooding through me when Daisy slows to a stop.

"You're still alive," Lark teases, reaching over to pat my knee. "And you didn't fall off."

"Pure luck," I manage, my heart still racing. "I think I left my stomach back there somewhere."

Lark dismounts gracefully, tying Onyx's reins to a low branch. "Come on, city boy. I'll help you down."

My legs are shaking when I hit the ground, but I'm grinning. "That was . . . actually kind of exciting."

"Nothing like a good gallop to clear your head." She steps closer, smoothing my wind-tousled hair. "Though maybe next time we'll stick to a trot."

"Next time?" I catch her hand, drawing her against me. "You're assuming I'll get back on a horse after that."

Her eyes sparkle with mischief. "I'll make it worth your while."

When I kiss her, she tastes like morning coffee, the blueberries we devoured at breakfast, and adventure. The horses snuffle quietly nearby as I deepen the kiss, my hands sliding down to her hips. I want to lay her down on the grass and continue where we left off last night. My hands go under her shirt and tug her bra cups down so I can palm her breasts.

When my thumbs stroke her nipples, she moans against my mouth, and I feel desperate. My desire ramps up from where it's been simmering since last night to a boil. In a flash, my veins are running hot, pumping blood to my cock.

Finally, I draw back and take a look at the ground. Tree roots and ants meet my gaze, and I doubt Lark would appreciate being on her back. We could always try—

"Look," she exclaims, interrupting my lascivious plans. Instead of staring at the uninviting scratchy grass, she's pointing to the sky. A hot air balloon seems to hover in the brilliant blue, but in fact, it's coming our way. Another reason not to throw caution out the window and give in to the urges building inside me.

"We should head back," she says, killing any lingering hope I have of a quickie out in nature.

"Why?" I ask.

"More ranch work. Gramps would appreciate that. And I could vacuum the house for Nan and work in the garden."

"You really like the chores, don't you?"

"Beats being in an office any day. I bet there's something we can do in the stables, too."

"I can think of a few things," I say, swooping down to nip at her bottom lip.

She relents, melting against me as we make the most of our private moment under the eucalyptus tree. When we finally break apart, her cheeks are flushed and her lips are swollen. I wonder whether we can ride back on the same horse. Maybe we can try a certain position that gets its name from—

"Race you back?" she suggests, giving me a wicked smile.

*Denied again.* "Not a chance," I say, because I can tell my ass cheeks are already tender. "I'm walking Daisy home."

I relent, of course, and climb onto the mare, who trots back to the stables behind Onyx. Enjoying the view, I love Lark's relaxed vibe, the way she keeps turning to check on me, giving me a saucy smile. Against all odds, our anonymous one-nighter has turned into a . . . friendship, one where we can be comfortably quiet together.

The rest of the day passes swiftly. After the ride, I get *up close and personal* with Onyx, Daisy, *and* their stablemates, brushing the horses before cleaning the four occupied stables under Lark's tutelage.

Taking every opportunity to pull her close, each time I kiss her until she sags against me. Basically, I'm driving myself crazy and getting a serious case of blue balls.

For lunch, we have sandwiches at a picnic table under a gum tree. It's the very essence of the word *idyllic*, watching sheep in the pasture, with bees buzzing around. The warmth of the Henleys' family life wraps around me like a comfortable blanket. Maybe a bit too warm.

With sweat trickling down my back, I'm ready for a refreshing swim. Her grandparents join us this time. I honestly can't believe how spry and agile they are. After the pool, there's work to do in the garden, which has an astonishing variety of fruit, vegetables, and herbs.

Then at long last, I get my hands on Eleanor's swanky kitchen. Not original to the house, it's macked out with stainless-steel and professional-grade appliances. A hand-painted tile backsplash banishes any industrial look, keeping it eclectic and welcoming.

As evening approaches, I prepare a lamb roast, working with fresh herbs and vegetables from the garden. The kitchen fills with mouth-watering aromas as I cook, and I catch Lark watching me from the doorway more than once. Eventually, after folding laundry with her grandmother, she comes in and sits at the kitchen island, pouring both of us a glass of wine.

"Smells amazing," she says.

We clink glasses and have a drink. "This wine does go with everything," I echo her words from last night. But I can't stand and chat. I've got a feast to finish. Although the meat is the star, I have a few knock-out supporting dishes— garlic and sweet red pepper roasted potatoes, fresh garden peas that I'll steam for barely a minute and dress with mint sauce, and some spicy, fresh-from-the-oven, curry-infused dinner rolls.

She steps closer, dipping a finger into the sauce I'm reducing. "*Mm*, faultless."

"Of course it is," I say with mock offense. "Did you expect anything less?"

Her answering smile makes my heart skip. "Never."

The night unfolds as I expected. My dinner is a success, ensuring Lark's Nan continues to think me a *keeper*. The conversation flows easily, and Pat's wine pairs beautifully with the lamb and veg. I even had time to make dessert, thick custard spooned over berry crumble. Neither is exactly haute cuisine, but they satisfy everyone's sweet tooth.

Besides, I wasn't going to mess around with chocolate in the presence of these masters.

Instead of another swim, we play cards. I feel as though we joke and laugh and chat through the entire hour, and I've decided I'll try to corral my own family into doing the same next time we're together. Working hard on the ranch has me yawning early, which Lark finds hilarious.

"Restaurateurs and bar owners can usually keep their eyes open past nine o'clock," she teases.

"They don't usually get up at the crack of dawn and spend hours putting in fence posts," I protest. But with my limbs feeling heavy, I have the growing notion this evening isn't going to end in a passionate encounter.

I'm more certain of it when we all say our goodnights half an hour later. Lark sends me an inscrutable look before disappearing down the hallway toward her childhood bedroom.

After another shower, I'm fast asleep as soon as my head hits the pillow.

But I'm just as wide awake sometime later when I hear movement in my room.

By the position of the moonlight streaming through the windows, I know I've slept for a few hours. Sitting up abruptly, I hope some wild kangaroo hasn't invaded the cottage, ready for a fist fight.

Then I see her. Lark, at the end of the bed, wearing nothing but a smile.

Instantly, I'm rock hard and ready for whatever she wants. In fact, I'm extra prepared, having brought her a couple small gifts I know she's going to love.

# 15

## Lark

My bare feet are silent on the cool wooden floor of the guest house's small living room. In the darkness, I make my way to the bedroom, stopping at the foot of the bed on the soft area rug. The only sound apart from the gentle whoosh of the paddle fan above us is Mitch's gentle snoring.

With the shades left open, moonlight streams through the windows, illuminating his sleeping form. He's on his back, one arm curled up, the other stretched out, leaving his broad chest and flat brown nipples on display. The sheet covers him from his hips downward. *Pity!*

Part of me feels guilty for sneaking away from the main house, but that's the leftover teenager in me, thinking my grandparents will care or be shocked. The adult woman I've become sheds her nightshirt and drops her phone on top of it. Its flashlight app was a necessity so I wouldn't end up in the pool when I could no longer resist my yearning for Mitch.

I've been craving him, *all of him*, since last night's stupid disruption.

Pausing in this calm moment, I watch the steady rise and fall of his chest. He looks younger when sleeping. I suppose we all do. For a moment, I'm struck by how quickly this man has become important to me, the way he slipped past my defenses so firmly in place the night we met. The night I didn't want him to know who I was.

I'm starting to think he's the one who could know me on a level no man ever has. What's more, here, away from Sydney, away from our businesses, it's easy to forget why I've kept a real relationship at arm's length for so long.

He stirs. Perhaps because I nudge his toe with my knee. I need him to awaken and do wild things to me. When his eyes flutter open, confusion gives way to recognition and even more swiftly to lust as he takes in my naked body. Merely my silhouette, yet it causes a slow grin to appear on his handsome face. I feel savage and beautiful at the same time.

"You're not a dream," he murmurs, voice husky with sleep.

"Not unless we're having the same one."

He sits up. "I didn't think tonight was happening. Not after I conked out." He holds out his hand.

Crawling onto the bed, feeling the mattress dip beneath me, I am light and happy when I put my hand in his, letting Mitch draw me down on top of him.

"I waited for Nan and Gramps to go to bed," I explain. "They may suspect what's going on between us, but I'd rather not be crude about it. Also, I wanted to give you some time to rest."

Mitch is skimming his hands along my curves but freezes. Then he laughs. "Time to rest! Like I'm a hundred years old."

"You were sound asleep when I came in. Even snoring."

"OK, woman." He rolls me onto my back. "So I needed a brief nap after playing ranch hand and cowboy all day and chef all evening."

"Two and a half hours," I point out, unable to keep from smiling. "I couldn't wait any longer for you to finish your beauty sleep."

"You are mouthy tonight," he says. "At least, I hope so."

His teasing words make my stomach flutter.

"Whatever you want, I'm ready," I confess, meaning it. After all, last night, I walked out on him after a rather intense orgasm. It's his turn.

Mitch's mouth claims mine, gentle at first, almost teasing, before his tongue demands entrance, letting me know his desire matches my own. Relishing the feel of his body on top of me, I squirm beneath him to part my legs so he can settle between them, against my sensitive mound.

For long, wonderful moments, we simply kiss. If an all-parts-tingling kiss can be called *simple*. My body remembers exactly how good we are together and goes from anticipating to pulsing excitement within seconds.

"I brought you something," Mitch whispers against my neck.

Intrigued, I try to push him back so I can look him in his gorgeous blue eyes. "What is it?" I sound like an impatient kid.

A mischievous smile plays across his lips, then he climbs off the bed and goes over to his leather duffel bag on the dresser. In a moment, he's back. This time, he straddles my thighs, resting on his knees and shins, looking down at me.

"A little something to enhance our fun *and* your pleasure."

He holds up a small velvet pouch. His fingers work the drawstring, then he tips the contents into his palm—two delicate metal clamps connected by a thin chain.

"Oh!" Recognizing what they are, I'm instantly aroused. And wet.

"Nipple clamps," he confirms, his eyes darkening as if he's as eager to try them on me as I am to enjoy them. "Nothing too intense. They're adjustable."

His fingers trace my collarbone, then drift lower. He adds, "They increase awareness. Make everything feel . . . *more*."

Heat pools between my legs at the thought, and the light pulse of my clit becomes a steady throb.

"I've never . . . That is, I haven't bought them because it seems so . . ." My tongue is tied and my face feels hot. "I wasn't ever sure I wanted my partner to know."

"We don't have to use them," he assures me quickly. "Just thought it might be fun to try."

I consider the steel clamps, the way they catch the moonlight. I trust Mitch, and the idea of trying something new with him sends a thrill through me.

"Put them on me," I say. "Please."

His expression turns serious, as he rests the clamps on my bare skin before cupping my breasts. His thumbs circle my nipples until they harden beneath his touch. I arch into his hands, already aching to test out his gift.

"First," he murmurs, "we need to make sure you're ready."

I nearly scream, "I'm ready!" But I don't want to miss out on anything he's doing.

Taking his time, Mitch replaces the slow circles of his fingers with his tongue until I'm squirming beneath him, my nipples taut and receptive. Only then does he reach for the first clamp, applying it to my right nipple.

There's a moment of sharp pressure that makes me gasp, quickly giving way to a delicious, tightness. He watches my face carefully as he fine-tunes the tension, looking for any sign of discomfort.

"Good?" he asks.

"Yes," I breathe, surprised by how much I like the feeling. *Better than a chip clip, that's for sure.*

He sucks my left nipple between his lips, licking, sucking, driving me wild, and then applies the second clamp with the same care.

"*Oof,*" I say as he tightens it a little.

The silver chain now hangs below my breasts. Their breath-stealing pinch plus the sight of the clamps adorning my body is fiercely erotic.

"You look incredible," Mitch says, his voice low and lusty. "How do they feel?"

"Intense," I admit. *Almost too much, but not quite.* "I like them. Thank you."

His fingers caress my sides, my stomach, my thighs, carefully avoiding the chain. "They'll make everything more stimulating," he promises. "Every touch."

He's right. When his fingers finally slide between my legs, finding me already slick with wanting him, my hips come off the bed. My nerve endings seem heightened, connected somehow to the exquisite tension applied to my nipples. He strokes me slowly, deliberately, watching as I writhe beneath his touch.

"Please," I whisper, not even sure what I'm begging for.

Mitch understands. He positions himself between my thighs, the head of his cock teasing my entrance. "Ready?" He knows I am, but he's torturing me.

"God, yes," I hiss.

In one smooth thrust, he fills me completely.

I gasp, on the edge of pain and pleasure. I have to deal with his massive length and girth, which still takes my breath away, my pussy stretching to accommodate him. On top of that, his movement causes the chain to sway, tugging at my nipples, causing an extra sting.

I clutch at his shoulders, digging my nails into his skin.

His groan sounds like a growl of desire. Then Mitch sets a rhythm that has me seeing stars. With each deep penetration and withdrawal, the chain moves, creating a counterpoint of raw sensation that drives me higher.

When he dips his head to lick around one of the clamps, I have to bite the pillow to muffle my scream.

His pace increases, his breathing ragged against my neck.

"Touch yourself," he commands softly.

I slide a hand between us, finding my clit. The combination of his thrusts, the clamps, and my fingers is overwhelming. Within moments, my climax has built to bursting, a tidal wave I can't escape.

"Mitch," I gasp in warning.

"Let go, beautiful," he urges. "I want to feel you come around me." Then he takes the silver chain between his teeth and tugs.

I hear my voice keening with a sound I've never made before. His words and his skilled movements push me over the edge so hard I can't breathe. My back arches as ecstasy crashes through me, more intense than anything I've ever experienced. The clamps amplify everything, making my orgasm seem endless.

Through the haze, I feel Mitch's rhythm falter and freeze, his cock grinding deep inside me as he follows me, his body tensing with his own release.

He collapses beside me, his sweat-slicked skin pressed against mine. With gentle fingers, he removes the clamps. When the blood rushes back, serious aftershocks flutter through me, making me quiver.

"That was . . ." I struggle to find words.

"Yeah," he agrees, pressing a kiss to my temple. "It was." Then he adds, "I didn't want to push it, but I could get a clit clip, too. Attach it to the same chain."

My imagination easily conjures that third pinch, and I groan as my lady bits instantly tighten.

"I'm game to try," I confess.

Lying together in comfortable silence, our breathing gradually slows. His fingers trace patterns on my skin, and I realize I could get used to this—falling asleep in Mitch's arms, waking up beside him. The thought is both thrilling and terrifying.

"Stay," he murmurs, as if reading my mind. "Stay until morning."

I should say no. I should slip back to the main house before dawn, maintaining at least the pretense of propriety for my grandparents' sake. But his arms feel too good, and my limbs are too heavy with satisfaction.

"Just for a while," I concede, nestling closer.

I don't mean to fall asleep, but Mitch's steady heartbeat under my ear lulls me into a deep, dreamless slumber. When I next open my eyes, early morning sunlight is streaming through the windows, and my phone is vibrating insistently with a low buzzing somewhere in the bedroom.

Mitch stirs beside me, his arm tightening around my waist.

"Ignore it," he mumbles into my hair.

But something—instinct, maybe—has me scrambling out of bed and finding my phone recklessly left on the floor next to my nightshirt. The screen shows Charlotte's name, and my stomach drops. My VP wouldn't call on a Sunday, certainly not at this hour, unless something was wrong.

"I have to take this," I tell Mitch, already hitting accept. "Charlotte?"

"Lark, thank God. I'm sorry to call so early, but we have a situation." Her voice is tense, professional—none of her usual casual warmth.

I am suddenly wide awake. "What's happening?" I ask, sitting on the end of the bed so I can cover myself with the end of the crumpled sheet.

Mitch raises himself on one elbow, concern etched across his face as he watches me.

"There's unusual activity with our stock," Charlotte explains. "A significant number of shares have been purchased, a relative trickle over the past few weeks but a lot since Friday. Various buyers, all behaving in synchronicity."

My blood runs cold. "You're thinking shell companies?"

"I am," she says.

"How significant?" I ask, although my mouth has gone as dry as red Outback dust.

"Almost twenty percent so far. Tracking it now, but it looks coordinated."

*A hostile takeover.* The words echo in my mind, though neither of us has said them aloud. Twenty percent isn't enough to seize control, but it's a substantial foothold—and enough to cause serious trouble if someone continues buying.

"Any idea yet who's behind it?" I ask, my mind already racing through competitors who might want to acquire Henley.

"We're still digging, but David's really good," she says, mentioning our crack CFO. "He's traced the shell companies back to a European conglomerate called RWI." Charlotte pauses, and I can hear her typing. "They operate primarily in luxury goods—fashion, jewelry, and recently they've been expanding into premium foods."

My stomach tightens. RWI isn't a name I recognize, but their strategy is clear. Buy up stock when no one's watching, over a weekend when market response is delayed. Classic predatory move.

"I'm coming back today," I say, already mentally packing my bags. "Can you arrange an emergency executive meeting for this afternoon? I want everyone there—legal, finance, strategy and development, even PR. And of course, we need to alert Luke and my dad."

"Already on it," Charlotte assures me. "Three o'clock at headquarters. Should I contact the board?"

I hesitate. The board needs to know, but I want to have a strategy in place first. "Not yet. Let's assess and formulate our response before bringing them in."

"Understood. And Lark? I'm sorry about your weekend."

The irony isn't lost on me. The first time I let my guard down since becoming CEO, and this happens.

"Not your fault. I'll see you at three."

Ending the call, I sit still for a moment, sheet clutched to my chest, trying to process what's happening. Mitch's hand settles warm on my back.

"I heard the words *shell companies*, so it must be big trouble," he says quietly.

When I turn to face him, my heart squeezes. Reality comes crashing back, and I don't see how he can be a part of it, of my real life. Not when he's one massive distraction. The truth is that I'm getting all tangled up with a guy whose biggest plus is that, at some point, maybe soon, he'll be jetting off to open a restaurant far away.

On the one hand, I don't have to worry about Mitch disrupting my focus forever.

On the other hand, if I let myself fall for him, I can only imagine how messed up I'll be when that day comes. Will I be sobbing in my office by day and spending my evenings at the F6 Tavern, wishing he'd walk through the door? *Ugh!*

"Someone's buying up Henley shares," I say, already feeling hollow, even while we're still on the same mattress. "Looks like a hostile takeover attempt."

His expression grows serious. "Shit. Who?"

"Some European conglomerate called RWI." I run a hand through my tangled hair. "I need to get back to Sydney right away."

Mitch nods, already throwing back the covers. "I'll drive you."

"We came in separate cars," I remind him, reaching for my nightie, glad it's the long cotton T-shirt style that won't be embarrassing if I meet Gramps or Nan before I get to my room.

"I *want* to drive you." He gets out of bed, looking glorious in his nakedness.

"I appreciate it," I say, although I don't, which carries over into my tone.

He crosses his arms. "But?"

"But I'm not some trembling flower who can't drive my car because there's trouble at work. I run the damn company, after all."

Surprisingly, he grins. "I get it. I was going all macho man when my capable lady doesn't need it. And I respect you for that."

A weight lifts off my shoulders. He understands. Except I'm not *his* lady.

"Still," he says, "I bet you're leaving as soon as you've had a cup of coffee and a bite to eat. I don't want to stay here without you. It'd be awkward, so I'm going to follow you down the driveway."

The efficiency with which he moves, pulling on clothes, gathering his things, reminds me that Mitch is no stranger to crises. He runs multiple restaurants and must be accustomed to pivoting when things go sideways. At this rate, he'll be ready long before me.

"Slow down, hotshot. You have time to take a shower. I intend to have one. My meeting isn't until three."

Last night seems like a dream now, distant and surreal compared to the sharp edges of this new reality. The clamps Mitch brought lie on the nightstand, and I feel a flush creeping up my neck at the memory.

"OK, then. Shower time," I say, striding through the guest house the way I came in, with only my nightshirt on and my phone in my hand.

"I'll meet you in the main house," Mitch calls after me. "If I get there first, I'll make us coffee and something to eat."

I don't turn but lift my hand in agreement, sending him a little wave over my shoulder before hurrying outside. I'm grateful for his calm. I'd half expected him to make a joke or try to lure me back to bed.

I'm also thankful not to meet either of my grandparents on my way in the side door nearest my room. I've already had an amazing heart-to-heart with Nan, putting some things in perspective.

A minute later, I'm in the shower, trying to organize my thoughts as the hot water cascades over me. Nan already said she doesn't blame me for any of the "cock-ups" that've happened, especially not while I'm trying to innovate and make beneficial changes.

"Reckon I'd do the same as you, love," she'd said, pouring me a cup from her old teapot yesterday afternoon. "Never got to run the company past this ranch, but every year I switched things 'round as the choccie business grew. Think on it, Lark, we don't do things here like we did when I first wed Pat. Different ways to manage this estate, tweaks to gardening and ranching and making wine. Why should you keep doin' things the same at your office?"

Still, as I dry off and dress, I can't help wondering if I'd kept a more careful eye on business, the way I did in New York, whether someone would've managed to secure close to twenty percent of Henley Confectionery. It's a significant chunk, but not insurmountable. We still have the family's controlling interest, but if RWI continues accumulating stock, they could gain enough influence to make serious trouble—force board changes, push strategic decisions that benefit them, even attempt to oust me or Luke.

*Not on my watch!*

By the time I've packed my small overnight bag, anger has replaced my initial shock. *How dare they!* Henley is our family's legacy, built from nothing right here under my very feet. I'll be damned if I let some faceless European conglomerate snatch it away.

In the kitchen, I find Mitch making breakfast while my grandmother packs up snacks for each of us for the two-hour ride home.

"All right, love?" Nan asks. "Mitch says you need to get back to Sydney urgently."

I consider downplaying it, but she deserves the truth. "There's a situation with the company. Someone's trying to buy up majority shares. You remember our VP, Charlotte Bauer. She thinks they're setting up for a hostile takeover."

Nan's expression hardens. I sometimes forget that beneath her grandmotherly softness lies the same steel that built Henley Confectionery from a kitchen operation to an international brand.

"You'll stop them," she says with absolute certainty. It's not a question.

"I'll do everything I can. Executive meeting's at three." I take a sip of coffee. "Where's Gramps?"

"Out checking the irrigation system. If he's not back before you leave, I'll let him know what's happened." She squeezes my arm. "I have no doubt you and Luke will handle this."

There's something steadying about her confidence, like a foundation beneath my feet. And I'm glad she mentioned my brother. After all, I'm not in this alone. Then we three eat eggs, bacon, and pancakes, barely talking since we don't know anything else.

When it's time to leave, I tell her, "I'll call you later with an update."

Giving her a tight hug, I breathe in her familiar Nan scent.

"You'd better. Anyway, Pat will probably call you five minutes after the meeting has started. He'll want to be in on it."

She turns to Mitch, surprising him with a hug of his own. "Take care of our Lark. And yourself."

"Yes, ma'am," he answers solemnly.

Twenty minutes later, we drive out like a convoy of two, winding our way toward the highway, then speeding toward Sydney. I call Luke, finding out he's already been filled in and is on standby for three o'clock our time, one in the morning for him and for Dad.

After we've been driving for a while, my phone rings, and I press the answering button on my steering wheel.

"You OK?" Mitch asks.

*Am I?* "Just thinking."

"About?" he probes.

"Whether I could have prevented this." The thought has been gnawing at me since Charlotte's call. "If I hadn't been away for the weekend, if I'd been more vigilant—"

"Stop," Mitch interrupts firmly. "This isn't your fault. Companies face takeover attempts all the time. It's part of doing business."

"I know that intellectually." I sigh. "But it feels like I've failed somehow. This wouldn't have happened under my father, or Luke's watch."

"You don't know that." I hear the annoyance in his voice. "And it is happening under Luke's watch. What happens to Henley Sydney happens to Henley NYC, right?"

"Yes," I agree. That makes me think I might be responsible for taking the whole company down with me.

But Mitch isn't done with his pep talk. "Even if you'd been in the office, what would you have done differently? Stock trades happen. You couldn't have stopped them."

There's truth in what he says, but I can't shake the feeling that I've been caught off guard, that I should have seen this coming. I could've studied the business sheets more closely, seen who was looking for an acquisition.

On top of that, I wouldn't have been so distracted if I hadn't tried to put my personal stamp on things that were working fine before I got here, like the sugar supplier and the processed beans. And then there's Mitch and the Franklin Darkly mess-up. And Jules.

"You still there?" he asks. "Believe me, OK?"

"Maybe," I concede, though doubt still gnaws at me. A second call is coming in. David Park, our CFO.

"I need to take this call," I tell Mitch.

"OK, Lark, hang in—"

But I've already hung up on him and answered the call. Henley Confectionery is back to being my number one priority.

# 16

## Mitch

I've texted three times, asking Lark how her meeting went. Left two voicemails to find out how she's holding up. No response. Nothing but silence since we parted ways on Sunday. I get that she's busy. *Hell!* Someone's trying to take over her family's company. But a simple acknowledgment would be nice.

"You're brooding, mate," Ravi says, coming up behind me while I'm dicing onions in the kitchen of Franklin 6. I almost never go to F6's kitchen, because that menu has no challenge for me. Neither does dicing onions, but it's just the beginning of the dish I plan to make.

"I'm focused," I counter, not looking up from my work.

"*Hm.*" He positions himself on the other side of the prep table, arms crossed. "That's why you've been hacking onions for five minutes? Your ninja-like focus?"

I set down my knife and glance at the piles of minced onions spread across half the cutting board. Maybe I am brooding a little. What's more, I'll have to switch up my recipe because my onions are too small.

"Doors open in four hours," Ravi continues, glancing at his sous chef, then back at me. "You're the boss, but I'm head chef. If you're here, I need you present. The kitchen is no place for someone whose head's stuck in corporate Sydney."

"Corporate Sydney can kiss my—"

"Good afternoon!" A cheerful voice interrupts what would've been some colorful language about Lark's priorities.

When I turn around, I'm met with a sight that literally stops me lifting my knife. Standing in the kitchen doorway, looking calm and beautiful, is Camille—my ex-girlfriend from Le Cordon Bleu days.

Her jet-black hair is somehow artfully up yet down at the same time, and she's wearing a dress that my sister might've modeled this season on some fashion runway. It's form-fitting where it needs to be and yet softly flowing, too. And it must have cost more than most people's monthly rent.

Last time I was with her, she wore torn jeans and T-shirts when she wasn't in chef's whites.

"Camille?" I manage to say after my brain catches up with my eyes. "What the hell?"

She laughs, a pretty sound that used to make me smile.

"Is that any way to greet an old friend?" Her French accent has softened considerably since we last saw each other.

*When was that, seven years ago?*

Wiping my hands on a towel, I approach her. "I'm just . . . surprised." That's putting it mildly. Shocked might be more accurate. Flummoxed, if I want to get fancy with it.

She accepts my awkward hug, kissing both my cheeks in European fashion.

"I heard you'd opened *another* successful place. This one, I had to see for myself."

*Why?* "How did you even find me?" I ask.

Our split was not easy, at least for me. We didn't keep in touch beyond my boxing up anything she'd left behind and dropping it on the doorstep of her fancy new address. I didn't even ring the bell since I had no wish to meet her new lover. Rich, established, restaurateur, Henri Laurent.

"Instagram is a magical thing," she replies with a smirk. "Plus, you've long since been a major name in the industry, Mitchell Franklin. Opening restaurants that actually succeed, unlike so many others."

Glancing around, I suddenly recall we're not alone. "This is Ravi, my head chef. That's Bobby, our sous chef, and—" I start to point out the rest of the kitchen staff, listing off their names like a military sergeant.

But it's only to Ravi, I add, "This is Camille Durand." I use her maiden name, not knowing whether she and Henri ever married. "We were at Le Cordon Bleu together in Paris. And she's head chef at Chez Henri."

Ravi's eyebrows shoot up as he extends a hand. "The famous ex who graduated while the boss here didn't. I've heard stories."

*Well, shit!*

"All good ones, I hope," Camille says, shaking his hand.

"Mostly about your knife skills," Ravi says diplomatically.

I clear my throat. "So, you're in Sydney because . . . ?"

She gestures vaguely. "Business, pleasure. Both. Thought I'd surprise you."

"Consider me surprised," I say. Another kitchen worker enters through the back door, reminding me this isn't the time to chat. "We're prepping."

"Terrible Tuesday," she murmurs, knowing the drill of how much there is to do after being closed on a Sunday and Monday. "Perfect timing then," she adds, looking around the kitchen appraisingly, "if you need an extra pair of hands."

Ravi's and my mouths drop open. No way she's working in here dressed like that. Her laughter peals out again.

"I am teasing," she says, her words lilting with her French pronunciation. "But I would love to catch up properly. Perhaps dinner after your service tonight?"

Before I can answer, Ravi jumps in. "You should take her up on it, mate. Closing is covered, and you need to get your mind off . . . onions," he finishes, nodding at my prep station.

I hesitate. Camille isn't a friend. Spending time with a former lover who saw me at my worst *after* she told me she was moving on sounds about as inviting as a trip to the dentist. At the time, she didn't even bother with a pretense of regret.

Now, she's staring at me with her dark eyes, looking like butter wouldn't melt in her mouth. And Ravi's eyes are boring into me because he's aware Lark has been messing me around.

"Sure," I find myself saying. "That would be nice." *Nice?*

Camille beams. "*Merveilleux!* I'll come back around . . . ten?"

"That works fine," I agree, already regretting it. Given our history, I have a suspicion she wants something besides dinner.

Leaning close, she kisses my cheek again. "It's so good to see you, Mitchell."

Her accent always makes it sound like she's saying *Me-shell.* I used to love that.

As soon as she sashays out the door, Ravi's on me like white on rice.

"That's the sheila who smashed your heart in Paris? The one who picked some rich restaurateur over you?"

I wince. "I may have been a bit dramatic when I told that story. And drunk." But he has the gist of it.

"She's a stunner," Ravi says, stating the obvious. "And pretty clear she still has a thing for you."

I shake my head, returning to my station, ready to switch over to chopping tomatoes. It's not my job. We have a prep cook for this, but chopping, mincing, julienning—all the grunt jobs—are my favorite for spacing out. Almost meditative. However, at the wrong time, like earlier, they make it too easy to start ruminating.

"Ancient history," I say. *And I intend to keep it that way.* "We wanted different things."

She wanted security and a fast ticket to status in the culinary world. I wanted adventure and independence.

"If you say so." Ravi doesn't sound convinced. "But she didn't rock up here just to say g'day and eat your grub."

That's what bothers me. Camille always has an agenda. *Always.* Back in our culinary school days, I was too infatuated to see it. Her decision to leave me and move in with Henri Laurent—twenty-three years her senior with a small empire of bistros—had been calculated from the minute she met him.

I don't blame her any longer. In fact, seeing her stirs up memories of good times together, studying, cooking, exploring Paris. I carefully avoid dredging up feelings of a knife to my gut. In retrospect, it was for the best. Our relationship had been passionate but volatile. Two strong personalities in one tiny apartment.

"*Oi!* Earth to Mitch," Ravi says, waving a hand in front of my face. "Where'd your head go this time?"

"Wondering why she's really here," I admit. "There's no way she needs a job." How ironic if she did and came to me of all people! She'd be yet another woman who wanted something from me because of what I can offer and how much money I have.

"Guess you'll find out at ten. We'll save a couple steaks for you two," he adds. "Reckon she likes hers rare."

I roll my eyes. After he has a good laugh, he steps back into professional mode. "Now, can we focus on getting this kitchen ready? The produce delivery is late, and Jamie called in sick, so we're down a chef de partie."

Straightening up, I'm grateful for the distraction. "I'll have Marco cover for Jamie. And we'll modify the menu if the delivery doesn't come in time."

For the next several hours, I manage to keep thoughts of both Lark and Camille at bay as we prepare for service. The restaurant buzzes with the familiar energy of a new week—front-of-house catching up after the break, learning any menu changes and specials. There's always last-minute cleaning, the hiss and sizzle of the first dishes on the grill. This is my element, where everything makes sense.

Unsurprisingly, the night runs smoothly despite the hiccups. My staff is well-trained, and the updated menu items are a hit with our regulars. I lose myself in the rhythm of the kitchen, calling orders, tasting sauces, plating dishes. It's nearly ten when things slow down, and I retreat to my office to check my phone.

Still nothing from Lark.

I stare at our last text exchange from Sunday when I peeled off to the waterfront, heading home while she'd driven downtown to her office:

*Keep me posted.*

She replied:

*Made it to the office. Talk later.*

Except *later* never came.

I start typing a new message, then delete it. Type again, delete again. After all, I've been trying to get a response out of her now for forty-eight hours. Finally, I settle on something simple:

*Hope everything's OK.*

I hit send before I can overthink it, then toss my phone onto the desk. This isn't like me at all. I don't chase after women. Well, not after the initial catch, anyway. But Lark has gotten under my skin in a way I didn't expect. I've certainly never bought sex toys before!

A knock at my office door pulls me from my thoughts. Ravi pokes his head in, wearing a knowing grin and his street clothes.

"Your date's here. At table fourteen with the nice wine—the Margaux—and a couple of our primo ribeyes. Should do the trick."

"It's not a date," I remind him, standing and shrugging off my chef's jacket. Underneath, I'm wearing a simple black T-shirt that's reasonably presentable. "And the Margaux is excessive."

"Too late. Already uncorked and decanted." He steps into the office and lowers his voice. "Look, mate, I know you're hung up on candy girl, but maybe this is the universe offering a distraction. Anyway, I'm heading home."

I roll my eyes. "Candy girl" is what Ravi started calling Lark after I told him about our first meeting, when I didn't know who the hell had just blown my socks off.

"The universe can keep its distractions." I grab my phone, check it one more time—*nothing*—then jam it into my pocket, irritated. I'm really getting sick of my own unwelcome neediness. If she can't spare the fucking time, let her breathe.

The main dining room is nearly empty when I emerge. Two couples, each lingering over their desserts, are at the far end of the dining room. Camille sits at a corner table, illuminated by the soft glow of candlelight, sipping wine.

Her raven hair, always kept short for kitchen work, has grown out to a sleek, glossy curtain that skims her shoulders, over a strapless metallic-silver dress that shimmers across the swell of her breasts. *Damn!*

Whatever she's been doing between surprising me earlier and now, it hasn't involved getting hot and sweaty over a stove.

"There you are," she says, smiling up at me. "I was beginning to think you'd stood me up."

"Sorry," I say, sliding into the chair across from her. "Service ran a bit longer than expected."

"No apologies necessary. I know how it is." She holds up her glass. "This wine is exquisite. Your sommelier has excellent taste."

This dinner feels unnatural, like I've taken someone else's seat. If I'd never seen her again, it would've been fine with me.

Taking a sip then another, I nod. The wine is excellent—rich, complex layers that unfold with each taste. But it's no Henley Reserve. Or maybe, it's my dinner guest that makes the expensive Margaux come up short in comparison to enjoying Pat's chardonnay with Lark.

"To old friends," Camille offers, clinking her glass against mine.

We were lovers and rival students, more than we were ever friends.

"What brings you to Sydney?"

"A bit of a sabbatical, actually." She sets down her glass, tracing its rim with one perfectly manicured finger, a pale-gray polish. Classy, but I prefer Lark's signature palette of warm chocolate colors.

Besides, it looks out of place on Camille, whose nails were always very short and unpolished at Le Cordon Bleu, as required for any culinary student.

"After Henri and I went our separate ways, I needed a change of scenery."

This catches my attention. "You and Henri broke up?"

"About eight months ago." She shrugs elegantly, tilting her head and allowing her silky black hair to spill across her cheek.

Out of habit, I nearly reach out to tuck it behind her ear. Instead, I sip my wine.

"It was time," she adds. "We wanted different things."

The irony of her echoing my earlier words to Ravi isn't lost on me.

"Sorry to hear that," I offer, though I'm not entirely sure I mean it. Henri had always struck me as controlling, the type who wanted a trophy girlfriend more than a partner.

"Don't be. It was amicable. He kept me on as head chef for six months after we ended things, until I decided I needed a complete break."

A server brings our steaks, and Camille looks appreciatively at the perfectly cooked meat.

"This looks divine."

We spend the next few minutes focused on our food, making comments about the seasoning, the sides, the wine pairing. It's comfortable territory for both of us, and I find myself relaxing incrementally. It's good to talk to someone who understands the nuances of running a restaurant. Then she kills the vibe by getting personal.

"I'm surprised you didn't know I'd left Henri," she says, setting down her fork.

My mouth opens, but I can't say, "Because I didn't care enough to keep tabs on you."

Instead, I close it and shrug, then add, "I never kept tabs on you. It's a guy thing." It sounds lame, but she nods.

"Meaning you moved on and didn't want to feel any old feelings for me, good or bad." Camille sips her second glass of wine, her blue-black eyes staring right into mine.

There was a time I could lose myself in that darkness and never want to surface. Now, I'd rather watch Lark's golden eyes as she unravels beneath my touch.

"Yes," I say, thinking her reasoning sounds better than what I would've said.

She smiles. "Well, I wasn't afraid to see you again, even if all the old feelings crop up. I have a proposition."

Here it comes. *Not happening, lady.* But I'll let her down gently.

"Look, Camille—"

"You've conquered Sydney. What's next for Mitchell Franklin?"

There's something in her tone that makes me hesitate. The arched eyebrow and determined look tell me we're shifting topics, and the current one isn't about reconnecting with me for a roll in the sack after all.

"I have my next venue in mind," I say carefully. "But no immediate plans to leave Australia."

"You used to get so restless," she presses. "You couldn't wait to leave Le Cordon Bleu so you could travel and cook. Cook and travel. You always said you had to experience different cuisines firsthand. You were going to conquer Tokyo, New York, Bangkok."

"I did some of that," I remind her. "Worked in New York, kicked around in Singapore, but once I got Franklin 1 well and truly on its feet in Boston, I picked and chose my venues with an eye to restaurant success, not just what suited me." I look around the dining room.

"This is definitely one of my favorites."

"Don't tell me you've settled?" she says, putting a hand to her cleavage in a mock gasp.

My gaze skitters away from the deep V between her breasts, returning to her lips. *Were they always so pouty or has she done something to them?* I can't hold back the sigh.

Looking at Camille makes me miss Lark even more. *You desperate idiot!*

"That's not the Mitchell I knew," she says. "*Sédentaire.*"

Taking another sip of wine, I try not to be irritated by her assessment.

"Not sedentary, just taking time to enjoy myself before moving on. I found something that works for me—creating unique dining experiences that reflect the neighborhoods they're in. I like building teams, mentoring young chefs."

She leans forward, her dark eyes suddenly intense. "What if I told you I have an opportunity that would tap into all of that?" She gestures with her hand, like she's stirring a sauce.

And there it is. *Her agenda.*

"I'm listening," I say, setting down my glass.

"I've been approached by investors looking to develop a new dining concept on the west coast of the United States—specifically Santa Barbara. They want something innovative, chef-driven, based on French cuisine with exotic influences."

She reaches down by her feet and pulls a slim portfolio from her oversized handbag, which I thought was some crazy style of large.

Sliding it across the table, she says, "All the details are in there, but essentially, they're offering substantial backing for the right concept . . . and the right team."

I understand what she's saying. Out of courtesy, I flip through the portfolio, scanning architectural renderings, location details, projected financials. It's thorough, professional, and clearly represents serious money. I even play along and ask a question, despite already knowing the answer.

"And you're bringing this to me because . . . ?"

"Because I think we'd be spectacular partners," she says. "You with your business acumen and vision, me with my culinary expertise and European connections. We always worked well together in the kitchen, Mitchell."

I close the portfolio. "We haven't cooked together in a long time, Camille. And our relationship wasn't exactly built on mutual trust and respect by the end."

She has the grace to look slightly abashed. "I handled things poorly back then, I admit. But we've both grown up, haven't we? As you said, people change. This would be strictly business."

"Would it?" I challenge, maintaining eye contact.

Her hand reaches across the table to rest on mine. "Unless you want it to be more," she says softly. "I've missed you. More than I expected to. I'm single. I would certainly welcome you back into my life. Whatever you want."

The Camille I knew in Paris would never have been so direct. She preferred subtle manipulations with a face for winning at poker. This forthright approach is new—and somehow more unsettling.

"I'm seeing someone," I tell her, gently removing my hand from beneath hers.

"Oh?" Her eyebrow arches again, a trait I'd forgotten until tonight. "Is it serious?"

It's none of her business, and I nearly say that. But I hesitate, thinking of Lark's silence over the past two days. "I'd like it to be."

Camille studies me for a moment, then smiles—a small, knowing smile that makes me uneasy.

"Well, the business offer stands regardless. And if you're not interested in Santa Barbara, perhaps something closer to home? The west coast of Australia, maybe? Perth has a thriving food scene these days."

My phone buzzes in my pocket, and I resist the urge to check it immediately.

"Wait, are you saying this entire 'new dining concept' can be moved from Santa Barbara to Perth in the blink of an eye?"

"No," she says, pulling the folder back toward her side before tucking it down by her feet. Then her gaze flicks upward, catching and holding mine as if we're lovers again.

*How many times did I look into those dark eyes while stripping her naked?*

"It would have to be something more . . . intimate. The two of us against the world, I guess. We could open the best damn restaurant ever. Utterly unique, quintessentially us, and blow the socks off the culinary critics."

I have whiplash with how quickly she's pivoting from one idea to the next, and from work to play, if I'm reading her right. Time to shut all this down. Now.

"I appreciate the *professional* offers, both of them, but I don't need or want a business partner. Not to be rude, but I gain nothing by hitching my reputation and name with yours. And I'm focused on my existing restaurants right now. There's still plenty of work to do here in Sydney."

Not true, but Lark is here, and I'm not done with her yet. Although her silence is worrisome. Maddening. Bad-mannered. And exasperating as hell. But then there's the night we spent together before Charlotte's phone call. No way that was the end.

Camille's lips have straightened, pressed together into a displeased line. She shouldn't have come here, even in that dress, hoping things would go her way.

"I'll decide when the time is right for my next place," I add. "But I doubt it'll be in Perth."

Leaning back, she swirls the last of her wine. "I understand. Though I have to say, I'm surprised. The Mitch I knew could never resist a new challenge."

*A new tactic.* But I'm not biting.

"Maybe that's the difference between the floundering man you knew and the person I am now," I reply, surprised by the edge in my voice. "I choose my challenges more carefully these days."

Her laugh is soft, almost musical. "Fair enough. The offer remains open, should you change your mind. Now dazzle me with dessert while we rake mutual acquaintances over the coals."

I can't help laughing at how she seems to genuinely shift from the intense, life-altering moment of seconds ago to gossiping about people we both knew.

By the time we finish dessert—a chocolate soufflé, which I think Ravi ordered for us to drive the screws into me—we've covered mutual acquaintances from culinary school, changes in the global restaurant scene, and our travels over the past few years.

The restaurant is entirely empty. The last of my staff has left, knowing I'll hose down the remaining dishes and cutlery before doing a final visual sweep of all the stations before lights out.

"I should let you close up," Camille says, gathering her things. "Thank you for dinner. It was lovely catching up."

Outside, the night air is cool, but not yet crisp enough to signal autumn. We have a lot of summer left. A lot of beach and pool nights, hopefully with Lark.

Camille turns to me, her face partially illuminated by the restaurant's exterior lights.

"I meant what I said, Mitchell. About the opportunity." She steps closer. "And about missing you."

Before I can respond, she rises onto her tiptoes and presses her lips to mine. For a fraction of a second, I'm too surprised to react. Then I gently place my hands on her shoulders and step back.

"Camille . . ."

"Had to try," she says with a small shrug, seemingly unbothered by my rejection. "Whoever she is, she's lucky." Reaching into her huge purse, she pulls out a business card.

"My number, in case you reconsider. About the restaurant venture. Or anything. As long as I'm still in Sydney, I'll pick up."

Taking the card out of politeness with zero interest, I watch her walk to what is most likely a rental car. I shake my head at how the sight of a gorgeous woman in a liquid silver dress that hugs her shapely ass is not the least bit tempting. My only thought is, *What's Lark doing right now?*

Damn me if my candy girl hasn't totally tamed my usual urges for *new* and *next*.

Then remembering I received a text, I head back inside to read it.

# 17

## Lark

I slam my car door with unnecessary force and hit the gas pedal, letting Mitch's restaurant fade in my rearview mirror. I'd stupidly caved in to my longing for this man, despite my smarter self knowing that I need to get Henley Sydney fully under my control for at least twelve months.

*One full year of being a great CEO before I can divide my attention.*

But I went looking for him anyway. Late. Because I'd changed my mind half a dozen times. I went to his apartment first, then to the restaurant. Franklin 6 was closed, but seeing his car, I couldn't resist trying the door. It opened to an eerily quiet foyer.

Beyond that, past the maître d's station, on the far side of the dining room, Mitch was enjoying a candlelit meal with a beautiful woman who was dressed to seduce.

The way she leaned into him, her hand on top of his, the easy familiarity between them—it cut deeper than I expected. I whirled around and left. *Unnoticed, thank God!*

Without thinking, I press the button on my steering wheel. "Text Mitch Franklin." When it beeps, I say, "Three nights later? Really? I'm done with you and your games."

"Send," I tell my smart car before I can rethink it, then immediately regret sounding like a needy, jealous bitch. After all, I'm the one who has been ghosting him since we got back from my grandparents' ranch. But couldn't he have given me a little time, knowing how my company has been threatened, about to be snatched away from my family?

*Did he have to start chasing pussy again before the sheets were even cold?*

It's even more galling when he doesn't respond to my text immediately. I guess he doesn't have time for me. Not with his new raven-haired friend.

Eventually, about half an hour later, I receive a single question mark from him.

*Wow! Way to play innocent!* My stomach churns thinking about what they were doing during those thirty minutes.

Two hours later, when I'm going to bed, there's still no real response from Mitch. Three separate texts spaced about thirty minutes apart, each with a question mark, managed to infuriate me.

If I hadn't seen him with my own eyes, I might've continued playing a risky game with a guy who made me feel like I was the only woman he wanted. *One billion percent.*

Clearly, I was just another hook-up. Switching off the light, I wonder how I'll get to sleep, but eventually, I do.

As it turns out, not very well and not long enough for the awful day I'll be facing tomorrow.

$♥$♥$♥$

Running on caffeine and determination, I drive to Wetherill Park again to finally confront Jules. He returned yesterday, while I was still obsessing over Mitch.

*The philanderer.*

After a brief talk with Jim, I climb the stairs to the test kitchen like I'm climbing the steps of the gallows. Hesitating with my hand on the door knob, I look through the glass door. Henley doesn't put out a billion new products a year. Some years, we do little more than tweak an older recipe, if sales have fallen off. But our master chocolatier is always creating in our spotless, state-of-the-art kitchen.

Jules is mostly kept busy creating holiday and seasonal treats, as well as exclusive creations for corporate clients. A month ago, he made hibiscus-infused white chocolate for a high-end perfume client who sells hibiscus-scented eau de parfum. The confectionery was divine. Those custom chocolates rarely if ever make it into our regular production line.

All of that is why the HLC was so damn exciting to me. A new product that would blow the proverbial cobwebs out of our boxed assortments.

When I open the door, my lungs fill with the sweet aroma of chocolate. Some people find it overwhelming, but I could live in here. I could bathe in the stuff! My mind goes to Mitch pouring Franklin Darkly over my body, and I shake my head to stop the long, lascivious memory from playing like a movie.

The kitchen is buzzing with activity, despite their being only two people in it, Jules and his assistant, Rudy. Steam rises from a double boiler, Rudy is chopping dates on a slab of marble, and Jules is whisking a concoction in a porcelain bowl while the two men talk a mile a minute, not yet noticing my entrance.

I'm used to the intensity of what goes on here. We have a second team in NYC, equally small and dedicated.

"Hello, gentlemen." They both look up.

"Lark!" Jules exclaims. "I didn't expect you out here today. Are you my welcoming committee?"

*Damn,* this is hard.

"I need to talk to you," I say, gesturing toward the sample room, which is through a connecting door on the other side of the test kitchen. "Privately."

A flicker of concern crosses his face before he nods and leads the way.

Following him, I step into the best room in the factory, like an extraordinary miniature chocolate shop, with marble counters and stainless-steel trays and drawers, containing small-production chocolates.

Luke and I used to sneak in here whenever we worked at the factory and gorge ourselves like little piggies, trying one of everything.

Once the door closes behind us, instead of getting straight to the point, I ask, "How's your brother doing?"

"Much better," Jules says, his voice sounding relieved. "They moved him out of intensive care. Thank you for asking and for being so understanding about my absence last week."

"Family comes first," I say automatically, despite struggling with that concept lately.

Family means Henley Confectionery. Family means duty and work. My ill-fated attempt at balancing my work life with a little fun in the form of Mitch Franklin has blown up in my face.

Sinking into one of the two industrial white plastic and chrome chairs, I say. "I'm glad he's improving."

Jules nods, then moves to a small refrigerator in the corner. "I've been working on some new praline fillings for Christmas. Would you like to try one?"

Part of me wants to dive right into the interrogation, but I realize I need to approach this carefully. He's been with Henley for a long time, and despite how things look, I trust him entirely. More than that, we are professional colleagues.

"Sure," I say, accepting the small chocolate he offers. It melts on my tongue, releasing hints of caramelized hazelnut and something else—a spice I can't quite place. "Cardamom?"

He grins, pleased I've identified it. "And a touch of pink peppercorn. Does it work?"

"It's intriguing," I say honestly. "Bold, but not overwhelming. I like it."

"That's high praise coming from you," he says, selecting another piece for himself. "Your palate is exceptional."

His compliment makes me feel even worse. I take a deep breath. The small talk can last only so long.

"Jules, I need to ask you something, and I hope you'll be honest with me."

His smile fades as he studies my face. "This sounds serious."

"It is." I lean forward in my chair, gathering my thoughts. "The chocolate sauce featured at all of Mitch Franklin's restaurants—Franklin Darkly?"

He doesn't blink or startle at the name.

"What about it?" he asks.

"Have you tasted it?"

Jules shakes his head. "No, I've never tasted it. Is it good?"

I study his face for any sign of deception. "It's remarkably similar to the HLC batches you've been developing."

"Is it?" His surprise seems genuine, and he still looks relaxed as he sits in the other chair and rests his right ankle on top of his left knee. "That's an unfortunate coincidence."

"It is," I agree. "Because the flavor profiles aren't similar, they're *identical.* If I gave you Franklin Darkly, you would swear it's HLC. It's also made with coconut sugar, which is kind of amazing, don't you think?"

His expression shifts from mildly interested to understanding, then to outright indignation.

"Are you suggesting I took their recipe and have been testing it here? Passing it off as my own work?"

He jumps to his feet. "Do you think I'd risk my reputation and that of Henley for one product? I certainly wouldn't send you out to Taste of Sydney with it, not with Franklin 6 becoming the in-spot."

I hadn't expected this reaction. "I'm simply trying to understand how two chocolate sauces could be identical when developed independently. Right down to the Mexican vanilla."

"Lark," he says firmly, "I've been with Henley for nine years. I've created hundreds of original recipes. Why would I need to steal from a restaurant, even a good one?" He sighs. "I have to tell you, this is not making me happy. Not what I wanted to come home to after last week."

I nod. "It's not a conversation I wanted to have either. Mr. Franklin sampled HLC at Taste of Sydney, and he went ape-shit, to put it mildly. So how do you explain the similarities?"

"I don't think I have to," he snaps, then Jules runs a hand through his blond hair, visibly frustrated. "I don't know. Maybe great minds think alike. I promise you, Lark, I've never even tasted his damn sauce."

I sit back and close my eyes. "If I don't come up with an explanation, he will sue Henley Confectionery to stop us creating HLC."

Mitch will say it's nothing personal. He can probably keep the lawsuit separate from, say, purchasing nipple clamps for me!

"It's such a departure for us," I point out. "No one's going to believe *immaculate conception*, are they? You were at home in your kitchen—"

"I was at my friend's place," he clarifies.

"And—*bam*—you made outstanding chocolate sauce?" I try not to sound doubtful. "I simply wish you had created it here, even if you'd brought a friend *into* the test kitchen. Anything done on Henley property seems more legit."

Jules makes a face. "I don't need my creations to *seem legit*," he says, using air quotes. "They *are* legit. *Mon Dieu!*" He throws his hands in the air.

Then I perk up. "Wait. The friend you mentioned. The one who wanted chocolate sauce on her crepes. She's an eye witness." My heart starts pounding, but with relief this time. "She can swear you made the chocolate sauce, right?"

His expression clouds over. "We're not together any longer. I don't even know where she is."

*Jeez!* First his brother has an accident and now he's lost his girlfriend. Not exactly a happy-go-lucky chocolate maker. "I'm really sorry."

"It's OK. Short and sweet," he says a little wistfully.

Then I add, "No, I'm *really* sorry. We're back to no proof. Also, I didn't tell you but the short run of HLC that I took to Taste of Sydney were produced and bottled at the same factory that Mr. Franklin uses."

"*Merde.*" That single word, softly uttered, which means merely "shit" makes me more nervous than anything else. Even Jules knows we could be in trouble.

I open my mouth to ask whether he can get in contact with this mystery woman, when a factory-wide alarm goes off. Both our glances go to the red blinking light in the uppermost corner of the room.

"Now what?" I wonder.

Together, we go through the test kitchen, nothing on fire there, and head downstairs. All the commotion is at one of the production lines. Or rather, on the concrete floor beside one of the conveyor belts where someone has collapsed.

"What's happening?" I ask, when the small group of workers moves out of the way.

Jim is already there, kneeling beside a man whose name I don't know, although I feel that I should. Still wearing his hairnet, his face is ashen and he's clutching his stomach while moaning in pain.

"What happened?" I ask Jim.

"Don't know yet. An ambulance is on its way."

Another worker speaks up. "Eddie suddenly said he was feeling crook. Next thing I know, he keeled over and disappeared. I scrambled under the belt and flicked off his line."

"Good thinking," I say. Then I kneel beside Eddie, afraid of how ill he looks. "Can you tell us what happened?" I remember when my sister got appendicitis. Clover looked similarly pale and sweaty.

"I ate . . . off the line," he manages. "About ten minutes ago. Maybe less. Tasted a little . . . metallic."

My blood runs cold as I lock eyes first with Jim, and then swivel to Jules. We all know instantly this is going to be a major problem. Scrambling to my feet, I race for the wall phone and press in the code for the speaker system.

"Attention all employees. Do not eat any product. We have a possible serious contamination. Again, don't eat any chocolates from the line." Then I add, "Or from the sample room. Nothing. Anyone who does will be terminated."

*One way or another,* I think grimly.

Hoping my announcement turns out to be total overkill, I return to where Eddie's condition is deteriorating rapidly. He's writhing in pain, and his breathing is becoming shallow as he curls into himself, still clutching his stomach.

Panic threatens to overwhelm me, but I force it down. I am the CEO of Henley Confectionery. People are looking to me for leadership, even Jim. I don't think I've ever seen our factory manager look so freaked out.

"Anything helpful in a first aid kit?" I ask him while he stares at Eddie, a strong man in his mid-twenties.

Jim's eyes dart to mine, and he swallows. I doubt anything like this has ever happened in our manager's long tenure. Broken bones, head injuries from slipping, but toxic poisoning? *My guess is no.*

When he shrugs, still silent, I look around for the shift's employee health-officer, easily spotted by the special green-and-white vest.

"Della, grab that first aid kit." I point to one hanging on the pristine white dairy-tile wall beside a fire extinguisher. "Maybe there's something useful."

Jules, still beside me, is on his phone. "Don't induce vomiting. That's not considered safe any longer, especially if you don't know the cause."

"Not helpful," I mutter, hating inaction. "How can you search for proper treatment for an unknown problem?" I almost said *poison*.

Workers step aside as Della jogs back with a red-and-white plastic box under her arm and hands it to me. *Me!*

She shrugs, explaining what I already know. "I can do CPR and even stitch a wound, but . . ."

Hoping Eddie doesn't need her services in the next few minutes, I gingerly open the lid and rifle through the contents.

"Would an EpiPen help?" I wonder aloud. Perhaps he's having an allergic reaction.

"Eddie," I say, "do you have any food allergies?"

He doesn't speak, replying with the barest shake of his head.

Jules is still searching. "Can be dangerous to use if he doesn't need it. What else is in there? Any charcoal tablets?"

"Bingo!" I say. "Charcoal tablets! We need a glass of water," I add calmly. "Right now."

One of the other workers has a wide-mouth water bottle in her overalls pocket. She hands it to me. *Again, me!*

Soon, I've mixed up a charcoal cocktail, and with Jules holding up Eddie's head, we manage to get some into him. He swallows and grimaces.

"Stabbing cramps," he says, then he turns on his side and throws up.

So much for vomiting not being safe. Regardless, I stay with him and rub his back, thinking of Eddie's family, oblivious to what he's going through.

And then he passes out.

"He's turning blue," Della says in high-pitched tone.

"Shit!" I exclaim. She's right. His lips seem dusky blue. Placing my fingers on his neck, I find his pulse, which is erratic, but hasn't stopped. If anything, it's fast. What's more, I can see that he's still breathing.

Luckily, the sirens are in our parking lot. In another minute, we've turned Eddie over to the professionals, along with some of the candy he was eating.

This is the lowest day in the history of Henley Confectionery, at least that I'm aware of.

"This can't be happening," I whisper, but then I straighten my spine.

"Where's the QA log for this batch?" I ask Jim.

He logs into the system at the nearby computer terminal. "Batch number HE-527J. It's been on his belt for the past hour."

That doesn't mean whatever was in that chocolate isn't also an ingredient in other products, which employees are free to eat all damn day if they want to. Although no one ever eats more than a piece here and there, not after their first week anyway. That's when workers usually gorge themselves and vow never to eat chocolate again. Until the next day.

Standing beside Jim, we scroll through the quality assurance records for the batch in question. Everything looks normal until we reach the materials sourcing section. There's a notation of a last-minute switch in the freeze-dried raspberry powder cartridge. The previous one ran out a day earlier than expected, and it was switched yesterday.

I want to fist my hands, squeeze my eyes shut, and scream to the rafters high above. That's potentially a lot of confectionery. However, if the raspberry powder is the problem, then we've been extremely lucky that Eddie was the first to be taken ill. Even luckier that the likelihood is very low any of the chocolates have left the factory.

"When was this line due to be tested?" I ask Jim.

Every day, all day, chocolate products are put through quality checks, randomly but also consistently.

He looks toward Derek, the manager in charge of four production lines, including this one. Derek consults the schedule on his tablet. "Thirty-five minutes before the next test."

My phone rings, jolting me from my concentration and making me jump. Irritated by the spike in my adrenaline, I glance at it. It's Mitch.

*Super bad timing, buddy.* I almost want to text him an exclamation mark to go hand-in-hand with his stupid string of question marks from last night. Instead, I simply swipe to ignore the call. Then I contact Charlotte.

"We have a serious situation," I say without preamble before explaining what happened to Eddie. "I'm going to check the production logs next and see if any of this batch or any other raspberry-infused chocolates were produced from that cartridge of raspberry powder. If they've been packaged and shipped, which is unlikely given the time frame, we might need to issue a public recall."

"We'll cross that bridge if and when," she says. But I can hear the worry.

Not only are these chocolates a ticking time bomb if any have left the factory, but a recall will create a publicity nightmare of panicked customers.

Worse in my mind, what if someone right now is about to eat one and get sick?

"What can I do?" Charlotte asks.

"I'm sending copies of the logs to you. I'll look them over here and you do the same. We'll have to locate every chocolate that used any of the same ingredients as the batch on Eddie's line, until we verify it's the raspberry powder."

I pause, considering whether I've covered everything.

"And Charlotte, we can't miss a single damn chocolate. Is that clear?"

"Yes," she says, her voice small.

I sigh. I've never had an employee sound like that in response to me, and I don't like it.

"Thank you, Charlotte. I trust you right now to be my second pair of eyes."

"I hear you. I'll stay all night if I have to."

$♥$♥$♥$

It's just turned midnight when I pull into the underground parking of my Sydney apartment, utterly exhausted. The sound of the ambulance sirens had barely faded when I'd already sent the raspberry powder, along with half a dozen of the chocolates from Eddie's line to our in-house lab and to an independent one to figure out what the hell had gone so horribly wrong.

Then with Charlotte's help and our combined detective work, we determined that the freeze-dried raspberries had been used in only two products. We checked and double-checked. And none of those chocolates had left the factory. I think my brother on another continent could hear my loud whoop of happy relief.

On the other hand, to be safe, we're doing the same cross-reference for every other ingredient, raw or processed, in that particular batch, finding out what other products shared them.

That was more of a nightmare, basically tracking down every cocoa bean. Hopefully, by tomorrow, I'll have some answers from one of the labs. In the meantime, I shut down all the lines as if it's Christmas Eve.

And then, before the drive home, I went to the hospital to check on Eddie. He was stable, his wife was with him, and from what I could tell, none of the doctors think he's in danger of dying. Beyond that, we don't know. Not until tomorrow and the analysis comes back.

Yawning and stretching in the driver's seat, I recall that tomorrow is already today.

Climbing out of the Audi, I feel older than my years. My phone rings again, and Luke's face appears. I've already spoken with him twice today, but I answer anyway as I make my way indoors.

"How're you holding up?" he asks, concern clear in his voice.

"Fine. I won't know for sure until the labs do their thing, but if the freeze-dried powder's the culprit, then no recall will be needed. Corporate crisis averted. Here's hoping."

"And Eddie? You said before he's out of danger."

"Yes, still the case, but . . . ," I trail off, entering the elevator.

"But what?" he asks, sounding more brotherly than fellow top executive.

I finally confess how I'm feeling. "It seems like everything's falling apart at once."

Luke doesn't know about the chocolate sauce debacle or the wildly premature poured concrete slab at the factory for a production line that will never happen. He also doesn't know how my emotions have been wrung out of me by one Mitch Franklin, or his lawsuit threat.

Naturally, Luke focuses on the two things he does know. The takeover threat and the poisoned employee, and says that we're handling both just fine.

"I'm also on probation for the sugar fiasco. You remember that we used a contaminated shipment, right? Happened to be on some super important chocolates."

"Frankly, I'm stunned they had the gall to put you on probation," he says quietly.

"At the time, I was, too," I agree. "But now I intend to get through it and prove them wrong. Unfortunately, I can't seem to catch a break."

"Is there more?" Luke asks, sounding like he doesn't want to know.

*Ugh!* I never should've kept any of my grand schemes a secret from my brother.

"You probably haven't heard, but the factory accepted delivery of a burned batch of cocoa beans."

"We don't use *pre-roasted* beans," he says, as though they're disgusting.

"It was a pet project, an expensive one," I confess. "And the board doesn't know about that yet, either."

Silence. Obviously, he's processing the growing list of fuck-ups. When I've reached my front door, he says, "You've got this. And you've got me right beside you."

"Thanks. I'll keep you posted."

But because he's my older brother, he can't leave it at that. "How about you tell me shit in advance instead? Or at least run your ideas by me?"

"I'm not asking your permission," I say, "for my decisions." *What an ineffective leader I'd be!*

"I don't have the power to give it," he snaps back. "But I can be a good sounding board. No one knows this job and this company better than us, except Dad. Even Gramps was dealing with an entirely different animal than what we have now."

"You're right. Sorry, I know you're trying to help."

After ending the call, I sink onto my couch, too wretched even to ask my smart-wired home to turn on a light. Sitting alone, going over the emergency at the factory, personally administering the activated charcoal, I feel a lump form in my throat. I'm capable of a lot, but this day stretched my limits.

Despite the call from Luke, who understands the pressure but is ten thousand miles away, I feel utterly alone. I could call Clover or my mother, both are also half a world away, but their unquestionable, familial support isn't what I want. I think it will come with platitudes and verbal pats on the head.

Scrolling through my contacts, I pause at various names of friends, wanting someone who really *sees* me. Not one of them, not even the Belgian master chocolatier I spent hours talking to at a European conference last year, is who I want to talk to.

Despite everything—seeing Mitch with another woman, his possible lawsuit against my company—he's the only person I want to be with right now. We connected on so many levels over the weekend. I dial before I can stop myself.

*Am I crazy? Or just exhausted?*

I nearly cancel the call.

I never get the chance.

"Lark."

When he answers on the first ring, simply saying my name as though he's relieved, the sound of his voice breaks something in me.

"I need you," I whisper, surprising myself with the raw honesty.

Without even a split second of hesitation, Mitch says, "I'm there in ten."

# 18

## Mitch

"I break a few traffic rules as I navigate Sydney's Point Piper. The urgency in Lark's voice—that broken whisper of "I need you"—has me gripping the steering wheel like it might fly out of my hands.

After days of silence following her puzzling text that she was "done with me and my games," nothing could stop me from answering her call. Obviously, something has gone very wrong in her world.

The night air whips through my open windows as I navigate the final turn to her building. My mind keeps cycling through possibilities. *Is she hurt? Is this about her company's takeover threat? Did something happen with her family?*

Pulling into the visitor parking, I kill the engine and skip the elevator. Taking the stairs two at a time until I'm at her door, I find it's not even locked. When I let myself in, the place is in darkness.

"Lark?"

Flicking on the front hall switch, I make my way through to the living room. In the silent shadows, I see her on the couch.

"Alexa, turn on living room light."

Lark rises off the couch, and the absolutely defeated look on her face makes my heart clench. It's not her wrinkled work clothes or her smudged makeup. It's her haunted expression.

Without a word, I close the gap between us and pull her into my arms. She melts against me, her body trembling slightly as she presses her face into my chest.

"Hey," I whisper against her hair. "I'm here."

She doesn't respond, just clings tighter for a few long moments. Eventually, when Lark tries to pull away, I barely loosen my hold before she slides from my grasp back onto the sofa. Settling beside her, I wrap my arm around her shoulders and wait.

For several minutes, we sit in silence. I don't push her to talk. Her breathing gradually steadies, and I feel the tension in her muscles begin to ease. My fingers trace circles on her shoulder, a gentle reminder that she's not alone.

"I've had the day from hell," she finally says, her voice small and raw.

"I figured."

She shifts, tucking her bare feet beneath her and leaning more heavily against my side.

"One of our line workers at the factory got poisoned by our . . ." Her voice hitches like she's about to cry before she finishes, "Our chocolate."

*Jesus.* That explains the devastation in her voice. "Is he OK?"

"For now." She says nothing more.

Picking up her limp hand, I intertwine our fingers. "How did it happen?"

"Dunno. He's lucky, though. It could've been . . ." She doesn't finish the thought.

I squeeze her hand. "But it wasn't. You handled it."

"How do you know?"

"Because you're Lark Henley," I say simply.

"I did handle it," she says quietly. "I happened to be at the factory."

Then she groans. "What's coming next?"

There's a vulnerability to her question that I've never heard from her before. Lark doesn't do vulnerability—at least not *outside* the bedroom.

"Everything's falling apart, Mitch. Everything I touch lately turns to shit."

"Not everything," I say, bringing our joined hands to my lips. "Not this."

She makes a sound that might be a laugh or a sob. "I would say, 'give it time,' but I think it's too late."

"Too late?" I ask. "I'm here."

She shakes her head and draws her hand slowly from mine.

"I shouldn't have called you. You're not mine. I'm not yours. I just didn't know . . . I just . . ." Lark falls silent.

The self-doubt in her voice twists me up inside. This isn't the confident, take-charge woman who stormed into my life. I turn to face her properly, bringing my hands up to frame her face. Her gaze is down, though, and all I see are long eyelashes on her pale cheeks.

"Look at me," I say.

A second or two later, she does. Her eyes are pools of golden-bronze shadows.

"Have you eaten?" I ask, realizing she probably hasn't had a proper meal all day.

"No, but—"

"Let me cook for you. Take a hot shower and it'll be ready when you come out."

She doesn't move, so I stand and pull her to her feet. Then I lead her through her bedroom, ignoring the lightning-hot memories.

Pushing her gently into her bathroom, with its carved stone sink and huge rain shower, I leave her standing motionless in the middle of luxury.

Turning to leave, I realize she's still shut down, like a dog who's been left at a shelter.

"Come on, lady. Snap out of it." My tone is no longer cajoling. I'm switching into my executive chef mode. With a no-nonsense manner, I rotate her to face me, unbutton her blouse, and slide it off her arms.

I have to take a beat before unzipping her skirt and tugging it down her slim legs that seem to go on forever. Trying not to get turned on and failing, I keep my eyes on her face while she simply stares back with soulful eyes.

"Fine," I mutter, as if she's challenging me.

Undressing her *is* a challenge. I intend to keep my fingers neutral and not trail them across any part of her as I battle my own baser nature. Whatever I have to do, including close my eyes, I don't intend to take advantage of Lark in this fragile state.

With my gaze locked on hers, I reach around and unhook her lacy bra, drawing it down her shoulders and letting it fall. Her eyes widen slightly, but that's the only reaction. I wish mine were as subtle. My cock is rock hard, and I do, in fact, close my eyes when I strip her panties down her legs. My blood pounding through my veins, it's a relief to turn away and yank the handle in her shower.

About to shove her under the spray even though the water is doubtless still cool, I halt when she puts her hands up to ward me off.

"OK," she says. "I got this."

Nodding, still keeping my eyes averted, I'm already closing the door behind me when she says, "Thanks, Mitch."

With a smile on my face, I stride back down the hall to her kitchen. Flipping on the lights and opening the refrigerator . . . *Damn!* Does this woman ever eat? The fridge contains little more than condiments, some wilted greens, and—*thank God*—eggs.

In the pantry, I push aside dried pasta and a box of cereal, grabbing a small can of spicy chopped peppers. It's enough.

By the time I hear the shower shut off, I've put a lid over what is essentially an omelet, although I managed the density and height of a frittata thanks to the last-minute discovery of a can of evaporated milk. I don't plate it until Lark emerges from her bedroom, looking less run down, but by no means happy.

Her still wet hair is pulled up into a bun, and she's wearing pajamas. A deep burgundy, short-sleeved silky top and matching shorts that show off her legs. *Have mercy!*

Despite her previous distress, the sight of her, mixed with the vivid memory of having recently stripped her bare, makes my pulse race.

"Smells delicious," she says without enthusiasm, climbing onto a kitchen stool at her island as if she's climbing Mt. Everest. Her weary eyes track the fragrant egg concoction, dusted with salt and pepper, as I slide it onto a plate and push it in front of her.

"I didn't know eggs could look so fancy," she says softly.

"You had the essentials," I say, leaning my hips against the counter opposite. "Eat. You'll feel more human."

She nods and takes a bite. Her eyes close briefly as she savors it. "God, that's good."

"Comfort food," I say, watching as some color returns to her cheeks with each bite. "Better than an energy bar for dinner."

That earns me a small smile. "You don't know how close you are to the truth. At the factory, none of us wanted to snack on candy. At least not Henley confectionery. Luckily, in my car, I had a granola bar, and at the hospital, I bought a cup of coffee for the ride home." Then she notices there's only one plate. "You're not eating?"

"I ate at the restaurant after the last service ended, about two hours ago."

An inscrutable expression covers her face. She continues to eat. Because the silence isn't strained or tense, I don't try to fill it while I wash the pan and cooking utensils, leaving them to dry on some paper towels I've stacked on her peninsula, since she doesn't have a dish rack.

Eventually, she says, "Do you eat dinner at Franklin 6 most nights?"

I shrug. "No. I eat at the bar, too, or I try my competitors, or I cook. If I'm already at the restaurant, yes. I don't work in the kitchen that often, though. Maybe twice a week. But I use an office there to run all of my restaurants. I do the same wherever I am, find some desk space. I work better there than at home where I'm more likely to test recipes."

My long-winded answer, rambling to distract her, yields nothing but a nod. I don't press her for details about her day or what pushed her over the edge, knowing she'll share when she's ready. And I don't want to stare while she eats. Instead, I take a few minutes to wander around her apartment, noticing things I didn't before.

The minimalist furniture in shades of tan and dark-brown seem classic Henley. I know she shared the spacious place with her brother, so the art on the walls could be his style for all I know. There are framed photos on the mantel, one of her grandparents, one of her parents whom I recognize from photos at the ranch. In another, Lark is about a decade younger, sandwiched between her brother and sister, all displaying the expected family resemblance.

Even knowing she and her brother have owned this apartment for years, the lack of food or even a dish rack makes it seem like a temporary rental rather than her home.

When she sets down her fork, her plate utterly empty, I return to the kitchen. "Better?"

"Yes." She's still a shadow of herself, way too quiet. Her gaze meets mine as I reach for her plate. "Thank you for cooking. For coming over. For . . ." she gestures vaguely, "not asking a million questions right away."

"You're welcome." Rinsing her plate, I leave it in the sink. When I turn back, she's watching me with that same unreadable look I saw earlier.

"What's up?" I ask. "I don't mean regarding Henley Confectionery. I mean us and that text you sent."

"I saw you," she begins, her voice hesitant. "You were dining with someone at your restaurant, holding hands."

*I was dining with someone? Oh!*

"You came to the restaurant?" *Dumb question.* Obviously she did. My brain recalls the setting, the candlelight, Camille's dress, the table for two.

She blinks and waits.

"If I'd seen you," I tell her, "you would've had no reason to be upset. I'd have introduced you. What you saw was nothing but a dinner between old . . . friends."

"Friends?" she asks, catching my hesitation.

I shouldn't sugarcoat it. "That was Camille," I say, rubbing my hand around the back of my neck, recalling the weird-ass, unwelcome kiss at the end and very glad Lark hadn't seen it.

"She's an ex-girlfriend from culinary school days in Paris. She graduated and then became a head chef. Yesterday, she showed up unexpectedly."

Lark's expression tightens almost imperceptibly. "The hand-holding looked pretty cozy for an *unexpected ex.*"

It's such a non-issue, I laugh. A short one, but Lark bristles, and I realize I'm not being fair. This wonderful woman, who's had a crappy day, doesn't know that I feel absolutely nothing for Camille. Although knowing how it bothered Lark to see her with me means there's hope for us.

"Actually, before she touched my hand, she made a business proposition." I move back around the island, taking the chair next to hers. "And before you ask, yes, she tried to make it more, but I turned her down flat."

"Really?" Lark's tone is skeptical, but there's a flicker of belief in her eyes. I can work with that.

"Really," I confirm. "The only woman I'm interested in called me at midnight because she needed me. And here I am."

She studies me for a long moment, then her shoulders relax slightly.

"Here you are," she echoes, her voice little more than a whisper.

"Now," I say, reaching for her hand, "if you want, tell me about this day from hell."

The story spills out of her then—the employee collapsing, the frantic search for the source, the fear of a public recall. As she talks, I understand more fully why she looked so shattered when I arrived. It wasn't just the incident itself, but the weight of responsibility, the dread of dragging down her family's legacy. The idea of a billion consumers suddenly not wanting to buy Henley chocolates.

"You did everything right, Lark. You were there, and you took immediate action."

"But it shouldn't have happened at all." Her hand tightens around mine. "None of the problems I've had lately should've happened. First the sugar contamination, then the burned cocoa beans, this HLC mess with you, and now poisoned chocolate? The board already put me on probation after the sugar incident." She shakes her head. "This could be the final straw."

I blink in surprise. "They put you on probation? You never told me."

"I was trying to handle it on my own." A rueful smile crosses her face.

"How's that working out for you?" I ask gently.

Her laugh is small but real. "About as well as you'd expect." She leans forward, her forehead resting against my shoulder. "I'm so tired, Mitch."

I stroke her damp hair, feeling a swell of protectiveness. "Then let's get you to bed."

She gazes up at me with big eyes and a wry smile, and I shake my head.

"So you can sleep. I have a feeling you've got another busy day tomorrow, once you get the lab reports back."

Lark stands, wavering slightly with exhaustion, and reaches for my hand.

"Stay with me?"

She didn't have to ask. The only reason I didn't offer was not wanting her to think I was making an ill-timed move.

Nodding, I squeeze her hand, leading the way into the bedroom. In here, we don't bother with the lamps. The light behind us spills across her massive bed with its satin duvet, and I swallow, feeling awkward. This is not a usual situation for me.

When she goes into the bathroom and I hear the sound of her electric toothbrush, I strip down to my boxer briefs.

"I have spare brush heads," she calls through the half-open door.

By the time I've brushed my teeth, she has snuggled under the covers. But she hasn't conked out yet. Instead, she watches me with those sad eyes. Sliding in beside her, I'm careful to leave some space between us. The last thing she needs right now is to feel pressured.

To my surprise, she immediately shifts closer, molding her body against mine. Soon, I've got an arm around her and am cradling her head on my shoulder. Her hair smells of coconut shampoo, and her skin is warm through the thin silk of her pajamas.

"This is nice," she murmurs, one hand resting on my heart. "Just being with you."

"I know," I say, pressing a kiss to the top of her head. I'm still dealing with the weirdness of being in a woman's bed without having sex. *A platonic sleep-over!* But the simple intimacy of holding her feels more significant than I expected. We've had wild, passionate sex on multiple occasions, yet this quiet moment of trust connects us more profoundly than offering one another our bodies.

"I'm sorry I'm so tired," she mumbles. "Didn't sleep well last night."

Her breathing gradually slows and deepens. When I think she's asleep, she whispers, "I didn't want to call anyone else."

The admission tugs at something deep inside me. "I'll always come when you call, Lark."

She makes a small sound of contentment before drifting off completely, her body going limp against mine. I lie awake for a while longer, listening to her breathe, feeling the steady rise and fall of her chest. Eventually, my own eyes grow heavy, and I let sleep claim me, still cradling her close.

$♥$♥$♥$

I wake to subtle movements beside me. Morning light filters through the partially closed blinds, painting stripes across the bed. For a moment, I'm disoriented, then remember where I am. And who I'm with.

Lark is awake, propped up on one elbow, watching me with an intensity that makes my pulse quicken. Her eyes are clear now, the haunted look replaced by an entirely different kind of energy.

"Hey," I say, my voice sounding rough with sleep. I clear my throat. "How are you feeling?"

"Better," she says, trailing a finger down my chest. "Much better."

The temperature in the room seems to spike as her hand continues its lazy exploration, moving lower across my abdomen, circling my navel. I catch her wrist, searching her face. "Lark . . ."

"I know what I want, Mitch," she says, her voice husky. "I want to forget everything else. For a little while anyway." She leans down, her lips hovering above mine. "I want you to make me forget my own name. You've done it before."

236

Her kiss is electric, sending a current of desire zapping straight through me to all parts south. There's a hunger in the way she presses against me, a desperation that matches the fire building in my own veins. My restraint from earlier evaporates when she straddles my hips, her silk shorts riding up to reveal the smooth skin of her thighs.

"Please," she says. "Take control. I don't want to think. I don't want to decide. I just want to feel."

The raw need in her voice triggers something primal in me. In one swift movement, I roll us over, pinning her beneath me. Her eyes widen with surprise and unmistakable arousal.

"Is this what you want?" I ask, my voice a low growl as I capture both her wrists in one hand, stretching them above her head.

"Yes." She breathes out the one word while arching against me.

Taking my time despite her urgency, I slide my free hand under her silk top to caress her breasts, feeling each nipple harden beneath my touch. She whimpers, tugging to free her arms, testing my grip.

"Patience," I murmur, lowering my head to kiss her neck. Quickly, the kiss becomes a nibble. I manage to undo the silk-covered buttons of her pajama top with one hand and part it, revealing her body, inch by delicious inch. Each newly exposed patch of skin gets thorough attention from my mouth and hands until she's writhing beneath me, breathless with wanting and straining against my hold of her wrists.

Unfortunately, I have to release her arms. Tossing the sheet and blanket to the side, she groans at the agonizing lack of speed as I strip off her silken shorts, sliding them slowly down her legs. Lark groans when my fingers glide along her inner thighs to her ankles, before I toss the burgundy silk aside. Removing my boxer briefs much more quickly, I let my erection spring free and climb between her legs.

"Please, Mitch," she begs, reaching for me. "I need you inside me."

But I'm not done with her yet. Parting her legs with a light touch, I settle between her thighs and raise her knees, threading my arms under them. From this position, pinned at the hips, she has no option but to splay her legs, while I open her pussy lips.

With the first touch of my tongue to her clit, Lark's back arches off the bed. At the first flick of my tongue, she cries out. I devour her like a man starved, savoring her taste as she builds toward release. When she's about to crest, I pull back, earning a cry of frustration. She even slaps the sheet beneath her.

"Not yet," I tell her, moving up her body to capture her mouth in a fierce kiss. She tastes herself on my lips, moaning into my mouth. "Turn over," I command softly.

She complies without hesitation, getting onto her hands and knees before looking back at me over her shoulder. The sight of her like this—offering herself completely—nearly undoes me. I reach between her legs and let my fingers glide along her drenched pussy, making her buck. She lowers her head to one of the pillows and screams into it, making me grin at her frustration.

My cock in hand, I tease her with the tip, watching her fingers clutch at the sheets in anticipation. Or desperation.

"Now, Mitch," she demands, pushing back against me.

I grasp her hips firmly, holding her still. And then, to up the ante, I slap her ass.

"I'm in charge, remember?"

Her whimper turns to a sharp gasp of pleasure as I finally thrust into her, roughly filling her until I'm sheathed up to my balls. Then I set a deliberate pace—deep, thorough strokes that have her meeting each thrust with increasing force.

She lifts her head. "Please," she begs.

She's playing the game, and doesn't want to direct me, but I know what she wants. What she needs. "I'm going to fuck you harder."

Again, she moans into the pillow, and I feel her sweet, slick channel clench around my cock.

"And I'm going to go faster."

"Yes," she hisses. "Yes, please."

Increasing the tempo, I'm driven by her frenzied cries and the way her body grips mine. Reaching around, I slide my fingers between her pussy lips and circle the delicate bundle of nerves with my thumb in time to my thrusts.

She's still on the edge, squirming. Recalling her words from the first night, I pinch her clit.

"Oh, yes," she screams, her inner walls beginning to tighten around me. "Don't stop. Please. Don't. Stop."

"Come now, Lark," I urge, feeling my own release approaching. "Let everything else go."

Releasing her clit so the blood rushes back, I go back tugging and stroking the sensitive area around it.

Her orgasm catches her like a wave, her entire body shuddering. The sound of her climax, as she cries out first nonsense, then my name, the feel of her pulsing around me, sends me over the edge. Following her into ecstasy, I bury myself deep as my release explodes.

Afterward, we collapse onto the bed, our limbs entwined, hearts racing in tandem. Gathering her close, I press a kiss to her damp forehead.

"Did you forget?" I ask, a hint of smugness in my voice.

She laughs, the sound light and free—a complete transformation from the broken woman who called me last night.

"Forget what?" she asks with mock innocence.

I stroke her hair. "Mission accomplished."

We lie there in comfortable silence for several minutes, basking in the afterglow. Eventually, she shifts to look up at me, her expression suddenly serious. *Uh-oh.*

"I've been thinking about something," she says, tracing patterns on my chest with her fingertip.

"*Hmm?*" I say encouragingly, although I don't really want to step back into reality so quickly. And I can tell by her tone that we're diving right into the thick of something.

"This thing with Jules and the chocolate sauce." She props herself up on one elbow. "That's why I was at the factory. I spoke to him yesterday, right before the chaos with Eddie."

I stiffen slightly, remembering our last conversation about the sauce hadn't ended well. "And?"

"He swears he created it independently. Jules was making it for his girlfriend at the time. To put on their crepes."

This is new information, and it totally surprises me. "I guess if she can corroborate that he came up with this," I begin. But Lark shakes her head.

"First of all, she may have had some small input, like asking for chocolate sauce in the first place and maybe suggesting some of the ingredients. Secondly," Lark hesitates, then finishes, "she's not around any longer."

"Convenient that this mysterious girlfriend cannot confirm or deny," I say, unable to keep the edge from my voice.

Lark sighs. "I know how it sounds. I promise you I do. But Jules has never given me or anyone at Henley reason to doubt him." She hesitates. "I trust him, Mitch. I wish you could trust me enough to believe what I believe."

Sitting up against the headboard, I run a hand through my hair. "You're asking me to let it go, to chill out about something that means the world to me. Not because of the money it makes, but because of my father."

My chest tightens at the memory. "Even when I had nothing more than a food truck, and before that when I was studying to be a Cordon Bleu chef, I already had that chocolate sauce. It didn't have a name at the time, but it was my family's."

"I understand what it means to you," she says, reaching for my hand. "But it's possible that a master chef and a master chocolatier could arrive at similar formulations independently."

"The odds are astronomical, Lark." I pull my hand away gently. "Coconut sugar instead of cane? The precise balance of vanilla to chocolate? The exact technique for the silky texture, meaning boiling it for the same amount of time? It's not just one coincidence—it's too many."

"I know it sounds crazy, but Jules is simply that good." Her eyes plead with me.

Looking at her, all soft and warm in the morning light, I want to believe her. I want to give her this. But the doubt gnaws at me, persistent and unrelenting.

"I wish I could accept that explanation," I say. "But I can't. Not when it comes to this."

The light in her eyes dims. "Where does that leave us?"

It's the question I've been avoiding. I swing my legs over the side of the bed, feeling a sudden need for distance. "I don't know."

"Mitch . . ." She reaches for me, but I'm already standing, gathering my clothes.

"We're incredible together, Lark. When it's just us, like this." I gesture to the rumpled bed. "But then daylight comes, and we're right back where we started."

She sits up, clutching the sheet to her chest. "Why does it have to be this way?"

"You believe your chocolate maker." I pull on my boxers, then my jeans. "I believe my sauce recipe was stolen. We're at an impasse."

She doesn't argue, which somehow makes it worse. The silence stretches between us while I finish dressing.

"So that's it?" she asks finally, her voice wavering. "We . . . walk away or do you sue me first?"

I turn to look at her—this woman who has somehow become essential to me in such a short time.

"You are not going to produce HLC, and I won't sue you. Agreed?"

With the slightest hesitation, she nods.

"As for us," I say, "I don't know. It was never going to be more than one night, right?"

Her eyes glistening, she says, "Right."

"We could keep doing that one night over, but I—"

"But you have more restaurants to open somewhere in the world," she reminds me.

Leaning down, I press my lips to her forehead. To hell with prudence, I full-on kiss her mouth and hope it expresses to her how I feel. Eventually, I draw back.

"For what it's worth, last night meant a lot. Having you call me. Letting me be there for you when you needed someone. I'm honored."

"It meant a lot to me, too." She catches my hand, squeezing it briefly before letting go.

I consider offering to be her sex partner for the time I'm here in Sydney, as long as we promise to leave everything else at the bedroom door. But we both understand that won't be enough. We'll want more. We'll probably find ourselves in a relationship. I'll want her to back me over any employee, and she'll want me to let go of a principle that I simply can't relinquish.

Ultimately, I'll resent the hell out of her for letting Julian Cartier continue to work for her.

But as I walk away, there's no anger, no dramatic accusations from either one of us. We seem to share a quiet acknowledgment that sometimes wanting isn't enough.

At her bedroom door, I pause for another look. She's still in bed, watching me go with those expressive eyes that hide nothing.

"Take care of yourself, Lark Henley," I say softly.

"You too, Mitch Franklin."

I clear the thick emotion from my throat. "Call if you need me."

I hate to think of her calling me, needing me, once I'm thousands of miles away.

She merely smiles.

When her front door closes behind me with a soft click, I'm left in the hallway, wondering how something that feels so perfect can be so impossible.

# 19

## Lark

At 9:59 a.m., the test results arrive via secure email from our own quality-control lab. I nearly spill my coffee in my haste to open the attached PDF, my heart hammering against my ribs. Charlotte hovers in the doorway of my office, her face a mask of carefully controlled anxiety.

"Come in," I say, waving her toward the chair across from me. "They're here."

She crosses the room in three quick strides but doesn't sit. She comes around my desk to stand beside me as I click through the file. The first page confirms what we already know—the chocolates from Eddie's line contained a contaminant. My eyes scan over the chemical jargon, searching for the culprit.

"Sodium nitrite," I read aloud, my brow furrowing. "High concentrations of it."

Charlotte looks puzzled. "Isn't that used in curing meats?"

"Yes," I say slowly, scrolling further down. "And it has no business being in our chocolates." The report goes on to detail the effects, how sodium nitrite oxidizes iron in the blood's hemoglobin, converting it to methemoglobin, which can't carry oxygen.

"As oxygen delivery plummets," I read aloud, "tissues begin to suffocate, even if the lungs are working perfectly."

The words on the screen blur slightly as I recall Eddie's face—the bluish tinge to his lips, the way he clutched at his stomach. It all makes horrific sense now.

"That's why he turned blue," Charlotte murmurs, reading over my shoulder. "Cyanosis."

I nod grimly. "The hospital report confirms methemoglobinemia. They treated him with oxygen and methylene blue." I close my eyes briefly, a wave of relief washing through me. The activated charcoal I managed to get into him before he threw up helped in his recovery.

"I feel a little sick imagining what might have happened if Eddie hadn't eaten a chocolate," Charlotte says, moving around my desk to collapse into one of the chairs. "He didn't realize he was a guinea pig, but think of how many people he might've saved."

A notification flashes in the lower right of my screen. "The independent lab results just arrived," I tell her.

She waits while I scan the document. "The report confirms the contamination was specifically in the freeze-dried raspberry powder." I shake my head at the analysis of the contaminant's concentration. "At these levels, it wasn't accidental cross-contamination."

An eerie silence descends between us as the implications sink in. Someone deliberately contaminated our product. The thought sends ice water through my veins.

"Why would someone poison our confectionery?" Charlotte finally voices the question hanging in the air. "It could have easily killed a child."

I shake my head, the pieces refusing to fit together in any logical way.

"I have no idea. Although, even without Eddie's unwitting help, we would've tested that batch within the next half hour. The sodium nitrite would've been detected and all the product scrapped. If someone wanted to sicken a bunch of people, there are easier ways than contaminating a single ingredient."

"Unless the goal wasn't to cause massive harm," Charlotte says, "but targeted disruption."

"To make me look incompetent. To undermine my authority," I suggest.

The takeover bid suddenly looms larger in my mind.

"We need to trace that raspberry powder," I say, straightening in my chair. "From production to delivery, and then every step from the moment it entered our facility."

Charlotte is already on her feet. "I'll call Jim and have him pull the delivery records."

"And security footage," I call to her retreating back.

Forwarding the report to our legal team, I add a note about potential sabotage. The word feels melodramatic as I type it, like something from a bad corporate thriller. *But what else could this be?*

I pace the length of my office, thoughts racing. First the sugar contamination, then the burned cocoa beans, now this. Each incident on its own could be explained away as bad luck or supplier error. But taken together?

The only one that can't be neatly tied in is the inconceivable coincidence of the chocolate sauce.

Charlotte returns, her face grim but resolute. "Jim's already reviewing the footage. And our factory security team is doing a full onsite investigation."

"Good." I pause, staring out at the Sydney skyline. "Do you think the lab can make any connection between these results and the sugar contamination?"

"You think they're connected?" she asks.

I shrug. "I don't know how, but I guess it's worth checking."

She nods and makes another note. "The board is going to want a statement."

"I'll handle them," I say, though my stomach clenches at the thought.

Another crisis, another explanation. My probation already leaves my position as CEO hanging by a thread. Anxiety over my place in the company is a decidedly odd feeling, since I've never before feared for my job. Not any single one of them that I've performed at Henley from the time I was a teenager. From a factory worker, learning how every line works, to the most boring time I spent in the accounting department.

We spend the rest of the day basically spinning our wheels. We trace the path of the raspberry powder, establishing that it was delivered a couple weeks ago, passed initial quality control, and was securely stored until yesterday. When the other cartridge ran out ahead of schedule, the contaminated one was loaded into the machine.

"I wonder how they're doing with the security footage," I say to Charlotte. "Call Jim and tell him to make sure to look at the ingredients room. I want to know everyone who entered that room since the raspberry powder was delivered. And I want our remaining stock isolated and secured as evidence."

After giving the lab time to compare the two contaminations, instead of my suspicions crystallizing, my confusion increases.

"Look at this," I say, pointing to the chemical composition analysis. "The sugar contamination is still considered to be a naturally occurring one. Geosmin is simply soil bacteria. For all we know, it happened during the sugar beets' farming, and we were really unlucky. But this . . ." I tap the screen showing the sodium nitrite levels. "This is different. More targeted, more precise."

Charlotte's eyes widen as she follows my logic. "You think someone's escalating their attacks on Henley's reputation?"

"I think someone's getting desperate," I say. "To me, it's clear that the intent is to drive down the value of the company. And there's only one benefit to a weakened company—the ease with which we can be taken over."

By the end of the day, between the two of us, we're sure it's a case of sabotage. Unfortunately, the security footage from today and yesterday shows nothing overtly suspicious. But they have a lot of hours to go through because I told them not to stop until they find something.

Of course the visitors' log has no one suspicious listed. The only visitors in a month have been the safety inspector and a group of children from a day camp for a tour and tasting. We're checking out the two adults who came with them nonetheless. But it's not like I thought some corporate spy would write in the log and say, "Had a great time on the factory tour."

When my phone rings with Luke's number, I answer immediately, putting him on speaker.

"Any news?" he asks without preamble.

I lock eyes with Charlotte over my desk. "Sodium nitrite. High concentration. Someone put it there intentionally. We're treating it as deliberate sabotage."

"Jesus, Lark, this is serious," he says.

"No shit." *Did he think I thought it was a game?*

"Hey, Luke, it's Charlotte," our VP says. They had a great working relationship when he was CEO here. "We're going with the theory this is connected to the takeover attempt, so you should keep your eyes open in New York."

"Agreed," Luke says. "I actually hope it is. Otherwise, what the hell is going on in Sydney?"

He's quiet for a moment. "Lark, Dad's already worried. When he finds out this was intentional, he's going to want you to fly back to New York. Why don't you let me handle

Sydney until this blows over? We'll switch places for . . . two months, tops."

My jaw clenches. "I'm not running away."

"No one's suggesting you're running," Luke says carefully. "Just a strategic retreat."

"It amounts to the same thing." I take a deep breath, steadying my voice. "If I leave now, it looks like I can't handle the pressure. The board already has doubts. Luke, I need to stay and fight this."

Charlotte silently gives me a thumbs up from across the desk.

"You're sure?" Luke sounds conflicted. "I'm worried about you, too. For Dad, you're his baby girl. For me, you're my little sister. Put yourself in our shoes."

"I appreciate both of your concern, but no one has come after me personally. This is about the takeover and weakening us to the point we're happy to be bought. They'll pretend to be our benefactors, pushing the narrative that new ownership would restore any public concerns over the safety and quality of our confectionery."

He's silent a moment. "I think you could be right."

"Absolutely," I say, but my mind is racing ahead, inadvertently spilling the proverbial beans. "Besides, I still need to handle the HLC situation. I can't do that from New York."

Watching Charlotte's eyes widen, I realize I've said something I shouldn't, forgetting for a moment who knows what.

"HLC? What's that?" Luke's voice sharpens with curiosity.

I sigh, recalling I've been keeping yet another crisis from my brother. "Henley Liquid Chocolate. Our newest product that I was showcasing at Taste of Sydney," I explain. "It went over like a champion."

It would've been awesome to pull this out of my hat, like a magician's bunny, *a big chocolate one!*

Charlotte waves a silent goodbye and closes my office door behind her. She's not abandoning me so much as letting two siblings hash it out. Luke's not going to be happy at being kept in the dark about any of this.

"Don't you think an entirely new product is rather a large secret to be sitting on," he says, not sounding warm and fuzzy at all. "I mean, if it's a go, then all of us in New York should be in on it."

"It's definitely *not* a go." Just saying so makes me sad because I had such high hopes for this.

Feeling a tension headache forming, I rub my temple. "I made a horrible discovery at the event. Turns out our sauce is identical—and I mean completely identical—to a popular product called Franklin Darkly."

"Never heard of it." Luke is on the move, by the sound of his footsteps. I can picture him walking down one of the Henley office hallways in bleak, wintry Manhattan, and am glad I'm in warm and sunny Sydney.

"Maybe not, but you'll most likely have heard of its creator, Mitch Franklin."

"The restaurant guy?" Luke's tone shifts as he's realizing I'm talking about impinging on a heavy hitter.

"The very same. He owns Franklin Restaurant Group. And he's not happy about the situation, which is putting it mildly. He's threatened to sue."

Luke makes a scoffing sound. "You know as well as I do how rare a recipe patent is, so I'm assuming this guy is blowing smoke."

I wince. Mitch is definitely serious as a heart attack.

"How'd he find out anyway?" Luke asks.

Might as well tell him the truth. "Because I personally gave him a sample at Taste of Sydney."

My brother lets out a low whistle. "Trouble is certainly dogging your heels, sis. How the hell did that happen?"

"That's what I'm trying to figure out. Jules swears he created it independently, with some input from a girlfriend who's no longer in the picture. They apparently made it to put over their crepes."

"His word is good," Luke says. "I trust him completely."

"Agreed. Personally, I think it's the mother of all coincidences. But the recipe is identical, down to using coconut sugar instead of cane sugar and Mexican vanilla."

"That's insane," Luke says. "We've never used coconut sugar before." His tone makes it clear he doesn't believe in coincidences that extensive. Then trying to make me feel better, he adds, "At least you didn't get into production."

I sigh. "Only as far as breaking ground on the factory expansion for a bottling line."

"Lark!" he exclaims, and I wince again, feeling every inch the little sister who has screwed up.

After a pause, he asks, "How far did you get?"

"The concrete pad, but I also put in an order for bottling equipment that's only two-thirds refundable." Then I confess the last nugget. "Even worse is that I used the same local factory for production and bottling of our small test run that Mitch . . . Mr. Franklin uses for all his production in Australia."

"*Oof,*" Luke says. "Bad luck!"

"Massive understatement," I say.

"Is Franklin threatening legal action?"

"He was. We've come to an understanding, as long as I don't produce HLC."

"Pity. Henley Liquid Chocolate has a nice ring to it," Luke says, commiserating with me. "Was it worth all the trouble?"

For a moment, I think he means my short fling with Mitch. I nearly blurt, *God, yes!* Then my I realize what he means. "HLC would've been spectacular. First of all, it's out-of-this-world delicious. Secondly, Mitch sells a ton from his restaurants and online. Imagine how we could sell something like that with our distribution channels for all things chocolate already in place."

"You're right." I can almost hear Luke's wheels turning. "Can we switch out an ingredient without losing the quality and taste? Or maybe he'd be interested in licensing his sauce to us and letting us rebrand it."

"No, I'm a billion percent sure Mitch wouldn't go for that. Franklin Darkly is important to him. He has his pride, and then there's the fact his dad originally developed it before Mitch tweaked it. It's a family legacy issue."

Into the short silence, I think I may've given away my hand as to how close Mitch and I have become. Sure enough, Luke's next question is asked in a curious tone.

"How do you know Franklin anyway? You seem pretty familiar with him, on a first-name basis."

I hesitate, not wanting to get into the complexities of my relationship, especially since it just fizzled out. "We've . . . crossed paths several times since I moved to Sydney."

*"Hmm,"* Luke says, picking up on my evasiveness. "And this crossing of paths, is it purely professional?"

"Luke . . . ," I warn.

"Because if this guy is giving you trouble, professionally or otherwise, I can have the company jet prepped and I'll be on it in an hour," he says, going from inquisitive CEO to protective big brother in the blink of an eye. "Say the word, and I'll come punch him in the face."

Despite everything, I laugh. "That won't be necessary."

"You sure? Because I'm hearing something in your voice, Lark. Something that tells me this guy matters to you more than you're letting on."

His perception catches me off guard. "It's . . . complicated."

"It always is." His voice softens. "But I don't like the sound of a guy who'd threaten to sue you, not if there's anything more between you than business."

When I say nothing to that, he adds, "Just know that I'm here, half a world away, but still right here. And if Jules did steal that recipe, I'll back whatever decision you make. Even if it means cutting him loose."

The words sting, though I understand the necessity. "I know. I'll handle it."

Another moment of sibling silence before I say something I've never said, "I don't know if I'm really cut out for this."

"Bullshit!" Luke fires back before I've even taken a breath. "You had Henley NYC running so smoothly, I didn't have to do anything when I took over but slide behind your desk."

"A minute ago, you told me to come home and let you take over," I remind him.

"For your safety," he insists. "Not because even for a second do I think you can't run either division of our company."

"It's good to hear you say that," I tell him. "I've felt rather . . . adrift." Then I wonder. "Have you ever wanted to do something different with your life?"

"You mean not be involved in Henley Confectionery?" Luke asks, sounding totally shocked.

"Yes," I drop my voice to a whisper. "Precisely."

"Honestly, sis, not for a minute," Luke says. "I'm happy coming to work every day."

"That's great," I say, trying to be enthusiastic while not feeling the same. Not even close.

"Lark, if being CEO of Henley Sydney doesn't make you happy, what would?"

Tears prick my eyes. I wasn't ready to be asked that. My first thought is Mitch. Mitch makes me ecstatic. Of course, I can't say that. Besides, even if I quit my job and showed up at his penthouse, I'd still need to do something.

"Forget I said anything, Luke. I'm just frazzled."

A few moments of silence. "OK. But don't forget. Call if you need me."

After we hang up, I lean back in my chair and close my eyes. My thoughts turn to Eddie. I can't go rogue this time.

I have to speak with the board before I speak to him. We'll discuss any potential damage control. After all, news of what happened—a Henley factory worker felled by a poisoned chocolate—could get out. The Fairfield Hospital staff know what happened, as do all the factory workers, and the independent lab we hired, too.

Then there's the ambulance crew and Eddie's family. Any one of them might go to the press. The board is probably going to order me to offer him a big bonus on the condition he doesn't sue us. And rightly so, too.

As if the universe hears my ruminations, Jim calls from the factory to tell me he had a call from Eddie's wife. I grip the phone tightly, until he says Eddie's still doing well but has to stay in the hospital another day for monitoring, repeat labs, and observation in case he has "rebound methemoglobinemia."

"There's a word I never thought I'd need to know," I say to Jim.

We both sound grim, but I'm feeling more than that. I'm starting to feel beaten. As I hang up, I get an email from Charlotte.

"Nothing conclusive yet. Security footage review continues, but there's nothing to see in the ingredients room. Many more hours to go through for the rest of the factory. Should we bring in an external investigator? I've attached the footage you requested."

She's attached the video I requested to show the board. My anxiety spikes as I relive the awful minutes of Eddie's collapse and what came next. When I see myself kneeling beside him, I close the screen and send Charlotte an approval for an external investigation.

Getting up from my desk, I pace to the window, gazing out at the Sydney harbor, wondering why exactly candy has become this complicated. For that matter, when did my life and my heart become so conflicted?

At the beginning, coming to Sydney had felt like a fresh opportunity. A chance to help out my brother's love life while getting away from a toxic social scene in New York. *But now?* Now, I'm drowning in corporate intrigue while my personal life lies in tatters. I want a man who I can only have if I fire a loyal employee. And even then, that man will be on a plane sometime in the near future. It's a hopeless situation.

I call Jules.

"How's Eddie?" he asks.

"He'll be fine." I pause, then add, "As far as I can tell, the contamination was deliberate."

His sharp intake of breath echoes through the line. "Why? How?"

The headache has blossomed into a whopper that no amount of temple-massaging will fix. I have no intention of going over the possible takeover with my master chocolatier, but I tell him the truth in a nutshell.

"Besides this incidence, there've been other issues recently that lead me to believe someone is trying to weaken the company."

*"Mon Dieu,"* he mutters, slipping into his native tongue.

There's a beat of silence and then I take the tiger by the tail. "Let's have one more, and hopefully *last,* discussion about HLC."

"Lark, I—" he begins.

"It would really help me if you could find your friend, the one who was there when you created your chocolate sauce."

"I'm already trying," he says. "I figured this would come up."

We don't waste time on chitchat, both of us having important things to do. But my stomach growls, reminding me I haven't eaten since . . . Mitch's omelet.

With the superior Henley break room at my disposal, I go downstairs to make use of it. Besides the boxes of assorted free chocolates and high-quality coffee machine that makes every kind of coffee drink, including those needing steamed milk or froth, we have a well-stocked fridge.

I snag a ubiquitous Aussie fave, a bottle of Lemon, Lime and Bitters, a chilled and crunchy apple, and a yogurt, knowing I need protein. At the last minute, I also take a cheese-and-ham sandwich. I've been running on empty for too many days, and maybe that's why the past few weeks have seemed overwhelming.

I'm out the door and heading back up to my office when it hits me. For the first time that I can remember, I didn't grab a Henley chocolate. I couldn't, not with the image in my mind of Eddie crumpled on the factory floor.

My first love . . . Henley Confectionery . . . has become tainted. And it pisses me off.

At my desk, while I eat, I scroll through the emails that aren't catastrophe related, which seem to be very few. My probation status hangs over me like a dark cloud as I work. If the board decides I'm not handling this crisis adequately, they could remove me entirely.

*Would that be so bad?* The thought slips in unbidden. If I stepped away from the company, I don't know what my life would look like. I couldn't even give Luke an answer about what makes me happy.

For a moment, I allow myself to imagine a different path—one where I'm not CEO of either Henley division, where I could pursue . . . *What exactly?* I'm not sure. My entire life has been about our confectionery company, about growing into someone worthy of running it. I did that effortlessly in New York. Here, I'm floundering rather than finding my groove.

Even before the night I met Mitch, I was already wondering if I'd made a mistake by leaving Manhattan.

It's not yet five o'clock, but it's been a long day. I came in right after Mitch left—*was that really this morning?*—and I decide I can leave early too, if I want. I'm the goddamned CEO! For the first time I can remember, I leave at five sharp.

On my way home, I want to call Mitch. I want to hear his voice. I want to invite him over. I want him to hold me the way he did last night, like I mattered more than anything or anyone else in the world. But the way he last looked at me, with regret and longing in equal measure, I know that's not possible.

The silence of my apartment is oppressive. Dropping my purse onto my hall table, I kick off my shoes and stride to the window, gazing out at the beautiful harbor. *Is this what I want?* An endless cycle of crisis management and corporate maneuvering?

My grandparents built Henley from nothing because they loved chocolate, loved creating something that brought joy, and loved doing it together.

The only thing making this second and the next and the one after that bearable is knowing Mitch is merely minutes away, either at his restaurant or his home. And considering we're not a couple, and I have no intention of seeing him again, that's a pretty thin lifeline to hold onto.

# 20

## Mitch

The pounding on my door drags me from a dreamless sleep. I squint at my phone—7:15 a.m.—and groan. With nothing and no one needing me elsewhere, I stayed till closing at Franklin 6, then had a few drinks with some of the staff. None of us left before one in the morning.

The knocking continues, more insistent now. *Lark!*

The thought of her has me wide awake.

"Coming!" I yell, dragging on sweatpants as I race through my apartment.

When I yank open the door, disappointment hits me instantly.

"Expecting someone else?" Camille asks, taking in my expression and my half-dressed, disheveled appearance with a smirk.

Today, her midnight-black hair is swept back in a high ponytail. She's wearing a loud, red pantsuit and impossible-to-miss, thick, silver hoop earrings. She looks somehow dangerous. Maybe because I was dead asleep a minute ago, and she's like a stick of dynamite.

I fight the urge to tell her *yes, I was hoping for someone else entirely*—someone with honey-streaked hair and golden tawny eyes that haunt me. Instead, I run a hand across the back of my neck, yawn, and step back, letting her in despite wanting to go back to bed.

"It's kind of early," I grumble, thinking I've got to speak to the doorman about how he lets every female stroll right past him.

"Today, I had to be an early riser," she says.

As she enters, I catch the scent of strong, musky perfume, another change from our days at Le Cordon Bleu, where fragrances were forbidden. She manages to run a polished fingernail down the front of my bare chest as she passes. It's definitely sexy but fails to get a rise out of me. *Any* part of me.

I hope Lark appreciates how she's ruined me for casual sex.

Camille strides into my living room like she has a right. Same old go-getter, who got herself a sugar daddy and a top chef job in one go. All she had to do was abandon *us* and spread her legs for a guy known as an exploitative predator. Henri was infamous for poaching from his bevy of female waitstaff. This time, he poached my lover and made her his head chef.

I guess Camille managed to do the exploiting, though. Suddenly, I'm cheering her for besting the old coot. I hope she made out like a bandit when they split.

After looking around my place, she leans on my kitchen's granite countertop and fixes me with her dark stare. "You look terrible."

"Thanks," I mutter. "Some of us still work in a restaurant and keep late hours."

She laughs, tapping her fingers along the edge of the counter. "Still cranky in the mornings, I see. Some things never change."

I don't like her pretending to know me so well. Moving to the coffee machine, I punch buttons with more force than necessary.

"What do you want, Cam? You didn't come by at the crack of dawn to reminisce."

"You're right, I didn't." She slides onto one of the bar stools. "I wanted to give my offer one more chance before I leave town. I'm heading home soon."

The coffee machine whirs to life, and I lean against the counter, studying her. "Where's home?"

She sends me a cat-ate-the-canary smile that I used to find mysterious but now recognize as evasive. "That depends."

"On what?" I press her for more info.

"On whether you'll change your mind and join me." Her voice softens, taking on a persuasive tone I recall. She used to be able to get me to do just about anything.

"I meant what I said at dinner," she continues. "We could open something spectacular together. Wherever you like."

I pour two cups of coffee, sliding one across to her. "Wherever I like? You don't care and your nameless backers don't care, either?"

"No backers if you don't choose Santa Barbara. Me and you alone, Mitchell." We stare at one another, neither of us looking away. I have to admit she has balls of steel for coming to me. Again. After I told her I didn't need or want anything from her.

Wrapping her hands around the mug, she says, "Look, Mitch, I know things ended badly between us—"

"You literally left without bothering to break up with me first," I interrupt flatly. "Not even a goodbye."

She flinches. "I was young and stupid. But that was years ago. We've both grown up."

She was old enough back then not to have been a first-class twat, and I don't think her age had anything to do with her mercenary behavior. Besides, I don't like being included in her assessment of our maturity, although I have changed a lot. Mostly through sheer hard work and long hours.

Regardless, I never would've done what she'd done, not to secure a fucking job. Not at any age.

It still blows my mind that she sold herself basically for chef's whites. And I'm back to no longer cheering her for getting the better end of the deal with Henri Laurent. They deserved one another, and they both got what they wanted. I'm glad she opened my eyes.

Coming back to earth, I realize she's still talking, still trying to sell me on a deal that will never happen. "And we've always worked well together professionally."

That much is true. Camille has an undeniable talent, not for cooking alone but for pairing and menu development. During the brief time we collaborated in Paris, we created some extraordinary dishes. But our personal relationship imploded so spectacularly, I could never trust her in any partnership ever again.

I take a sip of my coffee, letting the bitter warmth clear my head. Yesterday, I'd toyed with the idea of leaving Sydney. Not with Camille. *God no!* But thinking it's time to move on. I've already got the plans and the place picked out. The instantaneous fresh perspective from the moment I land is a head rush I enjoy. And I've done it enough times to know what I'll be getting into.

This time, however, I wouldn't be moving for the excitement of breaking ground on a new restaurant but to escape the irresistible pull of one difficult, elusive, stubborn woman. A pointless exercise since anywhere I go, I'll be thinking of her.

Camille, with her curves and her gloss and the way she's leaning on her folded arms to show me her cleavage, leaves me cold. After she screwed with my mind—and I guess with my pride—I engaged in the risky and childish behavior of one-night stands, blaming it on my schedule and my transient life.

That didn't change until Lark Henley showed me that a second night and a third are even better. With the right person.

So, I might as well be here, at least for a few weeks longer, even if I'm chasing smoke. There's a chance I'll see Lark, and that's enough.

"I'm staying in Sydney," I tell her, setting down my mug. "For now."

Her expression flickers with something. *Annoyance? Disappointment?* Don't know, don't care.

"If you're staying for Lark Henley, don't bother."

The name hits me like a slap. "What the hell does that mean?"

Camille rolls her eyes, then puts on the most dead-pan expression I've ever seen.

"I have to go. Plane to catch, *in a day or so*," she adds, even more strangely.

Unease trickles down my spine because, suddenly, Camille's polish seems cunning and her words, vaguely threatening.

"How do you know Lark?"

She merely raises an eyebrow before sliding off the stool. "Thanks for the coffee. If you change your mind about my offer, you know how to reach me." Then she pauses at my front door with a cock of her head. "If you still have my card. Otherwise, I guess this is goodbye."

Then she's gone, the door clicking shut behind her, leaving me with the strangest, unsettled feeling. Standing in my kitchen, coffee cooling between my palms, replaying Camille's words. The way she'd said Lark's name—casual, but with an edge. I'm beyond baffled.

After a quick shower, I try to rationalize away my unease. Lark and I were briefly in the news after I went ballistic at the Taste of Sydney event. Camille might have caught wind of that if she was in Sydney at the time. But why would she interpret that debacle as me being interested in Lark?

I decide I'm overreacting. Today, I'd planned to catch up on sleep—already ruined—and then work up some new dishes. I have a video conference planned with my head chef in Boston, and a live one with Ravi about what dishes he's ready to test on our Sydney customers.

The task of developing menus is one of my favorite things about owning restaurants, and because I'm up so damn early, I head to the Saturday open-air markets for inspiration and supplies.

Starting at my farthest stop, the Carriageworks Farmers Market, I go a little nuts. The first stalls are a feast for the eyes, colorful fruit and every type of veg. I buy pounds of local produce before finding the stall with the olives we serve at Franklin 6. In the next row, I buy avocados at various stages of ripeness, as well as some tomatoes.

I purposefully avoid the artisan chocolates as that would be like cheating on the woman I lo—*like* a whole lot. Buying a jar of raw honey for my next cup of coffee at home, I also grab a croissant for right now because the freshly baked aroma wouldn't let me pass the baker's stall. But I'm not done yet.

With my car already stuffed, I hit the Rocks Market, close to my apartment. I don't let myself get distracted from my quest by the intriguing plant-based baklava or the singing bowls, or by watching a glassblower. But I do stop at the stall selling Turkish gozleme, buying both savory and sweet examples, as well as purchasing a bottle of small batch gin before hitting up my main reason for stopping, the Mediterranean style BBQ stall.

I buy a to-go bag of skewered marinated octopus and garlic-infused prawns. Visually appealing, I hope they taste as good because I'd heard they were fantastic and I'm inspired.

With a small ten-minute detour to the aptly and simply named Sydney Fish Market, I head home for a day of cooking, inventing, and tasting—*not* eating. Just tasting.

Hours later, when I've opened a beer, stretched out on my couch, and turned on the TV, I . . . still miss Lark and wonder what she's doing. Before I can talk myself out of it, I call her. When she answers, I realize I need a pretense besides *I want you. Right. Now.*

"Mitch," she says, her voice neutral, even as my heart starts thumping. At least she answered her cell.

"Hey, how are you?"

"I'm not very good company right now. What's up?"

*What's up?* I can't confess to simply enjoying the sound of her voice. I need a real reason.

"Do you remember the woman I had dinner with the other night?" I slap a hand to my forehead. *Why did I go there?* Maybe because Camille mentioning Lark has been bugging me all day.

"Yes," Lark says, the word ending on a soft hiss of annoyance.

"Do you know her?" I ask.

A pause. "No, only that she seemed to have thick ankles."

"She doesn't," I reply automatically, then smile at the jealousy, thinly veiled as criticism.

"Oh. I mean, yes, she does. But are you sure you don't know her?"

"I promise you I don't. I have to go, Mitch."

I can hear the strain in her voice. I want to ask what's wrong, whether she's doing OK, and how her board meeting went, but I know she won't tell me. Not now, not like this. But maybe . . .

"Maybe we could share a meal . . . tonight." I glance at my destroyed kitchen and dining room table, looking like the lab of a mad scientist, or in this case, a mad chef.

She hesitates, and I hold my breath. Then with her tone flat, she says, "I'm not firing Julian Cartier."

I hesitate but make a decision. She's more important than my pride or even my chocolate sauce. I'm more than a little shocked to discover this fact.

"We won't talk shop."

"Are you sure you have time?" she shoots back. "Maybe your old friend wants to eat with you or offer you another chance to open a restaurant with her."

*Wow!* Talk about woman's intuition.

"She already did," I confess. "Camille came to my apartment."

Lark makes a noise of pure exasperation. "Why are you telling me this?"

"Because I have nothing to hide from you." It's true. I haven't felt this way about a woman . . . perhaps ever. I want Lark to know everything about me, even the uncomfortable truths. Mostly to prove that old girlfriends mean nothing to me anymore.

"I don't think it's a good idea to eat together," she says, but her tone is more amenable. "You know what will happen after."

I sit up and put my feet down off my couch. *Is she saying what I think she's saying?*

"Do I?"

"Yup," she says.

I guess she's as into me as I am into her. If we're alone, sparks will fly. Wild sex will ensue. But I don't want that to be a deal-breaker over eating together.

"It doesn't have to," I say calmly. Naturally, I hope it will.

"It probably will," she says, sighing, as if having sex is an inevitable fate.

"Then we should let it happen." I want her more with every syllable she speaks.

I hear her growl of frustration. "I have to go." And she hangs up.

*Damn.* Talk about blowing hot and cold. I stare at my phone, torn between frustration and an absurd desire to laugh. We're like magnets, constantly pulling toward each other and then forcefully pushing apart. It's exhausting. It's exhilarating.

I can't get her out of my head. I go over what she said. In the end, I don't think she said no to dinner. It's only five, and Ravi knows I'm not coming in to help with the weekend crowd. Saturday night service is always busy, and we're fully booked as usual but Franklin 6 runs like a well-oiled machine with or without me. And because of my impending departure, it has to do it *without* me more and more, until I'm totally redundant. As it should be.

Putting on a local channel, I listen to a show about sharks swimming near Byron Bay, while cleaning up my apartment, although how I'll get Lark over here, I'm not sure. I suppose I could pack up some of the prepared food and hope she's home.

Despite the grim background story of people swimming in shark-infested waters, my mind keeps drifting back to Lark. When I've got my place looking presentable again, I think about what she needed when she was at her lowest point the other day. She *needed* the burden of a choice taken from her.

Fingers crossed I know her well enough by now, I jump in my car. In approximately seven minutes, I'm at her home, but I don't go upstairs. Instead, I call. As before, she picks up.

"Come downstairs, lady. We have reservations for a superb meal. Everything's ready, and I'm not taking no for an answer."

When she hesitates, I'm not worried because I swear I can hear her smile.

Finally, she asks, "How should I dress? I'm wearing leggings and a T-shirt so wherever—"

"That's fine," I say. "I'm in jeans. But you better feed your goldfish since you won't be home tonight."

This time, she laughs, knowing I know she doesn't have any pets. The wonderful, earthy sound is utterly genuine, making my heart feel light and happy.

"I'll be right down."

$♥$♥$♥$

We make it through a smorgasbord of my test dishes until Lark groans.

"I'm stuffed. Not another bite."

"But there's another dumpling in the pan," I joke.

"Help," she says and leaves my dining table for the sofa. "How do you not weigh five hundred pounds?"

Laughing, I take the other end of the couch and pull her feet on top of my thighs. "Because I'm not usually so manic. I got carried away with ideas today. Not just for Franklin 6, but some of these are for Miami and for Amsterdam."

"Franklin 2 and 5," she says, then adds, "I did my research once I found out who you were."

"I'm impressed. Sometimes even I can't keep them straight." I'm joking again, but she beams at me, plainly amused. "What's so funny?" I ask.

"I don't know," Lark says. "I didn't expect this, so it's nice. Really nice. You know?"

"I know." I think about how the day started with a rude awakening, and this ending was the last thing I expected too.

"Ms. Henley, do you like foot rubs?" I ask, since her feet are wiggling on my lap.

"Who doesn't?"

"Some people," I say. "Me for one."

She refrains from asking why. Instead, Lark stretches and says, "Well I do, so have at it. And tell me which dish was your favorite and why."

I start to rub the soles of her feet. "I think I'm supposed to ask you that."

"You're the expert."

Regardless, we have a lively back and forth over what should definitely make it onto the menu, truffled lamb shank pie with a crisp herbal crust, which she declares as "comfort food elevated to art." And which needs more work, the pan-seared barramundi with native finger lime beurre blanc.

"The fish was great," Lark says, "but the lime butter overpowered it, in my humble opinion."

"You're right. It was too sharp."

"Honestly," Lark says, giving me an intense dreamy stare, "I don't know how you do it."

"What?" I ask.

She looks so delicious, I can barely focus on food, which never happens to me.

"Create such amazing recipes, and you seem never to run out of ideas."

"Easy," I say and tell her my secret. "In my mind, I always want to make the kind of meal I'd make for someone I care about. What do I want to give them that will make them feel nourished, happy, and satisfied."

Her mouth opens. "That's kinda magical and deep, Mr. Franklin."

"That's me," I say smugly. We both laugh. When we stop, it's because I've managed to lean over and kiss her. It's a stretch, because I have to span the length of her legs. I'm ready to get more comfortable with her on my bed.

"Did you feed your goldfish?" I ask.

She giggles, something I've never heard her do.

"Even better. I put my toothbrush in my purse. And nothing else."

That wipes the silly smile off my face. "Nothing else?" I manage to say, my voice suddenly rough. "Bold of you to assume I'd have everything you need."

"I'm counting on it," she says, her gaze locked with mine.

The playfulness from moments before has transformed into something intense, like a switch was flipped.

I shift, drawing her toward me until her legs straddle my lap. Her fingers trace the line of my jaw, hesitant at first, then with growing confidence.

"Yesterday was awful," she whispers. "Today too. Until now."

I brush a strand of hair from her face. "Want to talk about it?"

She shakes her head. "Not tonight. Tonight, I want . . ."

"What?" I urge when she trails off.

"You." The simplicity of the word, the naked honesty in it, steals my breath. "Just you."

Standing, I lift her with me. Her legs wrap around my waist, and she hides her face in the crook of my neck as I carry her through the apartment.

It feels different this time—no pressure. We don't have to prove anything to one another. We've done that a few times over. We know what each other likes and how to satisfy our partner. Now, we can simply relax and do it.

My bedroom is bathed in the soft glow of Sydney's night lights filtering through the curtains. I lay Lark gently on the bed, taking a moment to look at her—her light caramel-colored hair fanned out against my pillows, her eyes reflecting the dim light like amber caught in sunlight.

"What?" she whispers when I stare too long.

"I'm memorizing this," I tell her. "Just in case."

Her smile fades slightly. "In case of what?"

Instead of answering, I lower myself beside her, propping up on one elbow. "In case tomorrow we go back to being stubborn." I trail my fingers along her collarbone, feeling her shiver beneath my touch. "In case this is all we ever get."

She reaches up, pulling me down until our foreheads touch. "This is pretty great," she whispers. "This is a lot. This is better than anything I've ever had before."

*Whoa! So much for no pressure.* The one thing I would hate to ever do is disappoint this exceptional woman.

"Stop it," she says.

"What?"

"Thinking. You get two little lines between your eyebrows. We got this," she jokes. "We can do it splendidly, even with our eyes closed."

Our lips meet in a kiss that starts tender but quickly deepens. There's no desperate urgency since we have all night, and tomorrow is Sunday. We take it slowly, deliberately. It's an exploration rather than a conquest. Sliding my hand beneath her T-shirt, I trace the soft, warm skin of her stomach, feeling goosebumps rise in the wake of my touch.

She tugs at the hem of my shirt, and I help her pull it over my head. When I do the same for her, the sight of her nearly stops my heart. It's not merely her beauty—though God knows she's beautiful. It's when I look in her eyes and see the vulnerability, the trust. I don't think any woman has ever given me so much in return for so little and in so short a time.

"You're incredible," I murmur against her neck, trailing kisses down to her shoulder.

Her fingers thread through my hair as I go lower, leaving a path of kisses across the swell of each breast. I take my time, savoring every soft gasp she makes, every subtle arch of her body toward mine. When I reach the waistband of her leggings, I glance up, seeking permission.

Lark nods, lifting her hips. Slowly, I peel the stretchy fabric down her legs before pressing my lips to the inside of her ankle, then her calf, working my way back up her body with unhurried devotion.

"Mitch," she breathes, my name a plea on her lips.

I return to her mouth, swallowing her soft moan as our bodies press together. Her hands explore my back, my shoulders, pulling me closer as if she can't bear any space between us. I understand the feeling completely—I want to memorize every inch of her, learn her body so thoroughly that I could recreate her from memory alone.

When I finally nudge her legs apart, our eyes lock, and something unspoken passes between us—something that feels dangerously close to a promise. I thrust inside her. We move together in a rhythm that is ours alone, picking up speed toward an inevitable release.

It's happened between men and women since the beginning of time, but I can't help thinking it's also remarkably singular.

"Stay with me," I whisper, demanding she close in on her orgasm at the same time as I do. But I also mean something more.

Her answer is in the way she holds on tighter, the way her body trembles beneath mine. When she comes apart, it's impossible not to follow her over the edge, her name a soft prayer on my lips.

"Lark."

Afterward, we stay wrapped up in one another, her head on my chest, my fingers tracing lazy patterns on her back. The city lights cast moving shadows across her skin, and I'm struck once again by how right this feels—her in my bed, her heartbeat against mine.

Even to me my thoughts sound like some romantic idiot, but they are what they are.

"What are you thinking?" she asks softly.

I consider lying, saying something light, but what comes out is the truth. "That I don't want to lose you."

She props herself up to look at me, her expression serious.

"We don't make sense on paper, you know. My roots are deep here, probably forever, and you're a guy from Boston who's just passing through. Even if that's a six-month pass."

"Since when has anything good in life made sense on paper?" I ask, tucking a strand of hair behind her ear.

A small smile touches her lips. "Fair point."

"Besides," I continue, "forget the logistics. Think of us as two nuts from the same tree. Two stubborn, passionate people who care too much about our work and not enough about playing by other people's rules."

She laughs, the sound warming me from the inside out. "When you put it that way . . ."

I pull her closer, pressing a kiss to her forehead. "I'm glad you're staying the night."

"And why is that?" she asks, settling back against my chest.

"Because I'm not done with you yet."

We fall asleep like that, her pale bare skin resting on my dark bare skin, the problems of tomorrow temporarily held at bay by the sanctuary we've created in each other's arms. If I could figure out how to keep tomorrow from coming for a few years, I'd do it.

# 21

# Lark

I wake to sunshine filtering through unfamiliar curtains and the solid warmth of Mitch's body pressed against mine. For a moment, I allow myself to pretend this is normal—waking up in his bed, his arm draped over my waist, the gentle rhythm of his breathing against my neck.

It's Sunday morning, and I have nowhere to be. No emergencies to handle. No factory workers in the hospital. No board members breathing down my neck.

*Just this. Just us.*

Trailing my fingers along Mitch's forearm, I trace the slight rise and fall of veins beneath his skin. Last night was different from our previous encounters—less frantic, more intimate. The way he looked at me, the way he touched me . . .

It was a shift in the depth of whatever this is between us.

"You're thinking too loudly," Mitch murmurs, his voice husky with sleep. Pulling me closer, he buries his face in my hair.

I smile despite myself, feeling close to bliss when he kisses my shoulder and asks, "What time is it?"

I reach for my phone. "Nine already." Then I drop it back onto the nightstand.

"Perfect time to eat," he says, making no move to get up. Instead, his hand slides up to cup my breast.

A shiver runs through me. "I thought you were hungry."

"I am," he says, his lips finding the sensitive spot behind my ear. "Not for food."

Turning in his arms, my body is already responding to his touch. Our lips meet in a slow, languorous kiss that promises to lead to so much more.

My phone starts buzzing.

"Ignore it," Mitch whispers against my lips.

I want to—*God, how I want to*—but the professional responsibility ingrained in me won't allow it. "It might be important."

He sighs, releasing me with obvious reluctance. "Go on. Save the chocolate world."

Reaching for my phone, I'm surprised to see it's Luke. Concern ripples through me as I answer.

"What's wrong?"

"Wow. Braced for the next disaster?" my brother quips. "I want you to come meet me for brunch."

Sitting up straight, I belatedly drag the sheet up to my chest. "You're in Sydney?"

"Surprise! I landed an hour ago. Dad thought you might appreciate some back-up."

My heart sinks. Dad sent Luke. Without asking me first.

"I . . . Where are you staying?" Suddenly, I wonder if he's let himself into our jointly owned apartment. In which case, he already knows I'm not home.

"Didn't want to cramp your style in case you had a guest. I'm at the Langham. I've got a table reserved at our usual place in thirty minutes," he says, referring to our favorite breakfast spot when we were both learning the ropes by running Henley Sydney together.

I'm understandably speechless, having been torn from incredible sex by someone I thought was ten thousand miles away.

"Can you make it?" Luke asks into my hesitation.

I glance at Mitch, who's watching me with curiosity. "I'll be there," I say, knowing Luke didn't fly all this way simply for a good fried egg and a plate of rösti.

After I hang up, Mitch raises an eyebrow. "Everything OK?"

"No idea. My brother's in town. Unexpected visit." I make a sour face, even though I love Luke.

Sliding out of bed, I take the sheet with me, leaving Mitch's fabulous body on display. With regret at the ruin of our Sunday morning sex, I turn away, looking for my clothing.

"I said I'd meet him."

"Right now?" There's no hiding his disappointment.

"Sorry," I say, genuinely meaning it. "Luke being here means something important is happening. I'll make it up to you later," I promise.

He watches me dress with a wry smile. "We're good at that part—making up." His tone is light, but there's an edge to it. "Not so great at the staying together part. At least not first thing in the morning."

I pause, my leggings half on. "I'd invite you to come, but . . ."

"It would be awkward," he finishes, running a hand through his sleep-mussed hair as he gets out of bed. "I'll drop you home."

Lost in Mitch-world, I'd forgotten I didn't have my car. "Good thing we're waterfront neighbors," I say.

He nods, his expression unreadable. Ten minutes later, a half-dressed Mitch, sweatpants only, opens the car door for me in front of my place. It doesn't help that he looks like sensual, rumpled sex on muscular legs that could've been sculpted from marble they're so firm. I want to climb him like he's my own personal oak tree.

But Luke will be at our fave spot soon.

"Thanks for feeding me," I tell Mitch. "Again."

"No problem." His voice is morning gruff.

As I'm about to go inside, he catches my wrist, pulling me hard against him for one last kiss—insistent, wicked, promising more.

"I'll talk to you later," he says.

In the next instant, I'm regaining my balance as he speeds off.

$♥$♥$♥$

I spot Luke immediately when I enter the Kooka's Nest. He's at a corner table, wearing a suit, which seems super weird on a weekend, unless . . . there's a business meeting about to happen. The hair on the back of my neck prickles. Something is definitely up.

Despite his clothes, my brother always seems at home anywhere he goes—a trait I've always envied. Currently, he's chatting animatedly with the server who's making googly eyes at him, not knowing his heart is spoken for as is the rest of his body. I wish his wife, Morgan, was here, then I'd know this wasn't a serious visit.

"Hey, sis!" he says, standing to envelop me in a bear hug. When he lets me loose, he adds, "God, you look . . . Actually, like you just rolled out of bed."

I smooth my hair self-consciously. All I had time for at home was to brush my teeth and put on a clean T-shirt.

"It's Sunday. Some of us were sleeping in."

He gives me a knowing look but mercifully changes the subject.

"I ordered coffee. And mimosas. I figured we both could use one."

"You have no idea," I mutter, sliding into the seat across from him. "Or maybe you do, and that's why you're here. Did Dad send you to check up on me?"

He winces. "Not exactly how I'd put it."

The concern in his eyes softens my irritation. "I'm handling things."

"Are you? From what I hear you're juggling more than your fair share. It's like a crime show with a poisoned employee, contaminated ingredients, and a hostile takeover all happening at once."

"And I'm dealing with all of it."

"I know you are," he says quickly. "But family shows up when one of us is in the shit. And in this case, the takeover affects all of us. You know we're working on blocking it, too. You and Sydney HQ are not alone, but we owe David big-time for spotting this when he did. I want to meet with him before I leave."

Our drinks arrive and we put in our food orders—eggs benedict for Luke, an omelet for me. Before jumping into anything more serious, we tap our champagne glasses and chug down the bubbly orange drink. We have a brief chat about how his wife is, how well Nan and Gramps are doing, our sister's fabulous Boston life, and our parents' latest adventure to Egypt.

I've had more than enough time to collect my thoughts by the time our food is set before us. Luke digs in, but mine tastes more like sawdust than eggs. With my nerves frayed from not knowing why he really rushed across the world, I tackle the elephant in the room.

"I appreciate your concern," I say. "It was sweet of you to come here, although you've left Henley NYC vacant of its CEO while we're involved in this battle for control of our company. Regardless of that, I wish you'd listened when I told you I didn't need you to drop everything and ride to my rescue."

"I *needed* to be here," he says, talking around a bite he's stuffing into his mouth as only a big brother can get away with. "You did me a huge favor, switching places last year. All these problems should be on my plate, not yours. So I'm here to help."

I can tell there's something more, but he's easing into it.

"Maybe they're on my plate because I inadvertently piled them on," I suggest.

"That's bullshit. The way you ran New York is proof."

"This is different," I say quietly, pushing my omelet around before spearing a chunk of potato. "Sydney is . . . It's more personal being where Gramps and Nan started everything. Don't you agree? The stakes feel higher."

Luke nods. "All the more reason for me to be here."

I feel a rush of gratitude toward my brother, even as a small part of me resents his help.

"There's something else," I confess. "The board ordered me days ago to approach Eddie with what amounts to hush money. They want an NDA, or I'm supposed to terminate him."

Luke's eyebrows shoot up. "Did you do it?"

"Nope." I can't help the little defiant laugh that escapes me. "I've run out of fucks to give, apparently."

Luke grins, but then he says, "You know, what the board wants you to do is pretty standard procedure."

"The man almost died on our factory floor. I think the board's focus is hasty and disgusting," I say without hesitation.

I give up toying with my food and put my fork down. "The board keeps calling emergency meetings. They've called so many lately, they need to rename them 'regular' meetings."

Luke's expression hardens. "I know. There's one scheduled for today at three."

*What the hell?* Now it makes sense.

"That's why you're dressed like you're going to a funeral. Mine."

He shakes his head. "I'm simply here if you need reinforcements."

"Apparently, you already know that I will, or you wouldn't have come all this way."

Luke stares at me with eyes so like my own. "If this gets hairy, and the board starts talking about suspension or worse, I need to know if you want to fight this."

He catches me off guard. "What do you mean?" I'm still thinking about *suspension or worse.*

"Our last conversation," he reminds me, "you said your heart wasn't in Henley anymore. Not a hundred percent."

I glance away. "I was tired. It was a moment of weakness."

"Was it?" He studies me with the perceptiveness that always made it impossible to lie to him when we were kids.

Before I can answer, my phone buzzes with a message from Charlotte about the board meeting today, three o'clock. My stomach drops.

"The board has just informed me what you already knew. I have a feeling they didn't want me to have time to prepare a defense. Not that I need one. I didn't do anything wrong."

*Apart from going rogue a few times.*

Luke checks his watch, with its super-cool transparent face that reveals its inner workings of dials and whatnot. It's so him, I can't help feeling relieved. My big brother is here.

"We still have a few hours to create a strategy. And for you to put on a power outfit." He points his fork at my T-shirt.

"I hate this shit!" I declare childishly.

Despite everything, he smiles, and I shake my head.

"You don't mind dealing with the board, do you?" I ask. "Maybe you thrive on it."

Luke shrugs. "It has a certain excitement to it. But sometimes, I'd rather be in the factory or the samples room."

"Me, too," I mutter.

Nodding, he shovels in the last bite of his breakfast. "That's because chocolate is in our blood."

$❤$❤$❤$

I'm still thinking about that when I walk into our deserted office building. Alone. We decided Luke's being here would be better as a surprise to the board, like it was to me. More effective if we need to rattle them.

My footsteps echo across the lobby floor that I've been walking on since I was a child. First to play in the break room during the months we were visiting my grandparents. Later, when I came to work in every department. Finally, to lead the Sydney division.

I'm beyond conflicted, feeling a tightness in my chest, so I detour to the break room and snag myself a couple pieces from one of the boxed assortments. I don't even care which ones. I've always loved them all.

Although when I bite into a soft-centered raspberry chocolate, I get a jolt of fear that I quickly brush aside.

Feeling a little defiant, I cram the second one in while I ride the elevator to the executive floor. This one is a solid chunk of coffee-infused dark chocolate, dusted with cocoa. Checking my face in the mirrored elevator, I don't see any remnants on my mouth, but I also don't see a happy woman.

When I walk into the board room next to my office, it's 2:59 p.m. Nine pairs of eyes turn to me. Some are sympathetic. At least one pair is calculating. Neville Wembley sits at the head of the table, his silver hair perfectly coiffed, his expression unreadable behind wire-rimmed glasses.

"Lark," he says, his tone cordial but cold. "Thank you for joining us on such short notice."

I take my seat, noting the empty chair beside me where Charlotte would usually sit.

"Of course, Neville," I use his first name, despite how overly familiar it sounds, almost disrespectful, but I'm simply following his lead. "Although I'm surprised by the urgency of meeting on a Sunday."

"Recent events have necessitated immediate action," he replies smoothly.

"Have they?" There've been so many, I don't hazard a guess as to which he's referring to.

Before we go any further, the door opens again, and Luke strides in. The surprise on Neville's face is almost worth the tension in the room.

"Mr. Henley," Neville says, recovering quickly. It doesn't escape me that the chairman uses my brother's surname. Either because a male CEO immediately receives more deference, or because Neville was momentarily flustered.

"We weren't expecting you," the chairman adds.

"Obviously not," Luke says, unsmiling until he greets the rest of the board with handshakes. Then he addresses Neville again. "Given the circumstances, I thought it important to represent our family's interests directly."

Neville's jaw tightens. "This is a Sydney board matter."

"This is a Henley Confectionery Company matter," Luke states flatly, taking the seat beside me. "I'm sure you understand my family's concern."

A tense silence falls over the room. I fight the urge to smile, grateful for my brother's commanding presence.

Neville clears his throat. "Very well. Let's proceed." He addresses the entire room. "We're here today to discuss the recent series of incidents and to evaluate whether current leadership is equipped to handle these challenges."

I straighten in my chair. "I'd be happy to brief everyone on the steps I've taken to address each issue. Advanced spontaneous quality checks, new security protocols, and a private investigation into the—"

"We've read your reports, Lark," Neville says dismissively. "The question is not what you've done *after* the fact, but how these situations were allowed to occur in the first place."

"Are you suggesting I'm responsible for deliberate sabotage of our products?" I ask, keeping a check on my anger.

"I'm suggesting that under your watch, our company has become vulnerable to such attacks, as well as to a hostile takeover. That speaks to a fundamental failure of leadership."

Luke leans forward. "That's a serious accusation, Neville. Do you have evidence to support it? Meaning, how do you know any or all of this wouldn't have happened if I was still here and Lark was still in New York?"

Neville's eyes narrow. "The evidence speaks for itself. In the span of two months, we've had contaminated sugar, burned cocoa beans, and now poisoned chocolates. Not to mention the wasted resources on a product line that had to be scrapped due to intellectual property concerns. The latter has left us open to being sued under the Uniform Trade Secrets Act."

My cheeks burn at the mention of HLC, wishing I hadn't had to come clean about that. But I did, because the damn concrete floor was sitting there and the expense was listed in the quarterly reports anyway. Still, I hold my ground.

"Each of those unusual occurrences has been investigated or is in the process of such. My guess is that, aside from product development gone awry, the other issues are to do with the hostile takeover you mentioned. RWI is trying to wreak havoc with Henley, devaluing us, weakening us, and hoping for this exact meeting today with one outcome in mind."

"Speculation," Neville dismisses.

"Reasonable inference," I counter. "Deliberate sabotage is the most likely explanation. As for the intellectual property of Mr. Franklin's chocolate sauce, the situation was unfortunate but caught before significant resources were committed."

"After breaking ground on a factory expansion," another board member interjects.

I take a deep breath. "A minor expenditure in the grand scheme of things, and one that can be repurposed for future production needs."

Neville removes his glasses, pinching the bridge of his nose—a signal I've come to recognize as a precursor to his most cutting remarks.

"Lark, while we appreciate your optimism, the board's concerns are for the here and now. They go beyond individual incidents to a pattern of distraction and impulsiveness that has become increasingly apparent."

"What pattern?" Luke demands. "Lark has implemented every security measure recommended by our professional team. She's working with investigators to trace the sabotage to its source. What more would you have her do?"

"Perhaps focus on her duties rather than her social life," Neville says, his gaze fixing on me with uncomfortable precision.

While my throat feels tight with anger that he would bring up my personal life, my stomach drops at it being mentioned. Like I've been caught doing something I shouldn't be.

"I don't understand what you mean," I say stiffly. Although I fear that I do.

Neville slides a folder across the gleaming surface toward me, but he speaks directly to Luke.

"You asked for evidence." He gestures for one of us to open the folder.

I do it. Inside are photographs—Mitch and I driving together, me entering his building, him entering mine, me storming from his restaurant.

The final image—*oh my God!*—shows a shirtless Mitch clasping me against him after he drove me home this morning.

We've been captured mid-kiss in a merciless close-up.

# 22

# Lark

"What the hell?" I demand, jumping to my feet as if I'm sitting on hot coals. Rage and humiliation flood through me in equal measure.

"Please take your seat, Lark. I didn't mean to upset you," Neville says, his voice dripping with false concern.

"Then what is this?" I slap the folder. "Why are you prying into my life outside the company?"

"Your relationship with Mitchell Franklin seems to have coincided with many of our recent troubles," Neville says calmly.

I glance at Luke, who's learning about this for the first time. He's giving me severe side-eye, so I try to stop seething and retake my seat. I know, however, that no one would have dared question my brother when he was wooing his now-wife, right here in this very office building where she worked alongside him.

"This isn't the 1950s," I point out, knowing my cheeks are red. "My personal life has nothing to do with my ability to run this company."

"It does when it involves a potential litigant against Henley," Neville says.

*Shit!* That obviously does look bad.

Luke places a warning hand on my arm, sensing my rising fury. Then he goes to bat for me.

"This is outrageous." His voice is quiet, controlled but fierce. "These photos constitute an invasion of my sister's privacy. She could sue this board as easily as the 'potential litigant' you're speaking of. I demand to know who authorized surveillance of one of Henley's CEOs, and *without* the majority shareholder's consent."

Invoking our father is a good move, but Neville waves his hand dismissively.

"Those were provided anonymously," he insists. "But the point remains that Lark has been *involved* with a man who threatened legal action against our company. Not only didn't she tell the board about the threat initially, she didn't tell us about the new product she was rushing to production."

Neville is certainly getting his body blows in. But I keep my mouth shut until he's finished.

"Lastly, her being in a relationship with Mr. Mitchell represents, at the very least, a conflict of interest. Is she acting in the best interests of Henley Confectionery, or bowing to the pressure of outside sources?"

*That's it!* That's the final straw. I find my voice, determined not to be bullied.

"For the record," I glance at the board secretary in the corner taking notes for the official meeting minutes, "Mr. Franklin and I met *before* the situation arose with the potential new product. Since then, we've reached an understanding—no litigation will be pursued as long as Henley doesn't produce the chocolate sauce."

"How convenient," Neville says with a thin smile. "And we're simply to take your word that your personal relationship hasn't compromised your judgment?"

My face burns, but I meet his gaze steadily. "Yes. Because that's the truth."

The board member to Neville's right, Eloise Parker, clears her throat.

"While I understand the concerns, I must say I'm uncomfortable with this line of inquiry. Ms. Henley's personal life should remain personal unless there's concrete evidence of impropriety."

"Thank you, Ms. Parker," I say, grateful for the support.

Neville's jaw tightens. "Very well. Let's set aside Lark's distractions and focus on the facts. Henley Sydney has recently faced unprecedented challenges that threaten our market position and public reputation."

"Which is exactly why strong, stable leadership is essential right now," Luke interjects.

*My champion!* Except I'm starting to see the door to freedom crack open, and I'm shocked at how appealing it is. Part of me wants to blow that door wide open and off its hinges.

"Or perhaps why a change in leadership is necessary," Neville counters. "I move that we take a vote of no confidence on Lark Henley's continued role as CEO."

His words make me catch my breath, as a ripple of tension passes through the room. This is happening faster than I expected, and I feel unmoored but not panicky.

"I second the motion." This comes from Walter Graves, an old ally of Neville's.

Luke straightens, his expression hardening. "This is premature and reactionary. Lark has been CEO for less than six months."

"Six months of escalating problems," Neville says.

"Hardly that," I correct him. "Of the *five* months that I've been in Sydney, we've had about two and a half of what

I now consider to be targeted sabotage." I can't let Luke do all my fighting.

"Sabotage that, I remind the members of the board, coincides with RWI's interest in acquiring us. If you read the stock report I provided, you'll see when they started to invest. It was about the time we had the first problem with our sugar. They want us weakened, and they want our shares to drop in price."

Neville all-but ignores me. "Those in favor of removing Lark Henley from the position of CEO, effective immediately?"

Hearing those words feels like a physical blow. The room falls silent. Walter and another two immediately raise their hands. *Three votes.* Despite the morning's preparation with Luke, my heart pounds in my chest as my termination starts to unfold.

"Those opposed?" Neville asks, far too smugly considering how few voted against me.

Eloise raises her hand, along with two other members. *Three votes.* Two board members remain undecided, their expressions conflicted.

"Ms. Cooper?" Neville prompts.

Jennifer Cooper, a relatively new board member, glances between Neville and me. "I abstain," she says finally.

Wembley's mouth thins with displeasure. "Mr. Davis?"

Charles Davis, the oldest board member, sighs heavily. "I've been with this company since Luke and Lark's father ran it," he says, his voice weary. "I've never seen anything like the challenges we're facing now. But I've also never seen such a blatant attempt to undermine a CEO." He pauses, his rheumy eyes finding mine. "I vote against removal."

I would be in the clear. Uncomfortable as possible in my tenuous position, but safe with four votes, nonetheless, if it weren't for Wembley having not yet voted.

As expected, he now announces, "I vote for Lark Henley's removal. We are tied. However—"

Not missing a beat, Luke says, "I vote to keep Lark Henley as CEO, breaking the tie."

Neville bristles. "While you're welcome as an observer, Mr. Henley, you do not have voting rights, neither on this parent board, nor on New York's."

My brother's expression is as chilling as I've ever seen it.

"I'm well aware. But my father does. And I have his proxy."

Neville's confident expression falters slightly. "Richard Henley has not named a proxy for today's meeting."

"Check your email," Luke says coolly. "He sent formal documentation an hour ago."

Neville pulls out his phone, scrolling through his messages. His face tightens when he finds what Luke has described.

"This is highly irregular," the chairman mutters.

"But entirely legal," Luke says. "This farce is over."

The tightness in my chest and stomach eases with relief, because being the first Henley sacked from the company is not how I want to be remembered.

Neville's lips are pressed in a thin white line. "What I was going to say before you interrupted me, Mr. Henley, is that we have a board member absent. Per our company bylaws, I will call for a second vote again in a few days when Mrs. Gable has returned from vacation. You're welcome to stay in Sydney," he tells Luke.

Like I'm on a rope swing, my stomach drops again.

But Luke parries. "My father's proxy vote will be the same, whether I'm here or not," he reminds Neville.

"True," the chairman says, "but I believe I know which way Mrs. Gable will vote. And then, it will be up to Ms. Cooper to do the right thing."

The board member who abstained looks petrified at having the spotlight shone on her. But the chairman has dug in his heels, and he isn't going to give up until he has removed me.

I've been on tenterhooks through the entire board meeting. *Will they or won't they?* Now, like a light switch flicked on, I see clearly how I'm letting other people dictate the course of my life. And I don't like it one bit.

Before I can stop myself, I say the words that are in my head . . . and in my heart.

"That won't be necessary. I resign as the CEO of Henley Sydney effective immediately."

Just like that, I'm no longer a Henley executive. I can't look at my brother beside me. I know I'll see shock and disappointment. Instead, I address the board.

"I recognize your authority to call this vote," I say, standing once again. "And I respect the inevitable outcome. Before I leave, however, I want to be clear about what happened here today. You've allowed fear to guide your decisions. Fear of change, fear of challenges."

Neville's expression remains impassive, but the other board members glance at one another, perhaps reconsidering.

"For the record," I continue, "I believe this company is under attack from an outside force. Instead of standing together against that threat, you've chosen to fracture our unity at the most vulnerable moment. I hope you actually have good intentions, Mr. Wembley."

"What are you trying to say?" Neville demands.

Luke answers for me. "The Henley family would hate to find out that you deliberately chose this moment to disrupt our company's leadership because you have ulterior motives."

I know he and I are both wondering if someone got to him. Perhaps a sweetheart deal with RWI. Stock options and a secure place on the board if they take over.

Luke adds, "I hope we won't be needing to investigate you next, Mr. Wembley."

*Wow!* Way to threaten the chairman, big brother. I'd high-five him, but I'm heading for the door with nothing more to say to the pompous clown who chairs our board. Luke's footsteps are a few seconds behind me as he follows.

"Lark, wait," he calls once we're in the hallway.

Remaining silent, I keep walking. Not as pissed off as I expected to be, but feeling utterly drained, I enter the sanctuary of my *former* office.

Luke catches up. "That was a setup. The photos, the rushed meeting. Wembley had this planned."

"Obviously." My voice is tight with suppressed emotion. I take the folder he holds out to me, glad that my brother snatched it up. Still, I'm humiliated at how many people saw my private life in full color.

"We can fight this," he insists. "Dad will be furious. We can call for an extraordinary general meeting so Wembley can't—"

"No." The word comes out flat, final.

Luke blinks, caught off guard. "What?"

I take a deep breath, surprised by my own serenity. "I'm not going to fight. Later, I'll type out my resignation officially. Probably with a big glass of wine at hand."

"But—"

"Luke, I *have* been distracted. Unfocused." I look at him directly.

"Because of Mitch Franklin?" he asks, appearing angry again. "That's why you took your eye off the ball and threw away your job."

"Wrong order," I protest. "If I wasn't feeling restless, I never would've let Mitch into my life. He might seem like the catalyst, but it was really my own doing." I shrug. "I know Mom and Dad and even Clover are going to take it hard, but maybe it's for the best."

My brother runs a hand through his hair. "I can't believe this just happened. And I can't believe you're giving up." He studies me for a long moment. "You're serious?"

"Completely," I say, a weight lifting from me as I admit it out loud. "I'm not happy here. The company deserves someone who loves it the way it should be loved. The way you love it."

Luke's expression softens. "What about you? What do you deserve?"

*Good question.* "I don't know. Not yet," I admit. "But it's time I figured that out."

He pulls me into a tight hug. "Whatever you decide, I've got your back. You know that, right?"

I nod against his shoulder, grateful beyond words for his unwavering support.

"I know," I say, feeling a thick ball of unshed tears clog my throat.

"So what now?" he asks as we separate.

Holding up my hand, I take a second to recalibrate and let my emotions settle. Then I take a breath.

"Now," I say, "I need to call Charlotte before she hears the news from someone else. By the way, our VP would be an excellent CEO, don't you think?"

Luke looks amenable, so I add, "You're welcome to help me clean out my office if you like. After that, I'm going to talk to a friend about some chocolate sauce."

$♥$♥$♥$

When I knock on Jules's door in the trendy section of Surry Hills, I think I should've called first. I've only been here, in his personal space, twice for parties. Both times were while I was still learning the ropes as co-CEO with Luke here in Sydney. My brother would've come with me, but he said he had some business to take care of.

Our master chocolatier is surprised but opens his home to me, offering coffee.

"No, thanks," I say. "I simply wanted you to know I've quit. The board was going to remove me as CEO anyway."

*"Merde!"* Jules exclaims. "Now I must insist you sit and have something stronger than coffee."

Since I have no pressing business for the rest of my life, I take him up on his offer.

"It's after five somewhere," I say before making myself comfortable.

When we're both holding a gin and tonic, Jules says, "Are you going to tell me why?"

"Official reason? Leadership failure—mine—leaving us open to or directly causing our recent string of disasters."

I laugh without humor. "Unofficial reason? I've been sleeping with Mitch Franklin."

He frowns. "The restaurateur. Wait!" His eyes widen, as it dawns on him. "The Franklin Darkly guy?"

I shrug, too emotionally spent to be angry anymore about the board overstepping.

"It is what it is. I'm not supposed to have a life. Anyway, I wanted to tell you personally about why I'm disappearing as of today. But more importantly, I want you to know that I never believed you stole that recipe. Girlfriend witness or not, I totally trust you."

Jules runs a hand through his blond hair, his expression troubled. "Actually, I've made progress on that front, and it's pretty bizarre. I was coming to see you tomorrow."

"Here I am," I quip, the top-shelf gin already making me feel chill.

Turning on his laptop, he taps at the keyboard.

"I had to use facial recognition software since nothing came up for Milly Cook."

"Milly Cook?"

"Yes. That was the name she told me. But I had one photo on my phone, and I found her using it."

He turns the screen toward me. I'm staring at an elegant professional profile—and my breath catches in my throat. The woman smiling confidently at the camera is unmistakably the same person I saw at Mitch's restaurant.

"Camille Durand," I read aloud, my mouth suddenly dry. "Head chef at Chez Henri in Paris."

Jules sighs. "Not the name I knew. Nor the profession. And she certainly never wore her chef's whites. We even joked about her last name, since she claimed utter hopelessness in that area."

He gazes at the screen. "It's like I was catfished, but in a good way since she never did anything bad to me."

"I've seen her," I say slowly. "She had dinner with Mitch Franklin at his restaurant last week."

Looking startled, Jules says, "That's one coincidence too many. She dated me and is now dating the guy you're seeing?" He shakes his head. "That's fucked up."

"No, they're not dating now. They broke up years ago." I lean closer to the laptop, as if I can learn more by seeing her up close. "When did you meet her?"

He thinks for a moment. "About two months ago. She and I literally collided when I was coming out of a bar. Naturally, I went back in with her and bought her a drink."

*Naturally.* What man wouldn't? She's strikingly beautiful.

"What was she doing here in Sydney?"

Jules's expression is sheepish. "She said she was on an extended holiday."

"By herself?"

He shrugs.

"That didn't seem at all weird?" I ask.

"To be honest, I was happy to hang out with her. It was nice to speak French again."

"Milly Cook was French?"

"Belgian," he says wistfully. "She was fun and . . . stacked."

A bark of laughter escapes me. I'm seeing a new side of my master chocolatier. Knowing how quickly Mitch captivated me, from his physical appearance alone, I understand where Jules is coming from.

"And then one morning," I say, "she wanted chocolate sauce for her crepes, but had no idea how to make it. Right?"

Jules winces. "I was at her place, a short-term rental with a full kitchen. That seems odd now since she said she never cooked. She was pleased with herself at having bought everything I needed to make crepes." He sips the gin tonic and stares into the middle distance.

"Then for the sauce," he adds, "Milly put out on the counter what she had."

"Including the coconut sugar?"

"If I recall correctly, she asked if I'd ever tried it. I said it would add a more complex flavor. *Voilà*, she pulled out a bag from her cupboard. And the only vanilla she had at her place was—"

"Mexican," I finish, "although nearly everyone uses vanilla from Madagascar." My heart is pounding now. "Did she ever mention knowing Mitch or anything about Franklin Darkly?"

"Never," Jules says, looking increasingly disturbed. "But she was very curious about my job and about Henley."

Pulling out my phone, I quickly search through the comprehensive files that Charlotte has already put together on RWI, the European conglomerate attempting to take over Henley.

"Jules, did Camille ever mention her family?"

He shakes his head. "Not really. She intimated her father was in finance or something. Said he was quite successful, which was why she didn't have to work."

I find what I'm looking for and feel a chill run through me. "Stephen Durand," I read from my phone screen. "Board member, RWI Holdings."

Jules's eyes widen. "You think she's his daughter? That this was deliberate?"

"I think," I say slowly, "we're being played. All of us. Camille as Milly Cook gave you Mitch's recipe. She knew exactly what she was doing to stir up the pot."

Jules looks stricken. "I swear when I think about it, it still seems like I created it myself." Then he drains his drink and sets the glass down.

"There's more. I gave her a private, after-hours tour of the factory," he confesses. "Weeks before Eddie collapsed, but still, she might've taken a moment to—"

"*Poison* the raspberry powder?" I whisper.

He nods. "That doesn't explain the cocoa beans or the contaminated sugar, but—"

"But what?" I ask.

"A beautiful woman can gain access to places, distract a man."

I picture her at the bean roasting facility, pressing up against some hapless dude until he doesn't know what he's doing, while he's letting my precious cocoa beans burn. Maybe she even mixed up her own spray bottle solution containing geosmin, which I've since learned is water-soluble. The beet sugar would quickly absorb the residue.

"Where is she now?" I wonder.

He shrugs. "No idea. One minute, we were making crepes—"

"And chocolate sauce."

"Yes," he agrees, "and the next, she said she was heading home."

"Which is where? Belgium?"

He rolls his eyes. "She was a little vague." Then he grins. "But she was—"

"Stacked, I know." I get to my feet. *Men!* But why did she go see Mitch and pitch him a restaurant proposal?

"Are you taking this to the board?" Jules asks. "Do you think it'll result in your being reinstated?"

A little voice says, *I hope not.*

On the other hand, I'd love to smash all these findings right in Neville Wembley's smug face.

"Don't say anything to anyone," I tell him.

Jules grins. "You're technically not my boss anymore, but I'll pretend I don't know that."

His comment strikes me with unexpected force. I'm not anyone's boss now. For the first time since I can remember,

I have no title, no responsibility to the company that bears my name. The realization is both terrifying and liberating.

"I may not be CEO anymore," I say, "but I'm still a Henley. And someone is trying to hurt my family's company. That makes it personal."

I gather my things and head for the door, but Jules calls after me.

"Lark? Be careful. If what we suspect is true, these people aren't messing around."

I nod, appreciating his concern. "Neither am I."

# 23

## Mitch

One of my waitstaff pokes her head around my office door. "Boss, there's someone asking for you. Says he's Luke Henley."

Unexpected and not the Henley I've been hoping to hear from all day, but I say, "Send him in."

She hesitates. "He looks like he wants to punch someone. Maybe you." She sends me a saucy smile, already picturing the testosterone-laden situation about to ensue.

*Great.* "Send him in anyway." Just what I need on a day of nasty surprises.

After dropping Lark off to meet her brother, my brunch manager at the F6 called, sounding uncharacteristically frazzled.

A faulty electrical issue took out the fridge and freezer inventory. Thank God it wasn't in the middle of a Friday or Saturday night. We closed, which was a pity since Sunday brunch service, running at the tavern for the past few weeks, is gaining traction.

I stand as Lark's brother enters my space. He has Lark's hair color *and* the same golden-brown eyes as his sister. However, his gaze lacks even the barest spark of warmth when looking at me. He's wearing suit pants and a wilted dress shirt with the sleeves rolled up, sporting a watch that probably costs more than most of my staff make in six months.

Basically, Luke Henley strides in like a guy who knows his worth and expects others to recognize it too. Confidence laced with . . . hostility.

"Mr. Henley," I say, extending my hand. "What can I do for you?" He ignores my hand, letting it hang out there. Almost nothing worse than that trick.

"Let's skip the pleasantries," he says. "I want to know what your game is with my sister."

"I don't play games with women." Actually, that's kind of a lie. I've certainly enjoyed the fun of nameless one-night stands, but only if they were into it. The way Lark was the first night we met.

*Except with her, everything changed.*

"Not with Lark," I add, realizing it sounds like I'm hedging.

"Really?" He pulls out his phone, swipes a few times, then holds it up showing a photo of me and Lark kissing outside my building this morning.

*Why the hell didn't I take the time to put on a shirt?*

"Because this looks an awful lot like a game to me," he says. "Embarrassing her in public."

My jaw tightens. "That photo means someone has been following your sister. That should concern you more than who she's seeing."

"Oh, it concerns me plenty," he says, sliding his phone into his pocket. "Especially since several similar photos were plastered across a boardroom table this afternoon while Lark was fighting for her job."

That hits me like a punch to the gut. It explains why he's dressed like he was at a business meeting. Because he was.

"What happened?"

"She didn't tell you? My sister just resigned as CEO of Henley Sydney after the board used your relationship as evidence of her 'unfitness' to lead."

"That's ridiculous," I say immediately. "Lark is obviously capable of doing whatever the hell she puts her mind to."

"Which begs the question, *why isn't her mind on business?* She's been so distracted lately she has missed what's happening right under her nose." His gaze is accusatory. "Be honest with me. Are you the reason?"

I take a deep breath, reminding myself that he's doing his brotherly duty, being protective.

"You should ask your sister that question."

"I'm asking you."

"I may be one of the reasons," I say, watching his face cloud over. "But not because I've been messing Lark around. I genuinely care about her. A lot more than I expected to, frankly."

Luke studies me for a long moment, his expression unreadable. "She's had her heart broken before. I can't stop that from happening again, but I can certainly give a world of pain to anyone being reckless with my sister."

"I'm not here to hurt her." And if I could punch the heart-breaker in the nose right this instant, I would.

"That remains to be seen." He glances around my office.

It's not luxurious, although it could be. I simply don't care enough about my own work surroundings outside of the kitchen and the customer areas. Those, I care about down to the color of the bathroom walls, the safety mats under my chef's feet, and the ergonomic comfort of each chair in the dining area.

"I've done my research on you, Franklin," he continues. "You never stay in one place for long. Four months in

London, three months each in New Orleans, Amsterdam, and Barcelona. What's keeping you in Sydney?"

I could lie, make up some bullshit about business opportunities or the Australian food scene. But I opt for honesty.

"Right now? Your sister."

That seems to catch him off guard. He reassesses me, folding his arms.

"Today, she quit as CEO of the family company she loves, and I think you have something to do with this."

Thinking how Lark confessed to me a sense of fulfillment in her job, I shrug.

"She's fierce and could run the company with her eyes closed. If she wants to be the CEO, she'll be the CEO. If she doesn't, that's up to her."

Luke doesn't like my answer. "I'm warning you. If you're playing with her, there's no place far enough for you to run."

I roll my eyes. "I have a sister, too. I know what you're saying, but you don't have to go all caveman. Lark and I can deal with one another on equal footing. We always have. She knows how I feel about her."

"I know Lark is strong," Luke says, "but I'm not sure her judgment when it comes to men is as honed as it is for business."

Then he narrows his eyes. "She was royally rolled by a guy back in New York. A first-class prick."

"What did you do to him?" I ask, curious because the man standing in front of me is bristling with the need to clobber someone on his sister's behalf. I cannot imagine he would let Connor Whittel off the hook.

Luke shakes his head and sidesteps the answer. "I was here, running Henley Sydney. No one told me anything in time to keep her from making some huge and costly mistakes." Then he adds, "She simply has too much heart."

*Like that's a bad thing?*

"Too much heart for chocolate?" The question slips out before I can stop it. It probably sounds flippant.

He leans forward, menacingly. "It's a cutthroat business and has been since its inception. Ask anyone about the old-boy network of Cadbury, Rowntree, Lindt, Cailler, Tobler, and, of course our U.S. brands, Ghirardelli and Hershey. Those are just the first few that come to mind."

"I understand cutthroat as well as the next guy," I tell him. "Restaurant kitchens can be a nest of vipers."

Then I consider Lark going up against any man, even the chefs I've known who were egomaniacs. And I tell her brother what I think.

"Lark could kick ass working at any of those companies you mentioned, but maybe she doesn't want to deal with tedious executive shit any longer."

He considers this, and I have a feeling Lark has said something similar to her brother. For the first time, he speaks like we're on the same side.

"Right now, her head isn't in it. I don't know if it will be again," he confesses. "Or if she's done."

Since he's speaking freely, I will, too. "I know about what happened with that Whittel guy in NYC," I admit.

Luke's eyebrows shoot up. "Lark told you?"

"No, my sister's a model. High end. She rubbed elbows with Lark in New York." I try to say this delicately, but my face must express my disgust. "And she rubbed more than that with Connor *after* he broke up with your sister."

Luke looks appalled. "Well, that's . . ."

"Awkward," I finish for him. "Even gross, if I think about it too much."

"And you're not anything like him?" Luke shoots back.

"I can promise you I'm not."

"Good," he says, nodding. "My business is confectionery, but that doesn't mean I'm soft and sweet. You asked what I did to Connor. I tell you. I tanked his investments, shredded his reputation, and let the SEC clean up the rest. Ultimately, it cost him seven figures and a career. He's living out west somewhere, *after* his stint in prison for insider trading. If you let Lark down, I will do everything in my power to destroy your reputation and your restaurants."

We stare grimly at one another. I nearly counter with something combative and stupid such as, "I'd like to see you try." But I don't, in fact, want to see him try. I don't want to be at odds with Lark's brother or anyone in her family.

The reason is clear. I'm falling in love with her, and I want her family to like me, not try to ruin me.

"I've never given Lark reason not to trust me," I say firmly. "And I don't intend to start now. I give you my word."

I think I surprise him by sticking out my hand again. We're about the same height, six-three, and I'm not sure which one of us would win in a fight, especially if we're both fighting for Lark.

After a beat, he takes it and we shake. The tension dissipates between us, and Luke Henley seems satisfied, for now.

He drags a hand across his eyes, his expression no longer aggressive.

"Glad that's settled. I hope no one else pisses me off today because jet lag has caught up with me. If you hear from Lark before I do," he says, pausing to yawn, "remind her I'm flying home in the morning."

"Will do." I'm feeling relieved he trusts me enough to give his sister a message. "Although I haven't heard from her all day."

Luke nods, heading for the door. "My sister tends to circle her wagon of one. Always has done. It's just her way of dealing with the world—by pulling back and closing herself off."

After he leaves, I drive directly to her apartment, wanting her to know I have a sturdy wagon, too. Her car isn't in its usual spot. Regardless, I let myself in with the keycode she gave me when she was drunk and knock on her door. She's not home, and when I call her phone once more, it goes straight to voicemail. Again.

"Pick up the damn phone," I mutter, pacing outside her building before heading home.

Now that I know she walked out of Henley's boardroom leaving her job behind, I need to find out if she's OK. I love her independence, but I also love how the opposite is true in my bed. When she goes from tiger to purring, compliant kitten.

But, man, it's hard to deal with the way she disappears whenever something comes up.

If I did that to a woman, I'd be called *emotionally unavailable* or something equally derogatory. "You're running a masterclass in emotional minimalism"—that was from a woman I met about a month before Lark. I can't believe how much I've changed. How much she's changed me.

I try her number again when I get home. Nothing. My apartment feels emptier than usual. The spaces Lark filled last night and this morning seem to echo with her absence.

I've poured myself an Aussie favorite, a Carlton Draught, when there's a knock at my door.

Hope crashes hard when I swing the door open. *Camille!* Like last time, seeing the wrong woman on my doorstep yields the most severe disappointment.

This time, however, she's holding a small overnight bag and wearing a practiced expression of distress.

"This day just keeps getting better," I say sarcastically, leaning against my door frame and sipping my beer.

"I missed my flight the other day," she explains, her voice softening. "It took a while to sort out, but I got another ticket and need a place to stay for one night."

"There are about a billion hotel rooms in Sydney," I point out.

Looking up at me with those big, dark eyes, she bites her lip, a move that once had me wrapped around her finger.

"I've been lying to you," she confesses. "I'm out of money. After leaving Henri and the restaurant . . . I made some bad decisions."

Her words don't add up. "What about the Santa Barbara restaurant start-up?"

She blinks. "They only want me if I can bring you. You're the star restaurateur, after all."

Now I know why she was so persistent. On the other hand, there's her family money. Her father is Belgian, as I recall, and loaded.

"But your dad," I say.

She goes pale, her expression suddenly guarded. "What about him?"

"Can't he help?"

She swallows, like the words are sticking in her throat. Looking away, she whispers, "He has disowned me.".

I straighten. "That sucks. I know you two were close."

Camille shrugs. "Look, I need to stay one single night," she says, edging closer to the doorway. "Then I'll be gone. I promise."

"First, tell me why you made that remark about Lark Henley."

Closing her eyes for a long moment, she confesses, "Pure, unadulterated jealousy. I heard about you two, and then you were pushing me away. I said what I said. Now that I've humiliated myself, may I stay?"

I hesitate. My gut's telling me something's off. But because of what we once shared, combined with her apparent vulnerability, I feel my resolve crumbling.

"I'll give you money and put you up in a hotel, but you're not staying here." Luke Henley would definitely disapprove of an ex-lover spending the night.

Camille's expression hardens for a split second before melting into pleading.

"*S'il te plaît*, Mitchell." Hearing Camille plead in that tone tears at my heart, despite everything from our past.

"I'm emotionally and physically exhausted," she continues. "You are the only person I know on this entire continent, and I've come holding my hat, despite knowing you might turn me away."

"I think you mean *hat in hand*," I correct her.

Her lower lip trembles. "I could use a friend. Just for tonight."

I exhale heavily. "Fine. You can put your things in the room down the hall on the right."

Relief brightens her face. "*Merci*," she thanks me. "You won't even know I'm here."

Highly doubtful, but I step aside, letting her in. As she passes, however, her new perfume wafts over me, reminding me she's more of a stranger now than a friend. We did have good times before she left me for Henri.

Yet even then, she had no qualms about placing a goodbye note between our bed pillows and sticking me with a monthly rent I couldn't afford at the time.

Rolling my eyes at my own stupidity, I close the door and follow her inside.

Retreating to the kitchen, I try Lark again. It goes straight to voicemail. I text her, feeling increasingly aggravated.

*Luke came to see me. I know what happened. Call me. Please.*

No response. Her disappearing act has left me pacing the room, hating above all else this feeling of uselessness. I start to cook without even thinking, and before I know it, I've made Fettuccine Alfredo, while leaving two more messages for Lark.

Perhaps lured in by the aroma of the nearly finished sauce, Camille wanders into my kitchen.

"You didn't have to go to all this trouble," she says, knowing the dish is about as simple as falling off a bar stool. To me, it's a tastier version of the old standard comfort food, mac and cheese.

"You know I barely did more than boil water and emulsify a few ingredients."

"Wine would be nice with this?" she says, eyeing my wine selection.

I sigh. How the hell did I end up playing house with her? I think of Luke and my promise.

"You know what? No to wine, and you can help yourself to a bowl of fettuccine, but I'm heading out."

"Don't be so uptight," she says. "We used to have fun, remember?" But she enters my kitchen anyway and starts to plate a good-sized portion for herself.

"That was a long time ago," I remind her, already pocketing my keys.

"It doesn't have to stay in the past," she says, her voice smooth as béchamel sauce. "Don't go. Eat with me."

I'm about to tell her that she needs to back off when another knock comes at the door. Given my luck today, I expect it to be Luke Henley with a baseball bat. But the universe has something even worse in store.

When I open the door, Lark stands there, looking weary but by no means broken. Her eyes aren't even a little red. *No crying over spilled chocolate milk for my woman!*

"Hey, I'm sorry I didn't answer," she blurts immediately. "I had a bunch of stuff to take care of. Then I went to the beach to clear my head and left my phone in my car."

I'm trying to focus on her words, but my skin is prickling with the awareness of Camille behind me, perhaps already chowing down at my island. This is not going to make me look good. When I don't let her in, Lark frowns.

"Are you mad at me?" she asks.

"No. Not at all. I'm sorry I was blowing up your phone, but I was concerned. Do you want to go get something to eat?" I ask. "And talk."

After all, my keys are in my pocket. If I can just get Lark to back up a step, I'll be able to close the door. It's shitty of me, but I don't want her to get the wrong idea and feel hurt in any way. Over nothing.

"Whatever you're cooking smells amazing," she says. "And I'm not really up for going out."

She looks up at me, expression open and guileless. Maybe I'm being cowardly.

"I have to warn you," I say, coming clean. "I have a houseguest, but come on in."

Opening the door further, I step back. Lark strolls ahead of me across the marble entry hall, and I follow. Until she stops short, and I nearly plow into her.

Looking over her shoulder, my gaze lands on Camille at the dining room table. Set for two with two glasses of wine and two steaming plates of food. *Damn*, she's quick!

"You've got to be kidding me," Lark says, her voice calm and steady.

From behind her, I say, "It's not what it looks like."

"It never is," she replies coldly. At least she's moving forward again.

*Stalking* is the word that comes to mind, like a big cat going after its prey, straight into the dining room. I can't see Lark's face, but Camille can. She stops mid-chew, her eyes widening.

"Lark, please—" I begin, needing to defuse this ASAP.

"Hold up," she cuts me off, still staring at my ex-girlfriend. "I came here to tell you something rather startling."

"Tell me what?" I demand.

But Lark says nothing more. I move around her, so I can take the heat off Camille, who may be a pain in the ass, but has nothing to do with whatever sent Lark into this menacing behavior.

At last, I get a good look at her expression. *If looks could kill* . . .

"She's not eating dinner *with* me," I say, realizing how lame that sounds.

This finally draws Lark's attention to me. She cocks her beautiful head as if I'm speaking Greek and raises an eyebrow. Then she reaches forward. Camille flinches, but all Lark does is take the other full glass of wine from the table.

I anticipate her tossing it over one of us. She takes a sip and a deep breath, then says, "Go on."

"What I mean is, I made dinner, obviously, but not for her. Not for anyone, really. Besides, I was just leaving. To go look for you." I draw my keys from my pocket as if they're proof, because I desperately don't want this to explode into something crazy.

Lark looks at my keys, sipping more wine. Then she returns her attention to Camille.

"Shall I tell him, or do you want to?"

For the second time in a minute, I ask, "Tell me what? Lark, what's going on?"

Camille stays silent, looking more uncomfortable by the second.

"Your ex-girlfriend is working for the people trying to take over my company," Lark says. "She's been a one-woman demolition derby. And she's the one who stole your Franklin Darkly recipe."

Her words don't make sense. I turn to Camille, who slowly gets to her feet.

With a shake of her head, she says, "Elle est folle." *She is crazy.*

It doesn't help matters when she comes over to stand behind me as though I'm going to protect her. As if I'm going to take her side.

I'm not, but this is too weird, and I'm trying to wrap my brain around it. Camille is a trained chef, not a thief.

*What the hell is going on?*

"That can't be possible," I say. Because I don't want it to be true.

Not that I give a damn about Camille, even as she wraps her fingers around my arm, like I'm her savior. What I can't stand is the notion that anything or anyone from *my* life is responsible for causing Lark an ounce of pain or trouble. It makes me sick to think about it.

# 24

## Lark

Camille's hand grips Mitch's arm tightly. I want him to shake it off. To shake *her* off. He doesn't, but he does peel her fingers from his bicep—the bicep that rested over my naked body while I slept beside him last night. Then he takes a step away from her.

*Smart man!* I think, until his next words.

*Of all the defenses, this is what he came up with?* I can't help it. I laugh, quick and sharp, despite there being nothing funny here.

"Camille Durand is Jules's *friend* Milly Cook," I tell him since she's not going to. "Her father is on the board of RWI, the company buying up Henley shares."

Watching Mitch's face carefully, I trust the man with my body and, as it turns out, with my heart. *But with my family's company?* I have to be sure he had zero knowledge about any of this.

Sure enough, he appears to be utterly floored.

"She hung out with Jules, slept with him, made him trust her," I continue. "All so she could give him your recipe, *accidentally*, by having only those ingredients available when she asked him to whip her up some chocolate sauce."

The same fury I worked through earlier today rises to the surface again. Maybe because Camille is still standing here, near *my* man, and she doesn't look as scared as she ought to.

Finally, though, Mitch is getting the picture. Turning to his ex-lover, he asks, "Why would you do something like this when you're so talented? And why put me in the middle of it?"

Camille lifts her chin, lips firmly closed. Apparently, she isn't in the cooperating mood. Maybe I can help explain why she involved him.

"By using your sauce, she killed two birds with one stone, trying to get my company involved in a lawsuit while also throwing me off my game by involving the man I was sleeping with. It certainly messed with my head when I should've been focused on company shares being purchased."

Mitch's luminous blue gaze locks with mine, and a shiver runs right through me. He knows what I'm leaving unspoken. What makes this so devious isn't that we were having sex. It's that our hearts were rapidly becoming involved as well. If they hadn't been, Camille's interference wouldn't have amounted to a hill of cocoa beans. Sabotaging production would have been enough.

"You can spin whatever lies you want," she says, edging around Mitch. "I guess you have to make excuses for losing your job today."

And there it is—confirmation of everything I've said.

"How would you know that?" Mitch asks my question for me.

Camille pales and moves farther away.

*How did she find out so quickly?* Someone on the board, perhaps, or maybe she has made friends with the board secretary. It's a loose end I'll tie up eventually. There are others.

"I wonder who she slept with to get my cocoa beans burned and my sugar contaminated," I muse. "But Jules took her to the factory, himself, so I know how she poisoned the raspberry powder."

Mitch's mouth drops open. At the same time, Camille tries to dart toward the hallway, but I don't let her sneak by. I block her, not yet finished giving her a piece of my mind.

"You're toying with people's lives," I remind her, keeping my voice low and controlled, the way my brother would. "It doesn't matter about me. I'll land on my feet. But one of my factory workers was seriously ill. He has a family. It could've been a lot worse. The same with the sugar contamination. You're a chef. Don't you have some oath about not tampering with food?"

Camille doesn't answer, and she keeps her expression entirely neutral. We both look at Mitch, who's processing a lot in a short time without the benefit of a few hours on the beach like I had. For his sake, I feel sorry that he has to find out someone he once cared for is basically a piece of shit and whoring for her father.

Ignoring her, he's looking solely into my eyes when he speaks. "I am *not* sleeping with her. Just so we're clear."

"Oh, I know that," I tell him. "There's no way you'd go back to this . . . this gas station candy bar, not after you've tasted gourmet chocolate."

He delivers a full-blown laugh, while Camille's face contorts with rage. "Let me pass. I'll get my things and leave."

I simply want to put my arms around Mitch and lean into him. But this isn't over.

"You wanted to get out of the kitchen and play in the corporate world? Then you should've picked someone else to mess with. Does Mitch know that you saw the police at the airport today, that you didn't dare approach your gate?"

He shakes his head. "She said she missed her flight but has one tomorrow."

"Indeed, she does. Her father is sending a private jet, but she's not going to make that flight either." I get out my phone. "The police will want to know where she is so she can be arraigned."

"You have no proof," Camille spits out.

"Jules took you to my factory. Camera footage doesn't lie. You were in the ingredients area, doing something very naughty with my master chocolatier. When he left to get you a tissue, you're on tape tampering with our powdered raspberry supply."

It took a while to find the nine minutes, but once I told the factory security team the date, they found the evidence.

"I didn't know anyone could get rug burn from a rubber safety mat," I say. "And the way you used that pallet jack." I leave it to Mitch's imagination.

Camille makes her move again, this time toward the front door.

Mitch reaches it before she does. Grabbing her by the arm, he takes her down the hall. She's struggling all the way until he puts her in the guest bathroom and stands guard.

"Mitchell, you can't seriously believe her," Camille yells from her makeshift cell. Then she lets loose a string of French swear words. I recognize a few from Jules.

I dial 000 and get a dispatcher almost immediately.

"Can't she have her chef's diploma stripped from her, or something?" I ask him. "Maybe never be allowed to wear one of those silly hats again?"

Finally, this evokes a small smile from him. "It doesn't work that way, but I wish it did. And they're not silly hats. Not when I wear one."

That makes me smile back at him, because I haven't seen him in chef's whites or the ubiquitous hat, but I bet he looks sexy AF.

Camille has fallen silent, then she says, "My father won't be happy to hear how you're helping her."

For the first time, I consider that Mitch may suffer repercussions, but he doesn't appear worried.

The police come quickly, with the detective on the case pulling up behind the patrol car. In a few minutes, I hope I've seen the last of this bitch, when she disappears into the backseat in handcuffs.

"Her father will post bail. He might get her out before you and I finish dessert," Mitch says, taking me into his arms for the first time.

I melt against him, something inside me settles. "She messed with Henley Confectionery. In Sydney," I remind him. "She's not going anywhere. Besides, even if Monsieur Durand whisked her away to freedom somewhere in Europe, I believe discovering her crimes will put an end to RWI's takeover, one way or another. We have some top lawyers on it."

"I heard what happened at the board meeting," he murmurs into my hair.

I lean back to look up at him. "You left a message that you talked to Luke."

"He came to see me. Your brother wanted to make sure my intentions were honorable."

I can't help smiling. "And are they?"

"Some of them." Mitch waggles his eyebrows, like a cartoon villain and I laugh.

"Not all of them, I hope."

"Definitely not," he promises. With that, he kisses me. A perfect Mitch kiss that I feel down to my toes. It gets my heart racing and my juices flowing, but instead of leading me to the bedroom, he takes me to the kitchen.

"Sit," he orders. "Do you mind lukewarm Fettuccine Alfredo or shall I heat it up?"

"Wow," I say. "I can't believe you've relaxed enough around me to offer less-than-perfect food. I'll take it. Just not *her* leftovers," I add, jerking my thumb toward the dining room table.

After he scrapes her dinner into the trash, we sit side-by-side, chowing down in silence for a few minutes.

"So," he says as I'm taking a sip of wine, "I hear you had a bad day."

I laugh so hard the wine squirts out my nose, resulting in Mitch thumping my back while I cough.

"Sorry," he says, when I've recovered.

"No, don't apologize. You can make me laugh anytime you want."

We smile at one another, and I know the red wine dribbled on my shirt is a new level of intimacy for us. Like seeing me during my period in my comfy underwear.

Then I tell him, "I *thought* it was the worst of bad days. At first. After quitting the job that I've been born and raised for and finding out from Jules who Camille was, it seemed like a personal low point."

Mitch rubs my shoulder, which is so sweet, so supportive, and a lot better than having him pound on my back. I continue, although, sitting beside him, my day doesn't seem terrible any longer.

"I talked to the investigator we already had working on the poisoning case, telling him what I knew. He found out about Camille's flight, and then it was out of my hands. I spent hours sitting on Bondi Beach, thinking, trying to untangle what I want."

He leans down and gently touches the side of his head to mine. "Did you succeed?"

"I'm here, aren't I?"

"Meaning?" But his eyes have a look I've come to recognize—happiness.

"Meaning I want to see how far we can go in the time you're still here. I have literally no idea what comes next in any aspect of my life. For some reason, right now, I'm OK with that. But the one non-negotiable thing is that I want you while that's still possible."

My voice goes from normal to husky as I repeat, "Basically, I just want you."

"Are you done?" he asks, his gaze dropping to my mouth.

My breath catches and my body starts to react as if he's already touching me.

"Meaning?" I echo him.

"Meaning if you've finished eating, lady, then I want to take you to bed. Those nipple clips are waiting in their little bag in my bedside table."

With my heart beating a speedy tattoo in my chest, I climb off the stool on quivering legs. He doesn't need to ask me twice, since his words have made me wet and ready.

Mitch reaches out as if to take my hand, but instead, he sweeps me off my feet, up against his built chest. Today, I may have lost my place in my family company, but at this instant, I feel so damn lucky.

In a few of his long-legged strides, Mitch carries me into his very masculine bedroom. My heart races when he lays me on his king-sized bed with a gentleness that belies the hunger in his eyes. The mattress dips beneath his weight as he crawls over me, his sculpted body caging mine.

"I've been wanting to get you alone all day," he growls, his voice a rough velvet that sends shivers down my spine.

His mouth claims mine in a kiss that's both possessive and reverent. When his hands slide beneath my blouse, skimming over my heated skin, I arch toward him, my body responding to his skilled touch.

"Too many clothes," I murmur against his lips.

With practiced efficiency, we undress each other, our hands exploring across newly exposed skin. When I'm naked beneath him, Mitch pauses to look at me.

"You're so sexy," he whispers, tracing a finger between my breasts. "And tonight, I have something special planned."

Reaching toward his bedside drawer, he retrieves the familiar small black velvet bag. My nipples pucker in anticipation, remembering the exquisite pressure of the clips he's used before.

"Do you trust me?" he asks, his blue eyes intense.

"Completely," I answer without hesitation.

He tips the contents onto the bed, and I gasp. Alongside the familiar silver nipple clips is something new—a third clip connected to the others by yet another delicate silver chain.

"What's that?" I ask, my voice so husky with desire I barely recognize it.

Mitch's smile is wicked as he lifts the chain for my inspection. "This, my gorgeous Lark, is going to make you feel things you've never experienced before."

Understanding dawns. "A clit clip?" The words come out breathless, my body responding to the mere possibility with an immediate throbbing ache.

"You said before you wanted to try it. Still game?" His question is serious despite the heat in his gaze.

"God, yes," I whisper, surprising myself with how eagerly I crave this new experience.

Mitch's smile is both tender and triumphant before he lowers his head to my breast. His tongue circles my nipple until it's a stiff peak before he gently attaches the first clip.

A jolt of delicious agony zaps straight to my core, directly between my trembling thighs. I moan as he repeats the process with my other nipple, the dual pinch making me writhe beneath him.

"Be still," he commands softly, trailing kisses down my stomach. "The best is yet to come."

His fingers part my folds, finding me already slick with wanting him.

"So wet for me," he murmurs appreciatively.

I gasp when his talented tongue flicks against my clit, teasing it to swollen readiness. The anticipation has me shuddering on the edge already.

"Please," I whimper.

With careful precision, Mitch applies the third little metal device, which slides over my hooded-and-hard clit rather than clips to it. He adjusts the clamp's tightness, and I nearly come undone, shaking with pure pleasure.

The pressure is intense—not painful, but overwhelmingly satisfying.

Every slight movement radiates through my lower body and up my spine. The chain connecting all three points creates a circuit of sensory tension.

"How does that feel?" he asks, his voice low with restraint.

"Incredible," I manage to say. "I feel . . . connected everywhere."

A flash of a smile, then he says, "What happens when I do this?" He gives the chain the gentlest of tugs. With. His. Teeth.

I cry out as lightning bolts of pain and bliss surge through me. My back arches involuntarily, which only intensifies the pinching of my engorged clit. Clutching the sheets, I anchor myself as waves of ecstasy threaten to sweep me away.

"Mitch," I gasp. "I need you inside me. Now."

He positions himself between my thighs, his impressive erection poised at my entrance. Then he eases the clit clip up and out of the way, making me groan. The movement adds to my pain, making sweat break out on my back, but also increases my enjoyment to the point of overwhelming me.

I start to pant, seeing stars.

With torturous slowness, he glides inside, stretching and filling me completely.

"Oh God," I moan when he begins to move, to rock. The swinging chain sends exhilarating pulses to my already sizzling nerve endings. It's too much to bear.

"Mitch," I cry out, wanting him to stop, but knowing I'd disintegrate on the spot if he did.

Each thrust creates a rhythmic tug on the three clips, building an overwhelming symphony of sensation. I'm climbing higher than I've ever been, suspended in a state of perpetual nirvana.

"That's it, beautiful," Mitch encourages, his gaze locked on my face. "Let go for me."

When my climax hits, it's cataclysmic, as if the world shatters around me. Wave after exquisite wave crashes through my body, radiating from all three points of contact and meeting in my very center where his long, thick cock has impaled me.

Again, I cry out his name, my pussy convulsing around him, the intensity prolonged by the continuous stimulation.

Mitch follows me over the edge, his powerful orgasm rolling through him. After his climax, he's careful not to collapse on top of me, mindful of the clips still attached to my vulnerable flesh.

With tender care, he removes each one, kissing the spots where they were. The rush of blood returning creates aftershocks that have me still humming in his arms.

"That was . . ." I struggle to find words.

"Just the beginning," he promises, gathering me against his chest. "We have all night."

I hope we have longer than that, but I don't say it.

As I curl into his warmth, I know that whatever uncertainty tomorrow holds, right now, this is exactly where I'm meant to be.

# 25

## Mitch

I go to bed with the woman I'm crazy about and wake up with a target on my back from the one who's already stabbed me in it. More than once.

Text messages from three of my restaurants about supply issues can't be coincidence. Camille's daddy isn't pleased.

Climbing out of bed slowly and silently, I let Lark sleep. Yesterday was emotionally draining for her, and I added to that with a physically demanding night. I've met my match in bed, that's for sure.

In the kitchen, I make phone calls, sort out the worst of the disasters, while a couple more crop up like dandelions. A chef quits in Louisiana, perhaps bought off by RWI. And I start to wonder if this will be the new norm.

How will I keep restaurants running if someone is out to sabotage them on a daily basis? Maybe I can expect poisoned food, too. *Not gonna happen,* I think. But how do I stop it?

I've been running various plans around in my head, including paying a visit to Camille in jail or even hopping a flight to see Monsieur Durand, whom I met once. But I have a feeling if I let him know this is getting to me, he'll simply go harder with the payback.

And if I ask what he wants to stop it, then I'll be beholden to basically a mafia threat for the rest of my life.

By the time Lark joins me an hour later, yawning and looking sexy wearing one of my T-shirts, I have something of a solution.

"Coffee?" I offer.

Instead of answering, she walks straight up to me, wraps her arms around my waist and kisses me. A siren as desirable as any in Greek mythology.

"Good morning to you, too," I say, squeezing her ass with both my hands.

She grins, a flicker of mischief dancing in those golden-tawny eyes, while a few sexy memories leave me grinning, too.

Releasing me, she says, "Yes, please," although I've forgotten my question.

"Coffee," she adds, eyebrows raised with humor, probably knowing she has me completely under her spell.

"Right! Freshly brewed," I say. "By my fabulous coffee maker. Wasn't it the reason you stayed in my bed the night we met?"

"Absolutely not," she says. "But this morning, I appreciate its fabulousness."

Once we're on the couch, with Lark looking like she belongs here, I ask about her problems instead of launching into my own.

"Any clarity come to you in your dreams? Do you want to fight the board or investigate that Wembley character?"

"No and no. I might fight and win, but I'd hate to have to keep looking over my shoulder, worrying when they might try to oust me again. As to Neville Wembley, I'll let my father handle any investigation, *if* he thinks it's warranted. If I did it, it would look like sour grapes. I'm just glad I resigned rather than letting them fire me."

"*Glad* mixed with regret?" I ask.

"I've been feeling trapped." She looks at me over the rim of her cup. "Even before I met you. Which is weird because I haven't been slaving away in Sydney for very long. It should've been a welcome challenge, not such a drag. Anyway, it's not the responsibility or the constant pressure."

"What is it, then?" I'm listening and want to know her thoughts. But to stop myself from touching her—stroking her leg, tucking her hair back, or holding her hand—I have to keep both hands on my coffee cup.

"I think it's the lack of . . . newness. Maybe. I don't know. I expected something to change when I left Manhattan." She shrugs, then adds, "Except for the accent, running Henley Sydney is pretty much the same."

Lark releases a sigh that almost breaks my heart, sounding so lost. Still, I hold my tongue, giving her time to think out loud.

"Luke said chocolate is in my blood, and I think he's right." She sends me a twisted smile. "I love it. I want to bring chocolate to the world. How can I *not* work for Henley when I know the business so well? But if being CEO doesn't make me happy, what will?"

She finishes with a shake of her head, as if she's truly baffled.

I finally take her hand, threading our fingers together. "What does make you happy?"

Her gaze drops to our interlaced hands. "I'm still figuring that out. But I know it involves more of this," she squeezes my fingers.

"I can work with that," I say, returning the squeeze.

Her smile doesn't reach her eyes. "I'm worried about Henley Confectionery being especially vulnerable right now. If sending a shot across RWI's bow by locking up Camille backfires, then they might step up their risky game, rather than stopping it."

"I tend to think they already have," I confess.

The color in her cheeks from my superb coffee drains away. "Why? What happened?"

When I explain the various disasters happening at my restaurants, she goes all GI Jane on me.

Jumping to her feet, Lark declares, "Let's go to the police right now."

"Won't help matters. Local law enforcement can't stop the harassment happening in the States or in Europe."

Not that I intend to stand by and let RWI run roughshod over me, either. No more than I'm willing to let a lot of people lose their jobs in my establishments. Which brings me to my tentative solution.

"How about we fight their bad PR with really good PR?"

"Go on," she says, resuming her seat but facing me.

"Let's merge."

Lark frowns. "Our companies?"

I laugh. She's the only woman I know who would say that.

"I was thinking something more personal, but a business merger of sorts would work in conjunction to what I have in mind."

"Which is?" she asks.

"Us declaring we're a couple. In public. Gorgeous, esteemed Lark Henley deigns to spend time with restaurateur Mitchell Franklin, having met by chance in Sydney. We're the happy couple, and the press will love it."

"I'm sniffing what you're cooking," she says, "but how does this help?"

"It's a fairy tale. Beauty and the Beast."

"You're the Beast?" she asks, then giggles. "That's a hard sell."

I try again. "The Boston-born brute." I flex my bicep, the same one she bit last night. "And the New York-bred babe?" Fluttering my eyelashes, I pout my lips.

She laughs even harder, then says, "How about the Princess and the Pea Soup Kitchen?"

"I do have the best recipe for pea soup," I confess. "It's all in the quality of the ham. Has to be dry-cured and hickory-smoked."

"Oh my God," she says. "I want a ham biscuit so badly right now."

"I'll see what I can do later. Back to my plan. Who doesn't love a fairy tale? No one, that's who. The public will be opposed to anyone or any company trying to destroy it. And what do we need to make the story complete?"

She scrunches up her nose, and I lean over to kiss it.

"You're thinking too hard," I say. "Come on, you know the answer."

Lark's eyes narrow. "I was going to say a castle and some magic, but I think the answer is . . . a villain."

"Bingo!" I exclaim. "Eggs?"

"What? Yes. Cook for me, but keep talking. And find me some ham."

We go back to the kitchen where I start to whip up breakfast. Unfortunately, with bacon, although it's Australia's thick shortcut bacon, so she should be satisfied.

"We have a super villain," I point out, "who likes to hide behind shell companies and even the skirts of a foolish woman who should've known better. So we bring it all into the light. We go full court press and fight what's happening to both our businesses in the public arena."

"You shouldn't have to," she protests. "This isn't your fight."

"It is now."

Lark studies me for a long moment, as if weighing whether to let me in by way of a public announcement or fight alone. At last, she nods.

"OK. But we need to be smart about this. RWI isn't just some corporate raider. They're strategic and obviously ruthless."

"We'll be that way, too."

"They're also huge," she reminds me.

"So am I," I say deadpan, sliding a plate of food in front of her.

She bursts out laughing.

"Are you mocking me?" I ask. "Do you need a reminder, lady? Right here? Right now?" Still holding my trusty spatula in one hand, I make a lewd rocking motion with my hips.

Lark shakes her head. "I love you."

*Whoa!* Her words detonate inside me, and my whole world grinds to a halt, before she clamps a hand over her pretty mouth, her eyes widening.

"I mean, I love your sense of humor and how you make me laugh."

"Nope. Too late. You can't take it back," I tell her. "Besides, I love you, too." I experience one of those Grinch heart-expansions. Man-oh-man does it feel good to say the words I haven't said to a woman for so long.

Her smile is breath-taking. We stare at one another for a long moment. I'm frankly surprised we don't end up having sex. But the food is in front of us, and it's hot, so we dig in.

Lark picks up a piece of bacon and chews it with obvious enjoyment. "See, this is why I don't cook. I'd probably eat something like this every damn day."

Wiping her hands on a napkin, she adds, "OK. Let's drag this whole mess into the light and see if we can get the cockroaches to scatter."

I shudder. "Please don't ever say that word around me. All I can think of is losing a Michelin star if a roach was ever seen in one of my kitchens."

"OK, we'll shine a light on the villain and see if RWI goes up in smoke, like a vampire."

After we eat, I have another restaurant problem. Boston lost power. *Boston!* Fuck RWI and Stephen Durand. My crack team at home has already got Franklin 1 up and running with a generator, but I'm seething.

For her part, Lark starts to make some calls. First to Luke, who has already left Australia, heading home to his wife and his Henley division, in that order. Then she calls Charlotte, who apparently is acting as interim CEO.

Listening to Lark's voice shift from personal to professional and back again, I'm so impressed by her ability to forge ahead, even after such a demoralizing day yesterday. When she explains our PR plan, she elaborates on it.

"RWI has been playing dirty, using personal connections to destabilize our company and Mitch's business. We're going to beat them at their own game, Charlotte. Every time they so much as break a glass in one of Mitch's restaurants or let one of our chocolates melt, we're going to shout about it."

Later, she's drinking iced tea on my sofa, literally doing nothing else—"This is so damn strange," Lark says, "not having any responsibility on my mind. I mean, beyond saving Henley"—when she decides to go home.

"I'll get some things and bring them back with me," she says, since we've decided to spend some quality, uninterrupted time together. "Or you can come stay with me over at my place?"

"You don't have any food," I remind her. "And I really like my kitchen."

She laughs as she's been doing all day, despite her uncertain world. Then she reaches for my hand. "Thank you."

"For what?" I ask.

"For not walking away. For jumping into my mess with both feet."

I bring her hand to my lips and kiss her knuckles. "Where else would I be?"

Her smile turns playful. "Well, most sensible men would be running in the opposite direction by now."

"I never claimed to be sensible," I say, pulling her from her seat and into my arms. "Besides, even before they started their attack on my restaurants, you weren't the only one with a score to settle. Camille used me, and I don't like being manipulated, especially by her."

Lark wraps her arms around my neck, going up on her toes so our hips nearly meet.

"What about when I use you? You and your chip clips."

I laugh, relief flooding through me that we can still find fun despite everything.

"That's different. You're not manipulating me—you're bewitching me. And I'm a very willing victim."

Her eyes darken. "Victim, *huh*? Is that how you see yourself?"

In a flash, I back her against the wall, my hands sliding down to grasp her ass. "Not even close."

When our lips meet, it's a frantic, desperate collision as if we hadn't had sex twice last night. She tastes like sweet tea, and all the comfort of a home I've been seeking in my restless life. I want to devour her.

"Stay with me," I murmur against her lips.

She pulls back slightly, her eyes searching mine. "I'll come back. I promise."

$♥$♥$♥$

I check my watch for the third time in as many minutes, standing by the window of my penthouse as the Sydney skyline transitions from dusk to darkness. She should have been back ages ago.

"I'll come back. I promise," Lark had said, her amber eyes looking directly into mine.

I'd believed her.

I tap out another text—the seventh one. Each message a little less casual than the last.

*Everything OK?*

*Did you get caught up in something?*

*Starting to worry. Call me when you can.*

And now:

*Lark, please just let me know you're safe.*

The three dots appear briefly, then disappear. My heart jumps, then sinks. She's seen my messages. She's choosing *not* to respond.

Luke's words from yesterday echo in my head. *"When things get intense, my sister tends to circle her wagon of one."*

Grabbing my keys, I head to Lark's. I've given her enough space.

Traffic is light as I make my way there.

Punching in seven, seven, seven, seven, in thirty seconds, I'm at her door. I knock. Once, twice. No answer.

"Lark?" I call out, not caring if neighbors hear. "It's Mitch."

The silence from inside is absolute. It feels like a band around my lungs. I knock again, harder. Maybe she's in the shower.

No sound. Nothing. Just the quiet apartment on the other side of the door, like it swallowed her whole.

I consider my options. I could call Luke or Charlotte, but that feels like tattling. I could wait here in the hallway for however long it takes. Eyeing the sturdy door, I imagine shoulder-checking it open, Hollywood style.

Instead, I lean my forehead against the cool wood. This morning, she was curled against me, her body soft and warm, hair spilling across my chest. Over breakfast, she said she loved me. And I said it back because it's true to my core.

So how are we already here, with her ghosting me mere hours later, the way she's been doing since the beginning?

My phone buzzes. I snatch it from my pocket, hoping it's—

It's not Lark. It's the manager of Franklin 3. Another supplier has suddenly "lost" our order.

"Fuck!" I slam my palm against the door.

I've spent years building my restaurants. Eighteen-hour days, missed holidays, failed relationships, and nonstop hustle. I've created spaces where people can come together over good food without pretension or gimmicks. Places that feel like the home I've been denying myself since Camille left me.

And now it's all being threatened because I fell for the wrong woman once and the right woman now.

The irony isn't lost on me that Lark—who I'm currently furious with for disappearing—is the one facing even bigger stakes. Her family legacy, generations of work. But still. We're supposed to be in this together now.

Heading back to my car, I slide into the driver's seat, remembering her reaction when she heard about the problems at my restaurants. The fierce determination. The way she immediately wanted to fight for me. *Where has that woman gone?*

Did she get a better offer? Run into some new information that changed her mind about us? Or is this what she does—retreat when things get real?

"Goddammit, Lark," I mutter, starting the car. "You promised."

Driving back to my empty place, I try to find some perspective. Maybe something happened. Maybe there's a legitimate reason she's gone radio silent. I should give her the benefit of the doubt.

But as I crack open a beer and stare out at the harbor, another possibility looms. What if this is truly who Lark Henley is—someone who can't fully let anyone in, even when she wants to? If that's the case, do I have the patience to wait her out each time she goes AWOL?

I think of those golden eyes, that clever mind, the way she feels in my arms. *Yes,* I decide. *I'll wait. I'll trust her.*

But I'm still going to be mad as hell when she shows up.

# 26

## Lark

When I slide my keycard into my door lock, I'm already planning what clothes to pack. Sexy sundress and bikini so we can go to the beach. Lacy bra and thong for in the apartment. Just enough for a few days at Mitch's.

The thought makes me smile—how quickly we've gone from strangers to lovers to . . . whatever we are now.

I guess we're partners in crime-fighting, literally, as we plot to expose RWI and the Durands.

Pushing open my door, I step inside, and that's the last normal moment I have.

A gloved hand clamps over my mouth, and I freeze with disbelief. A strong arm wraps around my waist like a vise, squeezing all the air out of my lungs, before I'm lifted off my feet.

My world narrows to panic, but I manage to kick backward, connecting with something—a shin, maybe. The intruder's grip only tightens.

"Stop struggling," a male voice hisses in my ear in accented English. "I'm not going to hurt you if you cooperate."

Fear floods my system with adrenaline. This can't be happening. Not in my secure building with its doorman and cameras and—

The man, who sounds Dutch or German, drags me through my own apartment and slams me down onto a dining room chair. Before I can react, he's binding my wrists to the chair arms with what feels like zip ties. Professional. Quick. Practiced.

"What the hell is this?" I demand, my voice steadier than I feel. "If you want money—"

"I do," he interrupts, stepping back to admire his handiwork. "But not from you."

Now I get my first good look at him. Tall, athletic build, wearing jeans and a casual shirt. Perfectly normal clothing for a day in Sydney, apart from the balaclava covering his face, exposing merely his eyes and mouth.

Nothing particularly menacing, except for the terrifying situation and the navy-blue ski mask.

"Who are you?" I ask.

He gives a theatrical bow. "You may call me Bill."

"Bill?" I mutter, realizing I'm experiencing shock. I'm too calm, even for me.

"Exactly. As in U.S. currency, dollar bills. Not your Australian Monopoly money." He sounds almost cheerful as he secures my ankles to the chair legs.

"Why are you doing this?" My mind races through possibilities. Ransom from my parents or Henley Confectionery. Trade secrets maybe? But we're a chocolate company, not a defense contractor.

"Bill" finishes securing me and steps back, pulling out his phone. "Say cheese."

The camera flash temporarily blinds me.

"Perfect," he says, typing something. "Now we wait."

"For what?" My heart hammers in my chest. "Who are you working for?"

He tilts his head, considering. "I think that information will remain with me."

However, his accent suddenly causes this unbelievable moment to make sense. Like him, I won't share my guess that Camille's father sent him. That piece of info might get me killed.

Bill moves around my kitchen with disturbing familiarity, opening my refrigerator and examining its contents. "Why is this always so empty?"

His words confirm that he's been here before, and I shiver, telling him nothing. Hopefully, he'll starve to death.

"Because you're spending all your time with your chef lover, I suppose."

Again, he'll get no confirmation out of me.

"Luckily, I brought provisions." To my dismay, Bill unpacks a cooler of food, which indicates he intends to be here a while.

"Is this about the corporate takeover?" I ask, testing the strength of the zip ties. They don't budge. In fact, they're too tight already.

My kidnapper laughs. "No. This is a personal matter."

Understanding dawns with sickening clarity. I made sure Camille didn't get on her private jet, and her father wants his little girl back. Bill has probably been in Sydney all along, helping when necessary.

"All you need to know, Miss Henley, is that someone must cooperate. If they do, then you'll be free to go." He pulls out the one edible meal in my fridge and sniffs it. "Smells good. What is it?"

"Green curry mixed with Pad Thai." The answer comes out of me automatically before the absurdity of the situation strikes me. "This isn't how things work in the real world. You can't just kidnap people and trade them like baseball cards."

"And yet," Bill gestures around at my current predicament, before placing my Thai food in the microwave.

My phone buzzes in my pocket. *Mitch.* I know it's him without looking.

Bill notices. "Boyfriend checking in? Don't worry, I'll let him know you're busy. Eventually."

*Ugh!* I hate that he knows about Mitch, because it puts him in danger, too.

Entering my personal space, this stranger leans close, and I shrink as much as I'm able. All he does is extract my phone from my back pocket, where I've practically been sitting on it.

He sets it on the kitchen peninsula, close but so far out of reach, it might as well be in NYC. Then he goes back to the microwave.

"I don't know about you, but I'm hoping we won't be here long. We need only a little cooperation from authorities, and then make the exchange. The photo of you tied to the chair should hasten things."

Then it clicks. "You took those photos of me and sent them to the Henley board, didn't you?"

He bows again, getting on my nerves. "Guilty as charged. I've been following you for weeks. Your security awareness is terrible, by the way."

My stomach twists at the violation. "How did you get into my building?"

He shrugs. "I'm a professional. Like you. You make chocolate. I do what someone pays me to do, and I do it well. Sometimes, I hide in plain sight because people see what they want to."

I test my restraints again, more subtly this time. He's as good as confessed to working for Durand, or RWI, or both. I hope he doesn't think that's reason enough to slit my throat.

"Divide and conquer." Bill says, sitting across from me, eating *my* leftovers. I guess he's referring to getting my own board to vote against me. "Nothing personal. Just business."

"Until it becomes personal," I point out.

"Exactly." He points his fork at me. "My client went a little . . . I think you would say . . . *off-script*. As did you, for that matter. You're not like other CEOs I've dealt with. *It's all good* though, as the Americans put it. We'll get there in the end."

I focus on his previous remark. Durand has gone rogue, maybe with everything Camille and Bill are doing. RWI might have no idea.

"This is very good," Bill says, shoveling in a mouthful of green curry. "Corporate intrigue is hungry work."

"And kidnapping," I remind him.

Bill shrugs, seemingly unconcerned by this distinction as he continues eating.

I try a different approach. "You know if you let me go, I can't ID you. My family would pay you whatever you're being paid by whoever hired you."

He looks thoughtful. "I'm almost insulted that you would make such an offer. I'm no turncoat."

*Maybe you're simply insane.* But my expression makes him laugh.

"It's not that I have scruples about where the money comes from, you understand. But if I switch sides, I'll be hunted down and never work in Europe again. I have a lucrative business. I'm not going to throw it away on one woman."

*What a prince!*

"And what if this doesn't work?" I need to know what's in store if the police don't play nice with Bill's demands. Personally, I don't believe the police will release Camille.

"It will work." He wipes his mouth. "Your family has influence. They can pull strings."

He may be right. We've never tried to use that type of power. "Even if they could, they won't negotiate with kidnappers."

Bill shrugs. "We'll see. After all, I'm not ransoming you. They're not losing a dime by setting free my client's daughter." He pulls out a soda from his cooler, then puts a few more in my fridge, making himself at home.

"Besides," he adds, "all that's needed is for Henley Confectionery to drop all charges against my client's offspring."

He still doesn't say this is about Camille, and I don't confirm that I know anything. I feel like it's an unspoken agreement that he's not going to harm me if I play along by not naming names. At least I hope so.

I'm weirded out by the way he takes time to wash up the dishes he used, dry them, and neatly put them away—all the time humming to himself. If he is the violent type, he probably cleans up after that, too.

Hours pass. Bill makes himself at home in my apartment, watching my TV, using my bathroom, even browsing my bookshelves. It's surreal.

Occasionally he checks his phone, waiting, I assume, for instructions as to my fate. In the outside world, someone must be talking to the Sydney police department. My own phone buzzes every once in a while with what I assume are Mitch's increasingly worried messages.

Finally, at dusk, perhaps from sheer boredom, Bill picks up my phone, whistling when he sees the notifications on the home screen.

"A couple voicemails and seven texts? Clingy much?"

I feel for Mitch. It's bad enough when I know what's going on. For him, it must be the strangest mind-fuck ever.

A knock on my door makes me jump. *Shit!* Bill is on his feet instantly and warning me with a finger to his lips that I better remain silent.

"Lark?" Mitch calls out. "It's Mitch."

Bill and I stare at one another. My heart is pounding, and for the first time, I think I'm going to cry. Hearing that beloved voice, knowing he's mere yards away from me.

We wait, all three of us. Then what must be Mitch's large palm makes contact with my front door. My heart breaks as I hear him swear in frustration.

When there's nothing more, Bill decides Mitch has left, and I'm inclined to agree with him. I'm starting to feel hopeless. Another hour later, Bill escorts me to the bathroom, standing in the doorway, keeping his eyes averted. I cannot think of anything to do to escape or even disable him.

*Flick him with a towel? Spray perfume in his eyes?* I should've adopted a dog, a great big one.

When I'm in my chair again, which is apparently where I'm going to spend the night, I appeal to my kidnapper's common sense.

"Look, let me text Mitch that I'm OK. Otherwise, by morning, if not sooner, he's going to call the police."

"That would complicate things," Bill admits. He considers me for a moment. "Fine. One text, but I'll type it." He picks up my phone again, which is set to stay helpfully unlocked in my "safe" apartment.

He navigates to Mitch's thread and types:
**Decided to go out with a friend. Talk tomorrow.**
It's so obviously not me that I laugh out loud. "Mitch will never believe that."

"Why not?" Bill asks.

"Because I would never be that vague. And I told him I was coming here to get clothes and going right back."

Bill frowns and deletes the message. "What would you say?"

*Should I help him fool Mitch?* If I keep Mitch away, this situation might resolve itself with Camille being set free, and no one will get hurt. If he comes over again, riding to my rescue, then something bad could happen. To him or to me.

Ultimately, it's an easy decision. I want to buy myself more time and hope the police cave. Other things could be happening, too. Luke might've just landed in New York, or he might be on his way back here already. With my father. I try to imagine Neville being helpful, and fail.

Stalling seems like my only option, and that means keeping Mitch away.

"Try this," I say. 'Charlotte popped over unexpectedly. Grabbing dinner together so I can help ease her into the new role. Sorry for earlier radio silence.'" It's still a lie, but at least it sounds like me.

"Add 'I'll call you when I'm heading to your place,'" I tell my kidnapper. Otherwise, Mitch might come over later for sex and snuggling in bed, like last night, but I don't explain that to Bill.

He types it in and shows me the screen before sending. I nod. It's the best I can do under the circumstances. And then I'm rewarded with a few sips of water before enduring a night alone with my kidnapper.

He takes the couch, snoring lightly almost immediately. Ultimately, I doze off, sleeping fitfully in the chair.

$♥$♥$♥$

A phone rings awakening me to the same nightmare, but now with my neck and shoulders aching. The morning light streams in through my windows, as Bill answers immediately, turning away from me to speak in hushed tones. In Dutch, I think.

When he hangs up, his expression is tight.

"Problem?" I ask, not sure whether to be hopeful or frightened.

"Change of plans." He paces my living room. "The police aren't playing ball. They've denied my client's legal team's request for expedited bail."

"Shocking," I say dryly.

Bill ignores my sarcasm. "We need to escalate the situation. But first, we eat. Or at least, I do. Good thing I brought food. I learned to do that early on, during one of my first assignments. Lasted four days, and there was nothing decent in the chalet apart from a freezer full of bratwurst."

I watch in bewilderment as he starts cooking bacon. The sizzling meat fills the apartment with its unmistakable aroma, making my mouth water. *How cruel is this after yesterday?*

Again, tamping down the urge to cry, I ask, "What do you mean by 'escalate the situation'?" I'm trying to sound casual while working my wrists against the zip ties. I know it's pointless but I have to do something.

"Maybe we send proof of life." Bill shrugs, turning the bacon with practiced ease. "Or maybe we up the ante and go to your grandparents' ranch. I hear your grandfather had a stroke last year. Be a real shame if something caused him to have another one."

My stomach tightens at this threat, but I keep my face neutral. I'd almost let myself believe my kidnapper was a *normal* guy, one who happened to take people prisoner on behalf of other people.

But now he's talking about involving Gramps and Nan. I should've taken the chance to let Mitch know I was in trouble. I might not get another one.

"We'll know soon," Bill says, putting bread in the toaster. "Eventually, someone will make the right decision. Self-preservation is a powerful motivator."

Bill makes himself an enormous bacon sandwich, seemingly oblivious to how the domestic scene contrasts with the criminal situation. My stomach growls despite my fear.

"Hungry?" Bill asks.

"What do you think?"

"Just asking." He takes a big bite, crunching it with obvious pleasure. "Can't give you any because, if I do have to move you, I need you weak as a lamb."

Deciding I better reserve my strength, I close my eyes on his ugly-ass eating. A minute later, three sharp raps at the door have my eyelids snapping open.

Bill stops chewing, sandwich frozen halfway between his plate and his mouth.

"Lark? You in there?" Mitch's voice carries through the door.

My heart leaps. I can't believe he came back after I gave him the brush-off. Bill turns to me, eyes narrowing behind his balaclava. Then he sets down his plate.

"Not a word," he whispers, pulling a taser from his duffel bag.

*Damn!* It's the first I've seen of any kind of weapon. At least it's not a gun. Moving cautiously to the door, Bill presses his back against the wall beside it.

"Lark?" Mitch calls out again. "I can smell food cooking. I know you're in there." His voice is light but with an edge I recognize. He knows something's wrong.

*"Kut,"* Bill mutters in his native tongue.

Mitch's knuckle-rapping becomes pounding. "Lark, if you can hear me, I'm worried. I'm going to call building security." It is so good to know he's on the other side of the door, I nearly blow it and scream for help.

"Answer him," Bill hisses, surprising me. I'm even more surprised to have the taser leveled at me. "Tell him you're fine. Tell him to go away."

I clear my throat. This time, I'm going to try to let him know I'm not OK.

"I'm fine, Mitch!" I call out, sounding as normal as possible. "Just cooking my breakfast . . . like I always do."

A moment's silence lets me know he's received my message loud and clear. Then he asks, "Can I come in?"

"Now's not a good time," I respond, eyes fixed on Bill's taser.

Another pause. "OK. Call me later?"

"Will do!" I force cheerfulness into my voice.

Bill watches the door for several moments before relaxing slightly.

"He bought it," he says, tucking the taser into the back of his waistband. "Sharp guy, though. I need to hurry this up."

Sitting on the edge of the coffee table directly in front of me, Bill gives me a thorough looking over to make sure I haven't been able to free myself. Then he pulls out his phone. As he begins typing rapidly, all my attention is focused on the door, even though I'm not looking at it.

I'd bet my life Mitch is still there. I may *actually* be betting my life. But it's so quiet, after a few minutes, my heart sinks. I was sure he knows I don't cook breakfast. Not ever.

Bill is distracted with his phone, and I have nowhere to look but past him, over his shoulder, at the endless blue sky floating over the harbor. My kidnapper has made contact with someone and seems to be in a heated texting exchange.

I'm losing hope fast when, to my astonishment, a shadow moves along the edge of my balcony. So quick and unexpected, I think I've imagined it.

A moment later, I see Mitch, a sliver of dark skin, as he peers between the floor-length curtains. My heart rate goes from zero to galloping, as if I'm one of Gramps's horses at feeding time.

And miracle of miracles, the sliding glass door is unlatched. I'd opened it yesterday to let fresh air in before I left. After all, it's a fourth-floor apartment, and there's nowhere to go from here.

Unless you're Mitch, scaling the outside of the building, like Rapunzel's prince. I guess he was right about the fairy tale!

Forcing myself to keep my expression bland, so as not to alert Bill, I watch Mitch draw out his cell and text. On cue, my phone buzzes.

"Your boyfriend seems persistent," Bill remarks, looking over at my phone on the counter. "He's texting again."

"He's protective," I respond, deliberately keeping my voice steady, realizing Mitch used it as a distracting tactic.

"Well, he won't find you here much longer anyway. We are moving within the hour."

That news gives me the chills. If Bill gets me out of this apartment, my chances of rescue drop dramatically.

Behind him, I see the sliding door inch open. Agonizingly slowly. After all, Mitch doesn't know whether I have a gun trained on me or a bacon sandwich. When I see his whole face, my heart tells me how much I love him, and I try to send that message with my eyes.

His expression hardens as he assesses everything, including me bound to a chair. But when our gazes meet for the briefest moment, I feel a surge of relief so powerful I nearly cry out.

Bill gets up, so I quickly refocus on him. "What's the plan? Bag over my head? Trunk of your car?" I ask. "How exactly does one transport a kidnap victim in broad daylight? Tell me there's no drugs or duct tape involved."

"You ask a lot of questions," he says, annoyed. When he draws his taser, I stiffen with fear, but he walks past me, and away from Mitch, to the front door. Bill peers through the peephole.

"I need to make sure your boyfriend actually left."

While his back is turned, Mitch slips inside, moving with surprising stealth for a muscular man his size. He puts a finger to his lips, probably because he can see the excitement on my face. I'm ready to jump out of my skin and scream.

"I think he has gone," Bill announces, straightening. "As for how I'm going to move you—"

He never finishes the sentence. Mitch has raced across the room like a football player going for the tackle, and does so with such force that Bill drops the taser as he's slammed against my front door.

In a flurry of blows and wrestling moves, they remind me of a cartoon tumbleweed. Ricocheting off the hall table, they crash to the floor, landing punches on one another. Mitch takes a hard elbow to the face that splits his lip open, blood trickling down his chin as they continue grappling for dominance.

Despite the bruising blow, in the next minute, Mitch overpowers Bill, ending up nearly at my feet. With that brute strength he mentioned yesterday, he pins my kidnapper face down on the area rug, with a knee between his shoulders and the man's arm wrenched behind his back.

Bill groans, and I'm desperate to be set free, but Mitch is already pulling out his phone with his free hand. Once the police are on their way, he and I stare at one another. I feel a strange detachment, as if this is happening to someone else. Maybe it's a second round of shock.

"Get up," Mitch says to Bill, dragging him to his feet before looking at me. He's looking around for some way to restrict Bill from fleeing at the first chance. "I don't think the bathroom will work this time. You've got a big window in there."

"I want to get you untied, Lark," he says. "I bet you don't have any duct tape."

"I do," I say triumphantly. "In the drawer next to the fridge. This was Luke's apartment for years, and all men have duct tape, don't they?"

But when the police arrive minutes later, Mitch has got hold of the taser and is pointing it at Bill while managing to have cut one zip tie with a dull kitchen knife.

"I can't believe you don't own scissors," he fumes. "Or a sharp knife."

Upon entering, one officer does a double-take. "You two again? Crikey!"

For some reason, despite the situation and still being trussed up like a calf at the Mount Isa Rodeo, I start to laugh. Sure enough, it's the same policeman who took Camille away yesterday.

As soon as Mitch hands off Bill, he slices through the rest of my restraints. Strangely, I'm totally peaceful when I stand on wobbly legs and enter the circle of his arms.

Yesterday, I was heading home to pack a small bag, excited but uncertain about my future. What did I want? What would bring me satisfaction? What would make my life feel meaningful?

Now, after almost twenty-four hours of fear, mixed with absurdity—and a lot of time to do nothing but think—I've never been more sure of my path.

# 27

## Mitch

When Lark has given her statement, texted her family and Charlotte, it's only the two of us again. I rub her chafed skin, needing to touch her. She has already used a wet paper towel to wipe the blood off my chin, and keeps thanking me for overpowering her kidnapper.

But I can't shake the feeling that I let her down by not figuring out she needed me sooner.

"I did most of the damage," she says, looking at the red rings circling her wrists. "I thought I could work free of thick plastic ties like some kind of superhero. But *you* were the superhero."

She looks up at me with those gorgeous eyes that make me want to give her the world.

"I can't believe you climbed up and over three balconies to get to me."

I wasn't a superhero, just a man desperate to get to the woman he loves. Putting my hands on her shoulders, I start to draw her toward me, but she moans.

"Sorry," she says. "But my shoulders ache the most. The muscles are burning from how long I stayed in that position. And my neck," Lark adds, running her delicate fingers under her hair and over her nape, "from sleeping in a dining room chair."

I'm an idiot for not thinking about that. Grabbing her hand, I stride down the hall to her bedroom.

"Shirt off and lay down on your belly," I order.

"If I wasn't in pain," she jokes, "I'd be turned on right now." But she does what I tell her.

"If you weren't in pain," I echo, straddling her beautiful hips, "I'd be thrusting into you already, I'm so damned relieved to see you again." I begin to knead her shoulders.

"*Ohh*, that's good," Lark says all husky voiced, making my cock twitch since she has said those exact words in the same way when I'm balls deep inside her.

"You make bread, don't you?" she asks. "I can tell."

I grunt out a laugh and continue a deep massage all over her upper arms and the smooth skin of her back. She starts to relax beneath me. I go softer on her neck, but work the tension out until she's totally limp.

When she falls asleep, I climb off her, slowly, carefully, trying not to disturb this sweet, brave woman who has been through so much. And then, because I'm scared at how something so crazy might've stolen her from me, I sit on a small tufted ottoman in the corner and watch her. I feel at this moment like I can never let her out of my sight again.

After about fifteen minutes, she snuffles and turns her head to face me. Her cheek is red and wet where she's been drooling on her bedspread, and it's the most beautiful thing I've ever seen. In the next instant, her eyes slowly open, and I see the thoughts flickering in their depths as she remembers everything. Then she smiles at me.

"You stayed," she says.

"A thousand men couldn't have dragged me away."

She sighs and stretches, then winces, making me pissed off at that creep again. But he's been taken care of, so now I need to focus on her. Lark turns onto her back and stretches again while I purposefully don't look at the deep V of her cleavage or the way her nipples show through the pale cotton of her bra.

"How do you feel after your cat nap?" I ask.

"Hungry," she says, her voice kind of scratchy.

I jump up ready to make her a feast.

"No, wait," she stops me. "I'm going to shower first. I want to scrub away the memories of the last eighteen hours, brush my teeth, and primp like a girl before I even let you kiss me."

While she showers, I am useless because there's nothing good to cook here, and I refuse to use the kidnapper's skeevy food I find in the fridge.

In the end, I stretch out on her bed and wait. Ignoring the texts pinging on my phone, probably more restaurant catastrophes, I consider Lark and me. It's easy to think of us as a couple after the last few days. It's even easier to think of us being together on a permanent basis. But I would have to be willing to live wherever *she* wants to live.

*Can I do that?*

The bathroom door opens, and she comes out in a towel, hair still damp, no makeup. And she looks amazing.

The answer is *yes*. I could live in a hut on a deserted island with this woman.

Seeing me, she smiles.

"What's up?" she asks, immediately stretching out beside me.

I groan at her nearness wearing next to nothing, smelling like an array of feminine scents from all her lotions and potions. I close my eyes.

"I know you're hungry, so you need to get dressed."

"I don't smell anything cooking," she points out, pressing herself to my side.

"I'm a chef, not a magician." I open my eyes and look at her, all warm and dewy. "Unless you want to eat Bill's food."

She wrinkles her nose disdainfully. Adorably. With that superhero strength she mentioned before, I manage to roll away from her and get off the bed.

"Dress and let's go," I order. "I've got everything you need and want back at my place."

"I see everything I need and want right here," she says, starting to unwrap the towel.

"Jeez!" I exclaim, as my cock hardens to the size and girth of a baker's rolling pin.

Stalking from the room, I close the door behind me and lean against it.

"I'm not taking advantage of a hungry woman," I call out. "It goes against my molecular structure. Hurry up so I can feed you and . . . fu—" I cut myself off.

I want to do both until she can't walk, but I don't want to be crude right now.

"And pleasure you," I say, which is more accurate to how I'm feeling. Her pleasure is more important than my own.

"OK, OK," she says. "I'm dressing."

"I didn't want to invade your privacy and go through your things, but you should pack some stuff."

She's quick for a female. Fifteen minutes later, we're carrying two suitcases of her *stuff* through my door. I take it all the way through to my bedroom.

"Unpack and dinner will be ready when you are." I've had a lot of time to think what I'm going to whip up. First will be some cheese and crackers to take the edge off and give me more time to make her something special.

But Lark is still standing in my bedroom, looking—if I'm reading her right—almost shy.

"Shall I open my cases under the window and live out of them?"

While that wouldn't bother me, I know it's not the way to treat a woman. Not this woman. In seconds, I'm lifting my clothing out of the dresser drawers and putting all of it on the empty shelf high up in my closet. "Enough space?"

"For now," she says, making something inside me melt.

It sounds like she'll be moving more of her things in, and I think that's fine. She can have the whole damn room as long as she shares the bed.

"Can we kiss now?" she asks.

I think Lark is surprised at how fast she finds herself enclosed in my arms and held tightly against me. Capturing her mouth under mine, we stand there for a long time, joined and touching.

When I hear her stomach rumble, however, I slowly release her. "I'll go make you a snack that'll hold you till dinner."

After taking her crackers and sliced aged cheddar with a big glass of milk, which makes her laugh, even louder when I say, "No alcohol on an empty stomach," I start to cook. It's easy to lose myself in the familiar rhythm of creation.

This isn't merely cooking—it's an offering, a declaration.

For Lark, I'm preparing a feast worthy of everything she means to me.

The sizzle of duck breast in cast iron fills my apartment with a rich aroma as I sear the skin to perfect crispness. Next, I reduce cherry and port into a glossy sauce, the deep ruby liquid coating the back of my wooden spoon. Wild mushroom risotto comes together in another pot, each grain of arborio rice surrendering to the process of slow absorption.

My hands move with practiced precision, but my thoughts remain on Lark—on how scary it was to lose touch with her for a day and a night. And then find her held prisoner.

I'm not a man who frightens easily, but, good God, I don't want to feel that way again as long as I live.

Basically, while making her a meal, I come to understand how completely she's transformed my world.

When she emerges from the bedroom in a simple sundress, her hair in a thick braid, the sight of her steals my breath. It's not just her beauty—it's the resilience I see in her eyes, the quiet strength that survived a night of terror and emerged unbroken.

"That smells incredible," she says, setting the empty plate and glass on the kitchen island.

"You *look* incredible," I counter. "Do you want to pour us a couple glasses?" I indicate the Pinot Noir on the island. "And then sit your pretty ass in the dining room, please."

Her cheeks flush with color as she pours the wine. "Is this why women fall for chefs? The seduction through food?"

"Is it working?" I ask, plating the duck with artistic precision, the risotto nestled beside it, vibrant microgreens scattered across the top.

"It worked weeks ago," she admits with a smile that warms me more than the stovetop ever could.

We eat by candlelight, because why not? It's two in the afternoon and feels like we've already lived through a really long day. The conversation flows easily, both of us deliberately avoiding the trauma of last night, focusing instead on safer topics—the origin of this dish, her favorite childhood meals, my first cooking disaster.

But beneath our words runs an electric current, a tension that builds with each shared glance, each accidental brush of fingers.

"That was . . ." she begins after the last bite, "possibly the best meal I've ever had."

"Possibly?" I joke, pretending outrage before standing and starting to collect our plates. Then her soft hand catches my wrist.

"Leave them," she whispers.

The plates clatter back to the table as I pull her into my arms. Despite having eaten, our kiss feels hungry—a confirmation that we're both alive, both here. Her hands slide beneath my shirt, exploring the contours of my chest while I back her steadily against the nearest wall. Every rational thought evaporates as I feel her softness yield to my hardness.

"I can't wait any longer," I spill out the truth in a growling tone against her throat.

"Then don't. Please," she gasps, hitching her leg over my hip in an effort to get closer. That's when I discover she's *going commando*, as my college roommate used to call it.

I can scarcely breathe with how much I want her. Releasing her to divest myself of my jeans and boxer briefs, I shove them both to my ankles. With one swift motion, I lift her, so both her legs can wrap around me. Then I thrust.

We both cry out with the initial joining. Her eyes close, her head tilts as much as it can with a wall behind her. My hands cradle her glorious ass, supporting her while I drive deep and fast.

"Touch yourself," I order, and she slides her hand between us to work her clit. I wish I could see it, but her dress is bunched up. I wish I could taste her. I wish I could suck her tits and clamp them the way she likes.

All of that will have to wait. Her body clenches around my erection so hard I see stars.

"I'm going to come soon," I warn, although I'll do my level best to wait for Lark to finish. I don't need to worry. Moments later, she splinters into a billion shards of ecstasy, crying out my name. *My lucky-as-fuck name!*

Lark makes me feel like the billion-dollar man.

Her body spasms, milking me as she climaxes, moaning when I follow her after a last fury of spearing thrusts.

Finally, we're still and momentarily satiated. Inexplicably, my cock is still hard and won't settle down, too turned on. But I lift her off, getting a glimpse of her pussy before her dress falls and covers her. She's trembling, her eyes glassy, looking unsteady on her feet.

After I yank my clothing up my legs, the couch becomes our destination. Tugging her with me onto the large cushion, enjoying the feeling of her warm curvy body on top of mine, we both settle and let our breathing return to normal.

"I thought I'd lost you," I confess, against the top of her head.

"I'm right here," she assures me, patting my chest. "I'm not going anywhere. At least, not today."

A few long minutes pass, until I undress her again. Just a quick sliding of her dress over her head reveals every inch of Lark's bare skin. Apparently, her bra got left behind with her panties.

*God, I'm a blessed man!*

Even more blessed when she tucks her bare back against my front, nestling her ass into my crotch, both of us looking out at the harbor in broad daylight. She takes my hands and places them on her breasts, inviting me to play.

I tug on her perfect, dusky-pink nipples until they're peaked, then spread my legs farther so she can settle her ass against the crotch of my jeans, her head resting back on my chest.

Cupping one of her full breasts, I stroke its nipple with my thumb while sliding my other hand down her flat stomach, past her sexy little sapphire navel piercing, before burying my fingers in the trimmed patch of her pubic hair.

Lark whimpers, making my cock stand at attention, or try to as it presses against her curves.

"I could do this all day," I say, gliding my fingers between her pussy lips to stroke her wetness and circle her taut clit. When I barely touch it, she bucks her hips, and I have to wrap my legs over hers to hold her in place.

"I want to give you everything," I say, stroking and flicking across her sensitive flesh, while her desire leaks onto my hand.

Switching it up, glad I have large hands, I use my thumb against her clit and slowly insert two fingers into her slick channel.

"Mitch," she moans.

Squirming on top of me, Lark is panting, lifting her hips so my fingers go deeper. As she moves up and down, I let her set the pace, until I don't. Then I take over the speed and depth of my fingers thrusting in and out of her, helping her along, until her body tenses, chasing the promised orgasm.

Instead of gently brushing her nipples with my free hand, I pinch one, just hard enough.

"Yessss," she cries out, on a long hiss of mindless pleasure, shuddering uncontrollably. I don't stop until her muscles relax and her body lies limp on top of mine.

I chuckle. "Dinner *and* a show."

She turns onto her stomach, burying her face into my neck. We're silent again, and I love feeling her heart beating against me. I love . . . her. Eventually, she stirs.

"I think I can die happy now," she murmurs, tracing lazy patterns on my chest.

"Don't even joke about that," I say, tightening my arms around her. "Not after yesterday."

Her phone rings from the front hall. With a groan, she climbs off me, belatedly realizing she's utterly naked.

"Don't look," she says, making me laugh as she retrieves her dress from the floor beside the dining table. By the time she's pulled it over her head, she's missed the call.

Shrugging, she returns to the couch, taking a seat at the other end.

"You've changed," I say.

Looking surprised, she asks, "How so?"

"The old Lark would've had to answer her phone, even if her hair was on fire. And the old Lark would've checked to see who'd called if she'd missed it and listened immediately to the voicemail."

She grins. "I'm not the old Lark. I quit, remember? No longer at the beck and call of any company." Then she crosses her arms.

I wait to see how long she can last. She puts one foot on the coffee table and starts to jiggle it. Sighing, she glances at me and smiles, then looks away. Her fingers start to twitch.

"It's killing you, isn't it?"

"Yes, dammit!" Jumping up, she runs to the foyer and gets her phone from her purse, which she dropped on the narrow table. She hasn't even made it back to the couch before returning the call.

"Charlotte? What's happening?" Her expression grows serious as she listens. Her eyes are wide as she stares at me, eventually dropping onto the couch again. "You're kidding . . . No, that's . . . amazing news."

"What is it?" I mouth.

She crosses her eyes, which tells me nothing but makes me laugh.

"Yes, I was . . . It's true! Kidnapped . . . I know . . . Held against my will. Yup." She smiles at me. "Yes, Mitch was heroic. Yes, I'll tell him."

When she hangs up, her eyes are wide with disbelief. "Are you ready for the big news? RWI is ceasing all efforts to take over."

I sit up beside her. "Really?"

"They've issued a formal apology to the entire Henley Confectionery family and withdrawn all acquisition attempts. Durand has been removed from their board and is facing charges."

She shakes her head in wonder. "It seems merely the notion of you and me putting up a united front and disclosing all the rotten things Durand had done to Henley and to your restaurants made them decide we weren't worth the PR nightmare. And that was *before* the kidnapping attempt."

"We're not going to wage war against them after all?" To be honest, I'm a little disappointed.

"No war necessary," she confirms, leaning back, echoing my thoughts with her next words. "Though it's almost anti-climactic after all the battle planning we did."

"Hold on," I say. "How did they know we were going to be a PR nightmare *before* we became a PR nightmare?"

Lark grins. "I fired off a text to Charlotte about your great idea, from my car, right before I went upstairs to my apartment yesterday. I suggested sending a memo directly to the Chairman of RWI's board as well as to their CEO about the burned beans, the contaminated sugar, and the poisoned chocolate. I told her to mention the Franklin restaurants' latest mishaps and Camille's connection to you. I wanted to make sure they knew she was sitting in a Sydney jail."

I'm impressed by her quick thinking. "How'd you guess they'd back down?"

"I'm that good," she jokes. "Seriously, I figured that even a big conglomerate like that wouldn't want to have it known how dirty one of their members could play, especially against a helpless female and her—"

"Helpless!" I start to laugh.

"And her heroic chef boyfriend," she finishes.

*Boyfriend* sounds solid. Better than her *lover*. Much better than her *one-night stand*.

But it occurs to me I'm not ready to give up on our public merger. An idea forms in my mind, crystallizing with unexpected clarity.

"We should still make an announcement," I say. "Not a negative PR blitz, but about something else entirely."

"Like what?"

"A partnership—between Franklin Darkly and Henley Confectionery. What if I keep the original Franklin Darkly sauce as is, but collaborate on a new product line? Franklin-Henley Liquid Chocolate."

She blinks, processing this, before bursting into laughter. "FHLC? Flick?"

"Does have a certain ring to it, doesn't it?"

"*Um,*" she begins, but I steamroll over her with my next words.

"I owe your chocolatier an apology," I say. "To make amends, let Jules take my sauce base and amend it to his heart's content. He can add chili pepper or coffee extract or raspberry extract."

Lark winces. "Maybe not raspberry," she reminds me.

"Understood, but what do you think?"

"I'm game," she says, then her expression sours. "But I'm not the CEO any longer, so you'll be working with everyone except me."

That dims my enthusiasm, too. Taking her hand in mine, I bring it up to my lips, so I can sear a kiss against her palm.

"You know you can have your job back in a heartbeat. Not only coming back strong as CEO but having single handedly fought off the takeover while bringing a new product line of the best chocolate syrup in the world."

I can see she's considering it. I sweeten the pot by appealing to the growth of her company.

"In fact, if I'm working with you, I'll sell an assortment of your chocolates at my restaurants, on every dessert menu. We'll pair a plate of four . . . no, six chocolates with a perfect dessert wine. What do you think?"

Her expression is thoughtful. "It's a cool idea. I don't know of any restaurant that serves chocolates. The Franklin Restaurant Group might be the first."

Yet I notice she neither agrees, nor disagrees to take her job back. I guess she's still conflicted about what she wants.

$♥$♥$♥$

At one in the morning, I wake with my heart pounding, from a dream in which I'm searching for Lark. But I feel her next to me, even before I see her. As my eyes adjust, aided by moonlight, I look down at her serene face.

Usually, to put myself back to sleep, I would create a dish in my head, thinking of each ingredient in minute detail, down to the smallest caper or teaspoon of spice. Or imagine a new venue, with tablecloths or bare gleaming wood, high-backed chairs or sofa seating, textured walls or tiles.

But I don't do any of that. For the first time in my adult life, I'm not thinking about the next restaurant, the next exciting city, the next food challenge. I'm not feeling the need to escape.

Instead, I'm thinking about putting down roots—with Lark.

I know I have to wait until she can see her next move.

Without waking her, I drape my arm lightly across her middle before closing my eyes again, determined to protect what matters most. What's mine.

Sleep comes slowly, but when it does, my dreams are of a future I never knew I wanted until now.

# 28

## Lark

I awaken in Mitch's bed, covered by his sheets, his scent all over my skin. For one blissful heartbeat, I forget everything—the kidnapping, the corporate drama, even my resignation. Then it all comes flooding back, and I sit bolt upright.

"Mitch?" I call out, but the apartment answers with silence.

A note sits on the nightstand, his handwriting bold and confident:

*Gone to get breakfast supplies. Back soon. Don't go anywhere without me.*

I smile at his protectiveness, which feels earned after everything we've been through. My phone shows seven missed calls—two from my parents, one each from Luke and Clover, and a couple from Charlotte.

The events of yesterday flash through my mind—being rescued by Mitch, learning that RWI had pulled out. It's like waking up after a storm to find the battlefield cleared of enemies.

But I'm still left without a position at my family's company, although I had an epiphany while tied to my dining room chair. I'm just not ready to move forward with it. Nor does it preclude helping to run Henley Sydney.

Charlotte's voicemail plays as I head into Mitch's kitchen. I can at least make my own coffee.

"Lark, I need you to call me immediately," she says, sounding frazzled. "The board is convening an emergency meeting this afternoon. We need to discuss our next steps—particularly what we're going to tell the press." Her voice drops. "We need you back, Lark. Call me."

I lean against the counter, running a hand through my tangled hair. The words "emergency meeting" have lost all meaning. I know one thing I need to do. That's teach my former VP not to jump every time the board makes a noise. Then I hear Mitch's key in the lock.

"You're up!" he says, when he finds me in the kitchen, his arms weighed down with grocery bags. "I was hoping to surprise you with breakfast in bed."

"Charlotte called," I say, pressing buttons on his coffee maker. "The board wants to meet today."

Mitch sets the bags down and comes to me, his hands settling on my hips. "They certainly snap their fingers a lot."

"They do, indeed."

"And you're thinking of going?"

I look up into his eyes. "No, I don't think so."

His kiss is warm and reassuring. "Whatever you decide, I'm with you."

While he makes us a breakfast of avocado toast topped with spinach, tomatoes and poached eggs—*I could get used to being pampered and fed regularly*—I think about my options. The old Lark would already be dressed and heading for the door, cell phone plastered to my ear and a sense of urgency to fix whatever needed repairing.

That woman seems like someone I used to know rather than who I am now.

"*If* I go back," I say slowly, cutting into my egg and watching the orange yolk spread across the toasted English muffin and avocado, "it'll be on my terms."

Mitch, sitting opposite, nods. "Sounds good. What terms are those?"

Tapping my head, I say, "Still working that out." I take a bite of my delicious breakfast and close my eyes at the perfection of it. "I know one thing—Henley Confectionery needs to control the narrative from now on and stop reacting. RWI tried to take us down, and we need to show the world we're stronger than ever."

"A press conference?" he suggests.

I point my fork at him. "Exactly. A *joint* press conference with me and you."

"Me?" He looks surprised.

"I may not be the current CEO, but I know a good business proposition when I hear it."

Reaching my hand out to him, he takes it, not understanding until I say, "Let's shake on the merger and the creation of FHLC."

Mitch grins. "Deal."

I'm thinking aloud. "We'll show a united front as two professionals who love chocolate and want to merge our companies to highlight the very best of the best. Charlotte can orchestrate the PR side. She's brilliant at it."

He looks thoughtful, then jumps up to grab a paper towel and a pen. Sitting back down, he sketches an interesting fusion of our two brands on the shape of a bottle label. "Presenting the Franklin-Henley Liquid Chocolate partnership."

"Precisely," I say, my mind conjuring the possibilities. "You're just lucky that HFLC is harder to say."

After breakfast, I call Charlotte. She answers on the first ring.

"Thank God," she says, sounding frantic. "Are you coming in?"

"Nope," I tell her. "But that's because there is no longer an emergency, and we need to stop letting the board jerk the C-suite around. First, take a breath. Then tell them that you need longer to prepare for yet another board meeting."

"I didn't know I could push back like that. *Can* I do that?" she asks, still talking fast.

"Are you breathing?" I ask. "Yes, you can and you will. Tell them you have an important task taking up all your time today."

"Do I?"

"Yes, you do. I'm not your boss any longer, but as a Henley family member *and* a shareholder, I hope you'll do what I ask. I need you to set up a press conference for tomorrow. Let's say one o'clock in the lobby. Then, as acting CEO, tell the board that you're requesting a meeting directly afterward."

"OK," she says, sounding a little uncertain. "What's the press conference about? We no longer need to rake RWI over the coals."

"You're right, we don't. But we should still tell the public how Henley Confectionery weathered a shit-storm that was not of our making. There may be a couple RWI-related announcements, after I speak to their CEO today. But the important announcement will be that Mr. Franklin and Henley Confectionery will be jointly developing a line of chocolate sauces using Franklin Darkly as the base. All we need is a microphone, our names somewhere, including the acronym FHLC."

"FHLC?" she repeats.

"Don't ask. I'll also text you Mr. Franklin's logo. Let's hang it up somehow as a backdrop next to the Henley logo."

I can practically hear her smiling through the phone. "Consider it done. But Lark . . . what's your role going to be? The board wants to discuss your status."

"I won't discuss that with them until *after* the press conference." I'm feeling more confident with each word. Hanging up, I find Mitch watching me.

"What's that look?" I ask.

"Impressed," he says simply. "You're remarkable when you're taking charge."

"Is that a turn-on for you, Chef?"

His answer comes in the form of him lifting me onto the kitchen counter and stepping between my legs. "Everything about you turns me on."

"Even when I'm being difficult?" I tease.

"Especially then."

For the next several hours, we forget about press conferences and corporate machinations, losing ourselves in each other.

"As fierce as you are when talking business," he says, lying beside me, still breathing hard as we recover, "you're so chill and submissive in bed."

"That's OK, right? I mean, if you want me to wear a leather corset and wave a riding crop around, then I will."

He winces. "I'd prefer not. Taking charge is in my DNA."

"Which is perfect," I tell him. "Because having you dominate me in the bedroom makes me wet just thinking about it, wherever I am, whatever I'm doing."

My words cause his cock to stir from its resting position on his thigh to an impressive flagpole. When Mitch reaches over and traces a lazy circle over my stomach with a single finger before heading lower, I fear I may not be able to keep up with this man. What's more, I think I'm totally ruined for any other lover. Ever.

Ten minutes later, still lying on my stomach where he flipped me before taking me fast and hard—with such toe-curling satisfaction—I allow reality to seep into my thoughts.

"The board will want me back after the press conference."

"No doubt," Mitch says. "They'd be idiots not to. Have you made a decision?"

I stare at the ceiling, searching for the answer in the shadows. "I can't go back to being that woman who was chained to her job, stressed constantly, and missing out on life."

The zip ties taught me that.

"So don't." His voice is soft but certain. "Turn it down or redefine the position. Make it what you want it to be."

The idea settles over me like a comfortable weight. I'm counting on a middle ground between abandoning the job I thought I always wanted and drowning in it.

"First," I say, "I need to make sure Henley Confectionery doesn't simply survive this string of crises. I want to make sure it's thriving."

$♥$♥$♥$

The next day, Charlotte has outdone herself. Henley Confectionery's lobby is packed with reporters. A backdrop featuring Henley's and Franklin Darkly's logos, side by side, hangs behind a podium. Both the Sydney board and the NYC board have received a packet of info on what we're doing. And Luke, my parents, and even my big sister, Clover, are all in on the plan and approve.

"Ready?" Mitch asks, squeezing my hand. We're hidden in the short hallway leading from the side entrance to the building.

I smooth the front of my royal-blue, tailored dress that always makes me feel like a billion dollars and take a deep breath.

"Born ready."

Charlotte introduces us, her voice carrying throughout the vaulted lobby with practiced authority. "Ladies and gentlemen, Lark Henley and Mitch Franklin."

Together, we walk to the podium, while camera flashes blind us. Mitch is wearing an impeccably fitted, lightweight linen suit in a cream color that sets off his coffee-colored skin. I couldn't be happier than I am to step to the microphone with this creative, intelligent—hot as hell—man by my side.

"Good morning. Thank you all for coming on such short notice. As you may have heard, Henley Confectionery has faced some unusual challenges recently. Some played out in public, some behind the scenes, including espionage against my company, product sabotage, and a hostile takeover attempt by a foreign conglomerate."

Murmurs ripple through the crowd.

"What you may not have heard is that this attempt included kidnapping. Believe it or not, I was the one held hostage."

The murmurs turn to gasps. I briefly outline the events of the past few months, careful to leave out details that might compromise ongoing legal proceedings. And, of course, I make no mention of Camille or her father by name. Nor do I blame RWI directly.

"Throughout all of this," I continue, "Henley Confectionery dealt with each new challenge by continuing to produce the highest-quality candy in the industry. And one thing became crystal clear: Henley Confectionery isn't just a company—it's a family. We protect our own but welcome new members, too."

I gesture to Mitch, who steps forward. "Many of you know me as the creator of Franklin 6 and the F6 Tavern here in Sydney, as well as the owner of the other Franklin restaurants. Normally, I only do a press conference to tell you about an upcoming opening, but I'm here with Ms. Henley to announce something very exciting. A joint merger."

The murmurs become loud again.

He cocks his head for me to take over.

"Henley Confectionery and the Franklin Restaurant Group are joining forces to create a new line of premium chocolate syrups. The Franklin-Henley Liquid Chocolate line will combine Mitch's family's legacy syrup, Franklin Darkly, with Henley's chocolate-making expertise. Our master chocolatier, Monsieur Julien Cartier," I gesture to Jules whom Charlotte invited, and he offers a small wave to the crowd, "will develop new flavors of chocolate sauce that pair perfectly with every ice cream, cake, and alcoholic concoction you can dream of. Because, as I've discovered in my life, *everything* is better with chocolate."

My memory goes back to Mitch licking it off my skin, and I shiver. Meanwhile, a forest of hands shoots up for questions.

"Ms. Henley," calls a reporter from the *Sydney Morning Herald*, "does this mean you're returning as CEO of Henley Confectionery?"

I exchange a look with Mitch before answering. "I'll be attending a board meeting after this press conference to discuss that. As soon as the board and I have come to an agreement, I'll let you know."

"Mr. Franklin," asks another journalist, "will you be closing your restaurants to focus on this new venture?"

Mitch shakes his head. "Absolutely not. I actually have plans for a new venue—"

"Franklin 7," someone yells out, and most of the room laughs. But I'm a little shocked, as it's the first I've heard of a new restaurant.

"That's right," Mitch says. "I'm predictable in both naming my eateries and in delivering the best dining experience on the planet. Going forward, I'll be featuring Henley chocolates at all Franklin restaurants, creating a unique dessert experience that showcases the best of both our brands."

The questions continue, and we field them together, our responses complementing each other's as if we've rehearsed for weeks instead of hours. I catch sight of Charlotte in the wings, her expression a mixture of relief and admiration. She gives me a subtle thumbs-up.

"Ms. Henley," calls out a reporter from *Financial Times*, "what are your plans regarding the European markets? Will this partnership help Henley compete against the established European chocolate manufacturers?"

I lean into the microphone, pleased to reveal what came out of a productive conversation with Rafael Würtz, the biggest of the big RWI cheeses.

"I'm glad you asked about Europe. I've negotiated a distribution deal with RWI through their European networks."

The room erupts with a surprised hum of comments.

"Yes, you heard that correctly," I continue, unable to suppress a small smile. "RWI will facilitate Henley's entry into key European markets, not only for our established confectionery but also for Franklin Darkly and the new FHLC line."

I point a little sheepishly at the acronym on a thick poster board with the name spelled out beneath it. Charlotte did her best within the short prep period, and we might as well start branding it now.

Mitch steps forward. "This means that high-quality Australian-made chocolate will soon be competing directly with traditional European brands. We're bringing the heat to their home turf."

A voice calls out from the back of the room. "Is this a revenge move against a bad actor?"

I laugh, and I'm not staging it. I feel genuinely happy to have done something helpful for both Henley and for Mitch. But I've been careful not to paint RWI as an evil conglomerate.

"Not at all. This is simply good business. RWI recognizes the value in our brands, and we've found a way to work together that benefits everyone." I pause deliberately. "Well, *almost* everyone. I imagine when word gets out, some European chocolate makers might be a bit nervous."

The press conference continues for another ten minutes, and by the end, the energy in the room is electric. Maybe that's due in part to the free boxes of chocolates and bottles of Franklin Darkly.

Ultimately, Mitch and I are shameless promoters of what we believe in. And together, we've transformed what could have been a corporate disaster story into one of resilience, innovation, and growth. As we walk toward the elevator, Charlotte falls into step beside me.

"That went well," she says, with wry understatement. "You ready for round two?"

We step into the lift and head up to the executive floor. "The board is practically salivating. Stock prices jumped fifteen percent during your presentation alone."

"Charlotte," I say, putting my arm around her and giving her shoulder a squeeze, "we couldn't have done this without you. The way you handled everything in my absence—you were amazing. And the set-up downstairs—"

"That was first class," Mitch interrupts.

Charlotte's cheeks flush with pleasure. "Just doing my job."

"About that," I begin, but she cuts me off.

"The board is waiting in the main conference room. They want to see you immediately." She looks at Mitch. "Both of you."

Mitch raises an eyebrow. "Me too?"

"The Franklin-Henley partnership is the talk of the industry already." She glances at her watch. "For at least the last half hour. Naturally, the board wants to be in-the-know."

As we make our way past my old office, I can see it's still untouched since Charlotte remained in her own corner office at the other end of the hall. I could simply walk back in and sit behind the desk. I could . . .

Despite the success downstairs, my gut tightens when we approach the boardroom. Everyone inside it falls silent as we enter. Chairman Wembley stands at the head of the table, his expression unreadable. The last time I was here, I was being pushed out. Now the dynamic couldn't be more different.

"Ms. Henley, Mr. Franklin," Neville greets us, and the level of respect has already ratcheted up a notch. "Please sit."

We take seats side by side, our hands finding each other's under the table. A small gesture, but it steadies me enough to speak before the chairman can say anything more.

"Please, Neville. Call me Lark. After all, this is a family company."

His nostrils flare, and I wonder how long he'll remain on the board, but then he nods.

"I think I speak for the entire board," he continues, looking me in the eyes, "when I say that we owe you an apology."

The admission hangs in the air, weighty and unexpected.

"The board acted hastily in voting for your removal and in accepting your resignation. We allowed ourselves to be manipulated by outside forces and failed to recognize what should have been obvious—that you are the heart of the Sydney division."

I keep my face neutral, though inside I'm thinking he's laying it on a bit thick. On the other hand, vindication is an excellent feeling, and I can be gracious.

"I appreciate you saying that," I tell him.

"We would like to formally offer you the position of CEO of Henley Sydney once again," he says, sliding a folder across the table.

I'm fairly certain this one doesn't contain photos of me and Mitch kissing, but I flinch the tiniest bit.

Opening the folder, I scan the document inside.

"Should I leave?" Mitch asks, correctly guessing I'm going to negotiate.

"No, you're fine," I tell him.

"I accept the board's offer," I begin, letting them all visibly relax, "with some adjustments, of course." They all sit up straighter. Neville looks worried.

After listing a few incidental benefits that I don't care too much about, I say, "I want a seat on the board regardless of my operational role. In perpetuity, a family board seat with succession rights. One seat designated for one of my descendants per generation."

They look stunned. "I also expect to receive full backing for this new partnership venture with Mr. Franklin."

Ultimately, they agree to everything I ask for, mainly because the new distribution deal with RWI will make us a cool bundle. I should be on Cloud 9, but something still doesn't feel quite right.

"And what about Mrs. Bauer?" I ask.

Today, Charlotte's back in her usual seat at the table, since I made sure it was an executive board meeting, rather than an emergency one called by the chair. "She's proven herself more than capable in my absence."

Neville shifts uncomfortably. "I assumed she would return to her role as VP of the company."

"No," I say simply. "Charlotte has earned more than that."

The boardroom grows tense. Charlotte makes a sound of surprise. Mitch squeezes my hand under the table—a silent show of support—and then releases it. Drawing my hands into view, I lace my fingers on the tabletop, hoping to look "above board," as well as commanding.

"What are you suggesting, Lark?" Neville asks.

"I agree to return as CEO, with Charlotte as co-CEO."

I hold up a hand as several board members begin to protest.

"Before you object, consider this: She thrives on the day-to-day operations and knows them inside and out. I'll take point on strategic direction, international expansion, and this new partnership with Franklin Restaurant Group.

Together, we'll be stronger than either of us would be alone."

Neville leans back in his chair, considering. "It's . . . unorthodox."

"So is having your CEO kidnapped by a corporate rival," I remind him. "These are unorthodox times. They call for innovative solutions. Besides, with my brother heading Henley NYC, we already have multiple CEOs and have done since he and I took over for our father. What's one more?"

After a moment of tense silence, Neville nods slowly. "I take it your father and brother have already given their approval?"

"They have," I say, sending Charlotte a smile.

Before I have to press the matter, Neville calls for a motion, and the vote is unanimous to raise Charlotte's position to co-CEO. Then our chairman looks at Mitch.

"And what about you, Mr. Franklin? Are you taking a position here at Henley, too?"

I can't tell if Neville is cracking a dry joke or serious. In any case, Mitch shakes his head.

"I won't be collecting a paycheck. No need for the board members to worry," he says, sending a winning smile over all of them. "However, to protect the interests of the Franklin Darkly brand and to maintain the standards that are maintained at my establishments, I've offered my services *pro bono* to Ms. Henley's master chocolatier. At least, during the initial creation of the Franklin-Henley Liquid Chocolate line. I wouldn't want my name on anything I didn't think of the highest quality."

*As if we'd make anything subpar.* But business is business, and I don't fault him for saying it out loud.

"I can speak for all of us," board member Eloise Parker fairly gushes at Mitch, "when I say this is an exciting new development."

"And the factory expansion is underway," I point out, deadpan, as though the prematurely poured concrete pad is a happy circumstance.

Eloise nods in agreement, barely listening to me. "I've enjoyed every meal I've had at Franklin 6," she tells Mitch.

"Thank you," he says, suitably humble.

"Is your company based in Sydney?" Charles Davis asks.

"No, sir. It's incorporated in Massachusetts where I'm from."

Briefly, I wonder whether I'll ever go to Boston with him. Since Clover lives there and Luke's wife is from there, it's not out of the realm of possibility that I might be visiting and stop in to see him and even meet his family.

Shaking my head, I've only been CEO again for five minutes and I'm already on a ten-thousand-mile trip outta here.

"Do you have a plan to leave Australia? A time frame?" Neville asks Mitch, riveting my attention back to the proceedings. "Because we would expect to have a local Franklin rep here in case need arises."

Mitch hesitates, glancing at me, then back at the chairman. "Regarding how long I'm staying, my plans are in flux, but I trust either my head chef or my restaurant manager to be my voice once I've left. I'll designate one when the time comes."

Everyone seems satisfied, although I'm starting to get antsy. More so, when Mitch directs his next words toward me. "The nature of my business means I need to go away, usually for long periods of time, when I open a new restaurant and get it stabilized."

"Long periods of time" sounds . . . lonely, for both of us.

That is, unless he plans to continue playing the game of having a woman in every port. I suppose it's time for a frank discussion.

# 29

## Mitch

Working with Lark over the past three weeks has been different than I imagined. She's remote at work, by necessity, I suppose. In fact, Jules and I are in charge of developing the exclusive new flavors. So, for the most part, when I work on the FHLC R&D, I'm at the Wetherill Park factory, in the test kitchen.

Today, however, I'm at the Henley Sydney HQ, in Lark's corner office after a meeting with her and Charlotte, along with their head of marketing. They've hired Clover Bonvier, Lark's sister, to create the packaging and labeling from her design studio in Boston. Given the time difference, we didn't video chat but watched a taped presentation.

I am blown away by her mock-ups, as well as her suggestions for the campaign.

Ready to leave, I intend to race my woman home and start making cioppino for her. When I move close to kiss her, she frowns up at me from her laptop, as if she has forgotten I'm here.

"What are you thinking?" I ask.

About a billion thoughts flicker behind those crazy gorgeous eyes.

"I'm thinking of a road trip," she says, which I did not expect. "I know it seems irresponsible at this juncture. Impossible really. But it might be the perfect time *before* the first drop of FHLC hits the shelves. And I have Charlotte to cover for me."

I open my mouth to ask the obvious question, not where she wants to go but whether I'm invited. However, she beats me to it with a question of her own.

"Everything running smoothly at Franklin 6 and all the others?"

That's a relief. She's including me after all. "Smooth as your silky skin."

She blushes, which is sexy as hell.

Two days later, I'm driving Lark and me around the north of Queensland. We stop off at half a dozen cocoa bean plantations. At each one, Lark is treated like royalty, which floors me. Not that she doesn't deserve it. But the way she handles it, setting people at ease, is ridiculously sweet.

Despite most of the farmers freezing when they hear her unmistakable name and read her business card, she asks all the right questions, goes out into the field to sniff the soil, and even chews a bean or two. I'm impressed by her graciousness and humility, making her seem wiser than her years.

What's more, we've learned something new from each of these experts about growing cocoa beans over the four days so far. I'm also discovering that the Henleys are a really big deal, even outside of Sydney.

"You've taught me so much about the essence of chocolate," Lark said to the last farmer, a forty-something female, who's been at it for twenty years, since she was a young "idealistic hippie."

Lark was delighted. And delightful. Now, we're heading home.

*Home.* Sydney feels almost as comfortable and familiar as Boston. At least when I'm with Lark, it does.

"Are you staying with me?" I wonder aloud.

"You mean tonight?" she asks, sipping water between snacking on dried mango strips in the passenger seat. "We may not make it back tonight."

"You're sexy when you're snacking," I tell her, making her laugh, before I clarify, "I meant, are you moving in with me or am I moving in with you?" I don't know exactly why I choose this moment to blurt out such a loaded question. While it's becoming harder and harder to set a definitive date for when I'm leaving, I do have to go. And, to me, it seems silly not to be together under the same roof until whenever that day comes.

She sits up straighter. Before we came away, Lark hadn't spent a single night at her own apartment since she was held there. Perfectly fine by me. But I'd like to know where we stand in that regard. We fell into cohabiting rather than making a conscious decision, and it's uncomfortably similar to how Camille and I ended up sharing a place.

There was no kidnapping catalyst in Paris, obviously, but she suddenly lost her small loft near the school. Since we were hanging out, spending our nights in the same bed, it was a no-brainer to find a better caliber apartment that we could afford together.

Only later did I find out that she had zero money issues because her father was topping up her bank account every week. Camille was with me for the red-hot sex and the cooking tips we traded, not because she needed help with rent.

I realize Lark might be with me for the same reasons, sex and food. I can't ask for more since I can't make any promises. On the other hand, if we were officially living together, then I'd start thinking of Sydney as my home-base.

And that would open the door a crack to something more permanent.

"I don't know," Lark says, in a neutral tone that tells me nothing. "Is that where we are?"

"We could be," I answer.

Then we fall into silence, both of us considering. I'd never planned on keeping my Sydney penthouse permanently, and she already owns an apartment with her brother.

"I'm ready to give up my place, to be honest," I tell her. "I'd be happy to keep you company at yours. Unless you don't want to go back there after what happened, which I totally understand."

Lark is frowning. "Give up your place?" she echoes quietly, and I wish I knew what was going on in that pretty head of hers.

"You're selling your apartment?" she asks, her voice rising slightly.

I glance over at her, trying to read her expression as I navigate the winding coastal road. She's staring straight ahead, lips pressed together.

"I was considering it," I say carefully, putting my gaze back on the road unfurling ahead of us, shimmering in the late afternoon heat. "My plan never included remaining in Sydney permanently. Franklin 6 is established now," I remind her. *Long since needing my help, in fact.*

Her silence wedges between us like a physical block.

"But if you sold it," she says at last, "you wouldn't have anywhere to come back to. You know, *after* you opened your next venue. That is, if you were intending to come back."

"I'd have your place," I point out. "And yes, I intend to come back. To visit."

She shifts in her seat, tucking one leg beneath her. "Mitch, you open restaurants all over the world. That's your thing. You're not close to being settled, right?"

Something in her tone makes me uneasy. "Are you saying you need me to declare myself ready to live here forever?"

"I'm saying I don't want you to give up anything for me. Not a single dream or a single amazing new restaurant." She turns to look at me. When I glance over, her eyes briefly search mine. "Especially when you're about to start a new one."

I grip the steering wheel tighter. Something else we haven't talked about.

"You mentioned Franklin 7 a month ago at the press conference," Lark reminds me. "I didn't know how far in the future that was, but I saw the blueprints on your desk the other night. Seems like it's ready for launch. The only thing holding it back is you not getting your butt to Bozeman."

"I was going to discuss it with you," I say, feeling oddly defensive. I've never had to be accountable to a lover before, not since opening Franklin 1. "And you're right. My CFO has been pushing me to break ground for months."

"So, what are you waiting for?" she asks, though I suspect she already knows.

I dodge the question, instead, telling her about the restaurant. "It's a concept I've been developing for a while—upscale rustic dining with local ingredients. The farm-to-table and wild-to-table movements are big there."

She nods, looking back at the road. "Montana is a long way from Sydney."

The unspoken question hangs in the air between us, *What happens to us when I leave?* It's something I've been avoiding thinking about—the inevitable pull of my next project, the demands that will take me halfway across the world from her.

"It's temporary," I say, though we both know my definition of *temporary* can and probably will stretch to months, even half a year. "Besides, you could visit. Maybe even stay a while."

"While I'm running Henley Sydney?" she asks, her tone not accusatory, just realistic.

"I guess you can't imagine, at this moment, being uprooted for months at a time." I often look forward to going somewhere new, but about a month in, it gets old being a stranger in a strange land. That wouldn't happen if Lark were with me. Then it would be sheer adventure.

We lapse into silence again, the only sound the hum of the car's engine and the occasional call of birds outside. The tropical landscape blurs past us, but the beauty of it feels distant now.

"Let's find somewhere to stop for the night," I suggest, spotting a sign for accommodations ahead. "We can talk more over dinner."

At an exclusive beach-side inn, we rent a suite with an ocean view and a small kitchen because I've hit my limit of how long I can go without cooking. I'm checking out the minimalist equipment when Lark steps out onto the balcony. She's leaning against the railing, staring out at the water.

Joining her, I wrap my arms around her waist from behind, and she leans back against me. As we stand silently, she strokes my arms with the feather lightness of the breeze coming in off the Coral Sea. For a moment, everything feels right again.

"I make a mean prawn linguine," I murmur against her ear. "The market we passed boasted fresh seafood. I hope you're hungry."

She turns in my arms, pressing her palms against my chest. "Always feeding me," she teases, but her smile doesn't quite reach her eyes.

"It's what I do," I say, stroking her cheek. "Take care of the people I—" I catch myself, suddenly uncertain.

We've taken a step backward from the "I love you's" from before we started working together.

Her expression softens. "The people you what?"

"The people I care about," I finish, cowardly but safe.

We head to the small local market, and I select ingredients with practiced efficiency—fresh prawns, garlic, chilies, lemons, and pasta. Then I relax into my element in the suite's basic kitchen. I've worked with less.

As I chop and sauté, Lark sits at the small counter, sipping a glass of local white wine.

"You know," she says suddenly, "I've been thinking a lot during this trip."

"I could tell," I say, sprinkling red pepper flakes into the sauce, stirring carefully.

"I could see owning my own cocoa bean plantation." She eyes me like she's thrown down a challenge, or perhaps she thinks I'll try to dissuade her.

I nod. "Tell me more."

"I could stay in *chocolate*, but differently," Lark begins. "I keep thinking how passionate the farmers were about growing the perfect cocoa beans."

Her eyes are bright, animated in a way I haven't seen in weeks. "I could create something that's truly mine. A place where people can see the whole process, from bean to bar. Tours, tastings, a real experience."

"Like a chocolate vineyard experience?" I suggest, and her face lights up with a huge smile.

She holds her wine up like she's toasting the idea.

"Exactly! But it would still be a real working plantation. It's unlikely I could ever grow enough beans to provide the Henley factory with what it needs for production. Besides it wouldn't have the flavor profile of those from Côte d'Ivoire via our Belgian importer/exporter. But I can certainly grow enough for my own use."

"Sounds like a good plan," I say, because she has the same energy I do with each restaurant I'm opening. Excited, dreaming, planning, the sky's the limit.

"And the tastings wouldn't merely be ground beans and generic chocolate," she continues.

"Of course not," I say, holding up a sauteed shrimp on the end of my spatula. As usual, she opens her mouth to receive a taste. "You would never do anything generic."

"I'd create my own signature chocolate. Lark Henley brand, *not* Henley Confectionery," she says, her gaze in the middle distance as she conjures up a passion project. "Although maybe a different name entirely. Why compete or cause confusion? My own brand," she repeats.

Her enthusiasm is contagious. I can see it so clearly—Lark in her element, teaching people about her love of chocolate, creating something unique and personal. But it also means another major change, another path diverging from mine.

"That sounds incredible," I say, plating our dinner. "Where would you do this?"

She frowns, and then it hits me.

"That's what this trip was about?"

"I don't know yet," she admits, accepting her plate with a grateful smile. "But somewhere in Queensland, I think. The climate's right. I can grow cocoa beans and still be within a few hours' drive of Nan and Gramps."

All at once, she shrugs dismissively. "It's just a pipe-dream of a cocoa bean farm, with me toiling dawn to dusk. Maybe I couldn't hack it anyway." This last part is said in jest, since she'd definitely hire workers.

Suddenly, I picture some well-built farmhand stopping by her farmhouse for a cup of water like it's early in the last century. He'll saunter up in his jeans and boots, and he'll flex for her. I know how this lady loves muscles on a man.

As we eat, she elaborates—a sustainable farm, artisanal production methods, a store on the premises selling small-batch chocolate. I listen, caught between admiration for her vision and a growing awareness that our paths may not align as neatly as I'd started to imagine.

Because after she decided to share the CEO job with Charlotte, I had half hoped Lark would come with me to help open my next restaurant.

Now, I can't help wondering if she has any real interest in remaining as co-CEO or being in a long-term, long-distance relationship with me.

First thing's first. "What about the CEO position?" I ask. "You fought so hard to get it back."

She twirls pasta around her fork, considering. "I'm not giving it up. Not yet. I needed to prove I could do it. That I wasn't a failure or the weak Henley link. And I've done that. Soon the new European distribution will be bringing in new revenue, and Jules has the FHLC product line moving along . . ."

She shrugs. "Besides, Charlotte's brilliant at running things. Better than me in many ways because she's more patient and seems to love the job. Like LOVE it!"

*The way I love her.*

"Anyway," she adds, "I'm not planning on going anywhere yet. I've finally got my Sydney groove on, and it feels pretty good."

After dinner, we take a walk along the beach. The moon is high, casting silver light across the water. Lark's hand fits perfectly in mine, her skin soft against my calloused palm.

"So," I say, breaking our comfortable silence, "about living arrangements. What did we decide?"

She sighs, kicking at the sand. "I'm moving back to my place when we get home tomorrow."

The words hit me harder than expected. "I thought you were avoiding it because of what happened."

"Partly," she admits. "But also because it was easier just to give in to being with you. Not to think about what we're doing or where we're going."

"And now?" I ask, stopping and planting my feet in the sand, which has started to shift beneath my plans.

She faces me. "I need to stay on the right path and get down to some hard work. And you need to build your new restaurant before someone beats you to it."

"You make it sound like we're breaking up," I say, trying to keep my tone light despite the bands clamping around my chest.

"No," she says quickly, reaching up to touch my face. "Not at all. Whatever we share, I can't break. But we've never been looking at a long-term future, right? All I'm saying is we rushed into a temporary living-together arrangement because of the circumstances. The kidnapping, the Camille sabotage, all the craziness with RWI pushing us together. Everything was so intense. We need to slow down a bit, don't you think?"

I want to argue, to tell her that there's no time to slow down. But I can't deny our relationship was forged in crisis, accelerated by danger and sheer adrenaline.

*What can we mean to each other when I'm hamstringing my own business in order to stay here longer with her?*

"Okay," I concede. "You go back to your place, I'll keep mine. For now."

That is, until I sell it and get on a flight to Montana, because that's the only thing I see on my horizon.

She stands on tiptoe to kiss me, soft and sweet.

Back in our room, our bodies collide with a hunger edged in desperation, fearing that we're near the end of something really great. For the past month, I've liked going to sleep with this woman beside me, knowing she'll be there when I wake up. More than liked it, I came to rely on it.

Now it seems like this is our last night. *For now.*

Tracing the moonlit patterns on her skin with the pads of my fingers, I end up gliding my hands over her entire body, committing her shape to memory. I trace every one of her luscious curves first with my fingertips, then my lips. When she comes apart beneath me, clinging to my shoulders, her nails dig in. Weirdly, I hope she leaves her mark.

Afterward, Lark lies in my arms, her head on my chest. No matter how tightly I cradle her, I can't hold on to what we have. Our real-world responsibilities are lining up at dawn to pull us apart.

"Tell me about Bozeman again," she murmurs sleepily. "And your new place."

It's not the first time I've told her. She said before that I describe my vision like a bedtime story. So I dive in, building the rustic lodge with my words, log by log and stone by stone. I explain in detail the open kitchen that guests can see from different vantage points. I list the menu items, local game and produce, a bar specializing in Montana whiskeys. I tell her about the local Bozeman glass-blower who's making all the lamps.

As I talk, her breathing deepens, her body growing heavier against mine.

"You should come see it," I whisper, though I think she's already asleep. "When it's ready."

$♥$♥$♥$

Once we return to Sydney, the change is immediate and jarring. Lark moves her things back to her apartment that very afternoon, employing the "ripping off the Band-Aid" approach. I carry her suitcases, even though each one feels like it's filled with rocks instead of clothes and shoes.

The empty spaces she leaves behind are like open wounds, cataloging what used to be. The penthouse instantly becomes just a temporary place to sleep and cook again, no longer feeling the least bit like home.

"It's not goodbye," she says, standing in her doorway after we've brought in the last of her things. "But it's best to face what's coming. I think it'll hurt less later."

*Doubtful.* I preferred when we talked about living a fairy tale, rather than facing a future without her in it.

For ten more agonizing days, I stall. We maintain a professional relationship. Jules, who lets me practice my forgotten French, develops two exclusive flavors for the

FHLC line. They're spectacular. The first is showy, an almond extract infusion with rich cherry essence that brings out the chocolate's depth. The second is more universal, a sure palate pleaser, with its hint of sea salt and caramel that makes the sauce addictively good on almost anything.

Clearly, Jules has it under control and doesn't need me.

During a final meeting in Sydney to go over marketing, distribution, and wholesale pricing, none of which I give a damn about, Lark is pleasant but distant. There's a new kind of tension between us, which is making us both sad.

When our hands accidentally touch, both reaching for the same sample, she pulls back as though burned. I notice the dark circles under her eyes and wonder if she's sleeping any better in her own place than I am without her in mine.

Clearly, Lark doesn't need me at the office, either.

I've completely pulled back from any kitchen work at Franklin 6, too. They are on the top of the restaurant scene, thanks to Ravi and his staff.

Meanwhile, my contractor in Montana calls daily, increasingly agitated about delays. The permits are secured, the materials are onsite for the renovation of the century-old building I bought, and the blueprints have been finalized for weeks.

All that's missing is me. And since I always have hands-on approval every step of the way, nothing happens without my being there.

I find Lark in her office late one evening, staring out at the Sydney skyline. The city lights reflect in her eyes when she turns and sees me.

"I need to leave for a while," I say without preamble. "I can't put it off any longer."

She nods, unsurprised. "I've been expecting this. Frankly, I need you to leave. This is too hard."

"Then come with me," I suggest, the words tumbling out before I can stop them. "See what I'm building there. Stay as long as you like."

But she's already shaking her head, like I knew she would. "I can't, Mitch. I have too much to do here."

The hollowness that has been growing in my chest makes it hard to breathe. I see her future. She's rooted and tied to her family's legacy. And I see mine—always moving, searching for the next perfect place to conquer, the next restaurant, the next challenge.

She notices my hesitation. Of course she does. She's been reading me like a recipe book since the day we met.

"If we hadn't moved so fast," she says softly, then her throat seems to close. Coughing to clear it, she starts again. "We need this breather to figure out what each of us wants."

"I know what I want," I argue, but even as I say it, I feel torn.

"OK, then move into my apartment here in Sydney and . . . I dunno, become the head chef of Franklin 6," she says. "Does that sound appealing? Will that satisfy you?"

Her tone is laced with anger now, and she's baiting me. I've told her before that I'd be stifled by one kitchen, one menu.

"We *want* each other," I state plainly.

"And the rest somehow works itself out?" she asks. "That's not how it is in real life." Her voice is thick with emotion, and I feel its counterpart like a tightening in my chest.

"Go, please," she says, like she's begging for mercy from an executioner. Her eyes are overly bright. In the next instant, she wipes at a tear. "Dammit!"

I'm utterly wrecked. But there's nothing I can say to make this better, and I can't do anything to change what's going to happen. So, I do as she asks. I walk out of her office

$♥$♥$♥$

Two days later, at Lark's insistence, she drives me to the airport. Our goodbye is painful in its polite restraint and lack of passion. No dramatic scenes, no promises to wait for each other.

Just a tender kiss at the curb that tastes like an ending.

"Thank you," she says against my lips.

I don't ask what for. I simply say it back to her. From the bottom of my soul, I tell her, "Thank you, Lark."

But I can't leave it, can't leave *her*, without trying to bind us together somehow. I'm not used to caring like this, to having a lump in my throat before boarding.

And I'm definitely not used to leaving behind someone I love.

"I hope you're up for some heavy texting," I joke. It falls flat as overworked dough.

Her gaze firmly fixed on mine, she tilts her head and takes a deep breath. "I think we should do our best not to hurt one another."

When she bites her bottom lip, I nearly get back in the damn car. I want to break every speed limit driving to anywhere with a bed or a floor or a wall. I want to settle between her thighs and sink deep into her. Right. Now.

And I want to howl, thinking about the distance I'm about to put between us.

"When I have time to visit," I begin, but she cuts me off.

"Let's not make foolish promises," Lark says, all tough and calm and sensible.

I don't protest. Deep down, I know she's right. Blowing up her phone when we can't touch one another, when we have zero plans for a future, that would be cruel. And pretending "Us, Part 2" is right around the corner, that's just stupid.

Back straight, she lets her gaze flick over me again, then our eyes meet for a long moment. Turning away, Lark hurries to escape, and a second later, she's speeding off.

As my plane takes off, Sydney falls away beneath me, and I'm trying not to think about Lark and how she's taking this on her drive home. Personally, I'm lucky. I have a whiskey in hand already.

I'm trying to scrounge up my usual excitement on a flight to a new place. And failing. Another Dewar's Scotch later, still the unfamiliar sorrow hasn't eased. I don't know if Lark will wait for me—or if I've already lost her. Besides, I couldn't even tell her if I'd be jetting back in three months or in six.

But I'm not ready to accept that this is the end. Maybe she's the "forever girl" my dad once told me about. "When you know, you know," he'd said, speaking about the day he met my mom.

All I know is, for the first time ever, I've left behind more than a city and a well-running restaurant. I've left behind my heart. No doubt about it.

# 30

# Lark

Late-morning sun pours through my office windows as I review our quarterly sales figures. Three months after taking back my position as CEO, Henley Confectionery's numbers are better than ever. *Through the roof,* as my father says.

The European expansion, facilitated by the distribution deal I wrung out of Rafael Würtz's RWI in exchange for not pressing charges against his company, has exceeded our most optimistic projections.

Of course, I nailed Camille and Bill, whose real name is Jan de Smet, to the proverbial wall. And while I couldn't touch Stephen Durand, Würtz did that for me.

I glance at two bronze-cast "cocoa beans" resting in a small, silver cocoa pod-shaped dish on my desk. Rafael sent me the bespoke sculpture out of the blue. We're like besties now. The heavy beans have become my latest fidget toys.

God knows I can't even look at a clothespin right now without being hit by the sadness stick, hard and repeatedly. Followed quickly by longing. And love. But no regret. Except for having to banish my old fidget toys under my kitchen sink.

*What is Mitch doing at this very instant?* Given the time change, probably in bed. I hope he's alone. Please let him be sleeping solo.

"Knock, knock," Charlotte says from my doorway, though she actually knocks at the same time. "Have you seen the latest numbers from Belgium? We're outselling two local brands now."

I smile, gesturing for her to take a seat. "I was just looking at them. It's almost unbelievable."

"Not really." Charlotte settles into the chair across from me. "Not with you at the helm. The board couldn't be happier."

*The board.* The same people who threw me to the wolves are now singing my praises. I should feel elated. Instead, I feel . . . empty. Their approval contributes nothing to my current state of mental well-being, such as it is.

"Jules wants to know if you've heard anything from Mitch about the newest flavor concept," Charlotte mentions, studying her tablet.

My heart does that annoying little skip it always does at the mere mention of his name.

"Not yet. I forwarded the samples to him last week."

Charlotte nods, not quite meeting my eyes. She knows better than to ask anything more, since I've become a little touchy when his name comes up.

Once she leaves, I take a stroll around my spacious office, which I try not to think of as a prison cell. As usual, I end up gazing out at the Sydney skyline. *Three months.*

Three months since Mitch boarded a plane to Montana.

Three months of throwing myself into my work.

Three months of pretending I don't check my phone fifty times a day looking for messages that never come.

I told him we needed a breather. I pushed him away, even driving him to the goddamned airport like a stoic martyr. *So why does it feel like I'm the one who was abandoned?*

My phone buzzes with an incoming call. For a heart-stopping moment, I think it might be him. That also happens daily, along with the disappointment when it's not Mitch.

Sure enough, the screen shows my brother's face instead.

"How's my favorite CEO?" Luke's voice comes through, warm and familiar from New York.

"Working too hard, as usual," I reply, settling back into my chair. "How's the Big Apple treating you?"

"Can't complain. The new boutique store concept is taking off. Dad's proud as hell, though he'd never admit it outright."

We chat about business for a while, the comfortable rhythm of siblings who understand each other's world. Then it dawns on me.

"Why are you awake?"

He laughs. "Took you long enough. I had a dream about you and woke up thinking I needed to call. Everything OK?"

"Sure is. I'm ending my fabulous workday in the beautiful city of Sydney," I say, wishing I didn't sound facetious.

"Work is work," he says, "wherever you are. But it has to feel pretty good when you look at the company numbers. You're blowing my German chocolate sales out of the water."

I can tell Luke has something else on his mind.

"Alright, out with it," I say. "You didn't get out of your comfy bed, leaving your lovely wife, in order to discuss quarterly reports with me."

There's a pause on the other end. "Have you heard from him?"

*Ugh!* I don't need to ask who "him" is. I also didn't need the question, and I certainly don't need to answer. But I do.

"No. Not beyond a few emails about the FHLC line, copied to Jules and Charlotte. Why? Don't tell me you're pen pals now."

"No, but . . ." Luke hesitates. "I saw some press about his new restaurant. Had a soft opening last week. Looks impressive."

I ignore the tight band that instantly circles my chest. "That's good. I'm glad for him."

"Lark," my brother's voice softens. "The week after Mitch left, you told me not to go punch him, because it was mutual break-up. But was it really? I told the guy he'd have to deal with me if he ever hurt you, and I hate to go back on my word."

Closing my eyes, I recall the conversation with Luke. He had called, going all *big brother* on me. Ready to hop a plane to Bozeman and defend my honor. I'd pretended to laugh it off, insisting we were adults making adult decisions.

I'm not laughing now. If anything, it becomes more painful each day.

*Damn. Am I ever going to be over him?*

"You most definitely don't have to 'deal' with him," I tell Luke. "We're both where we need to be."

"Are you? Because you sound about as happy as a chocolate Easter bunny in December."

I can't help but laugh at that. "What does that even mean? How happy does a regular bunny sound, never mind a chocolate one?"

He's a great brother. He actually made me laugh. I lie to him, so he'll go back to bed.

"I'm fine, Luke. I'm running the company better than ever. The European market is booming. The FHLC line has a new flavor. I'm—"

"Working yourself to death and sleeping at the office more nights than not. Yeah, Charlotte mentioned that part the other day."

"Traitor," I mutter.

"She's worried about you. So am I."

I sigh, rubbing my temples. "I appreciate your concern, but I'm okay. Let me bury myself in work for a while and grieve the natural and necessary ending of a pretty good relationship. OK?"

After I tell him I love him and we hang up, my own words echo in my head. *Am I really where I need to be?*

$♥$♥$♥$

Three months later, I stand on the front porch of my new home, breathing in the rich scent of earth and vegetation. The property stretches before me, acres of pure potential, waiting to be realized.

The previous owner had already planted several fields of cocoa trees, which have been neglected. Still, the farm is beautiful—both rolling hills and flat pasture covered in lush greenery, a renovated farmhouse that's modern with rustic touches, and enough space to build my dream.

"What do you think, Ms. Henley? Is it a go?" Andy, my burly contractor with kind brown eyes, asks after I hand him an ice-cold Victoria Bitter from my fridge.

I can't help drinking Mitch's favorite Aussie brew, since the taste on my lips brings him closer to me in a small way.

"I'm glad to hear the barn's floor is solid," I say. "I like its high ceilings, and I don't want to gentrify it too much."

Andy's been helping me plan the renovations. "I can convert it into a tasting room with minimal work," he agrees.

I nod, already picturing it. Visitors will sample freshly made chocolate while learning about the journey from bean to bar. "What have you got planned for the farm laborers' accommodations?"

"Got a nice spot for a seasonal bunkhouse over by the eastern ridge," he says, pointing. "Good view of the sunrise. Get 'em out of bed early."

I have the same view from my upstairs bedroom window, and I love it.

We spend the afternoon going over plans—where to expand the cacao trees, where to build the processing facility so it won't be a major eyesore, where to put the new horse stable. Because although this isn't that type of ranch, I want a couple of horses.

By the time Andy leaves, night is falling, and I'm alone in my new home. The seclusion hasn't fazed me yet. In a way, it's less lonely than being holed up in my apartment in Sydney, not wanting to go out. I'm over the nightlife, definitely not thinking of one-night stands, can't imagine going into F6 Tavern with no hope of seeing Mitch striding through the lively, noisy bar.

The two-level farm house is beautiful and was move-in ready. I haven't yet got the furniture to fill the spacious rooms. Haven't put area rugs on the red-toned, native ironbark floors. No curtains yet on the large windows overlooking the property. And least surprising, barely any cooking supplies in the modern kitchen that would make Mitch—

No. I won't think about him. Not tonight.

*Give your heart a break,* I tell myself.

Heating chicken soup from a can and wishing I'd inherited my grandmother's and my mother's cooking gene, I carry the bowl out to the large porch. The stars are incredible, away from city lights. The closest town, Sarina, is small but charming, with enough amenities to keep me from feeling stranded.

Like soup cans and microwavable dinners, but also a bakery, an ice cream store, and a pizza parlor. Basically, I'm all set.

The locals have been welcoming, although they're still adjusting to having a Henley in their midst. The town's other claim to fame is Buffy, the Big Cane Toad, which is . . . a big fiberglass statue of a cane toad by the highway. Gotta enjoy fun-loving Aussies.

Best of all, Sarina is surrounded by sugarcane fields, and in keeping with my interests, there's a small sugar mill and distillery nearby. They don't produce enough for my chocolate-production, but I appreciate knowing my peeps are here. I've already taken their tour.

Naturally, I'll direct people to the sugar mill once my own tours are running, and hopefully, they'll reciprocate.

Night falls quickly in the countryside. The darkness seems deeper, more absolute than in Sydney. Definitely more absolute than in Manhattan. I don't mind. After months of noise, chaos, corporate politics, loud celebrations over Henley's burgeoning profits, the silence is a balm.

My phone rings, interrupting my damn balm! I still get a shot of hope with each call, followed by the quick chaser of disappointment.

"Just checking in," Charlotte says. "How's farm life treating you?"

"It's perfect," I tell her. "You should visit once I'm more settled. When I have a bed in one of the guest rooms."

I left all the furniture in Sydney, apart from my bed. The memories were too good to leave it behind.

"I will," she says, although we both know she won't get away to come up here, not for months. "By the way, the board sends their regards. They're still in shock that you actually meant it when you resigned this time."

"To put that look on Neville's face, that was the main reason I left." We both chuckle. "Anyway, I think my dad was more surprised than anyone. But he came around after he saw my business plan."

"And of course, he *adores* your replacement," Charlotte adds, with a self-deprecating laugh. "I'm still getting used to being called CEO without the 'acting' or 'co' qualifier."

"Everyone loves you," I tell her. "You're an honorary Henley forever."

We talk a while longer. Charlotte still feels the need to update me on company matters that are no longer my concern.

"Well, you are a board member," she reminds me.

When we hang up, I feel a mixture of relief and nostalgia. I don't regret my decision to leave, but there's something bittersweet about closing that chapter of my life.

Carrying my empty bowl inside, I wash it by hand, since it would take a long time to fill my dishwasher. I'd be out of dishes before then. After pouring a second glass of red wine, I lean against my kitchen island, looking out the window.

All I see from this vantage point is the outline of the cacao trees against the night sky.

*My trees now. My dream.*

It's everything I figured out I wanted when tied to my kitchen chair.

*Why does it feel like something's missing?*

I know the answer, of course. Have known it since the day he left. But admitting it means admitting I made a mistake, and Lark Henley doesn't make mistakes. At least, that's what I tell myself.

The truth is, I was scared. Scared of how quickly things had developed between us, scared of the intensity of my feelings, scared of what would happen when his restless nature inevitably pulled him away *after* I gave my entire heart to him.

I would've left myself defenseless. Naturally, I pushed first, convinced myself we wanted different things. As it turned out, I was right.

Mitch has his restaurants, his nomadic lifestyle. I have my roots in the soil, my vision for a future that will keep me in one place.

But in the quiet moments, when there's nothing to distract me, I wonder if I was a little bit hasty, or altogether wrong. Still unable to see how we could've compromised, perhaps we would have found a way.

A week passes, then another. And I. Love. My. New. Life.

I throw myself into the renovation work, consulting with agricultural experts, interviewing potential employees, drawing up plans for the visitor experience.

During the day, I'm too busy to think about him. At night, going to sleep when my head hits the pillow, I dream of dark eyes and skilled hands, of whispered words and shared laughter.

I tell myself it gets easier each day, but that's a lie. It gets more familiar, this ache, but never easier.

One evening, I'm poring over the final color choices for the tasting room when my phone buzzes with a text. *Hope. Disappointment.* It's from Jules.

**The fourth flavor is killing it. Mitch said he knew it was the best yet.**

I stare at the message, feeling that familiar twist in my chest. I should be pleased—this is business, after all. The FHLC line is important to Henley's future. But all I can think about is Mitch tasting Jules's creation, probably in his gleaming Montana kitchen. Without me there to see his reaction.

I type a brief response:
**Great news!**

Setting my phone down, I try to focus again on the designer's sketches spread across my dining table. But my concentration is shot, and there are too many choices. I should send everything to Clover and ask her opinion. It would still be my vision, but with her experienced input.

*So why am I still sitting here, staring at nothing?*

Because the green-eyed monster has reared its ugly head, wondering if Mitch shared the chocolate sauce with another woman, in his special way. One of those women he once boasted about having in every restaurant city. That was when we were talking dirty and sexy during our one-night stand.

The thought makes me physically ill. I push back from the table, needing air.

Outside, sitting on the porch steps, I wrap my arms around myself against the cool night breeze. The stars above look the way they do from Nan and Gramps' ranch, mocking my ugly thoughts with their beauty.

How many times did Mitch wrap his arms around me while we looked at stars? Each time, I felt happy, until the last time when we were on our tour of the cocoa bean farms. That was the night I realized I had to pull back or be crushed under the overwhelming feelings I had for him.

"Stop it," I mutter to myself. "Just fucking stop."

My phone rings again, and I consider ignoring it. But it might be important. *It might be Mitch.*

It's my mother. My heart skips a beat. This is likely going to be a long, emotional session, ending with me confessing how much I miss my chef boyfriend. I take a deep breath. It'll be good to get it off my chest.

"How's my little meadowlark?" she asks. Her familiar, loving voice, so far away in New York, makes me choke up.

Half an hour later, against all odds, I feel better. She reminded me of all the blessings. How for the first time in my life, I'm simply Lark Henley, not *the* Lark Henley, in training to be CEO, not the millionaire heiress, not the kick-ass NYC CEO, or even the Sydney success story.

The way she makes me face it is both terrifying and exhilarating. And liberating.

"I can't wait to see what my baby girl is creating," Bunny Henley says, while I go back inside as the mosquitoes start biting. "We'll come soon, so make sure you have a firm mattress for your father's back."

"Sounds great, Mom." The promise of guests gives me a reason to buy some furniture. I've spent all my time and a shit-ton of money on the public areas of the plantation. Nothing yet on my own house.

I curl up on the sofa that was already here when I moved in. It's a high-back, fussy Victorian-era piece, which looks too small and precious for this living room. I fully intend to choose furniture soon, and this will be one of the first things to go, mostly because it's hard as rock.

Arranging the pillows I've added, I flick on the TV. Instead of dealing with business reports or spreadsheets, I can binge-watch my latest pastime, home renovation shows. Sometimes, I even take notes.

My ears perk when I hear the crunch of tires on the gravel outside.

I freeze, listening. I'm not expecting anyone. The sound stops, followed by a car door closing.

My heart begins to race. I live alone, miles from my nearest neighbor. Hardly anyone even knows I'm here except family and a few close colleagues.

Moving quietly, I retrieve the rifle my grandfather gave me for protection when I told him I was moving by myself to a farm. It's loaded—Gramps made sure I knew how to handle it safely—and the weight of it feels reassuring in my hands.

More sounds now. Footsteps on the path leading to my front door, up the porch steps. Heavy, purposeful. A *man's* footsteps.

My heart is racing, but it could be my contractor. Maybe Andy forgot something. Like his tape measure. Something he simply had to get tonight. *Sure.* I try to swallow but my pulse is thumping in my throat.

Positioning myself near the entrance, rifle ready, I hear the steps climb the porch stairs, then stop. No knock comes.

*Merde!* as Jules would say.

Instead, I hear movement along the planks of the porch, heading toward the side of the house. Toward the windows of the living room where I was just sitting, where a light is still on.

*Double shit!* Without curtains, whoever it is can see right in like I'm on a stage, but I can't see out at all. I am officially freaked out!

Deciding to circle around and get behind whoever this is, I creep to the side entrance. My heart nearly hammering out of my chest, I ease the door open. Maybe I should call out Andy's name so the intruder knows there's a man around here.

The night air is cool on my skin as I step outside, rifle held steady. The moon is half full, not casting enough light to see more than my socks on the wraparound porch and two-feet of wood planks in front of me.

I creep along the side of the house, listening.

There—a shadow moves by the corner, going back toward my front door. I raise the rifle, stepping into the light streaming from my living room.

"Don't move," I call out, my voice steadier than I feel. "I'm armed."

The shadow freezes, then slowly turns toward me. I adjust my aim, finger hovering near the trigger.

"Identify yourself," I command. "If your name isn't Andy, you're probably going to get shot."

# 31

## Mitch

*Andy! Who the hell is Andy?*

I take a step forward, hoping she doesn't shoot me, although I've carried around a hole in my chest for the past six months, where my heart used to be.

"Lark, it's me," I say, soaking in the welcome sight of her in the spill of light from her windows.

*Welcome, apart from the rifle.* "Would you mind lowering that weapon?"

But she's frozen, shocked. I can see the disbelief on her beautiful face. Her shaking hands and the instant shimmer of tears in her eyes wipes the slightly amused expression from my face. I feel the same emotion, bottled up and lodged in my throat.

"Mind not shooting me, lady," I say. "I just got off a twenty-three-hour flight to get here. Plus a half-hour car ride."

At last, she lowers the rifle while whispering my name.

"Mitch?"

It's so damn good to hear it on her lips.

"What are you doing here?"

I close the distance between us, pausing only to relieve her of the rifle and lean it against the house. Then I take her beautiful face in my hands, the one I've seen so clearly in my dreams.

"I thought that was obvious," I say. "I came to see you."

She puts a hand to my cheek, brushing her fingertips over the day's worth of stubble darkening my jaw, and examines me with bright, alert eyes.

*Not yet welcoming.*

"How did you even find me?" she asks, like her brain's trying to make sense of my being here.

"I have my sources." Then I confess, "Charlotte may have given me the address."

"Charlotte," Lark murmurs. "Of course."

I thought we'd be kissing by now, but I can tell we'll have to waste time on some words first. Besides, there's this guy Andy.

Lowering my arms, I simply allow myself to enjoy being ten inches from her instead of ten thousand miles.

"I have a billion questions, all trying to escape me at once," she says. "But I swear, I'm still in shock. You *cannot* be here, in Goldsborough."

"I hope it's a good surprise." I still can't tell if she's pleased, but I blurt out what I'm feeling. "I'm really happy to see you. You look great."

She glances down at herself. We both take in her worn jeans with dirt on the knees and a ratty, long-sleeve cotton T-shirt that's seen better days.

"You've never looked more beautiful," I tell her. "Farm life suits you."

She raises a hand to her hair piled high on her head in a messy knot.

"I'm not wearing any makeup," she says softly.

"Me, neither."

Finally, Lark cracks a smile.

"I wasn't expecting company," she says.

I glance at the rifle. "You seem prepared for it anyway."

"Gramps's idea. He wasn't thrilled about me living out here alone."

I nod. "Smart man, your grandfather." Then I have to ask, because this might make or break my world, "Who's Andy?"

Her eyes widen, and a second later, she bursts out laughing. The jealous band around my chest eases.

"My happily married contractor."

"Good."

She cocks her head. More silence stretches between us, until I slap at a mosquito on my neck.

"Are you going to invite me in?"

"Part of me wants to," she says. "Part of me wants to order you off my property. Why were you peering in my window instead of knocking on the door?"

I shrug. "I saw the light coming out and the flicker of the TV. Wanted to catch a glimpse of you in your natural habitat *before* you realized it was me. By the way, you should get curtains."

Lark nods and smacks a mosquito on her arm.

"Are you going to tell me why you're really here?" she asks, her voice steady now, stronger. *A little cocky.* "Or should I guess?"

"I could tell you I was in the neighborhood," I say, "but that would be a pretty obvious lie, considering the nearest town with a decent restaurant is forty minutes away."

"Speaking of which, I read about your place in Montana," she says. "Congratulations. Franklin 7 sounds amazing."

"Thanks, it is. Not boasting, but it's one of my best. That's partly why I'm here."

"Business?" she asks. "FHLC distribution issues?" Her words are clipped. I think her romantic feelings are hurt.

*Can this irresistible woman be so dense?* Would I really travel this far for some goddamned chocolate syrup?

"Unfinished business," I tell her. "Between us."

The simple word—*us*—hangs in the air. Strangely, she winces, like I delivered a physical blow.

"There is no us," Lark says, flatly. Her words sting. "Can't be. Not in the long-term. We established that."

"Did we?" I ask. "That's not how I remember it. I recall you pushing me away when things got complicated. You decided we wanted different things without actually giving me much choice."

"You left," she says.

"You told me to go," I counter. "You said we needed space to figure out what we wanted."

"And did you?" she asks. "Figure out what you want, I mean."

Something vulnerable flickers in her golden-topaz eyes. I hope she can see it in my eyes, too.

"That's why I'm standing here getting eaten alive by ferocious bugs after traveling halfway around the world."

I have to cut this discussion short and show her how I feel. Closing the space between us again, I wrap my arms around her slender, familiar body. Then I kiss her with all the longing I've suppressed. I want to howl when I taste her lips and smell her scent of vanilla and cinnamon.

It's like coming home. All the months of emptiness while I kept myself busy, pretending I didn't need her, hanging out with a new crowd of kitchen staff like they were friends when I only wanted to talk to her—they vanish in an instant.

She melts against me, her arms winding around my neck. I feel her fingers in my hair, and she kisses me back. That's the best part. For the first time since seeing her pointing a gun at my chest, I relax. I hadn't realized how worried I was that she wouldn't still want me. Her mouth and her body tell me she does.

I try to pour everything I'm feeling into this kiss, how hungry I've been for her. We cling to each other, both of us letting our hands begin to roam. It's sensual, but it's also purposeful. I need to feel her familiar curves, touch what I consider mine, and let her do the same.

*I'm yours, touch all of me.* I want her to remember how my body responds beneath her fingers, remember how my muscles are at her service.

When she pulls back, breathing hard, a little night air manages to get between us and cool my heated skin. She's trembling in my arms, and my entire body is humming with desire. In the silence of the night, my breathing sounds loud and ragged in my ears.

Suddenly, Lark slips out of my embrace, collects her gun, and grabs my hand, leading me to her door. When I open it for her, warm lamplight envelops us both.

"Come in," she says.

Once indoors, I try to take it all in, when I really just want to look at her. And touch her.

It's minimally furnished but has what my dad would call *great bones.* The flow of the rooms is good, the red-hued hardwood floors need merely a little polish, and the great room with its fireplace and lofty ceilings needs nothing but better-fitting furniture.

All in all, the farmhouse suits Lark far better than her Sydney apartment.

"Welcome to Bushlark Farm," she says, crossing the open concept hall to the living area, where she hefts the gun onto pegs over the mantle.

"Although I guess you'll see it all in the morning." Then she turns, her eyes like liquid gold beckoning me closer.

"Bushlark?" I ask, mesmerized by her, barely believing we're in the same room together, and grabbing onto the one word I heard.

She shrugs shyly, and the accompanying blush to her cheeks makes my cock stiffen with instant arousal.

"It's the only Australian species of lark. It seemed fitting," she explains. "A new beginning, a new identity." She sends me a wry smile. "Also called the *singing* bushlark, but adding that to my farm's name is a step too far."

I can't help smiling while I reach for her hand. "I know. I've heard you in the shower. Kept thinking you'd brought a feral cat home."

She laughs. *Hard.*

Just like that, we're comfortable enough for me to insult the quality of her voice and for her to snap back, "Don't forget. I've got a loaded rifle."

"Duly noted." I give her hand a gentle squeeze and start to pull her close again, but Lark slips out of my grasp.

"Do you want anything?" She's backing toward the kitchen.

My libido, which had been calming down, blooms again at her words. I've spent a lot of hours wanting her, and it's hard to believe we've been together for this many minutes and still have all our clothes on.

"To eat or drink," Lark clarifies, though her saucy smile tells me she knows what I'm thinking.

"I'm thirsty," I confess. "And a little hungry?" I make it a question because it's Lark, after all.

"I have freshly baked bread from this morning."

At my stunned expression, she says, "Someone else baked it. Obviously. But I bought it. Also, some local sharp cheddar. How about a side of pickled onions? This way."

In a weird turnabout, I sit at *her* kitchen island, made of beautiful green-gray granite. I can't help smoothing my hands over it.

"Caledonia granite, according to the real estate agent," she says, producing my favorite beer from her fridge and sliding it across the island. "Quarried from southeastern Victoria."

"You're gorgeous," I say. *What?*

She giggles, that rare girlish sound that I hadn't forgotten for an instant.

"I mean, *it's* gorgeous. But you are, too."

I'm enthralled watching her slice the round, perfectly golden country loaf. Seeing her in the kitchen, out of her comfort zone, is incredibly arousing. Maybe it's the novelty of it. Maybe I'm simply dying to spread Lark out naked on the granite island and reacquaint myself with every inch of her.

Soon, I have a plate with chunks of robust, tangy cheddar and perfect bread, chewy on the inside, crusty on the outside, spread thickly with sweet creamy butter.

"I'm impressed."

"You're silly," she says. "I didn't even turn on the stove." Pouring herself a glass of red wine, she comes around the island to sit.

"You talk," I say. "I'll eat. Tell me about everything you're doing here."

$❤$❤$❤$

When I can't keep my eyes open, couldn't even finish one beer, she leads me to her bedroom. An awkward moment ensues, as we both talk at once.

"My toothbrush—" I begin, as she says, "Your suitcase—?"

We start over. "I'll go get my case," I say, talking over her words, "I have a spare toothbrush, unless you need anything else."

We smile at one another before she says, "I'm going to take a shower. I've been getting up super early, and it's been an eventful day."

I find out it's *not* an invitation to join her when she gives me a couple towels and a washcloth, and sends me to find another bathroom.

But as soon as I hear her turn on the water, I hustle out to my rental car for my bags. I don't want to stalk around buck naked when we're still feeling one another out. And I refuse to wear the same clothes I had on for so many hours on the plane.

Showered, teeth brushed, clean T-shirt and boxer briefs, I feel more like myself, and go in search of her. She's in the bedroom, lights on, sitting upright.

*Looking uncertain.*

"Lark," I say.

She cuts me off. "Only one bed in the house."

"I noticed. But I can take the couch, until . . . until we talk more."

This makes her laugh. "Lie down, sleep. I won't jump your bones until you're up for it."

"That's funny," I say. "You're hilarious."

Actually, I'm relieved she has let me into her bed, but also sorry I'm not being given the chance to satisfy her. Even with my last breath, I'll still want to give this woman pleasure.

When I push my luck and draw her against me, her back to my front, and drape my arm over her hip, she doesn't rebuff me. We've always been good at spooning.

Tomorrow, there'll be decisions to make. I'm going to enter into negotiations with Lark Henley regarding compromises. It's daunting. If I wasn't so tired, I'd be nervous.

But for tonight, it's enough that I'm here, that she's in my arms again, and that we're willing to admit what we both want is each other.

I try to think of what I'll say to convince her I no longer want to be a nomad, but sleep starts to pull me under. For the first time in months, Lark's warmth isn't just a dream, and I drift off, holding my woman.

*Perfectly content.*

# 32

# Lark

Each time I stir in the night, I check to make sure Mitch is still beside me. That I haven't dreamed he suddenly appeared out of the darkness on my porch.

He's here, black eyelashes resting on his cappuccino-colored cheeks. His firm lips are slightly parted. At some point he raises an arm, covering his eyes with the crook of his elbow, while his other hand fists the sheets in his sleep.

The next time I wake up, it's early morning and he's looking at me with his aqua-blue eyes.

"Your mother's eyes or your father's?" I ask, not even knowing which of his parents is black and which is Caucasian.

"Mom's eyes."

I nod. It was a weird way to greet a man I haven't seen in half a year. But it didn't seem to faze him.

"Are you watching me sleep?" I ask.

"Yup."

"I watched you too, last night."

He grins. So handsome and happy-looking, his smile steals my breath.

"I'm over being sleepy," he says. "I don't do jetlag, so let's rock 'n' roll, lady."

"What?" I sit up and lean back against the carved wooden headboard. "Are you talking about . . . well, *talking*, or are you talking about sex?"

"Both," he says, "and in that order."

"Coffee first?" I ask.

He scrunches up his face and shakes his head. "I'm thinking, we dive right in."

"Sex or talking?" I ask again.

"Stop it," he says, "or you'll be stripped, clipped, and penetrated so damn fast, your pretty head will spin."

*Well, damn. Way to make me wet, throbbing, and needy.* "How am I going to focus on your words, with that promise of fun?"

"Did that on purpose," Mitch says. "I think I need to throw the former CEO off her game for this business meeting."

"Ha!" It's all I can muster.

Just hearing *CEO* makes me tense, for an instant, imagining being back in my office, wearing a skirt-suit and heels, staring at a monitor. I shudder then relax. Look where I am and, for heaven's sake, look who's with me.

Strangely, Mitch looks a little apprehensive.

"I mentioned last night, on your porch," he says, "that Franklin 7 is partly why I'm here. That's because while I was in Bozeman building it, decorating it, and planning the menu, I wasn't focused, barely half engaged. That's not me. Not me at all. I didn't even buy a place to live in for any significant amount of time. I rented a crappy little dive."

He nods to himself before scooting back and leaning against the headboard beside me.

"I actually asked myself a couple times, *what's wrong with you?*"

Shaking his head, Mitch gives his own answer, "Turns out I'm not the same person who landed in Sydney. There's nothing wrong with me, though. I've simply changed. I'm a man in love."

I gasp, not because I hadn't heard it before, but because he's saying it like five seconds after we're back in one another's company. That's either brave or crazy. Slowly, he turns his head, and we lock gazes.

"I haven't stopped being a woman in love," I concede.

*"Whew,"* he releases a breath, and then wipes his hand over his face.

I guess he really didn't know how I felt.

He pauses, gathering his thoughts, and I lightly rub his arm, waiting.

"Franklin 7 taught me a lot," he says. "That being an executive chef and a successful businessman aren't enough for me any longer. Finally, I'm getting to why I came back." His voice is rough with emotion.

"Because I can live without a lot of things, including street lamps and a nearby gourmet market, but I can't live happily anywhere in the world *without* you."

The words wash over me, healing cracks in my heart I hadn't fully acknowledged. I search his face, looking for signs of doubt or hesitation, but instead find certainty and . . . love.

But I don't see how we've improved our situation one bit.

"I've been here only a short time, but I love it," I say. "You're right about the lack of lighting outside or gourmet anything. No bar or club down the street, either. But it's where I want to be, even if I'm here alone."

Mitch was so honest, I have to be, too. I add, "If I could have it all, though, if I could have my heart's desire, I'd want you with me. That would make my life perfect."

"That's what we'll do then," he says. "Make me happy and make your life perfect."

"What about your restaurants? New and old? And the ones in the future?"

This is where he's going to make me choose to go with him or not have him in my life.

"I've restructured things, which is what kept me away so long. I hired an executive chef, super talented, to manage the seven restaurants—"

"Plus F6 Tavern," I remind him.

"Plus the bar, where I've bronzed the table we sat at and shared our first burger," Mitch adds. "And it has a little plaque with both our names."

He delivers this startling news with such a believable expression, that I ask, "You did?"

"No," he says. "But I could."

"Don't you dare." I give him a playful shove. "Go on. Tell me how absentee Mitch Franklin can still run the Franklin Restaurant Group."

"I'll still be involved, but not full-time, not handling the daily headaches. That'll be the new executive chef's job. I already have an amazing CFO, who watches out for my best financial interests."

Possibility blossoms in my heart, but there's still the issue of him going away for long periods of time. "What about new venues?"

He shrugs. "That's where I'm hoping I can negotiate with you, just a little. I vow to shave off the time I need to be onsite at a new restaurant by . . . delegating."

"Hard word for you," I quip.

"Very. But I have people I can trust who won't let me down. I'm happy to let them shine in my place."

"*Happy* to?" I ask, reaching for the familiar pendant resting on that perfect chest of his, running my thumb over the smooth surface.

Mitch pretends to be in pain at the notion of delegating, gritting his teeth while fake smiling.

"Not ecstatic at first, but I'm learning. I didn't have a Charlotte at my disposal," he says. "Now I have Taylor

Burina. He's the new executive chef, who'll be playing the part of Mitch Franklin."

"And he'll make sure the lesson of great-grandma's broken bottle isn't lost at any Franklin restaurant?" I ask, knowing how important that is.

He smiles, resting his hand over mind, holding it tightly against him so I can feel his heartbeat. "I believe he will."

"Where do I come into this deal?" I ask.

He rubs the back of his neck with his other hand. "That's the thing. I want you to come with me and make wherever I go bearable. At least, for some of the time that I'm away. Otherwise, it's all just shit."

I laugh at his summation. Then I squeeze his big hand, hoping he can feel it.

"So, most of the time you'll be here? With me?" The hope in my voice is embarrassingly transparent.

His long thumb strokes the side of my wrist, making me shiver.

"I'll be wherever you are, Lark. Whether that's here or Sydney or the moon. Though I have to say," he adds, "I like what you've started at Bushlark."

"Sex, please," I say without any more delay.

"I thought you'd never ask." He has me bare and beneath him in moments.

We don't goof around. This rekindling of a love affair is serious business, demanding a no-nonsense position, the perfect amount of foreplay for me, and deep-thrusting hip action from him.

"Wow!" I say afterward.

"Can you say 'pent-up'?" he teases. Then, Mitch asks, "Do you have any eggs?"

$♥$♥$♥$

After breakfast, I give him the full tour of what's already been done and what's planned. We wind up on a shady patch of pasture land. I point to the perfect spot for the stables.

"The horses will be over there."

He groans, tilting his head back as if beseeching a greater power.

"Don't worry," I say. "I'll get you a sweet mare for you to ride."

Mitch freezes, then looks at me. "There's only one sweet mare I want to ride."

"Oh, man," I say. "I forgot how . . . *enthusiastic* you can be in a single day."

With that, he sweeps me off my feet, making me laugh. It's as though I weigh nothing, like I'm back in that fairy tale he once mentioned. Holding me high against his chest, he sets out toward the farmhouse, and doesn't stop until we're back in my bedroom.

"Do you still have them?" he asks, setting me on my feet.

I know what he's asking, and my clit starts pulsing with anticipation.

Unsmiling, arms crossed, legs slightly apart, Mitch says, "Bring them to me and then strip off your clothes, right here." He taps the wooden floor with his toes.

I swallow. He's upping the ante a little with his dominance. And I love it.

Soon, I'm kneeling on a down pillow, utterly naked, with all three clamps attached to my most sensitive spots. I'm trembling. I'm wet. I nearly came when he carefully attached the last one to my clit.

"I'm going to feed you something *hugely different* than anything I've given you before."

I know what's coming. As he strips, I watch with a mixture of excitement and trepidation, biting my lower lip when his erection springs free of his boxers.

Mitch is the biggest man I've ever been with, and for some reason, I haven't given him oral sex yet. We somehow never got around to it.

*How the hell am I going to get that long, thick cock into my mouth?*

"Sit back on your heels," he orders, standing directly in front of me.

I almost say, "Yes, sir," but we're not at that point. Yet. Maybe I will next time. If we continue down this titillating path, who knows?

Instead, I just obey because I trust him completely.

Before Mitch does anything else, he reaches down and slides the chain connected to all my erogenous zones over his wrist. That movement alone makes me lightheaded. Then he glides his long fingers of one hand into my hair and cradles my head with his broad palm.

"Open your mouth," he commands, guiding the tip between my lips as soon as I part them. "Take hold of my cock."

My heart is pounding with excitement for what's to come as I encircle his shaft with one hand and gently take hold of his balls with the other. This frees his other hand to secure my head more firmly between the grip of both palms and all ten fingers.

He has me right where he wants me and is in full control.

Quivering, I take him into my mouth, inch by inch, until I can't take any more. At least, that's what I think. All I can do, then, is suck and lick the upper end of his shaft while tugging on the skin behind it, making him moan.

"That's it. God that's good, Lark."

It's better than that. It's great. Every movement I make is telegraphed down that magical, swinging chain to my nipples and my clit. Even better, his arm moves with my head as it bobs along his cock. His wrist tugs at the dangling, three-headed "torture" device, sending me into another world of sensation.

*Sweet mercy,* I've barely started pleasuring him and I'm going to come.

Recognizing my readiness, Mitch tests our relationship. "Don't come until I give you permission."

If I could speak with his cock in my mouth, I might protest. Instead, I squirm, which only adds fuel to my building orgasm. Nearly impossible to stop. *Nearly*.

"Do you want to come with my cock *in* your mouth?" He moves his hips a little, taking over. I can no longer suck the head. I can do nothing but receive, as he slides between my lips, letting my tongue caress the underside of his thick shaft.

*"Mm,"* I agree. *Yes, I want to come. Right. Now.* With his cock in my mouth or in my hand or deep in my pussy, I don't mind. *Just let me climax!*

Then he asks, "Do you want *me* to come with my cock in your mouth?"

Desire floods me and drips down my thigh.

*"Mmm-hm,"* I add enthusiastically.

I relax, telegraphing how much I want him to take charge, which he does. Holding my head still, he glides smoothly in and out of my mouth, steadily, going a little deeper, a little farther each time.

"Tilt your head back," he urges. "It'll be easier."

When I do, he thrusts, actually going down my throat, which I've never experienced before. It's frightening and thrilling. My entire lower body, centered on my throbbing clit, is aching with the desperate need for release.

"That's it," he coaches me, his voice husky. "Don't forget to breathe through your nose."

*My thoughtful bedroom dom.* I breathe and give in to the erotic enjoyment of having my mouth used this way.

In a few more seconds, though, I start to moan because I can no longer hold back my orgasm. At the same time, my hand on his scrotum feels his balls tense in preparation for his own.

"Now," he commands, and my body starts to shudder. My climax starts deep and spreads wide, sending warmth like a melting chocolate through my pussy and up to my breasts, finally making me see stars behind my closed lids. I'm floating through the Milky Way.

At the same time, Mitch is surging into my mouth, my lips stretched over the massive girth of his cock until he stills, holding me prisoner by my head. My nose is buried in his pubic hair as he sends his cum sliding down the back of my throat.

When he withdraws moments later and releases me, I am wrung out and wobbly. I start to collapse onto the floor, but Mitch scoops me up and lays me on the bed. He unclamps my nipples and clit, giving me a second rush of pleasure as the blood flows. It's amazing.

We both have to rest and recuperate before we can even speak. That's fine because I think we've said everything we need to, in words and with our bodies.

And I think I've demonstrated what I need him to know. I'm all in this time.

*One billion percent.*

# EPILOGUE

*Six months later*

## Mitch

I'm delighted by the expression on Lark's face, while her entire body hums with anticipation. Joy seems to radiate off her as the convoy of vehicles makes its way down our long gravel drive. It looks like a presidential motorcade gone rogue, minus the flags and with an assortment of rental cars instead of big, black SUVs.

She's been planning this reunion for months, checking and rechecking every detail until I finally had to physically remove the tablet from her hands last night. I replaced it swiftly with a glass of her grandfather's wine.

Now, we're standing together on the wide porch where we spend most of our evenings eating on the local, hand-crafted, outdoor furniture. But the cushioned swing is our favorite spot for star gazing.

"They're here," she says, stating the obvious and ending on a high pitch, making our dog Ramsey bark. He's been

414

our "practice puppy" for adjusting into an adulthood in which we care for people other than ourselves.

I bend down and pet his soft golden head with one hand. Lark is squeezing the other one so tightly, I might lose circulation.

"They're *all* here," she adds, meaning my family, too. "At the same time!"

I drop a kiss on her temple. "My family wouldn't miss seeing me 'settled down', as Mom calls it. And no way the Henley clan would miss the grand unveiling of your chocolate empire?"

She gives me a playful shove. "It's hardly an empire yet." Her joyful tone makes my heart happy. "Plus, you know it's *ours*."

"Thank you," I say. She has let me share her dream and be a big part of it. Lifting our gripped hands, I brush my lips across her knuckles. "Your family's going to see how you've exceeded even your own expectations."

Lark nods. I don't think she's listening to me any longer, as she confesses, "I'm a little nervous hosting your family. And I hope everyone doesn't feel too cramped."

"Crazy lady," I say. "They already love you. And no one's going to mind where they're sleeping."

The past six months have transformed Bushlark Farm from a neglected cocoa plantation into something quite special. The processing facility gleams with new equipment, the visitor center is fun and informative, and the first batches of our signature chocolates are curing in the climate-controlled aging room.

My contribution—beyond muscle, sweat, and occasionally placating the contractors when Lark's perfectionism drove them to despair—was helping design the tasting room and its kitchen. A chef knows how to stage a culinary experience. I also helped envision the retail space, which is now stocked.

And while we haven't done too much to the house beyond refinishing some floors, updating the plumbing, and buying furniture, we have enough room for everyone. Rooms with beds for four couples, one pull-out sofa, and an air mattress for the two children.

Speaking of which, Lark's sister, Clover, and her husband, Adam, emerge from the first vehicle. Their two kids tumble out after them, immediately racing toward the pen where we keep three friendly but naughty Nubian goats who needed a home.

I fear more animals will keep being added because of Lark's tender heart. At least with these, the two tan-and-white does provide a couple gallons of milk a day. And the third is a smug billy goat who keeps his ladies happy.

Adam Bonvier, a fellow Bostonian, looks around at the sprawling farm with an appraising eye.

"Nice digs," he calls up to us while Clover corrals their little ones. "Better place to work than a corner office."

"Agreed," Lark says to her brother-in-law. "Maybe you want to buy a neighboring property. Clover can trade in her stilettos for Blunnies."

"No, thank you," Clover chimes in. She and Adam come up the porch steps, each holding a child by the hand. "I'm quite fond of our brownstone, even in winter."

"You know my sister and her footwear," Lark reminds me.

We took a flight to Boston four months ago for a week, hanging out with Adam and Clover and introducing my "forever girl" to my parents.

"It's not that," Clover protests. "I'll put on a pair of Blundstones as needed. I'm even wearing boots today."

After the sisters hug, Clover sticks a foot out from under a mid-calf denim skirt, that somehow looks sophisticated and rustic.

I laugh because the pointed, shiny, black-leather ankle boot is ridiculously ill-suited to anything but the city streets.

"Gianvito Rossi boots," Clover exclaims as Ramsey gives it a good sniff. "A steal at $1300."

That stops my laughter, while her husband makes a choking sound.

"Go inside," Lark orders her. "Start doling out drinks and snacks."

My parents and my sister are the next to come up the steps. Hugs all around. I hope Riley and Lark get on well, despite the whole Connor Whittel connection.

My mother, still blonde with a peppering of gray mixed in, looks at me with that particular mix of pride and mild reproach she's perfected over the years. Her blue eyes, identical to mine and Riley's, take in everything before she leans close.

"Mitchell," she says, embracing me. "You couldn't have chosen somewhere a little closer to civilization?"

"Sorry, Mom," I say, hugging her back.

She and the rest of our guests all arrived sometime late yesterday, either by private jet or by car, and stayed at area hotels so they could come here by mid-morning.

I remind her, "The cocoa trees are particular about their climate."

My father, never one for excessive displays of emotion, gives me a firm handshake that transitions into a brief, powerful hug. "Looks like you two have built something special here."

"Still working on it," I tell him, but his approval means a lot. Like always.

As my mom moves aside from hugging Lark, he takes his turn.

"There she is." That's all he says, but it speaks volumes. He's thrilled that I've found the love of my life. After my family goes indoors, Lark takes a moment to grab my arm.

"This is so great," she says.

The third vehicle contains her parents. Richard grew up on the Hunter Valley ranch before going to start the chocolate division in New York. And Bunny Henley captured his heart in the States and raised three children, while agreeing to spend every summer of their early marriage Down Under. I need to have a word with her about how to adapt to this new world on a long-term basis.

Hugs and handshakes follow before they go inside. Ramsey, who has his nose attached to Bunny Henley's leg, seems to think she's Lark or the next best thing and goes in with her.

Luke holds the car door open for his pregnant wife, Morgan, who looks radiant despite the Australian humidity that has the rest of us already perspiring. Also riding with them are Pat and Evelyn, Luke, Lark, and Clover's grandparents.

They're the only ones who've seen Bushlark Farm in person, not in a video. They've come to visit twice already. As Pat likes to remind me, "It's a quick eighteen-hour drive."

Luke gives me a hearty slap on the back that nearly sends me off the porch.

"So, you survived your first six months of farm life," he says with a grin. "The gourmand in you missing anything?"

"I make whatever I'm craving," I tell him. "Although the town of Sarina has a decent meat pie and pasties shop."

For some reason, this cracks Luke up. I think he's enjoying my banishment to the north.

Lark hugs her brother and then Morgan.

"Honestly, living with Mitch is like dining at a private restaurant every night," she tells them, and I feel about a billion feet tall.

"All the city slickers are here," Pat teases his granddaughter once he reaches the porch.

"They're not all urbanites," Lark says, her voice softening the way it always does with them.

"Half of them grew up on our ranch," Evelyn reminds him, giving her husband a poke in the ribs.

With her arm around her grandmother's waist, Lark goes indoors, and Pat and I follow. He gives me a commiserating nod, and I'm glad to be considered a fellow farmer now. I can muck the stables with the best of them.

Once inside, I keep refreshments coming, while watching Lark with both our families, directing luggage to appropriate rooms, answering questions about the property, promising tours and tastings later. She's in her element here, surrounded by the people she loves, on the land she's chosen as her own.

"There are the clothespins," Evelyn says loudly, upon seeing the glass bowl on the granite island. "Making this a home. I can almost smell the wash drying on the line."

All three Henley siblings laugh, although Lark is the only one of them grinning at me. The wooden pins weren't out when I first got here. When I found them under the sink, I couldn't resist putting them on display as a memento. We don't need them for their emergency use, but Lark also never reaches for one as a fidget toy, either.

The tense, caged CEO I first met, the one who needed a risky, wild night to blow off steam, has vanished. In her place, this relaxed, radiant woman who figured out what she wanted and went after it. Fortunately, that includes me. Even more lucky, the wild nights continue unabated.

My sister approaches, having snuck by me on the porch. I hug her tightly, making sure she's not too thin. It will be my greatest honor and pleasure to feed these people over the next week.

"A half Black man willingly living on a plantation," Riley murmurs, too low for the others to hear. "Never thought I'd see the day."

I laugh out loud at her choice of words. "The irony isn't lost on me. But I've never felt more at home anywhere."

And it's true. I've found an unexpected peace here. The boredom I feared never materialized. Every day is a little different. And we keep discovering new things not only on the land—like how one row of taller trees with glossy, dark-green leaves turned out to be coffee plants—but also new things about each other.

Lark sprinkles cocoa powder on everything! Breakfast cereal, even oatmeal, in her coffee, and over something that should be sacred, like a peanut butter and strawberry jam sandwich.

How she hid this weirdness from me until after I fell for her, I'll never know.

"You do seem really happy, bro," Riley says, studying my face. "It's a good look on you."

"I am happy," I admit, watching Lark gesture animatedly as she explains something to her brother. "Disgustingly, ridiculously happy."

"About time," she says, bumping my shoulder with hers. "And the restaurants?"

"No complaints so far. Everything's thriving. I'm considering a second place west of the Mississippi. Most likely Austin. If it happens, Lark will come with me. But at the moment, I've no reason to go anywhere and no desire to."

Later, after everyone has settled into their rooms and had a light buffet lunch—goat milk cheese and smoked duck breast crostini, with some peanut butter and cocoa sprinkled banana sandwiches for the little ones, and mini passionfruit tarts for everyone—we start the official tour.

Lark leads the way, beginning with the more established part of the farm that basically sold her on the place.

"The original trees are about six years old," she explains. "We've had a full harvest from them this year." It's a good long walk through them before we get to the trees we've recently planted to expand our production capacity.

"Those new plantings should start producing in about three years."

Moving on to the processing facility, Lark explains the journey from fresh cocoa pods to finished chocolate with the precision of someone who's studied every step of the process and devoted her life to chocolate.

Her entire family could no doubt tell the same info, but she practices the tour for the benefit of the Franklin clan. At the end of the discussion, everyone claps, and she gives an exaggerated curtsy, looking down at the sterile concrete floor, hiding how touched she is.

Next, she gets to the "good stuff" that her family might not know.

"We're experimenting with fermentation techniques and our roasting process to draw out specific flavor notes. And we're loving the results of our stone-grinding method. It's creating what will hopefully be our signature smooth texture."

"Bushlark's going to give Henley Confectionery a run for our money," her father says, obviously thrilled.

Lark shrugs it off, but I can tell she's pleased by his praise.

"And this," she says, leading us into the climate-controlled room lined with shelves, "is where the magic happens."

The aging room is my favorite part of the operation. Rows of chocolate bars in various stages of maturation rest on cedar shelves, each labeled with production dates and flavor profiles. The rich aroma is intoxicating, a complex bouquet of cocoa, fruit notes, and subtle spices.

"We're aging our chocolates for a minimum of three weeks," Lark explains. "Except for our premium line, which will rest and mature for up to three months."

"The process develops deeper, more complex flavors," Luke explains to his wife.

"Like a fine wine," his grandfather says.

"Or a good bourbon," my father adds.

We end the long tour at the tasting room, where I've set up an elaborate sampling station. Varieties of our Bushlark Midnight brand chocolates are arranged on slate boards, accompanied by palate cleansers of sliced green apples and chilled cucumber-mint water.

"Why 'Midnight'?" Morgan asks, resting a hand on her rounded stomach, inside of which, as Luke has announced more than once, their second trimester baby is growing.

Lark glances at me, and a private smile passes between us. "Mitch and I always do our best *thinking* at midnight," she says.

We do quite a few things around midnight, but they all boil down to us connecting deeply on many levels.

Ignoring her brother's snort of laughter, Lark guides everyone through the tasting. I stand back, watching my family and hers blend seamlessly.

The kids are fascinated by the table-top melanger we display in this room, a small version of the grinder in the processing building. Its granite stones are constantly grinding a small number of cocoa nibs into smooth chocolate liquor, right before their curious eyes. They keep asking their father questions, even though Adam probably knows the least here about the process, apart from my parents.

Riley and Clover are deep in conversation, about shoes, if I know my sister. Our parents are laughing together, and I hear my mother mention something about beautiful babies, which startles me.

And Gramps and Nan are quietly tasting their granddaughter's third-generation chocolate. Approval is clear on their faces.

Catching Lark's eye, I send her a wink of solidarity and love. Then, when I clear my throat, a flash of nervous excitement crosses her face. *Has she guessed my intention?*

"Before we start thinking about dinner," I say, "I'd like to say a few words. And this room, surrounded by Lark's chocolate—"

"And yours," she interjects.

"And mine," I correct. "Anyway, surrounded by our labor of love, it's a fitting place for what I want to say."

The group quiets, turning expectant faces toward me. My mouth suddenly feels dry. I've rehearsed this speech a number of times over the past few days, but now, with all the people who matter so much to Lark and me gathered with us, I'm uncharacteristically nervous.

"First, I want to thank you all for coming to see what Lark and I have been building here," I begin, my voice steadying as I focus on her beautiful face. "It means more than you know to share this with the people we love most."

I take a breath, fingering the small velvet box in my jeans pocket.

"When I first met Lark, I thought I knew exactly who I was and what I wanted in life. I was a nomadic chef, a restaurant empire builder, priding myself on never staying in one place too long." I smile ruefully.

My mother rolls her eyes good-naturedly, and my father coughs something that sounds suspiciously like "understatement," loudly enough for everyone to hear. Most of them laugh.

"I knew she'd break you," Luke calls out. He's going to be a fun brother-in-law.

I shoot him a quick grin, glad I never gave the man cause to try to ruin my company, as he once threatened to do.

"Then this stubborn, brilliant, independent woman walked into my bar and turned everything upside down." I face Lark fully now. "You challenged me, Lark, and made me crave more out of life than I'd dared to imagine. Most importantly, you made me want to be a better man than I was."

Her golden-topaz eyes, not unusual in this Henley group, are filled with emotion, and a soft blush spreads across her cheeks.

I can't let her pink cheeks distract me the way they usually do.

"We didn't make it easy on ourselves," I continue. "We competed when we should have cooperated. We pushed each other away when we should have held on tighter. We nearly lost each other trying to protect ourselves from the very thing we both wanted most."

Stepping forward, I take her hand in mine and draw her into the middle of our guests. The rest of the room seems to fade away until it's just the two of us.

"But here we are, finally working together. You dreamed of this beautiful farm and were generous enough to include me. My own dreams have expanded into so much more than I ever thought possible."

Reaching into my pocket, I withdraw the small velvet box. A collective intake of breath sounds around us as I lower myself to one knee. Lark's eyes widen. I keep her anchored in place by one hand, half afraid my lark will fly away. Her other hand covers her mouth in surprise.

"Lark Henley," I say, opening the box to reveal the ring I spent weeks designing—a platinum band with a rare, chocolate-hued, radiant-cut diamond, circled by fiery white diamonds, like flawless stars in the midnight sky. "You once made fun of my fairy tale idea."

A few people chuckle. "That's Lark, for you," her sister says.

I ignore them. "Maybe it's because we were meant to create our own story. So far, I'm loving the beginning, and I can't wait to see what comes next. Will you marry me?"

For a heart-stopping moment, she's silent as tears start to spill down her cheeks. Then Lark smiles down at me.

"Yes," she says, her voice choked with emotion. "Of course I will."

I slide the ring onto her finger, then rise and pull her into my arms. Our families erupt in cheers and applause around us, but I barely hear them as I kiss my fiancée, pouring every ounce of love and promise into the fusion of our mouths.

When we break apart, we're immediately swarmed by well-wishers. Even Ramsey, picking up on the excitement, is barking loudly. I've planned for this moment—for Lark accepting me, because I've become such a hopeful guy—so I tell Luke and Adam there's a case of champagne in the tasting room walk-in fridge. They make quick work of pouring for everyone, and toasts, both serious and funny, are made.

All the women take turns examining the ring, but it's her Nan's mention of strong unions and a "fertile future" that makes me blush as hard as Lark.

My mother asks the question on everyone's mind. "When's the big day? We should probably book our return flights now."

I hope I'm not overstepping, but Lark has induced in me a seize-the-day mentality.

"Actually," I say, "if my fiancée of five minutes agrees, I was thinking we might do it . . . now."

"Now?" Richard Henley repeats, looking bewildered. "What do you mean, now?"

Lark squeezes my hand. "You're brilliant. Yes, let's do it."

"That's Lark for you," Clover says again, and we all laugh.

"What about a minister or a license," Bunny protests, though I can see she's on board with the idea.

"A JP from Sarina will be here in two hours," I tell them. "And I might have already taken care of the license last week."

Lark raises an eyebrow at me. "Pretty confident, weren't you?"

I shrug. "I prefer to think of it as optimistic planning."

She laughs, shaking her head. "You'll be impossible to live with after this."

"You love it," I counter.

"God help me, I do," she says. "At least, I love you beyond reason, so I guess I can adapt to your insufferable smugness."

What follows is a whirlwind of activity. Every female is ushered indoors with champagne in hand, to fuss over the bride and help her get ready. My impromptu posse of groomsmen help me transform a eucalyptus grove behind the house into our simple wedding venue.

I'd planned ahead, buying white folding chairs and a dozen vibrant red gymea lilies, each of them seven feet tall to mark the area, and lanterns to hang from the trees.

Moving on to the reception area, the main aisle of the new barn, I show the men the supplies I've amassed—garlands of pink waxflowers and golden billy buttons and yards of twinkling lights. I've even hidden a long dining table, set up since yesterday.

"We've got this," Adam says, although he's more into directing the others than decorating. "Go make yourself presentable for that pretty bride of yours."

With Luke and Pat's agreement, I head inside to get changed.

Before I know it, I'm standing in the eucalyptus grove, wearing a cream-colored, linen suit. Lark now knows the reason I recently insisted she buy herself a new dress.

"Just get something that makes you feel good," I told her a few weeks ago. "Then we'll have a night out."

"Where?" she asked, thinking our choices were limited in the area.

"We'll take a jet wherever you like," I said.

My father stands beside me as best man, looking suspiciously misty-eyed beneath his stoic expression.

"Well done," he says, meaning this entire spontaneous event that could've been a fiasco, but is working out perfectly.

The Justice of the Peace arrives and then all our guests take their seats. Even Ramsey lies down like a good boy, tired from the day. As the sun begins to set, painting the sky in brilliant golds and pinks that echo the flowers, soft music starts playing. Nothing fancier than a recording sent from my phone to outdoor speakers, but no one minds.

And then Lark appears, and for me, the world stops turning.

She wears a pale blue dress of lightweight fabric that floats around her like water. Her caramel-colored hair is loose, which it rarely is on the farm when we're working.

Someone's made her a crown of small white flowers, and her exquisite face, radiant with joy, takes my breath away.

Her father walks her down the makeshift aisle, clasping her arm, preparing to give his youngest daughter away.

As Lark moves toward me, I'm transported back to the first time I saw her, seated at a high-top in my bar. I remember thinking how beautiful she was. Actually, I recall my thoughts were more like "hot and fuckable."

Then her intriguing Henley gold eyes locked with mine, and I was hooked.

But I had no idea then that she would transform my life and become my everything.

The ceremony is simple, heartfelt. We exchange vows that we compose on the spot, promises that feel more genuine for their spontaneity. We both stumble a bit, but get through them.

When the JP pronounces us *husband and wife*, I kiss Lark beneath the wide-open Queensland sky. And then, she turns to our now one-big family and says, "Time to party!"

The caterers arrived while we were saying our vows, and with my careful instructions as to how they should prepare my recipes, they lay out a meal worthy of the occasion. I only wish I could've been the groom *and* the chef.

Today of all days, however, I know which one is more important.

The celebration that follows is everything a wedding reception should be—jubilant chaos, filled with laughter, a barking dog, shrieking children, and dancing that continues into the night.

There's a cake from a local Sarina bakery that's damn good, but the chocolate fountain featuring FHLC is the star, delighting the children and adults alike.

As we stroll out of the barn to finish a dance under the stars, I hold my wife close, still marveling at the words. *My wife*. Lark Franklin, though I'm totally fine with her keeping her own name, especially professionally.

In this moment, it doesn't matter what we call ourselves. We belong to one another, and that's all that counts.

"Happy?" I murmur against her hair as we sway to the music.

"Stunned, impressed, amazed is more like it," she replies, tilting her head back to look at me. "And yes, happy. You are one sneaky man. 'Buy a new dress,' you said. And I kept thinking, *where the heck in Sarina am I going to wear this?*"

I grin. "I promise to use my sneakiness solely for good and never for evil."

This makes her laugh, and it's a gorgeous sound, floating above the music and the farm's usual night noises.

"I love you, Mrs. Franklin."

She sobers and takes a deep breath. "I love you, Mitchell Franklin. More every day."

$♥$♥$♥$

*Another six months later*

# Lark

I blink awake to the morning light filtering through our gauzy bedroom curtains. My hand automatically reaches for Mitch across our rumpled sheets, but his side of the bed is empty. This doesn't happen very often, since his years as a chef left him with a late-to-bed, late-riser schedule. But I'm not bothered. The scent of coffee and something baking tells me where to find him.

Stretching unhurriedly, I savor the moment of peace before the day begins in earnest. Married half a year, and I still sometimes wake up astounded that this is my life—the cocoa farm thriving, our Midnight chocolates gaining recognition in specialty markets, and Mitch beside me through it all.

Three months ago, we had our first business trip together. Three weeks in Texas, to open his new Austin restaurant. His CFO said the project proceeded quicker, therefore cheaper, *without* Mitch micromanaging those who know what they're doing.

My husband scowled, but he understood that sometimes, in the past, he held up a venue until he could make each minute decision.

Regardless, even from afar, he designed every aspect of the place. And when we got there, his team had pulled it off to perfection. After he worked through the finishing details, the grand opening was outstanding. All I had to do was go shopping, eat delicious food, and see my man lauded as the best in his profession. The easiest business trip I've ever had.

Climbing out of bed, I head to the kitchen in my nightshirt. The sight that greets me stops me in my tracks—Mitch at the stove in sweatpants and a T-shirt stretched over his strong back. *That ass, those thighs!*

I'm so freakin' lucky.

He skillfully flips something in a pan. The kitchen island is already set for breakfast—fresh fruit, a French press of coffee, and what looks like a plate of his chocolate chunk scones.

This man, who made his home in kitchens all over the world, now seems perfectly content making breakfast in our farm kitchen. I hope it's enough.

"What's the occasion?" I ask, sliding onto a stool at the island.

Mitch turns, his face lighting up at the sight of me. Even after all this time, that look still makes my heart flutter.

"The occasion," he says, leaning across the counter to kiss me, "is that my wife has a doctor's appointment today."

I smile against his lips. "You didn't have to cook for that."

"I cook because I love you," he says simply. "The doctor's appointment just gave me an excuse to make your favorites."

He slides a perfect omelet onto a plate and places it before me. I inhale the mouth-watering aroma of farm-fresh eggs, herbs from our garden, and his homemade creamy goat cheese. And the special ingredient.

"Ham," I say on a long sigh of pleasure.

"You used to say my name like that," he jokes.

My mouth is already full so I don't answer except to wiggle my eyebrows.

He busies himself, putting a glass of mango juice in front of me, then a glass of milk, and lastly, he pours me a cup of coffee, preparing it precisely the way I like it—strong, with a good amount of cream, a teaspoon of honey, and some cocoa sprinkled on top.

"Nervous?" he asks.

I look at him from behind my beverages, hoping he's not going to give me any more.

"A little," I admit. "But I think I should be asking you that."

Sure enough, he fills me another glass, this time with spring water, and is about to set it down next to the rest . . . when he notices what he's doing.

"Sorry." He downs the water. "Yes, I'm nervous. And thrilled in a roller coaster way," he says. "Excited but with a little fear mixed in, to be honest."

I nod, and he plates himself the same breakfast. We eat in companionable silence for a few minutes.

"I had an email from Luke last night," I say between bites. "Morgan and the baby are doing great. They want to visit ASAP."

Mitch nods. "They can come anytime. Door's always open."

"That's why we have the rifle," I quip. In truth, I haven't felt a moment's apprehension since Mitch moved in. *Why would I?* It's like having my own personal bodyguard. With benefits.

"Which room shall we turn into the nursery?" he asks.

My lack of interest in prepping is starting to drive him crazy. He answers for me. "Probably the one closest to our bedroom. No brainer, right?"

My phone interrupts his domestic planning, buzzing with an incoming notification. I glance at it, then smile.

"The feature on Midnight Chocolates just published in *Gourmet Traveler.* Jules is already sending texts with fireworks emojis. And Charlotte says she'll put it on the Henley website."

Mitch leans close as I pull up the article on my tablet. The spread is gorgeous. Rich photos of our plantation, the processing facility, the finished chocolates in their elegant packaging.

The writer has captured everything we've worked for—the sustainable farming practices, the artisanal production methods, the unique aging process that gives our chocolates their distinctive character.

"'A chocolate revolution in the heart of Queensland,'" Mitch reads aloud. "'Former confectionery CEO Lark Henley and acclaimed chef Mitch Franklin, now husband and wife culinary powerhouse, have created something truly unique. A bean-to-bar operation that honors tradition while pushing boundaries.'"

"Not bad," I say, scrolling to see more photos.

"Not bad? It's brilliant." He kisses my temple. "Like you."

We finish breakfast and get ready for the day. I have farm chores that get me dirty and a tour to give. Mitch has meetings with our manager and a phone call with Clover regarding marketing. None of it can keep our attention today, however.

We have one singular focus, the doctor's appointment.

As we finally drive into town, I watch the landscape roll by. Our cocoa trees give way to the wilder bush beyond, and then the town of Sarina, with its quaint shops and five thousand mostly friendly residents who no longer stare when we walk by.

We've become part of the community here, hosting local events at the farm, which gives Mitch an excuse to dazzle with his cooking. In all ways, we're supporting regional businesses and building something that feels rooted and real.

"Back to the nursery," he says, his hand finding mine across the console.

"Andy said he'll start on Monday," I say, putting my husband out of his misery. "He can start on the structural changes first, that sagging floor and adding the new windows. I'll leave the decorating decisions to you."

Mitch nods, his eyes fixed on the road. "Sounds reasonable, except I know you'll overrule all my design suggestions anyway."

I laugh, squeezing his hand. "Only the ridiculous ones. We are *not* having a chocolate-themed nursery, Mitch."

"It would be educational from day one!"

"It would be brown. Entirely brown."

"Brown is a perfectly respectable color," he argues, his eyes twinkling.

"On you," I tease, "it's the sexiest, most perfect color." Then I shake my head. "On our baby's walls, not so much."

This playful bickering carries us all the way to the doctor's office, easing the nervous anticipation building between us. We've been here before, of course, for the confirmation pregnancy test. But this is the first ultrasound. This appointment feels different. More real somehow since our baby is eight weeks along.

"About the size of a raspberry," Mitch whispers in my ear as we sit in the quiet waiting room, with one other couple, who are both scrolling on their phones. But naturally, my chef husband is consulting a wall chart that relates the various fetal stages to food.

His statement makes me laugh.

"Let me know when it's the size of a watermelon," I say. "Then I'll take notice."

*"Ha,"* he says and falls silent. His knee bounces up and down, betraying his nerves despite his calm expression. I place my hand on his thigh, stilling him.

"It's going to be fine," I murmur.

"I know," he says. "It's just—this is happening. Really happening."

I understand completely. Despite the morning sickness that started early, with my first missed period, and shifted entirely to after-dinner sickness last week, and despite the subtle changes in my body, part of me still can't quite believe it.

Lark Henley, who once lived for nothing but the next quarterly reports, is sitting in an obstetrician's office with her husband, waiting to see our baby on an ultrasound.

"Mrs. Franklin?" the nurse calls, using the name that still gives me a jolt of joy whenever I hear it.

We follow her back to the examination room. Soon after, Dr. Campbell arrives, with her calm demeanor and gentle hands, greeting us warmly.

"Everything still going OK, Lark?" she asks.

"All good so far," I say.

"It's the big day," the doctor reminds us, getting down to business. She squeezes cold gel on my still-flat stomach, making me flinch slightly. "You ready, Mitch?"

"Yes," he says, sounding strangled.

"Then let's check on your little one."

Mitch's hand tightens around mine as I lie on the examination table, feeling the ultrasound wand gliding gently over my skin.

"Oh," Dr. Campbell says, her eyebrows lifting as she studies the screen intently.

My heart skips a beat. "Is something wrong?"

"Nope," she reassures me quickly. "Nothing wrong at all." She turns the monitor so we can see. "But it appears we have an interesting situation here."

I squint at the grainy black and white image, trying to make sense of what I'm seeing. Beside me, Mitch leans forward, and his familiar scent keeps me calm.

Dr. Campbell points to one and then another black blob with a little pale spot in the middle of each.

"Is that . . . ?" he begins before trailing off, rendered speechless.

"Two separate gestational sacs," the doctor confirms with a smile. "Congratulations, you're having twins."

"Twins?" I echo, my voice barely audible as shock washes through me. "Two raspberries?"

"Oh, shit," Mitch whispers, his voice thick with emotion before he makes a strangled sound beside me that's half laugh, half gasp. "Two babies."

Dr. Campbell adds to our amazement when she says, "We may be able to hear their heartbeats. Not always, so don't panic if we don't." And she turns a dial.

Two fast, fluttering beats fill the room, and Mitch and I stare at one another.

"Are they supposed to be that fast?" he asks the question before I can.

"They are," the doctor confirms. "About one hundred and sixty beats per minute. They sound perfect."

Two tiny humans that Mitch and I created are growing inside me. The reality of it hits me with full force, and I feel tears spilling down my cheeks.

"We're having twins," I say, reality crashing in. I'm drowning in hormonal emotions, which get ramped up by about a billion percent when I see Mitch's eyes widen with something that looks suspiciously like panic.

"Twins," he repeats. Then a smile breaks across his face, brilliant and dazed. "Double the trouble."

We keep our gazes locked for a long breathless moment before we burst into slightly hysterical laughter at the same time. The sound mingles with the steady pulse of two tiny heartbeats. Our family.

$♥$♥$♥$

"Everything looks perfect," Dr. Campbell assures us ten weeks later when my stomach looks like I've swallowed a whole cantaloupe. "Two healthy babies developing exactly as they should. Would you like to know the sexes?"

Mitch and I exchange a look, having discussed this already.

"Yes," he says at the same time that I say "No."

Come to think of it, I guess our discussion didn't end with a negotiated unanimous decision.

Dr. Campbell moves the wand, studying the screen.

"Last call," she says, cocking her head, waiting.

We smile at one another. That was what my sexy husband said to me the night we met, wanting to know if I needed another drink or was ready to get busy with him.

"Last call," I mouth the words silently.

Mitch raises an eyebrow, then he addresses Dr. Campbell.

"My wife wants to wait. We'll wait. *For now.*"

My mouth drops open. "You don't think I can hold out till the end, not knowing. Do you?"

"When I put something in the oven to bake, you always demand to know what it is," he reminds me. "If you can't guess from the aroma, you are ruthlessly persistent. 'Cake or cupcakes?' 'Mitch, do I smell raisins in those cookies?' 'Walnut or pecan brownies?' 'Is that Portuguese sweet bread?'" he mimics.

*All recent. All true.*

"But this is different," I argue, patting the roundest part of my belly. "This is more like a box of chocolates with two equally delicious flavors. We'll find out when we find out. Maybe we have two chocolate-covered vanilla caramel boys. Maybe we have two creamy dark-chocolate truffle girls. Maybe one of each."

"Stop, please," Dr. Campbell says. "I need to go in search of some candy. And next time you visit, you better bring me a box of chocolates."

Thanking her, we leave, hand in hand. "How does that always happen?" Mitch asks.

"What?" I ask innocently.

"You know what," he says, giving my fingers a gentle squeeze. "Wherever you go, you are such an ambassador for chocolate, you always make people want some. We need to start carrying a cooler of Midnight in the car."

I shrug. "I don't know what you're talking about. I'm just Lark He— Lark *Franklin*, carrying the twin babies of that fabulously talented chef and famed restaurateur."

Mitch's full-bodied laugh makes me join in.

Finally, he says, "You'll never be 'just Lark' anything, lady. And if I ever catch you hiding your fabulousness . . ."

"You'll what?"

He looks at me, considering. "I may have to tighten the clamps."

I shiver. Over the past year, he's become an expert at the timing of putting them on and taking them off and, of course, the amount of pressure to keep me on the edge of bliss.

Seeing my expression, he looks smug, appreciating the control I give him over my body. Then he opens the car door for me.

"Let's go home, so I can feed you and our growing family."

My mind isn't on food, and he knows it. My libido has grown along with my stomach, and as long as Dr. Campbell says it's safe, we'll continue to enjoy ourselves.

"Before we eat, Mr. Franklin, I'm thinking of marital relations."

"I know you are, Mrs. Franklin. And I aim to satisfy every desire."

A shiver runs down my spine, and he grins. I start to climb into our car, but he draws me close. The world falls away when Mitch claims my mouth under his.

Life doesn't get any sweeter than this. Not even chocolate compares.

*The End*

# ABOUT THE AUTHOR

Jane McBay is the pen name of *USA Today* bestselling author of historical romance, Sydney Jane Baily. She wanted to write about strong, sexy men who know how to treat a woman BUT aren't wearing top hats and shiny Hessian boots.

Trading carriages for limos and horses for private jets, she's dreaming up mouthwatering billionaires with big . . . hearts. They're paired with clever, passionate females who have a hard time resisting these intriguing men. *So why bother?*

Give in, have fun, fall in love.♥ They do. And you will too! *NO* cliffhangers. *NO* frustration. *ALL THE FEELS.* You're welcome!

Contact her through her website, JaneMcBay.com.